ELI B

Me Too

INDIE BEE PRESS

First published by Indie Bee Press 2021

First edition

ISBN: 978-1-9196361-0-8

Editing by Kylie Lynn
Cover art by Leni Kauffman

This book was professionally typeset on Reedsy.
Find out more at reedsy.com

For young Eli who just wanted to see herself in a love story–maybe not Nadia and Luca's fucked up story, but you get it.

Imagine meeting someone who wanted to learn your past not to punish you, but to understand how you needed to be loved.

Tiny Buddha

Preface

Content Warning

This novel includes depictions and descriptions of domestic violence, rape, panic attacks, anxiety, suicide and racism. Please keep this in mind and be safe while reading.

／
Acknowledgement

I want to thank my best friend Moie, who's always cheered me on and encouraged me to write. She's been there since day one, when Me Too was just a few sheets of looseleaf paper (she won't remember this, but you were there bestie!). My mom, who always told me I can do anything I put my mind to. Thank you for starting me on my writing journey with that scary ass alien abduction story we wrote together for a 5th grade English project! My brother, who read the first novel I ever tried to publish and was so kind even though it was a disaster. My dad, who told me to never give up, keep my head to the sky because the clouds are why. To Ivette, my Curvy Girl partner, thank you for pushing me to publish my novel on my own terms. Thank you to the amazing writers of The Tribe. It feels good to have a place for us! To Des, your journey inspires me every day. I'm in awe of the stories you create and the strength you have to persist in this industry. To CD, thank you for your daily words of feminist encouragement and the insane ability you have as a beta reader. Thank you to all my betas. This novel wouldn't be where it is without you. My editor Kylie and my cover artist Leni, you helped me bring this novel to life! Thank you to my partner, Mr. Eli, who doesn't bat an eyelash when I roll into bed at 2 or 3 am after an intense writing session. Thank you for listening to me when I'm frustrated and letting me cry on your shoulder when I feel like my writing isn't good enough. And last but certainly not least, thank you to my amazing patrons!

Patrons

A. McCullough
Desastr
M. Bateman
N. Lee
Kyondra
T. Eneh
Z. Hudson
K. Lewis
M. Barnes
Kiara
CD Pulley
JC Candanedo
L!ghtQu33n
JC Hurston
D. Copeland
K. W.
M. Fisher
Priscilla H.
M. Ceasar
Renee
M. Merritt
Q. Hayward
Jahniece
B. Wade
Skyesabove143
D. Ad
R. Mensah
J.M. Collins
Jazleen
Niamya
Remember Ir
Destiny
Nicole
Van
T. Hardy
Cera P.
S. Rieu
B
K. O'Neal
C. Green
Queen Shikongo
Tapiwa
A. Bora
G.Blast
Jazmine
S. Terrance
Tameka
N. Rambang
S. Morgan
lucystarx
Tasha
Hawa
T. Mbazumutima
E. Fef
S. Harris
Adelle
C. Whitmore
K. McKinney
S. Lindsay

Thank you for your support!

To my Little Bees, your love and support means the world to me! As always, thank you so, so much for reading!

Soundtrack

The official Me Too soundtrack is available on Spotify. Use the link or search: **Me Too Official Soundtrack**.

https://open.spotify.com/playlist/2EQkeei20Zs2FWtIorjEKB?si=14667ea236874beb

1. Bloom - Sultan + Shephard
2. Catching On - Elephante ft. Nevve
3. Balance - The Him ft. Oktavian
4. Hell and High Water - Major Lazer ft. Alessia Cara & Utiliti
5. Guilty - Chad Cooper ft. Robaer
6. Sway - Syn Cole ft. Nevve
7. Discover Love - Ryos, Envy Monroe & Kaidro
8. SOS - Avicii ft. Aloe Black
9. Good Thing - Tritonal ft. Laurell
10. White Lies - The Him
11. Crooked - Steve Void
12. Sunday Morning - Matoma ft. Josie Dunne
13. Woman - Andreya Triana
14. Little Love - Blinkie ft. Grace Tither
15. Undo My Heart - Karen Harding & Digital Farm Animals
16. Have Mercy - Chloe
17. Old Friend - Elderbrook
18. Kiss It Better - Rhianna
19. Need a Reason - Kelly Rowland ft. Future & Maejor
20. Like You Love Me - Conro, Disero & Alice France
21. Tell My Heart - Nora En Pure ft. Dani Senior
22. LaLaLa - Black Coffee ft. Usher
23. Breathe - Seinabo Sey
24. Underwater - Rufus Du Sol
25. Naked - Ella Mai
26. You Need Me - Black Coffee ft. Maxine Ashley & Sun-El Musician
27. Mother's Daughter - Miley Cyrus
28. Guess Again - Plan B
29. Ultraviolet - Fred V & Grafix
30. I Got U - Duke Dumont & Jax Jones

Chapter 1

Nadia cursed under her breath as she ran up the gray stone steps to the entrance of a towering black mirrored building. She pushed through the revolving glass doors, her heels clicking against the swirling black and gray-tiled floor to the bank of elevators at the far end of the spacious lobby. The decadent scent of fresh coffee wafted through her nose as she passed the little canteen near the oval receptionists' station. If she hadn't woken up late, misplaced her keys and her purse, she might've had a moment to indulge in the cup of coffee she so desperately needed. She tore her gaze away from the canteen and picked up her pace through the few employees littering the lobby to the elevator.

"Hold the - Ah!" she screamed as her damn heel caught in the fold of the pristine black and gold Shola Enterprises embossed rug. Her arms flailed as she flew forward through the doors and crashed into the hard chest of the unsuspecting man in her path.

"What the hell?" A deep voice grumbled as they slammed

backward into the wall and the elevator doors closed with a soft ding.

Nadia caught her breath and slowly looked up at the black suited man. He was so *tall.* She barely reached his broad shoulders in her three-inch heels and–oh dear. A fire burned over her cheeks, her throat dried as she stared at the man's tawny chiseled face and glaring gaze. "I…I am so sorry! I'm so clumsy," she said, laughing nervously as she pushed out of his arms.

"It's fine. Just look where you're going next time," he said, straightening his suit and smoothing a hand over his short midnight hair. "Are you alright?"

"Yeah." She cringed at her impeccable ability to make a fool of herself. "I'm sorry again."

"It's okay," he grumbled, moving around her. "What floor are you going to?" he said with his hand poised over the control panel, waiting for her answer.

She frowned. "Um…" She laughed. "I'm having a brain fart. I can't remember what floor I'm supposed to work on."

He sighed and checked the onyx watch on his wrist. "What department do you work for?"

Her cheeks burned up to her ears at his dry, disinterested tone. He clearly wasn't the type to find humor in her mishaps. Great. Not only was she running late, but she'd already annoyed the first person she met. "Um, marketing and investments. Cameron Ramirez is my boss." At least she remembered that.

His golden hazel eyes widened. Just a little, but enough to show he was interested. "You're the new International rep, Nadia Coleman, right?" he said, pressing the number six on the panel. "Cameron wouldn't stop talking about you yesterday."

She nodded. "Yes, that's me. So, what do you do here?"

He raised a thick black eyebrow and scoffed. "Not a good start that you don't know who the CEO is."

"Oh my God," she said, sliding a hand over her mouth. She'd studied Shola Enterprises enough that she should've immediately recognized his handsome features that were slapped on nearly every business and investment magazine. "You're Luca Shola. I'm an idiot. I promise I'm not normally this clumsy or forgetful."

A smug grin tugged at his lips. "Something tells me you are this clumsy, but the forgetfulness is probably because you have a hangover."

She choked out a laugh. How the hell did he know that?

"This is your floor, Miss Coleman." The elevator dinged, and the doors slid open, much to her relief. "Get yourself a cup of coffee," he said as he dug his hand in his pocket and held out a small packet of ibuprofen to her. "I expect to see good things from you."

"Yes, Mr. Shola," she said and took the offered painkillers. Her fingers grazed his warm skin and sent a tingle up her arm from the faint touch. "Thank you."

Nadia stepped off the elevator and stared at the tablets in her hand. She laughed as she slipped the medicine in her pocket. What a way to start her first day? She pushed through the glass doors of the marketing department into a bright beige office space with various posters on the wall in shining gold frames that boasted of the company's accolades from previous marketing and PR campaigns.

The space was oddly quiet save for the muffled voices in the offices behind frosted glass walls and the receptionist typing away at the smooth oak wood desk with a golden Shola Enterprises 'SE' logo embellished on the front. The young man looked up at her, his mouth curled into a pearly white smile that was a beautiful contrast against his dark brown skin.

"Good morning, Miss Coleman." The receptionist's brown eyes sparkled with excitement as he stood to greet her. "I'll let Mr. Ramirez know you've arrived."

"No need, Alex." A tall gentleman with russet brown skin and light brown eyes walked in a smooth rhythmic gait toward her, buttoning his pressed navy blue suit over his white shirt and salmon pink tie. "Good morning, Nadia." A dazzling smile spread over his lips as he checked the silver watch on his wrist. "I thought for sure you were going to be late."

"Good morning, Mr. Ramirez." She greeted, and the packet of ibuprofen burned in her pocket as her cheeks flushed from the memory of her embarrassing tumble. "I almost was."

He chuckled, tapping a finger to his head. "Yeah, did you have fun last night? Looks like a bit of the party came to work with you."

Alex stifled a laugh as he sat down and busied himself with whatever work her entrance interrupted. Nadia frowned at his reaction and slowly slid a hand to her hair. Her eyes grew wide when she felt a cluster of glitter in her curls. "I-I woke up late and I didn't have time to–I'm so sorry." How did she miss the damn confetti? She'd given herself a once over before racing out the door, but clearly missed the glittering silver and gold specks. She cringed. "I was in the elevator with Mr. Shola. He must've seen this."

"It's fine. I did the same thing when I got this job. I showed up here worse than you." Mr. Ramirez laughed. "Don't worry about it. I'm sure Luca thought it was funny."

"If you say so." Nadia sighed. "He didn't seem too impressed with me."

"Luca doesn't seem impressed with anyone. The fact that he talked to you tells me he didn't mind your appearance. You'll be fine."

"Fair enough." She patted the braid around her head. There was no way that glitter was coming out unless she washed her curls, so she'd just have to be the sparkling new girl. Another check in her 'how to fuck up on the first day' list.

"So, now that I've made my awkward entrance, what do you have planned for me today?"

"It's not awkward at all." Mr. Ramirez said. "We pride ourselves on being the liveliest department here at Shola. You're going to fit right in." He grinned and rubbed his hands together. "I'd like to do a few introductions to start and then you can take over the international side of things."

Nadia's eyes grew wide, her heart thumped in excitement. "You said you're going to hire other reps. You don't expect me to run this department, do you?"

He chuckled softly, motioning for her to follow him down the hall. "For now, yes. I think your qualifications and previous work experience make you perfectly suited to run the department. I have faith in you."

"I'm glad you do, Mr. Ramirez. I'm happy to be a lead rep for now," she said as they walked down the beige and brown speckled carpet into the main office behind the frosted glass.

"Cameron is just fine," he said. "I don't mind Mr. Ramirez from the younger employees, but we're practically the same age."

"Okay." She nodded, looking over the wide-open office of twenty plus employees tapping and typing away at their desks. A bright smile spread over her lips as Cameron introduced her to the team of internal and external marketing coordinators. This job was the opportunity she'd been waiting for. She had experience running start-up projects for smaller companies and she was fluent in several languages. This was her chance to finally take control of her life. She wasn't going to let anything or anyone stop her from doing what she came here to do.

There was too much riding on this and Shola Enterprises was her last chance to get it right.

Chapter 2

Luca stepped off the elevator and chuckled to himself. Cameron didn't mention anything about his new employee being such an attractive little mess. She was a damn hazard waiting to happen. She'd do well in Cameron's department of misfits.

"Mr. Shola, Miss Dagenham is waiting for you in your office," his assistant called as he walked past her desk.

Luca's humored mood plummeted into a pool of anxiety at the mention of that name. Ciara Dagenham was the last person he wanted to see this morning or ever again if he had the choice. "Thanks." Luca's hand shook, gripping the door handle. "Next time, make her wait out here." He pushed the door open to find Ciara's blonde head sitting in his chair facing the wide windows overlooking Boston's skyline.

"Good morning, Lu." Ciara swiveled around in his high-backed Italian leather chair. A smile graced her rose pink lips as she untied her tan trench coat to reveal her pale naked body–save for the red lace undergarments barely covering her intimates. "I thought we could have a little make up sex to start your day."

Luca grit his teeth. "We're not doing that, Ciara." He seethed, shrugging off his coat and hanging it on the rack next to the door. "And get the fuck out of my chair. I have work to do."

"Aw, come on. You're not still mad at me, are you?" she pouted, sliding her fingers over the hem of her panties. "I want to make it up to you. You know I didn't mean it."

"You always say that and I'm always the one who ends up hurt," he said, pointing to the door. "Get out."

Ciara's warm brown eyes turned cold as she stood from his chair, yanking her coat around herself. She marched toward him and he fought the urge to flinch in anticipation of her taking a jab at him. "You won't stay mad forever. You'll come crawling back to me. You have to." She grabbed his face, digging her crimson nails into his cheeks. "You're a weak man, Luca. You're lucky I still want you with your tainted blood and disgusting scars," she sneered, pushing his face away from her. "I'll see you tonight."

The door closed with a soft click behind her, and Luca let out the breath lodged in his chest, tugging his suit jacket closer around him. Half of his scars were from her and she made him feel like it was his fault she beat him.

Luca crossed the beige carpeted floor and slid a hand over his face as he slumped into his chair. He didn't want to go back to her. Looking at the photo of his family beside his computer, he heaved a deep sigh. But he'd have to. He was the only one standing between his family and his grandfather's power over them.

***

Chapter 2

Luca's heart churned as his phone buzzed on his desk. Picking up the sleek black device, he glared at the message scrolling across the screen.

Ciara » Come on, Lu. I miss you and Daddy's asking questions. You know I hate that. «

He'd been avoiding Ciara for three weeks. It was the longest he'd ever gotten away with it, but it looked like his time was up. Luca ran a hand over his face and tapped his reply.

Luca » I'll be at your fundraiser on Monday.«

Ciara »Fine. I'll give you the weekend, but my dad will be at the shareholders' meeting today, so don't say anything stupid.«

"Fuck," he whispered. He avoided her for too long if her father was coming to the office. If he didn't act right around him, his grandfather would be next. Ciara's father and his grandfather have worked together for years building up the lucrative Syndicate society and their lasting legacy. His grandfather would be furious if he thought Luca was getting in the way of that. He didn't need any more scars from him.

"Luca! Have you seen the reports?"

He jumped as his bubbly father burst into his office. "Yes, I was just looking over them. What are you doing here?" he asked, watching him take a seat in the leather chair in front of his desk.

His father usually left everyday business to him now that he was retired, but he still came around occasionally to see how things were going and raise morale with his presence. Everyone loved his impromptu visits and Luca usually didn't mind but knowing Ciara's father was going to be here today, his father's cheerful existence grated on his nerves.

"Well, I had to come meet the new International rep at the shareholders' meeting. I'm so pleased with these numbers so far." He beamed and his hazel eyes sparkled with joy as he spun the glass storm globe on the desk, which annoyed Luca even further. "And your mother wanted me to have lunch with you. She said she hasn't heard from you in a few days. She's worried."

A whisper of a smile tugged at Luca's lips. His mother was always worried about him. It was her guilt eating away at her for putting him in this position, but he couldn't be mad at her for following her heart. His mother disobeyed his grandfather when she was young and eloped with his father. She fell in love with the wrong type of man in his grandfather's eyes, and now Luca was forced to suffer her consequences. "I'm fine, but I wouldn't mind having lunch with you. I want to talk to you about some of these new investments – "

"Luca." He laughed. "We're not going to talk business. I want to talk about you. You've been holed up in your penthouse since you stopped seeing Ciara and even before that you hardly went out unless you were going to a Dagenham event."

Luca groaned. "If that's what this lunch is, I'm not going. You, of all people, should know why I live like this."

"I know." His father sighed and the light in his eyes dimmed. "Are you going to be okay at the meeting? I saw Arnold walk in with a few of the other shareholders."

"Yeah." Luca smirked. "I've already been warned not to say anything stupid."

"As long as he and your grandfather think you two are doing alright, we have nothing to worry about."

"I know," he said, grabbing the reports on his desk. "Do you want to chair the meeting? I'm sure everyone will appreciate it."

"Sure, I don't mind coming out of retirement for that." His father chuckled, following him out of the office to walk across the hall to the conference room. A startled cry coupled with a loud bang rang out into the hallway as they neared the meeting space. Luca sighed and shook his head. He didn't even need to guess who caused the commotion.

His father stifled a laugh as they entered the room. "Is that our new rep?" he whispered as Cameron helped up the curly auburn-haired employee sprawled out on the floor.

Luca's lip twitched, a slight smile tugging at the corners. "Yes, that would be her."

"I-I'm fine! I'm fine!" Nadia laughed as Cameron helped her into her chair. "Well, at least I didn't spill my coffee," her bubbly voice giggled.

"Goodness, what am I going to do with you?" Cameron chuckled as he rubbed a hand over his tightly curled black hair and sat next to her.

Luca's father turned to him as they took their seats. "I like her." He grinned and looked down the table at the young woman putting her papers back together. "That was quite a spill, Miss Coleman. I hope you're alright?"

Her bright sea-green eyes grew wide as she slowly nodded. "Oh, yes, I'm fine. Thank you."

Cameron struggled to keep a straight face and Luca bit his cheeks to fight the laugh itching to burst from his lips at the humorous sight. The feeling quickly faded when he caught Arnold Dagenham's unamused gaze. The steely look in his eyes made his stomach knot with anxiety.

Luca cleared his throat. "Right, let's get this meeting started," he grumbled. "For those of you who don't know, this is Philip Shola, retired CEO and owner of Shola Enterprises."

His father grinned, slapping a hand on his shoulder. "And Luca has kindly offered to let me chair this meeting for old time's sake. I hope you don't mind?"

"Of course not, Phil. It's good for us retirees to come out and show these young kids how it was done in our day." Arnold chuckled and cut his brown eyes at Luca.

Luca ignored the snide comment. There was no need to start a row with Arnold. He'd just keep his head down and let his father take over the meeting. He found little joy in chairing these, anyway. It was just a pissing match between the shareholders and management. Most of them hated that Cameron was the head of marketing and investments.

He was a black man in a prominent role and some of the legacy shareholders had a hard time accepting it, especially Arnold. That never ceased to amuse Luca since his father was Native Hawaiian, but until he took over as CEO, the face of the company didn't reflect their non-white roots like it did now.

Luca looked up from his notes to listen to Cameron's report and his eyes drifted to the beautiful brown skinned, auburn-haired conundrum next to him. He didn't quite understand her and he found himself a bit too drawn to watching her awkward antics around the office. Nadia tripped over damn near everything, and it humored and unnerved him at the same time.

He watched as she carefully brought her cup of coffee to her plump mauve lacquered lips and jotted down a few notes on the pad in front of her. The action was so simple, but he found it so alluring to watch her.

A buzz on his watch drew his attention to the message scrolling across the screen.

A. Dagen-douche » Staring a bit too hard, son. I'd hate to catch my daughter's boyfriend with wandering eyes.«

Fuck. Luca looked down at his notebook, tapping his pen against the pages in irritation. Arnold was just as bad as Ciara. He just hoped that minor slip up wasn't enough for him to tattle to his grandfather. That was the last thing he needed.

Chapter 3

"Next we have a report from our newest member of the team, Nadia Coleman." Philip smiled.

"Please don't fall," Cameron whispered to her.

She blushed and cut her eyes at him. "Shut up," she mumbled in annoyance as she slowly stood from her chair. "Hi, everyone. I'm Nadia Coleman, the International PR rep or the girl who missed her chair," she began, causing the room to fill with laughter. Nadia caught Cameron giving Luca an odd smile through her report, but she shook it off as them sharing a joke about her mishap. It didn't bother her. She was used to that.

When she concluded her brief, she nearly laughed at Cameron holding her chair steady beneath her. He'd become like a brother to her in the few weeks she'd been working there and he genuinely looked out for her. She'd never had a boss that cared like that and she loved the camaraderie they shared.

"Could I ask a few questions about your report, Miss

Coleman?" The graying blond-haired man smiled from across the table.

"Sure, what would you like to know?"

He tapped his finger over the notes in front of him. "What makes you qualified to project these kinds of profits? Your background is in small start-up companies, is it not? I also heard you left Hatch Engineering without so much as a notice. How can we trust you'll stay here to see this through?"

Nadia's heart thumped. She wasn't expecting a question like that or for someone to look that far back into her history. She cleared her throat and squeezed her hands in her lap.

"You don't have to answer that, Nadia," Cameron said.

"No, I think she should. Mr. Dagenham makes a valid point." Another older gentleman nodded. "We're putting a lot of energy into building the international department," he said and looked down the table at Luca. "We need to know the person you've hired is qualified to do the job and not because she meets some sort of *quota* you've imposed."

Nadia's eyes grew wide. Oh, hell no. He thought she was a *token* hire? She single-handedly revamped the marketing strategies of a few of the failing investments in the few short weeks she'd been there.

"Do you have a problem with the way I run the company, Mr. Sharpe?" Luca chuckled as he sat his pen down. "Let me remind you that shareholders only have a say in what we invest in, not how we operate the company, nor do you have a say in who my directors choose to employ," Luca said as he flipped through Nadia's report. "In Miss Coleman's first three weeks, she generated profit from three textile manufacturers that this group voted to invest in against my better judgment. All of which haven't turned a profit since we acquired them three years ago. I'd say she's qualified to do the job and not because she meets a quota," he said, turning to Nadia and his hard golden gaze sent a chill down her spine. "You're free to answer the questions posed to you, Miss Coleman, but know that you don't owe anyone an explanation for your background."

She cleared her dry throat and nodded. "Thank you, Mr. Shola, but I'd like to address my ability to project those profit margins," she said, turning to the steely brown eyed man. She knew Mr. Dagenham's type. The uber rich hedge fund entrepreneur who never worked an actual day in his life but had an opinion about everyone else's work ethic.

A grin curled over her lips as she explained how she planned to revamp the tired marketing strategies, restructure the money being poured into the failing communications plan and breathe life back into the products by utilizing her skills in social media to increase the profit margins of the companies in question. "And with the changes and improvements I'm going to implement, Shola should recoup the initial investment and earn a profit on these companies in the next fiscal year."

Mr. Dagenham raised an eyebrow. "Well." He clicked his tongue. "Thank you for explaining that, Miss Coleman."

"Yes, that's quite the robust plan." Mr. Sharpe nodded and tugged at his tie. "I believe you'll do well here."

Nadia cut her eyes to the aging pale faced man with a full gray mustache and receding hairline. "Thank you."

"Alright." Philip chuckled. "If those are all the questions and concerns, I think this is a good time to adjourn this meeting. We'll see you all next quarter."

Nadia stole a glance at Luca while the shareholders grumbled their goodbyes and shuffled out of the room. Her cheeks burned up to her ears when she caught his warm golden gaze, but the feeling soon passed as a pained look flashed in his eyes when Mr. Dagenham patted a hand on his shoulder.

Nadia dragged her eyes away from the scene, but not before she caught Mr. Dagenham's threatening glare. That didn't settle right with her, especially the way Luca's body tensed at his touch. She shook her head as she gathered her notes and turned to Cameron. "You didn't tell me these meetings got *that* extra."

"Yeah." He sighed. "I'm used to the things they say, but that was bad. Arnold shouldn't have asked you that. You told me you left Hatch for personal reasons, and that's all I need to know. You don't owe anyone an explanation for that."

"Miss Coleman, are you okay?" Philip asked as he and Luca stood from their seats to move closer to them. Nadia found it uncanny how similar they were. Same tall, broad physique, golden hazel eyes, and thick, short black hair. Luca was a shade lighter than his father's bronze skin tone and if it wasn't for Philip's graying hair, they could be brothers.

"I'm alright, Mr. Shola," she said as she and Cameron stood from their seats. "I've dealt with people like that before. Not as blatant, but it happens."

"I'm sorry about that," Luca said as he slid his hands in his pockets, making his muscles tighten against the sleeves of his crisp black suit. "Some shareholders can be a bit too outspoken for their own good."

"Yes, and it's always the same few," Philip murmured, crossing his arms over his chest. "I hope this doesn't make you feel unwelcome here. I'd hate to lose an excellent employee like you."

"If I'm honest, that meeting made me feel uncomfortable, but I feel very welcome here and I like the values of this company. However, from a public relations standpoint, having shareholders with that kind of mindset isn't a good look."

A slow smile spread over Luca's lips and the subtle change to his otherwise somber expression caused a flurry of butterflies tingling in her gut. "How many times have Cam and I told you the same thing?"

"Alright, well you and Cam can talk to me about it again at lunch," Philip said and his warm hazel eyes fell on Nadia and a smile graced his lips. "Thank you for your honesty, Miss Coleman. I hope we're lucky enough to have you here for a long time."

"Thank you, Mr. Shola. It was nice to meet you." She smiled. "Enjoy your lunch."

Luca moved to the side to let her pass. She took a step and she stumbled forward when her heel caught on the leg of the chair, naturally. Luca's hand shot out and grabbed her arm to steady her, as if he expected her to tumble. "You alright?"

"I'm fine." She laughed. "Damn chair is out to get me."

"I guess so," he murmured. "Watch your step out there," he said, letting go of her arm and leaving a warm tingle over her skin.

"Thanks," she said, moving past him to the door. She rubbed her arm where he touched her. That slight gesture sent a tingle down her spine and pooled in a place it shouldn't have.

Nadia shook her head and bit her lip as she took the elevator back to her office. She didn't need those kinds of thoughts clouding her mind.

Chapter 3

"You alright, Nadia?" Alex said, from his seat behind reception, dressed in a navy blue suit with a bright floral yellow bow tie.

She looked up and flashed him a smile. "Yeah, I'm fine. I, um, met the shareholders."

"They're a trip, huh?" He chuckled. "So, which Dagenham did you meet? Arnold or his daughter, Ciara?"

"Arnold, he's a bit much."

"Mm-hm, even more so that he apparently likes to keep tabs on Hades because of his on again off again relationship with Ciara or so the rumors go." Alex shrugged and she chuckled at the nickname everyone called Luca for his cold and distant demeanor around the office. It was fitting of his mysterious aura and the black suits he wore, but a twinge of jealousy tugged at her heart. Luca had a girlfriend.

"Anyway, Mr. Visser called for you. He'd like to schedule a meeting and you've got some junk mail," he said and held out a few magazines and letters to her. "Don't worry about Mr. Dagenham or the shareholders. We only have to deal with their tone-deaf asses occasionally."

"Thank God for that. You know they thought I was a token hire?"

Alex let out a bark of laughter. "Girl, they think half the damn workforce are token hires. They're not used to black folk knowing how to do a damn job," he said, rolling his eyes. "You coming to lunch with the team today?"

She nodded. "Yeah, I think I will," she said, taking her mail from him.

Nadia strolled down the hall to her office with envy still biting at her at the thought of Luca's girlfriend. She shook her head. Luca was just nice to look at and it was nice of him to stick up for her in the meeting, but that would be the extent of this tiny crush she had on him. A crush was the last thing she needed. Being single was safe and she had other things to worry about than daydreaming about Luca's gorgeous smile.

Chapter 4

Luca let out a long sigh as he and Cameron walked back to his office. "I'm glad you got roped into lunch with my dad. It'll keep him from talking about my personal life."

"You're not getting out of that." Cameron chuckled as they passed his assistant's desk and into his office. The morning light filtered into the space and brightened up the plush black leather couches and chairs Luca chose to fit his mood.

"Seriously, you too? You know why I'm like this. You saw Arnold in that meeting," he huffed, slumping into his lavish black leather chair.

"Yeah, I did," Cameron said, taking a seat in the chair in front of him. "But you need to stop letting them dictate your life, man. When was the last time you went out and had a drink with me? When was the last time you danced?"

Looking out the wide windows, Luca stared at the glittering skyline cast in the sun's warm morning haze. "I don't dance anymore and I just had a drink with you last weekend."

"Yeah, in your fucking penthouse." Cameron shook his

head. "You used to love to dance. That used to be your thing."

"Mm, it used to be," he mumbled. He and Cameron used to be the Dynamic Duo. They could dance anyone off the floor in the nightclub and he felt alive, but that stopped when Arnold and his grandfather's Syndicates, the secret nationalistic society full of wealthy and powerful business moguls, came for his family. "Now the business is my thing." Luca sighed. "Why are you bringing this up, anyway?"

Cameron shrugged. "Well, you broke up with Ciara again and you haven't gone back to her. I just figured something's changed in your situation since you've been eyeing up my new employee."

A blush scorched Luca's cheeks. "No, nothing's changed." He scoffed. "And I haven't been doing that."

Cameron raised an eyebrow. "We've been best friends for over two decades. You think I don't know when you're checking someone out?"

"I just..." he trailed off as his heart thumped at the thought of Nadia's striking green eyes and the way her body felt when she crashed into him. He shook his head to wipe that image from his mind. "She's so damn clumsy. How can't I notice her?" he grumbled.

Cameron nodded. "I know what you mean. I've never met anyone who can trip on air."

Luca chuckled. "How did she miss her chair in the conference room?"

They stared at each other and fell out laughing at the memory. Tears pricked Luca's eyes as his stomach clenched from laughing so hard.

"Oh, shit." Cameron wheezed through his laughter. "I

haven't heard you laugh like that in a long time."

Luca wiped his tears. "I know, but damn that was funny. Nadia's pretty interesting."

"Mm, that's another first for you," Cameron said and slid a hand to his chin. "Listen, I think I can help you with your situation with Ciara. I'm going to put a call into my friend. She's a special agent for the Feds, but does some PI work on the side." Cameron held up his hand. "Before you interrupt me. I know your ex-military guards have been doing an investigation on the Syndicates' black market dealings and connections, but just humor me. Raquel is really good at what she does. Maybe you need some fresh eyes on this. It couldn't hurt."

Luca thought about it for a moment and nodded. "That's not a bad idea. My family needs all the help we can get."

"I'll let her know," he said. "So when do you have to make up with Ciara?"

Luca sighed and looked away from Cameron to stare out the windows again. "Monday. She's allowing me the weekend."

"Alright, in that case you're going to Kani Kani with me tonight."

Luca slid his eyes to his friend's cheerful brown orbs. "Ciara wouldn't want me to go there. She doesn't like it when I dance."

Cameron scrunched up his face in disgust. "There you go, letting her rule your life. You're not together right now. Why the fuck do you care what she thinks?"

"Because I have to. You know my situation with the Dagenhams."

"Yeah, I know. You're stuck making amends for your

parents' forbidden marriage, but that shit shouldn't be your problem and the Dagenhams don't own you." He scoffed. "Come on dude, come out with me tonight. DJ D would love to see you and Ciara hates that area. You'll be fine."

Luca stared at him. Ciara hated Kani Kani. The area was too 'urban' for her liking and Cameron made a valid point. He was free. At least for a little while. "Fine, I'll go."

Cameron clapped his hands together. "Yes!"

"But I'm not staying out all night."

Cameron grinned. "Fine, fine, whatever. I'm just happy you're going."

***

Luca followed behind Cameron into the darkened night club. A comforting rush of excitement washed over him as the music bumped through the speakers throughout the two-storey establishment. The colorful strobe lights bounced off the mirrors and people dancing in the crowded space. The laughter and rumble of chatter were joyous and the drinks were flowing at the fully stocked bar.

A smile spread across Luca's lips at the dancing brown-skinned, pink-haired DJ on the raised stage above the dance floor. He loved this club and used to come here all the time when his family first moved from the west coast. It was where he used to hide to get away from the high-end parties Ciara liked to drag him to.

The club was for dance enthusiasts and prided itself on being the dance battle central. It was a great place for Luca to unwind and it was even better when Cameron moved to Boston. They tore up the competition in this club. No one could beat them in a battle.

"See, it's not so bad." Cameron laughed, handing him a drink.

"Yeah, but I'm still not–"

"Is that, *Nadia?*"

"What?" he said, following Cameron's gaze through the crowd to the dance floor. His heart stuttered at Nadia dancing effortlessly with a group of women. He couldn't tear his eyes away from her. The way she swayed her hips and her feet moved flawlessly to the beat of the music was like she lived and breathed the moves.

Luca took a slow sip of his drink to wet his dry throat. He had no idea she could move like this. She was far too clumsy to dance like that. He moved through the dancing bodies around him to get a better look because the woman out there couldn't be the same one that tripped all over the office.

"I can't believe what I'm seeing right now." Cameron laughed next to him.

"Neither can I," Luca mumbled, taking in Nadia's sultry attire. Her army green tank top matched her green eyes and showed off the smooth brown skin of her midriff. Gold chains wrapped around her waist above her tight denim jeans and he nearly bit his lip at the gold stilettos on her feet. His eyes trailed back up to her laughing face and the mane of auburn curls framing her head. Dear God, she was gorgeous.

"This looks like they're trying to start a battle," Cameron murmured, nudging him. "You too rusty to take them on?"

Luca slowly shook his head. "Nope." He had to challenge her. He was too enticed not to show her up. Maybe Cameron was right to drag him out tonight. He finished his drink and placed his glass on the tray of a passing server. He rolled his shoulders and a grin spread across his face. Maybe he needed this.

"Alright, the Furies aren't playing tonight! Do we have any challengers?" DJ D called out as the song ended and Luca was quick to raise his hand.

There was a soft gasp and then an excited squeal belted out from the DJ booth. "Oh, my word?" she said, with her bright pink braids and golden headphones glittering in the strobe lights. "The Dynamic Duo has graced my club again! You ladies better be ready."

Luca's heart thumped in anticipation as he looked across the floor at Nadia's shocked face while the sweaty dancers around them backed away as they walked out under the strobe lights to take on her crew.

The surprise on Nadia's face twisted into a smug look of determination and a devilish grin curled over Luca's lips as he baited her with his moves.

The battle was lively and Nadia's crew proved to be an excellent challenge especially with her as their fearless leader. At one point, Nadia and her friend broke away from their crew, stalked onto the dance floor, interrupting Luca and Cameron's set to mimic their moves. Every single one of them as if they'd created the damn routine themselves.

DJ D announced the battle a tie as the bumping tune faded and the Furies cried foul at the results. "You know the rules, ladies. All five of you needed to match them to win!"

Nadia laughed as she wiped the sweat beaded on her forehead and looked up at him with joy radiating in her eyes. "I'm impressed, Mr. Shola. I didn't know you were a dancer."

Luca cringed at the formality as he ran a hand through his damp hair. "It's just Luca and I'm impressed by you too."

"Whew! After that fiery battle, I think we could all use something to cool down," DJ D said as the soft piano melody and slow drum beats of Syn Cole's Sway filtered through the speakers.

"Enjoy your night Luca." Nadia smiled and followed her friends off the floor.

Luca grabbed her hand before she could get too far away from him. He wasn't sure what came over him, but he wasn't ready to stop dancing with her. A blush scorched his cheeks as he stared into Nadia's confused green eyes. "Would you mind another dance?"

A smile spread across her face, and a glint of mischief filled her eyes. "Sure, but do you think you can handle it?"

"Oh, I'm sure I can." He chuckled, slipping his arm around her waist. He didn't know what he was doing, but he couldn't let this moment pass him by. "How is this possible?" he said as they fell into the rhythm with each other.

"What do you mean?" she said as he twirled her around and held her back against his chest.

"You're amazing at this, but a complete disaster at walking." He laughed. "I'm so confused by you."

"Mm," Nadia mumbled as she leaned into him and he savored the way her curves felt, as if she were the piece missing from his puzzle. "Dancing is just my thing. You don't have to understand it."

"Fair enough." He grinned. "I'll just enjoy this rare moment with you."

She turned around and slid her hand to the back of his

neck as a beautiful smile graced her fuchsia lips. "It doesn't have to be. I like dancing with you."

His heart thumped, and his throat felt dry at that simple admission. "I like dancing with you too," he whispered, but she was wrong. This was a rare occasion because he couldn't do this again. Luca forced himself to stay in this moment with her as the music swelled around them. He'd cherish this and after tonight, he'd lock this feeling away because this couldn't last.

The song came to a gentle end, as if to punctuate his thoughts. The moment was over. He should just say thank you and walk away.

He leaned down to her, his lips nearly grazed her ear and the sweet jasmine scent of her perfume teased his senses. "Do you want to get a drink?" His eyes widened at the words that rolled off his tongue, and he was thankful for the darkened space to hide the utter embarrassment on his face.

"Yeah, I need some air," she said as she stepped away from him to move through the sweltering bodies dancing around them. He slid his hand to the small of Nadia's back and guided her toward the bar where Cameron was standing next to her friend.

They looked to be deep in conversation, and a smile tugged at Luca's lips. He could tell by the wide smile on Cameron's face that the brown skinned, curly haired woman clad in a short golden slip dress was just his type. The woman looked over her shoulder and giggled as she waved them over.

"Nadia, your very nice boss got us some drinks." She smiled as Cameron handed them both a glass of spirits.

"Thanks." Nadia grinned. "I see you've met my bestie, Cameron."

"Yes, I have and you two looked like you were enjoying yourselves out there," he said and winked at Luca, which made his cheeks flush.

"Yeah, what was up with that?" Nadia's friend laughed and held out her hand to him. "I'm Minerva, by the way."

He chuckled, taking her offered hand. "I'm Luca, it's nice to meet you."

"Well, you know I couldn't deny the loser a dance after that battle," Nadia said as she brought the glass to her plump lips.

"Loser?" Luca smirked. "I'm pretty sure DJ D called that a tie."

Nadia and Minerva looked at each other and burst out laughing. "We fucking won that battle and you losers know it," Minerva snickered.

Cameron looked at Luca, and they grinned. "I feel like those are fighting words," Cameron said. "Next time, how about you two ditch your crew and battle us?"

Nadia shrugged. "Yeah, alright, but we'll still win."

Luca and Cameron followed them to a table with the rest of their dance crew. They were a spirited bunch of women who wouldn't let him and Cameron live down the fact that Minerva and Nadia essentially beat them.

"You two seem alright to me," Minerva said as she sat her glass on the table and clapped her hands. "We usually go to another club after this and you're more than welcome to join us."

"Actually, I'm going to pass on that. I'm not really in the mood for that crowd tonight. I'm going to head home," Nadia said, yawning.

Minerva rolled her eyes. "Bitch, you getting old," she said as she looked at Cameron and Luca. "What about you guys?

Are you coming?"

Luca chuckled at Nadia's annoyed glare at her friend. He cleared his throat and shook his head. "No, I second what Nadia said. I think I'll just call it a night."

"So you're an old fart too, Luca." Minerva shook her head and turned her attention to Cameron. "Well, what about you? Are you too tired to hang out with us?"

He looked at Minerva and a grin spread across his lips at her hopeful smile. "Nope, I'll join you."

"Good," Minerva said, looking away from him. "Nadia, are you sure you don't want to come? I don't feel right not walking home with you."

She nodded. "I'll be fine. I'm just down the street. You don't have to walk me," she said, sliding out of the booth. "You guys go have fun."

Luca's heart thumped at the thought of her walking home alone. He didn't like the idea of that, but he shouldn't concern himself with it. He'd spent enough time with her already, and Nadia looked like she could handle herself.

"I can walk you home." The words slipped out of his mouth before he could fucking stop himself. Why? Why couldn't he just keep his mouth shut?

Nadia raised her eyebrow and he ignored the surprised look from Cameron next to him. Luca ran a hand through his hair as he stood from the table. "I, uh, agree with Minerva. You shouldn't walk home by yourself."

Nadia bit her lip and turned her surprised green eyes to Minerva. "See? No need to worry. I'll be safe with Luca."

He didn't know why that filled him with such a sense of pride, but it was true. He wouldn't let anything happen to her in his care, and he always wanted her to feel that way about him. And… he really didn't want this to end with her. Shit. He'd just walk her home and forget about these feelings.

"Mm-hm, you better look out for my girl, Luca." Minerva pointed her finger at him before she turned her glittering nail to Nadia. "And you better text me when you get home. I mean it, Nadia," she huffed.

"I will, Nervy." Nadia laughed as she tucked her phone into her back pocket and turned her amused gaze on Cameron. "I know you're my boss, but you better behave yourself with my friends."

He grinned. "Of course. You two get home safe."

Luca slid his hand to Nadia's waist and guided her back through the crowd of people dancing and pushing around them to get to the bar. He stole a glance at her and his heart pounded in panic. He shouldn't be taking her home. What was he going to talk to her about? What if they walked in complete silence? He wasn't exactly the debonair man he used to be when he exuded confidence.

What if Ciara's little spies saw him?

Luca took a deep breath before they reached the exit. Fuck them. It was just a simple walk. He wanted to be with Nadia right now, and that was okay.

Chapter 5

Nadia and Luca walked slowly down the street away from the swell of music spilling out from the bars. She looked up at him and a blush burned over her cheeks. She wasn't sure what to say to him now that they weren't around their friends. She didn't do things like this anymore. Looking away from him, a twinge of panic raced down her spine as she caught the reflection of three men trailing behind them and a black sedan inching along the street.

"So, do you go to that club often?" Luca said, breaking the silence and pulling her from her worrying thoughts.

Nadia looked up at his warm hazel eyes. He didn't look concerned, so she had to be overthinking. Those men and that car couldn't be following them, right? She nodded more to convince herself than to answer him. "Um, yeah, at least my friends and I have for the last couple of years. You seem like you know DJ D pretty well, but I've never seen you there before."

"I used to go to Kani Kani all the time, but I stopped going a few years ago." He shrugged.

"Oh, why's that? I mean, I feel like I'm too old to hang out there sometimes, but it's the only place that's more about dancing than just getting drunk, you know?" she said, wrapping her arms around herself to stop the slight shiver that prickled over her skin. The weather was changing, but the nights were still cool and she stupidly went out without a jacket.

"I do feel a bit old there, but that's not why I stopped going," he said, shrugging his jacket off and draping it over her shoulders.

She blushed at the sweet gesture and tugged the jacket around her. It was so warm and the decadent cedar and patchouli scent of his cologne filled her senses in a calming warmth.

"I was dating someone who didn't appreciate my love of dance, so I stopped going for them and I just never went back until now."

"Yeah, I know how that feels," she mumbled as her thoughts drifted to her ex and his dislike of her dancing or going out with her friends. A worrying chill slithered down her spine. Nope. None of that tonight. "Well, I'm glad you came out." She smiled up at him. "It's not too often I get to dance with someone as talented and sexy as you." She laughed as her eyes grew wide and she wanted to drown in the pool of embarrassment that washed over her. "I-I mean… not sexy. That was inappropriate."

Luca choked out a laugh and shook his head. "That's alright. I don't think that's inappropriate for the amount of drinks we've had tonight." He grinned and leaned down to her. "I haven't danced with anyone as talented or gorgeous as you in a long time either."

She bit her cheeks to hide her blush. Was he *flirting* with her? Sweet lord she didn't think her aloof boss had it in him. "I guess I'm just lucky to–Ah!" she let out a startled cry as her heel caught in the crack of the sidewalk. Her arms flailed as she fell forward and cursed her damn luck for ruining this moment. She was doing so well!

Luca burst out laughing, catching her around her waist and steadying her on her feet. "How is it you can dance so perfectly, but trip on air?"

She pursed her lips, but couldn't stop herself from joining in his laughter. "It's just my design flaw, okay? And I didn't trip on air. My damn shoe got caught in the sidewalk!" she said, pointing to her gold heel sticking out of the pavement as she held onto his shoulder to keep her balance.

Luca shook his head as he bent down and reached for the shoe. "But you're the only person who'd find this crack and lose her shoe," he mumbled, holding her leg still and slipping it back on her foot. He stood and her heart stuttered at the amused look in his golden eyes. "Your clumsiness is kind of cute, but it drives me crazy. You constantly trip and stumble all over the office. I don't know what to do with you."

He noticed her in the office? She shook her head. "You don't need to worry about me. I'm used to this. It's just the way I am."

"I don't know about that." Luca chuckled. "I feel like you need a team of bodyguards to follow you around just to make sure you don't hurt yourself."

Her heart thumped as she looked into a shop window and caught another glimpse of the men trailing behind them. Panic filled her again as she leaned into him. "Speaking of that," she whispered. "There's three men and a car that's been following us since we left the club."

Luca looked behind her and she grabbed his collar. "Don't look!" she hissed. "They'll know we've caught on to them. I don't know why they're following us, but we should probably try to lose them." Nadia hoped it was a coincidence and she'd chalked it up to her natural ability to over think these things, but she'd taken a few odd turns to her apartment just to be on the safe side.

A rumble of laughter burst from Luca's mouth and she stared at him in confusion. "This is serious!"

"Those are my bodyguards," he said as his eyes sparkled in amusement. "There's nothing to worry about."

"What?" She frowned as he waved them over and three plain dressed men jogged from their positions. Two came from across the street and one ran up the rear half a block behind them. The black sedan rolled to a stop and parked under a street lamp, blocking the view of the driver inside.

"Mr. Shola, is there a problem?" One of them asked as they approached. Nadia pressed herself against Luca's side. She was still unsure of the buff men surrounding them as if they were fending off a threat.

"No, there's no problem, but could you introduce yourselves to Miss Coleman? She's a bit unnerved by you."

"Oh, right," the man with short golden blonde hair and kind blue eyes laughed as he held out his hand to her. "I'm Gordon Anderson and the other two are Henry Lui and Oscar Smith."

She slowly placed her hand in his. "It's nice to meet you," she said and looked around him. "But what about the person in the car?"

Gordon looked at the black sedan. "Oh, that's Jack Hale.

He's one of us too. We've been working with the Sholas for years. We didn't mean to frighten you." Gordon chuckled. "It's not often that Mr. Shola's dates find us alarming."

Nadia laughed. "I'm not his date, but I guess it's nice to know you guys weren't about to mug us."

"I'm sorry. I should've told you about them when we left," Luca said. "I honestly didn't think you'd notice them."

"I've had a stalker before, so I'm pretty aware of my surroundings and people following me."

Luca raised an eyebrow. "Is that why you've been taking us down random streets? You said your place wasn't that far and we've been walking for a little while now."

A blush scorched her cheeks. "Yes, I didn't want them to know where I lived. I'm sorry."

"Don't apologize for that. That's completely understandable," he said as the guards laughed around them.

"Oh, I like you. You're tactful." Gordon smiled. "Would you mind if we escort you home now, Miss Coleman?"

"Yeah, but can you walk with us? It still freaks me out with you trailing behind like that."

The bodyguards looked at Luca and he shrugged. "It's fine. Whatever makes Nadia feel comfortable."

"Sorry if that's not protocol. I'm just not used to something like this," she lied. She was used to bodyguards, but Luca didn't need to know the extent of the stalking she endured.

"No need to apologize. It's my fault for not telling you." He smiled and she turned the other way to walk back down the street toward her apartment. "How long were you going to keep walking, though?"

She chuckled. "I would've walked all night hoping they would give up their pursuit."

Chapter 5

Gordon, Henry and Oscar burst out laughing. "Well, thank God you said something! We're well trained, Miss Coleman. We wouldn't have stopped," Gordon snickered. "You're definitely far more observant than Mr. Shola's previous lady friends."

She raised an eyebrow at Luca's blushing face. "Oh, so you do this often?"

"No, I don't. This is the most excitement these guys have had in a while."

"It's true. Mr. Shola is usually holed up in his penthouse like a hermit." Henry, the tall curly haired, brown-eyed guard, smirked which earned him a glare from Luca.

Nadia giggled. "Yeah, I get that. I don't go out too much either. Minerva usually drags me out."

Her heart thumped at the bright smile that lit up Luca's face. "It's nice to know I'm not the only one who gets dragged out. I don't feel so weird now."

"You're not weird. It's kind of refreshing to meet someone like me." She shrugged. "I just prefer to stay in and read most weekends."

"Oh God, he does the same thing," Gordon said and nudged Luca's arm. "You two should start a book club."

"Maybe, but I doubt we read the same novels. I read a lot of fantasy and I prefer indie authors over the mainstream ones," she said and blushed. She hardly thought this conversation was going to turn into her love of books. Luca was going to think she was such a nerd.

"Actually, I read a lot of fantasy novels, too. I'm guilty of reading mainstream, but now I'm reading Eyes of the Beholder by an indie author I just picked up."

Nadia's eyes grew wide. "No way." She laughed. "I just

started reading that, too. I didn't think anyone else was reading her work."

"You're not the only one who seeks out undiscovered gems."

"Maybe we *should* start a book club." She grinned. "It might be fun discussing theories with you."

"I think I'd like that. None of these guys like to read as much as I do and Cameron just thinks I'm a nerd."

Nadia's heart swelled at that. She liked a well-read man. "I'm pleasantly surprised by you, Luca. You're a dancer, you read, and you're not the stone-faced CEO that lurks around the office. You actually smile."

His guards stifled their laughter and he gasped. "I don't *lurk* around the office. I may not look excited to be there, but I don't lurk around."

She shrugged. "Mm, whatever you say, but your employees call you Hades because you act like the lonely King of the Underworld."

"Yes, I know what they call me." He sighed, but a grin tugged at his lips. "So would that make you Persephone? She wasn't clumsy like you, but you do bring some life into the office."

She choked out a laugh. "I guess so, but maybe you should show your employees this side of you. They might not think you're so cold and distant."

He shook his head, the smile fading from his lips. "No, I don't mind my reputation. It's better that way."

She tilted her head to the side as she stopped in front of a red brick apartment building. "That's a shame." She sighed and a devilish grin spread over her lips. "Well, if I'm Persephone, you won't be able to hide this side of you forever.

I'll bring it out of you."

A dazzling smile graced his lips and the warmth in his hazel eyes made her heart trip and skip a few beats. "You're welcome to try, Nadia."

Goddamn. Luca had to know how handsome he was when he smiled like that. She bit her lip. "Maybe I will. I'll start with that book club."

He nodded. "That sounds good to me."

She blushed, looking back at the apartment building behind her. "Well, this is me. Thanks for walking me home. That was really nice of you."

"It was my pleasure and I'm sorry about my bodyguards."

"That's alright." She smiled and waved to them standing near the waiting car. "It was nice to meet them, too. Enjoy the rest of your night, Luca," she said, turning away from him, but he quickly grabbed her hand.

"Sorry, um," he said, letting go of her hand. "Do you mind if I get your number for… for the book club?"

"Oh! Sure, that would make sense wouldn't it?" she said, pulling her phone from her pocket. "I feel like I'm fraternizing with the boss."

He grinned, taking her phone and putting his number in it. "There's no rules against being friends with the CEO," he said, handing her his phone and she did the same.

"Good," she said, shrugging off his black cotton jacket and she missed the warmth and delicious scent of it. "Thanks for this too."

"You're welcome," he said as he folded the jacket over his arm. "Have a good night, Nadia."

"You too," she said and walked up the stone steps behind her. The front of her heel nicked the last stair and she stumbled into the door. She sighed in annoyance and the beautiful sound of Luca's deep laughter filled the air. "Shut up!" She laughed, looking back at him.

"Goodnight clumsy." Luca waved.

"Goodnight." She blushed, shaking her head as she walked inside. She leaned against the door and looked at Luca's number on her phone. How the hell did she manage that? Nadia bit her thumb as her thoughts drifted to the way he danced with her and walked her home.

Shoving her phone in her pocket, she shook those thoughts from her mind. Luca wasn't part of her plan and she knew damn well she couldn't let him into her life. She learned the hard way not to open her heart to men like Luca. The last time she did that, she nearly lost her life.

Nadia ambled down the cream and oak trimmed hallway and up the creaking wooden staircase to her third-floor apartment. Luca could only be good for one thing; getting the information she needed to complete her mission. Nothing more.

Chapter 6

Luca grinned as he slid into the waiting car and stared at Nadia's number on his phone. He hadn't felt that content to sit in a crowded space with Nadia and her friends in a long time. He felt happy being around Nadia tonight. It felt good, and he didn't want to let that feeling go.

He tapped the message icon on the screen and sent her a text to make sure she got into her place alright. And since when did he feel confident enough to flirt like that?

"You're feeling bold tonight taking a woman home like that." Jack grinned as he watched him from the rear-view mirror.

"It's nothing. I just had a good night." His phone buzzed and a smile crossed his lips as he read the message.

Nadia » Ha ha... Yes, I made it into my apartment without tripping. «

Luca » I don't know if I believe that. I bet you tripped over an invisible crack and lost your shoe again. «

Nadia »... shut up. I didn't lose my shoe. «

Luca chuckled. That woman was such a mess.

Luca » I think you need bodyguards more than I do for your own safety. «

He started to put his phone in his pocket before it buzzed and a smile lit up his features again as he read her message. He ignored the smug 'mm-hm' Jack uttered under his breath.

Nadia » Very funny, but why do you have bodyguards? Maybe I should worry about your safety. «

Luca's heart clenched. She didn't need to know about Ciara or that he's had bodyguards all his life. It might scare her away. She already mentioned she had a stalker in the past and the thought of someone watching her like that filled him with an irrational compulsion to protect her. Maybe he should put a small security detail on her.

No, that was none of his business. She didn't need his protection–unless she asked.

Luca » No need to worry about me. I've always had bodyguards and being the CEO of a successful company comes with its own dangers.«

Nadia » Please tell me you're not in the mafia doing shady business deals?«

Luca » As if I'd tell you if that were the case.«

Nadia » Well, if you are, I don't want to have anything to do with you. I don't need that kind of drama in my life.«

He chuckled at her response as he got out of the car and walked through the underground parking garage of his father's towering, black mirrored building that sat at the edge of Rose wharf. It housed the family's separate security agency's workspace and living quarters and a top floor penthouse that overlooked the Boston harbor.

Luca » So, you'd quit your job if you found out I was in the mafia?«

Glancing up from his phone, Luca said goodnight to Jack and the rest of his bodyguards before he took the elevator to his penthouse. He checked his phone and his heart sank that Nadia didn't respond. Maybe he scared her away with that question or his cryptic answer. Luca shook his head, sitting his phone on the top of his dresser before going into the gray and black tiled bathroom to take a shower.

He needed to come back down to reality. He just had a good night. That was it. He couldn't let anyone new in his life even if Nadia completely captivated him with the way she moved on the dance floor and her excellent choice in reading material.

Shrugging off his clothes, Luca stepped under the warm water and rubbed his hands through his hair before washing the smell of the nightclub from his body. It was better that he kept to himself.

Turning off the shower, he stepped out to grab a towel on the warming rack. He dried his hair, wrapping the black towel around himself. He sighed at his reflection in the wide black iron mirror above the swirling gray marbled sink and traced a finger over one of the many jagged scars that marred his chest.

A tattoo of a black mandala hibiscus flower wedged between the tattoos on his pecs swept over his abdomen just above his belly button. The detailed ink camouflaged his scars, but it did nothing to hide Ciara's abuse. He still remembered every strike of her knife and damaging word she used to beat him with.

Luca gripped the edge of the sink and took a deep breath. He hated he had to endure her torment because of his grandfather and his fucking duty to become the next leader of the Syndicates to uphold his mother's Rodawson name. They were the reason he'd become this standoffish and unemotional person he didn't recognize in the mirror.

He pushed away from the sink and padded into the bedroom to shrug on a pair of sweatpants and a t-shirt. His phone vibrated on his dresser and a smile tugged at his lips. But then there was Nadia. The little conundrum that made him want to pick his head up from the shadows.

Nadia » It would be a shame if I had to quit, but I would. The mafia is dangerous.«

She wasn't wrong about that. The Syndicates didn't consider themselves an organized crime mob, but their disgusting group might as well be.

Luca » Well, then it's good I'm not involved in anything like that. «

He lied, but she didn't need to know about that, and it wasn't like he wanted to be part of the Syndicates.

Nadia » It sure is. Anyway, I'm going to munch on some popcorn. Thanks for a good night.«

His smile grew even wider as he shuffled to his bed. She had a good night with him. God, there was something so refreshing about her and it made him want to stay in her orbit.

Luca » You're welcome. I had a good night with you too.«

Luca » I usually go to South Street Diner with Cameron after a night out and you're welcome to join us tomorrow.«

His thumb hovered over 'send'. What was he doing? It was one thing to walk her home, but asking her to breakfast might be too much. He ran a hand through his hair. Cameron made a good point about not letting Ciara dictate his life and technically, he was still free for the weekend.

Luca took a deep breath and sent the message. Nadia would probably say no. Why would anyone want to be friends with someone like him? He wasn't like he used to be, but he just wanted to spend a little more time with her and hold on to this freeing feeling when he was around her.

Nadia » Maybe. I'll see what Minerva is doing. She might want to come if Cameron's going. Good night, Luca.«

Luca's heart swelled at her answer and a tingling rush of excitement raced through his veins. She didn't say no and maybe was good enough for him.

Luca » Good night, Nadia.«

Luca sat his phone on his bedside table and snuggled under the blankets. The slight smile on his face never left his lips as he closed his eyes. It was nice to feel like himself again even if it was just for a moment.

Chapter 7

Nadia groaned, sliding a hand over her face squinting at the sun streaming through her bedroom window. She picked up her phone that was incessantly vibrating next to her knowing it could only be one person at this hour in the morning. "What?"

"Well, good morning to you, too. Did I wake you up?"

"Yes, Nervy, what do you want?"

"I knew your ass would still be asleep," Minerva grumbled. "I'm at your door. You need to get up. We're going to brunch."

"What?" Nadia sighed, pushing her blankets off and rolling out of bed to trudge through her sunny apartment. Hanging up her phone, she crossed the small living room with her red couch and mustard yellow reading chair.

She picked a dead leaf from one of the potted plants sitting on the end table before she opened the door to stare at Minerva's too perky face. Her mixture of light and dark brown curls were swept up in a bun on top of her head and her baby hairs were perfectly laid. Her flawless make-up brightened her brown skin and her sheer white maxi skirt and yellow crop top were far too put together, as if they hadn't been out drinking last night.

"We're going to brunch!" She exclaimed. "Cameron said Luca asked you about it last night. So come on, you need to get dressed." She grinned, pushing past her into her apartment.

"Oh, the brunch thing. I don't want to go," Nadia said, shaking her head as she padded to the kitchen to fill a green watering can at the sink. "Last night was nice, but I don't think I want to get to know my boss like that." She turned off the faucet and began watering the spider plant hanging from the window and the rest of the foliage around the room while she ignored the annoyed look on Minerva's face.

Minerva crossed her arms and raised an eyebrow at her. "You're the one who wanted to do this in the first place. 'I'm going to ruin Jonathan and that fucking cult he belongs to!'" she said in a mocking tone. "You remember that? So, getting to know Luca is exactly what you need to do."

Nadia rolled her eyes. "No, what I need to do is get information on the Syndicates. Raquel didn't mention anything about using Luca to do that." She scoffed. "I'm not going. I don't need to befriend any Syndicate members. The plan is to snoop around Shola Enterprises for records and information on Syndicate members so I can take them down in court and once I destroy them, Jonathan won't have anyone left to protect him from getting the justice I deserve," she said, continuing her chore of watering plants. She didn't need Luca to get what she needed on the Syndicates. There was no need to get wrapped up in someone like him. That was a dangerous idea, especially when she found him extremely attractive. She already decided she was going to spend the rest of her weekend in her apartment, reading and watching TV like usual.

Minerva snatched the watering can out of her hands and it sloshed out and spilled onto the beige carpet. "Nervy!" Nadia gasped as she reached for it, but her irritating best friend held it out of her reach.

"Bitch, get in the shower," she huffed. "The best way for you to get what you need is to get to know Luca. He's the damn kingpin's grandson, for fuck's sake. You need him for this, and it's just brunch. It's not like you're going to be alone," Minerva said as her eyes softened and she put on her best pout. "Please come with me?"

Nadia crossed her arms and stared at her big brown puppy dog eyes. Minerva touched a hand to her arm, and her lip pouted even further. "Please," she whined. "I know you're hungry and I heard this place has the best pancakes in the city."

Nadia's stomach growled in agreement. Damn it. She was starving and she could go for a nice stack of pancakes. It might not hurt to see Luca again. If she were friends with him, it might make it easier to get the information she needed. She sighed. "Fine," she grumbled. "But just brunch and then I'm coming back home."

"Yay!" Minerva squealed. "I'll pick out something for you to wear," she said, pushing her toward the bathroom.

"Finish watering my plants too," Nadia said as Minerva nodded in excitement and closed the door.

Nadia shed her clothes and slipped into the shower. She slid her hands over her face, letting the water trail over her back. Her heart thumped at the memory of her conversation with Luca and that lovely walk home. She liked being around him, and she hadn't felt like this in a long time. Not since Jonathan.

She clenched her eyes shut as she shook under the warm water. Her breath came out in small bursts, her chest clenched tight and her lungs felt as if they were going to cave in. She whimpered and pressed herself against the white tiles of the shower to keep herself from sinking to the floor. She forced herself to take a deep breath before she recited the mantra her therapist taught her.

"Every man is not like him and he is not every man," she whispered repeatedly until her chest released and her breathing calmed.

If she was going to ruin Jonathan for good, she had to push aside her fears because a restraining order against him wasn't enough. Nadia took another deep breath. She had to do this.

"Nadia! Hurry up, girl!"

"Alright!" Nadia called back to her very impatient friend. She must've had a good night with Cameron if she was this eager to see him again. Nadia turned off the water and hastily wrapped a towel around herself before she padded down the short hallway to her bedroom. She frowned at her Sailor Mars figurine sitting on top of her kitchen island. "Nervy did you move this?"

Minerva looked up from her seat on the couch and shook her head. "No, why?"

"Nothing, it's just I never move Rei. She's always pointing at the Death Star," she said, crossing the living room and sitting the figurine under the lamp on the end table next to her reading chair.

"That's not nothing," Minerva said, sitting up and placing

her magazine on the coffee table. "Has anything else happened like that?"

"No, well, I misplaced my keys–" Nadia's eyes grew wide as she slumped in her chair and slid a hand over her mouth.

"Nadia, don't freak out," Minerva said as she knelt in front of her and grasped her hand tight. "We don't know what that means. Maybe you moved Rei last night and didn't realize it. You were drunk, but shit like this is why you need to do all you can to make sure Jonathan can't get near you."

A tear rolled down Nadia's cheek and she let out a breath. "I know, but what if it's him?"

"Then we'll change your locks and you'll tell your lawyer what's happening."

She nodded and squeezed Minerva's hand. "Can we change the locks right now?"

"Of course. You go get dressed and I'll get your tools," she said, standing up and going into her kitchen to open the drawer full of spare locks.

Nadia got up from her chair, biting her thumb as she went into her bedroom to get dressed. She walked around her room, touching her little potted plants on her shelves, checking to see if anything had been moved. Tears pricked the corners of her eyes as she sat on her bed next to the orange and yellow floral print dress Minerva laid out for her.

She wrapped her arms around herself and closed her eyes. Things moving and going missing was how it always started with Jonathan. He liked to toy with her mind. She moved too many times in the past three years to get away from him, but he always found her. Nadia wiped the tear rolling down her cheek. He'd never leave her alone unless she got rid of him and that fucking cult protecting him.

Chapter 7

All the research she'd done on the Syndicates pointed to Shola Enterprises as the epicenter of their activity. The kingpin or the Grand Duke, as they liked to refer to him, used the company to hide some sort of master list with every fucked up thing that cult did. If Nadia had that, she could take control of her life and ruin Jonathan and the rest of the sick members involved in the society.

If getting close to Luca was going to further her cause, then that's what she'd do. He may be nice and she felt safe with him, but he was just like the rest of those Syndicate fucks. Beautiful on the outside, but a controlling egotistical dick on the inside and she would take them all down.

***

Damn it.

There was something about him. Nadia couldn't put her finger on it as she watched Luca walk through the art exhibit holding two cups of coffee. Her heart skipped a quick beat at his short midnight locks that were a bit disheveled, as if he'd just ran his hands through his hair. She was intrigued by the black ink on his biceps that peeked under the sleeves of his faded blue UCLA t-shirt, which hugged his broad shoulders and perfectly defined pectorals. Luca looked far less disarming in this casual attire and the minute she sat down in the diner, one small smile from him washed away the anger she held for him and his kind.

Nadia surprised herself and Minerva when she didn't hesitate at brunch to say yes to joining Luca for a tour of the sold out cover design exhibit at the Museum of Fine Art. To be fair, she'd been dying to see the displays and he had the only ticket she could get her hands on. She reasoned with herself that hanging out with him would get him to trust her. It was a minor bonus that she found she genuinely enjoyed being in Luca's company.

Fuck.

"Are you enjoying yourself?" he said, handing her a cup of steaming hot coffee.

"I am, but I didn't realize your tickets were for a private viewing. You don't like crowds, do you?"

"Not really." Luca chuckled. "Not anymore."

"And why's that?" she said as they strolled through the exhibits.

"I don't like all the attention. It comes with unwanted drama."

"Fair enough. I guess for someone who has a dangerous job as a CEO that would be an issue." She teased. "You sure you're not a mafia boss on the side?"

He looked away from her and ran a hand through his hair. "I'm not in the mafia." He laughed. "Shola doesn't do shady business deals."

"Mm, okay." Nadia chuckled, but she knew better. Shola may be squeaky clean, but she was sure his family wasn't. "Speaking of CEOs, I never thanked you for sticking up for me in the shareholders' meeting."

"You don't need to thank me for that. They shouldn't have said those things and I'm sorry Arnold asked you those questions. He can be extra sometimes." Luca shook his head. "But I don't want to spend this afternoon talking about work. Did you see any pieces that you liked?"

"I did," she said, walking across the floor to another design of a black woman kneeling in front of a sword. Gold markings swirled over her brown skin as her gray eyes stared in determination at the horde of oncoming warriors. "I love this one. You don't see too many diverse characters in fantasy."

Luca checked the placard. "Falonia. I've never heard of this novel, but you're right. It's why I like Eyes of the Beholder. I love the way the author describes Miri. She's beautiful."

Nadia's heart thumped, and a devilish grin tugged at her lips. "Are you trying to say you find black women attractive?"

Luca choked out a laugh. "Is that a problem if I am?"

She bit her lip. "Nope, it's just interesting considering you're dating Ciara."

The smile fell from his face, and his eyes grew cold. "I'm not dating Ciara. Not really."

Her heart clenched. Shit. Maybe that was too probing. She definitely struck a nerve. "I'm sorry. I probably shouldn't have said that."

"No, it's okay. I'm sure you've heard the rumors around the office, but it's complicated. I'm not dating her or anyone. If that's what you're getting at."

Nadia shook her head. "No, not at all. I don't do relationships."

The smile returned to his face, and his eyes brightened again. "Oh yeah? Why's that?" he asked, but frowned at his watch blinking on his wrist. "I'm sorry, I have to take this call."

She smiled. "No, no, that's fine."

Luca nodded, taking out his phone and walking away from her. Or stalked, rather. His steps were tight, his back stiff as he rounded the corner of the exhibit. That call must be serious. Nadia looked around at the empty museum and itched to follow him. His call might be with the Syndicates, and she could get some information on their shady dealings.

No. She couldn't seem too eager for information. It was important that she played it cool. She learned a few investigation tips from her friend Raquel, who she was lucky to meet after Jonathan attacked her. Raquel was working on sex rings and human trafficking for the FBI, and Nadia convinced her to help her find a way to get Jonathan to pay for what he did to her. Raquel agreed, but only if Nadia and Minerva agreed to learn self defense.

Nadia took a sip of her coffee as she wandered through the rest of the exhibit, and a twinge of guilt tugged at her heart. Raquel taught them a few spy skills too, but she didn't like playing on Luca's kindness. He seemed genuine, but so did Jonathan in the beginning.

"Nadia, I'm so sorry, but I need to leave." Luca sighed in disappointment behind her.

"That's alright," she said, turning around and her heart sank at the pained look in his golden eyes. "Is everything okay?"

"Yeah it's just… an issue I need to take care of," he said, placing his hand to the small of her back to guide her toward the emergency exit. "We can't leave through the main entrance. I'm sorry."

She frowned. "This seems extra. Are you sure everything is okay?"

"It's nothing I shouldn't have prepared for," he grumbled, opening the door where his bodyguards were waiting for them. "Gordon will take you home. I'm sorry I had to cut our tour short."

"It's alright, you don't have to keep saying sorry. You just handle your business. I can find my own way home. I don't need a bodyguard."

Chapter 7

Luca ignored her request and looked over her head to Gordon. "Make sure she gets home and let me know when she's inside."

"Yes, sir." He nodded, sliding his hand to her arm.

"Hey! I said I don't need a bodyguard. I can make it home by myself," she snapped, pulling her arm out of his grasp. Gordon's eyes grew wide and he looked at Luca for guidance.

Luca sighed and turned her around to him. "I'm sure you can make it home by yourself, but in this situation I'd feel better if you let my guards take you, please?"

Goosebumps pricked her arms at his firm but gentle touch and the concern in his eyes was enough to make her nod in agreement. "Fine. I'll let Gordon take me home, but you owe me an explanation for this."

A whisper of a smile tugged at his lips. "And I promise I'll explain it to you. I just can't do that right now, okay?"

She stared into his golden depths and saw nothing but honesty behind the worry that plagued them. She wanted to know what was going on and she'd hold him to that promise, but she had to make him feel like he could trust her and letting his bodyguard take her home would do that. "Alright, well, thanks for a lovely day out, anyway. I had a good time."

"You're welcome," he said as his hands fell from her arms. "Maybe we can do it again sometime."

"Sir, we need to go," Henry said as he jogged up to them.

Luca took a deep breath and nodded to his guard. "I know, I'm coming," he said and looked back at Nadia with his eyes full of guilt. "Enjoy the rest of your weekend."

"You too," she said as the guards escorted them from the building to two waiting cars in the small alley behind the museum.

"Come on Miss Coleman, let's get you home."

"Just call me Nadia, Gordon," she said, sliding into the back of the car and watching Luca's furious expression as he spoke angrily into his phone. "Is everything okay? Luca doesn't seem too happy."

"Yeah, he'll be alright. It's nothing you need to worry about," Gordon said, closing the door and quickly getting into the driver's seat.

"Alright, but this seems kind of serious to me. I don't understand why you need to take me home."

He sighed. "I know it seems that way, but Mr. Shola's not taking any chances with your safety."

Nadia bit her lip and tugged at the hem of her dress. "Alright. Should I be worried about hanging out with Luca?"

Gordon's blue eyes slid to the rear-view mirror. "No, and I hope this doesn't stop you from seeing him again. Mr. Shola has a complicated past, but he's a good person and he could really use a friend like you."

A blush scorched her cheeks. A friend like her? Someone who planned to use him for information. "I, um, no. This wouldn't stop me from seeing him, but I'd like to know what happened."

She wouldn't make a good friend for Luca, but part of her wanted to. That look in his eyes reminded her of the fear she felt when Jonathan started playing his games.

"That's understandable, Miss Coleman. He said he'd explain it to you." He winked at her. "Don't let him get out of that."

"I won't." She chuckled. "And please just call me Nadia."

"Fair enough, but how about I call you Miss Nadia?"

A laugh sputtered from her lips at his pedantic response.

"If that makes you feel better," she said as she stared out the window and watched the sun-kissed streets leading to her apartment building. Her smile never left her lips as she waved goodbye to Gordon and walked up the steps to her building. She liked Gordon. He wasn't mean-spirited like Jonathan's henchmen that watched her every move.

Her smile fell at the thought of what Gordon said about Luca. A man with a complicated past who needed a friend like her. She dug her phone from her purse and unlocked the screen to tap a message to him.

Nadia »Just wanted to let you know I'm home and I hope you're alright. Thanks again for a wonderful day. See you at the office, Hades.«

The cursor blinked at the end of the message, and she hesitated for a moment before sending it. Tucking her phone back in her purse, she slowly took the stairs to her apartment.

Luca sounded like her.

She had a complicated past too, and she knew how hard it was to have friends who didn't understand what it was like to go through the trauma she'd endured. While she didn't know the extent of Luca's past, she wanted to be his friend. But how could she? And what would happen if he found out she was using him for his connections to the Syndicates?

Nadia closed her eyes and pushed open the door to her apartment. She couldn't be Luca's friend. She'd just get what she needed from him and keep her distance. It was safer that way.

Chapter 8

Broken glass crunched under Luca's feet and the smell of burned fabric assaulted his nose as he walked into his sister's dress boutique. "What the fuck, Jack? Why wasn't anyone here to stop this?"

Jack shook his head as he pushed a fallen clothing rack aside. "It must've happened during the security change over."

"Luca?" a voice sniffed from the back of the shop.

"Lacey?" Luca called, rushing through the burnt and ripped clothing to his raven haired sister, dressed in a simple green sundress, sitting on the floor in a heap of shredded fabric. "I told you not to come down here."

She gripped her hand-patterned fabric in her fists and looked up at him with her hazel eyes full of rage. "I had to see what they did."

"I'm so sorry," he said, kneeling down to her, placing his hand over her carefully crafted fabric. "This is my fault."

"No, it's not, and I'm tired of you blaming yourself for this shit," she said, tossing the fabric to the side. "I'm fucking livid, but I can make more clothes and fix my shop," she said, looking around at their guards picking up the fallen shelving and bricks strewn across the floor. "But our grandfather should be ashamed of himself. We're fucking family–"

"Yes, you are and you're lucky I even consider you part of my legacy," a deep voice grumbled. Fear dug its claws into Luca's spine as he and Lacey stood to face Gregory Rodawson, their formidable grandfather who filled the door dressed in his Saturday golfing attire. The pastel colors of his clothes were a sharp contrast to his pale stoic gaze.

"Oh fuck," Lacey cursed under her breath.

"Mr. Rodawson, it's not safe for you in here," Jack said, blocking the path between him and his grandchildren.

He scoffed. "Oh please. A little broken glass isn't going to hurt me," he said, looking around Jack. "Come with me, Luca. We need to talk."

Lacey dug her nails into Luca's arm. "Don't go," she whispered.

He slid his hand over hers. "It's okay. I'll be fine."

"Luca–"

"Stay here and wait for mom and dad," he said, hugging her tight. "We'll talk later."

"Okay," Lacey said, wrapping her arms around him. "E pakele," she whispered. "E ikaika, Eke."

Be safe, be strong. The words their Tutu always spoke to them and what had become their motto lately.

"Don't speak that shit around me. It's disrespectful," their grandfather huffed and crossed his arms. He never liked when they spoke their father's native language. He said it insulted everything he worked for. "Let's go," he said, motioning to his black sedan waiting for them on the street.

Luca squeezed Lacey's hand before he followed their grandfather out of the shop. He shoved his hands in his pockets to stop them from shaking as he slid into the back of the car.

"The Dagenhams aren't happy with you," his grandfather said, as he slid in next to him and promptly lit a cigar. "That means I'm not happy with you." He blew the smoke in Luca's face.

He coughed and covered his nose from the nauseating stench. "I'm sorry," he croaked.

Tapping his cigar on the silver ashtray in the middle of the seat, his grandfather sneered at him. "You will be."

***

Luca's grandfather took him to his countryside estate in the Berkshires where Luca was lectured about his place in the Syndicates and his duty to the Dagenhams while Arnold and Ciara sat with smug grins on their faces.

"What I did to your sister's shop is nothing compared to what I could do. Would you like to see her in the next Juliet auction? What about your mother?" His grandfather seethed from across the table.

Fear clawed at Luca's spine as he dug his fingers into his jeans, keeping his eyes averted. "No."

"I didn't think so. Now, apologize to Ciara for your disgusting behavior with that woman."

Looking up from the polished oak wood table, Luca stared into Ciara's smug brown eyes. "I'm sorry. It won't happen again."

"It better not," Arnold grumbled.

"Oh, it won't. Not after a nice beating to remind him," his grandfather said, standing from the table. "Let's go."

Luca kept his gaze on Ciara. He wasn't sure what he was hoping for in her eyes. There wasn't an ounce of empathy or remorse for what was going to happen to him. She never cared about him. She just liked the wealthy cushion of her father's money for being with him and the clout that came with being the First Lady of the next Grand Duke.

Luca's grandfather grabbed his arm and pulled him from his seat to walk down the familiar hallway to the steps of the private chambers below. The waiting guards cut his shirt from his body before tying him to a thick wooden whipping post in the center of a stone bricked room. Luca closed his eyes and hung his head as he waited for his grandfather to beat him for his disobedience. He'd been subject to this punishment a few times and it was always because of Ciara, but at least this time he didn't pass out.

Lying on a plush bed in one of the many rooms of his grandfather's home, Luca stared through bleary eyes out the window at the grounds bathed in the setting sun. His back was throbbing from the welts and slashes that covered his skin. He winced, biting the pillow clutched under his chin as his wounds were cleaned and bandaged by the nurse his grandfather kept for situations like this.

"I'm so sorry, Mr. Shola. I'm almost done," she said, taping the gauze in place.

"Get out," Ciara hissed, her heels clicking on the wooden floor as she neared the bed.

"Yes ma'am," the nurse replied, popping up from the bed and gathering her supplies. "He'll be sore for a little while, Miss Dagenham."

Luca sighed as Ciara sat on the bed next to him. "You did this to yourself. You shouldn't have been out with her."

"You didn't have to tell your father. You said you'd give me the weekend."

"Yes, but not to go *dancing* at that god awful place or take that woman home. An employee, no less. Do you know how embarrassing it was for me to see that happy fucking look on your face?"

Luca closed his eyes. "Why the hell does it matter to you?" he mumbled.

"Because seeing you with her reminded me of how we used to be," she said, brushing a lock of hair from his forehead. "We used to be happy with our arrangement and I miss that."

"But I'm a weak man who isn't good enough to be with you for my disgusting scars and tainted blood." He scoffed. "I don't miss any of that, Ciara. I'm only doing this to protect my family."

She slapped his back and Luca howled into the pillow as tears blurred his vision. Ciara clenched her fist in his hair and leaned into his ear. "I hope that fucking hurt," she whispered. "You're going to love being with me again. We're going to get married and have plenty of children to tie our families together like we're supposed to. Our children won't cleanse your tainted blood, but that's what I want now," she said, kissing his cheek before she stood from the bed. "I'll see you on Monday."

Luca sucked in gasps of air, drenching the pillow with his silent tears. He shouldn't have gone out. He never should have thought he could have a moment to feel free.

Reaching a shaking hand to the bedside table, he grasped his phone. His thumb quivered as he unlocked it and sent a message to his family letting them know he was alright.

But he wasn't and he didn't want this life.

An unread message sat in his inbox and a slight smile tugged at his lips as he read the text from Nadia, letting him know she was home. She didn't have to tell him, but it warmed his heart that she did. He started to respond, but stopped and clenched the phone in his hand. It was better if he didn't.

Luca held the phone to his chest and closed his eyes, but he could hold on to that comforting feeling he felt when he was with her. Freedom and comfort were what he deserved in this life and the reason he had to ruin his grandfather and the fucking Syndicates.

Chapter 9

Nadia checked her phone as she leaned against the small counter of the canteen in the lobby of Shola Enterprises. It'd been a few days and Luca hadn't responded to her text, nor had she seen him lurking around the office. It shouldn't bother her, but the way everything went down at the museum and that fearful look in his eyes reminded her of how she used to get with Jonathan. She just hoped he was okay.

"That's two fifty, Miss Coleman," the barista said as he sat two cups of coffee on the counter.

"Oh, sure," she said, popping away from the counter to dig in her purse for her wallet.

"I got it."

Nadia's heart thumped as she dragged her eyes up Luca's tailored black suit that hinted at the curve of his muscles as he handed the young man a crisp twenty-dollar bill. "Um, thank you."

"You're welcome," he said as he collected his change and picked up the other cup sitting on the counter. "It's the least

I can do for not answering you."

"Oh, it's fine." She blushed as they walked through the quiet lobby toward the bank of elevators. "So, where have you been, Hades? I haven't seen you lurking around." She teased, taking a sip from her cup.

"I just had some business to take care of," he said as he pressed the button to call the elevator and looked at her with guilt swirling in his golden depths. "I'm sorry."

"You don't have to say sorry." She shrugged. "But Gordon told me not to let you get out of telling me what happened," she said and the small smile that tugged at the corner of his lips made her heart simmer.

"Oh, did he?" He chuckled and sucked in a pained breath.

"You okay?"

Luca cleared his throat and nodded. "Yeah, I'm just a little sore. I, um, hurt my back carrying some stuff for my sister," he said as the elevator dinged and he stepped to the side to let her enter first.

"Mm, okay. Nothing to do with your mafia side hustle then? You weren't out capping knees and threw out your back?"

"No and who says capping knees?" He laughed, wincing as he pressed their respective floors on the control panel.

"I do!" She giggled. "I'm sorry. I should stop picking on you. It's not helping your back."

"It's okay. I need to laugh," he said, leaning against the back of the elevator. He looked down at her with a nervous gleam in his golden eyes. "So, about that explanation I owe you, would you... like to have dinner with me tonight and we can talk about it?"

Nadia's cheeks burned up to her ears. He wanted to have

dinner? Like a date? Before she could answer him, the doors of the elevator opened and a tall slender woman dressed in a powder pink peplum dress that highlighted her fake tanned skin and straight golden blonde locks.

"Luca!" she exclaimed, stepping on to the elevator and a thick tension filled the small space as Luca sucked in a breath at the blonde's presence.

"What are you doing here?" Luca said, his body stiffening next to her.

"I was visiting an old friend, but I'm glad I caught you." She smiled, sliding her hand up his arm, and her eyes flicked to Nadia. "Oh, you must be the new rep all the shareholders have been talking about. I'm Ciara Dagenham," she said, holding out her hand and the sound of her too sweet voice made Nadia's stomach turn.

She forced a smile on her face and took Ciara's offered hand. "Nadia Coleman. It's nice to meet you."

"Likewise," Ciara said, looking her up and down before she turned her brown eyes to Luca. "You have a moment to squeeze in a meeting with me, right?" she pouted, sliding her fingers around his tie.

"Yeah, of course I do," he mumbled.

Nadia felt sick at the way Luca trembled beside her and her throat dried up at the rising panic she felt for him. He was *scared*.

She trembled the same way when Jonathan used to corner her like this. Fuck. She should do something, but what? If she called Ciara out, it would just make it worse for Luca and she didn't even know if he was being abused. She was probably overthinking it, and it was none of her business. She should just leave it alone.

Chapter 9

Luca clenched his shaking hands when Ciara leaned up and kissed his cheek. Nadia's heart sank at the discomfort radiating from his body. Shit, she should do something. This wasn't right. The elevator gave a soft ding and Nadia's heart thumped in panic at the thought of leaving him alone with her.

"Isn't this your floor?" Ciara said, raising her eyebrow in question.

"Oh! Yes it is. Um, h-have a nice day. It was lovely to meet you," she said, smiling at Ciara before her eyes flicked to Luca's pained expression and she wished she could give him a sign to let him know she knew.

"Have a good day, Miss Coleman."

"You too, Mr. Shola," she said, giving them a small wave as she stepped off the elevator and slid a hand over her pounding heart as she walked through the doors of the marketing department. What the fuck was that?

"Good morning, Nadia!" Alex greeted from reception as he did every morning. "You okay?"

"Good morning," she said, forcing another smile on her face. "I'm alright. I just rode the elevator with Hades and Ciara."

"Oh, I didn't realize he was back in the office or they were back together," he said and cringed. "That must've been awkward." Alex shook his head. "They don't make any sense to me. Half the time, Hades looks in pain when she visits the office. It's hard to watch."

"Yeah it was," Nadia murmured and bit her thumb. She'd been that person trapped in a relationship by someone who couldn't let her go.

"Anyway, I left some mail on your desk for you and Ben

from IT is in your office setting up the new monitor you wanted."

"Oh good. Thank you." She smiled as she continued down the hall to her office. A man with short dirty blonde hair and bright blue eyes was sitting at her desk setting up the brand new monitor for her hard drive.

He looked up at her, and a smile tugged at his lips. "Good morning, I'm just about finished hooking this up for you."

"Thank you. Ben, right?" she said as she sat her coffee on the edge of the desk.

"That's right. It's nice to meet you, Nadia. I'm usually the go-to guy for all things IT. So, if you have any issues with your new setup, just let me know." He stood and held out his hand to her.

"I will and it's nice to meet you too," she said, shaking his offered hand.

"Alright, well, have a good day. I'm sure I'll see you around this place," he said as he picked up the empty box and plastic on the floor. "Enjoy that monitor. I have two of these babies. They're nice."

She laughed. "I'm sure I will," she said as he left and closed the door behind him.

Nadia sat her purse on her desk as she slumped in her chair. She put her head in her hands and a tear rolled down her cheek. She couldn't shake the worrying panic she felt for Luca and the way he reacted to Ciara's touch. The look of fear in his eyes brought back so many memories of her own abuse.

"Come to me, little kitten."

Jonathan's smooth voice and devilish smile pierced through her thoughts. She shuddered. His voice could elicit fear in her and make her feel the pain of his harrowing punishments before he even laid a finger on her.

Nadia shook her head to wipe those damaging memories from her mind and sifted through the few letters of mail on her desk. She frowned at a small black envelope in the middle of the pile. It was blank save for her name scribbled in gold ink on the front with no sign of who it was from or where it came from.

She carefully ripped the envelope open and pulled out a white card.

'No matter where you go. I'll always find you.'

Her hands shook as she dropped the card and dug her phone from her purse to call Raquel for guidance.

"Hey my little spy in training, what's up?"

"He knows where I work," she said, staring at the ominous card.

"Okay, we knew this was a risk when you took the job, but what happened?"

Nadia sighed. "He sent me a note. It didn't have a postage stamp. Someone brought it here and put it in my mail and... some of my things have been moved around my apartment. It's starting again."

"Alright, make a copy of that note. Give me the original, keep a copy for yourself and give the other copy to your lawyer. Have you changed the locks in your apartment or do you need me to do that?"

"No, Nervy and I changed the locks, but my lawyer thinks I should move again."

"Of course she does." Raquel sighed. "What do you want to do?"

"I want to stay. This is the first time I've unpacked

everything and I've made it my home. I'm not running anymore. That's the whole point of me doing this."

"You're damn straight," Raquel said, and Nadia could hear the proud grin in her voice. "You've come a long way from that woman I met in the hospital and I wouldn't agree to you doing this if I didn't think you could handle it. We're going to get him this time. We're going to get all of them."

"Yeah, we have to. I don't want to keep looking over my shoulder for him." Nadia sighed, tearing a corner of the black envelope and taping it over the camera on her monitor like Raquel taught her.

"Minerva mentioned that you two went out with Luca Shola and his friend. That's a good start. You should develop that friendship. It might get you access to other key members."

"That's what Nervy said too." Nadia bit her thumb. "Can you do me a favor and look into Ciara Dagenham?"

"Yeah, I can do that." Raquel chuckled. "That's the second request I've gotten to look into that family."

"Who else is investigating them?"

"Come on, Nadia. You know I can't give out that info. That's against my confidentiality policy."

"I know. I'm sorry." She sighed as a knock sounded at her door. "I've got to go. Keep me posted on anything you find out. I'll drop the card off to you after work."

"Alright. I'm going to have one of my guys keep an eye on your place."

"Thanks."

"No problem, you know I got you. I'll see you later," she said and hung up.

"Come in," Nadia called as Cameron popped his head into

her office.

"Hey, do you have a minute?"

"Yeah, what's going on?" Nadia said, shoving the card into her drawer.

"We've got that meeting with Luca at nine thirty and I've double booked myself. Do you think you can brief him on the Ono Medical stuff?"

"Oh, yeah sure," she said, checking her watch. "I almost forgot about that. I'll let him know you're terrible at time management."

"Ha. ha. He already knows, ya snitch." He laughed. "We can have a catch up afterwards. I'm sure he'll want us to get started on the pitch."

"Yeah, no problem. I can handle it."

"Thanks," he said, closing her door.

Nadia sat back in her chair and couldn't believe her luck that Cameron needed her to attend the meeting on her own. It would give her a chance to check on Luca and make sure he was okay. She bit her thumb. She hoped her suspicions about Ciara were wrong, but all the signs were there. Closing her eyes, Nadia shook her head as a wave of guilt washed over her. Using Luca for information was just another form of abuse wasn't it?

Chapter 10

"What the fuck do you think you're doing?" Ciara hissed, pushing Luca into his office chair and straddling his lap. "Did you think I wouldn't catch you flirting with her?"

"I wasn't –"

"Shut up," she seethed, wrapping her hand around his neck and digging her nails into his skin. "Now you get to make up for that," she said, grabbing the buckle of his pants.

"No." Luca choked, grabbing her hands and ripping them away from him. "I don't want this." He grit his teeth and pushed her off of him as he stood. "Get the fuck out of my office," he said, turning away from her and realized his mistake when Ciara popped up from the floor and drove her fist into his back.

He cried out and stumbled forward, falling to his knees from the shooting pain.

"I'm not leaving until I get what I want," she said, digging her heel into his side and pushing him over. He sucked in a pained breath as his back connected with the floor and she pounced on top of him. "I fucking own you, Luca."

He trembled beneath her and tears welled in his eyes as she wrapped her hand around his throat and pressed her lips against his. He felt paralyzed as she took liberties with his wounded body. Luca's mind tumbled into the depths of his memories of the first time Ciara laid her hands on him and he fought back, only to be sent to the whipping post after she cried to Arnold and he was beaten for laying a hand on her. He learned from that moment that she truly held all the power over him. She could get away with whatever she did to him and there was nothing he could do about it.

Ciara was right. He was a weak man.

***

Luca stared at the rays of sun casting its morning light over the beige ceiling. Tears stained his cheeks as he tried to grapple with what Ciara had done to him. It didn't last very long, but it felt as if hours had passed while he was pinned beneath her. He wanted to hit her and break the arm she used to choke him with while she got off on the power she held over him. But what was he supposed to do? If he fought back, she'd cry victim and he'd be the one accused of rape.

Guilt and shame tore at his heart that he let her take advantage of him. How could his body betray him like that? Luca slid his hands over his face to wipe his tears and grimaced at the pain radiating from his back. He never thought she'd do something like that to him.

"You need to get up, darling. You can't lie there all day," Ciara said as her heels clicked on the tiled floor in the ensuite bathroom. She crossed the room and stood over him. "I'm going out with a few friends tonight, so I don't want to be bothered by you." She smiled, bending down to him. "Mm, but you're such a good fuck. I missed that," she whispered, and he flinched when she kissed his cheek. "Have a good day, Lu."

As soon as the door closed behind her, Luca shakily zipped up his pants and dragged himself from the floor. His lip trembled as his chest tightened and his breath came out short. Clenching his eyes shut, he braced himself on the back of his desk chair and sucked in gasps of air to ease his constricting lungs. A wave of nausea overwhelmed him, and he stumbled into the bathroom. Falling to his knees on the cream tiled floor, he vomited over the toilet.

"Mr. Shola, your nine-thirty is here," His assistant called.

"Give me a minute," Luca grumbled, hurling into the toilet again.

"Are you alright? Do you want me to cancel the–"

"No. I'm fine. I just need a minute," he said, pushing himself from the floor. The last thing he wanted was to spend any more time thinking about what happened. He needed the meeting. He needed to get his mind off of the disgusting way he felt.

Dragging himself to the sink, Luca washed his mouth out and eyed the droplets of blood dripping into the white basin. He looked into the mirror at the puncture wounds and bruises forming on his neck. He winced and grunted as he tore off his shirt. The slim doors of the mahogany wardrobe shook from his trembling hands as he opened them and pulled out a crisp black dress shirt followed by the drawer with rows of makeup concealer.

He always kept an emergency stash of clothes and makeup for this reason. Only this was the first time Ciara–

Luca shook his head. He couldn't bring himself to think

of that word again. Fuck. His grandfather may rule the Syndicates and the Dagenhams may have a long-standing deal with him over some spurious business he had yet to uncover, but he didn't deserve to be treated like this–to be owned. He didn't care about the bullshit legacy they were trying to protect.

Shrugging the shirt over his shoulders, Luca grit his teeth when the fabric brushed against his throbbing back. He grasped a handful of napkins and stood in the mirror, pressing them to his neck to stop the bleeding. Carefully placing the concealer over the scratches and bruises discoloring his skin, tears pooled in his eyes again.

He wanted to be free.

Luca wiped the tear that rolled down his cheek and took a deep breath as he straightened and smoothed a hand over his hair. He ignored the nagging itch to rip out of his clothes and scrub Ciara's essence from his body. He'd do that later. Right now, he just needed to get through the fucking day.

Clearing his throat and smoothing his hands over his suit. Luca looked at himself in the mirror and hardened his expression before he walked out of the bathroom. Taking a seat at his desk, he pressed the intercom for his assistant. "I'm ready."

Chapter 11

Nadia stepped off the elevator, and her heart clenched at Ciara walking down the hallway toward her. She smoothed a hand over the pleat in her peplum dress and a bright smile curled over her glossy pink lips. "We ran over a bit, but you know how it is." Ciara winked, and the lustful look in her eyes made Nadia's stomach sour. "Have a good meeting."

"Thanks," Nadia murmured and nearly gagged at the smell of her sweet lavender perfume. It was like she'd drenched herself in the nauseating scent.

"Miss Coleman, Mr. Shola said he needed a minute. He's running a little behind today," Jayne, his graying brown-haired assistant, said in her cheerful voice.

"I'm ready," Luca's voice proclaimed through the intercom on her desk.

"Oh, go right in." Jayne smiled.

"Thank you," Nadia said, opening the door to Luca's office and stepping inside. He was sitting at his desk and his usual kempt hair was disheveled but not in the boyish manner like the museum. This looked haphazard, as if he'd tried to get his locks to stay in place but failed. His black suit looked off as if he'd dressed in a hurry and his shoulders were hunched like he was in pain.

"Nadia?" Luca asked as he looked at his computer and the color drained from his face.

"Hi, do you want to reschedule this? Jayne said you were running behind and Cameron double booked himself."

"N-no. It's fine," he said, tugging his suit jacket closer around him. "Have a seat."

"Sure," she said, crossing the room and settling into the black leather chair in front of his desk. "So, Cameron and I wanted to talk to you about Ono Medical," Nadia said, sliding a black folder across Luca's desk. "Hishimoto Ono owns a ton of businesses across Osaka. He's not new to the US market, but he likes to put out marketing bids to build hype around his companies and products," Nadia explained, looking up from her copy of the report to assess his reaction. Luca kept his bloodshot eyes downcast and tugged at the collar of his shirt.

She eyed the discoloration on his skin and bit her lip before she looked back down at her notes when he didn't add to the conversation. She started to explain the process of pitching a proposal to Mr. Ono, but shook her head and clenched her hands in her lap. "Luca, I know this isn't my place and I probably shouldn't pry, but are you okay?"

"I'm fine," he murmured, pulling at his collar again.

"Okay, well you missed a spot covering that hickey," she said and he froze, but his shaking hands gave away his panic.

"It's not... a hickey," he breathed and slid a hand over his neck.

"I didn't think so," she murmured. "Luca, you need to go home."

"Wh-what?" He looked up at her and her heart shattered at the tearful look in his eyes. The fear, guilt and *shame* reflecting in his golden depths was the same look she saw in the mirror the first time Jonathan took advantage of her.

Nadia took a deep breath and fought back her own tears and memories rising to the surface. She never thought she'd find a man in this position, but it was all the same. "I don't know what happened with you and Ciara and I may be overstepping a boundary, but I think you need to go home and if you need to talk to someone –"

"I can't," he said, shaking his head. "I don't - I'm sorry." Luca cleared his throat, trying to blink back his tears and angrily wiping away the ones that escaped.

"It's okay," she said. "Do you want me to call Cameron or Gordon for you?"

He shook his head. "I want to take a fucking shower."

"Okay, but that means you need to go home. Is there a way to get out of here without anyone seeing you?"

Luca nodded. "Yes," he said, standing from his chair. He winced and leaned against his desk as he sucked in a gasp of air.

Jesus, what really happened to him? She had a feeling that back pain didn't come from lifting anything. Nadia popped up from her chair and rounded his desk. "Are you okay? I can help you. Just put your arm around my shoulders."

"I'm fine," he grunted. "You don't need to help me."

"Okay," she said, backing away from him. "Do you mind if I walk you out? Just to make sure you get to your car?"

He looked up at her and a glimmer of light burst through

the swirling cloud of pain behind his eyes. "I'd like that."

"Alright then, lead the way."

Luca walked with hunched shoulders to an otherwise blank beige wall beside a short wooden bookshelf. He flashed his wrist over a slim black pad. The lock released and the wall creaked open to reveal a hidden stairwell lit up by soft fluorescent lights.

"Are you sure you're going to make it down all those stairs?" Nadia teased. "You could've installed an elevator for yourself."

"I'm wishing I did that now, but stairs are safer in an emergency. I'll be fine," Luca said, grasping the metal railing. "You don't have to come if you don't want to."

"Right, so I can sit in my office worrying that you fell and cracked your head on these steps? Nope. I'm coming with you."

He looked back at her, and a small smile tugged at the corner of his lips. "Thank you. I'm sorry, I'm sure this is weird for you."

"You don't need to say sorry and it's not weird."

"It is," Luca's voice cracked and he sucked in a breath as he leaned against the railing. "I can't believe I–that she..."

"Hey, you're alright." Nadia reached out to touch his shoulder, but pulled her hand back and bit her lip. "I... I know how it feels and you're not weird and it's not your fault."

"But it feels like it," he whispered.

She walked down a step and stood next to him. "Luca, it's not your fault. I promise you, you did nothing wrong."

He nodded as a tear rolled down his cheek. "Can you stay... n-nevermind."

"Do you want me to stay with you?"

"No, yes... I-I don't know." He took a deep breath and wiped his face. "I'm sorry."

"Luca, if you need me to stay with you for support, I will. You don't need to say sorry for that. For any of this."

"Okay," he said, taking another deep breath. "I need you to stay. I-I want to talk."

"And I'll listen."

***

Nadia sat in a stone alcove facing the sun-kissed water that crashed against the rocky shores of Marblehead. When she agreed to stay with Luca, she didn't expect them to drive an hour outside of the city to his cottage by the sea. She popped a strawberry in her mouth from the spread of cheese, crackers, fruit and cold cuts that lined the stone slab table in front of her while she waited for Luca to take a shower.

Her mind drifted to the silent car ride and Luca huddled against the car door. His body shook every so often and she wanted so badly to comfort him. He was a tall, muscular man, but at that moment he looked so small and it pained her to see him like that. God, she couldn't believe what happened to him. He didn't say the word, but he didn't have to. Ciara took advantage of him when he was already hurt and couldn't defend himself.

Shaking her head, Nadia wiped a tear rolling down her cheek. How did that make her any different? She was going to use him to get information on the society his family was involved in and take advantage of his friendship to do it. She would never touch him like that, but didn't that make her just as bad as Ciara?

"Hey, Miss Nadia," Gordon said with a sad smile on his face as he slipped into the alcove and sat next to her. "I wanted to thank you for coming out here with Mr. Shola."

"It's not a problem. I'm... I'm glad I was there."

"So am I." He sighed, picking a grape up from the tray. "I don't think he would've left the office if you didn't encourage him to. He's good at pretending he's okay when shit happens like this."

"Has this happened before?"

"Not this particular situation, but other stuff," Gordon said, looking out at the waves crashing against the shore. "I told you he has a complicated past," he said, running a hand over his golden locks. "This isn't the first time he's been hurt like this." Gordon looked away from her as Luca emerged from the wooden cabin dressed in a black shirt and denim jeans, and walked down the cobbled path to the alcove. "You're looking better," he said, standing up and a bright smile spread over his face.

"Thanks, I feel a bit more human now." Luca sighed as he ducked into the alcove. "Have you been keeping Nadia company?"

"Yeah, you've got a good friend here." Gordon smiled at her. "Let me know when you're ready to go home, Miss Nadia."

She nodded. "I will, thank you," she said and guilt tugged at her heart. She wasn't a good friend. She was deceitful, but she needed Luca for his ties to the Syndicates. God, she was fucked up.

Luca eased himself into the padded seat next to her and the bleakness in his golden depths tore at her heartstrings.

She shouldn't do this to him. He didn't deserve to be used by another person, but her life depended on the information she could get out of him. Fuck.

"So, I don't know what I'm doing or why I asked you to come out here with me," Luca said as he poured himself a glass of water and topped up her glass. "You didn't have to do this."

"I know I didn't, and you don't have to say anything. We can just sit here. This place is really peaceful," she said, leaning back against the pillows cushioning the stone behind them.

"It is. It reminds me of my home," he said, pulling a silver rectangular case from his pocket and sat it on the table.

"Oh, you're not from Boston?"

Luca shook his head and plucked out a thickly rolled blunt from the case. "Do you mind if I light this?"

A smile tugged at her lips. "Nope, as long as you share."

He pushed the case toward her. "Feel free."

"Thank you," she said, helping herself. "So, where are you from then?"

"Hawai'i," he said, passing her the silver Zippo lighter in his hand.

"Why the hell would you move here from that glorious sunshine?"

He laughed. "My grandfather. He... wanted us to be closer to him, so my parents moved the company to Boston."

"Damn, that's a pretty drastic move to be closer to family. Why didn't he just move out there with you guys?"

Luca scoffed and took a long toke from his blunt. "It's a long story, but basically what my grandfather says goes and there's no arguing with him."

"That sounds... nice. Would you ever move back there?"

"I'd love to. I own a few businesses on the west coast and my Tutu's lands. That's my grandfather on my father's side."

"So why don't you? It sounds like you're close with your Tutu and that's where you want to be."

"I was. He died when I was eighteen and I can't move back. I have… a responsibility to live here."

"Oh, another grandfather thing? I don't mean to be rude, but he sounds like a piece of work."

"You have no idea." He smirked. "He wouldn't approve of me having lunch with you."

"Why not? Am I too much of a commoner to hang out with the King of the Underworld?"

A genuine laugh escaped his lips and some light returned to his somber gaze. "I'm no king in my grandfather's eyes. I'm more like a pauper he has to deal with and he wouldn't approve of this because my attention should be focused on someone else."

Nadia took a toke from her blunt and let the smoke out slowly before she asked her next question. "Would that be Ciara?"

"Mm-hm," he said, taking a drink from his glass and tapping his blunt against the stone ashtray.

She shook her head. "Does he know how she treats you?"

"Probably, but our arrangement is complicated." Luca sighed and leaned back against the pillows as he sucked in a puff of herb. "I can't explain it all and I know this isn't exactly the talk you have with someone you barely know, but after what happened at the office and the museum, I think I should explain myself and I'd like to try if… if you don't mind listening."

"I told you I would. I made one of my best friends through

a talk like this. So, for me, this isn't strange at all."

Minerva had been there for her since they were kids, but Raquel had been there for her since the day Jonathan tried to take her life and they've all been best friends ever since.

The corners of Luca's lips curled into a small smile. "Thank you."

Chapter 12

Luca took a long toke from his blunt and tried to find the words to explain his situation. He wasn't sure why he even offered to tell Nadia, but she was here and she stayed with him when she didn't have to. She cared when she didn't have to and even though she said it wasn't weird; he knew it was. God, he was fucked up. She shouldn't want to be around a man who–

He closed his eyes and clenched the fabric of his jeans.

"Luca, it's okay if you're not comfortable. I'm not here for an explanation." Nadia's soft calming voice pierced through his mangled thoughts.

He looked into her serene eyes and something about the warmth in her depths filled him with a sense of security. "I know, I just don't know where to start."

She nodded and took a deep breath. "I don't tell too many people this, but I was in an abusive relationship too. It's not easy to talk about."

His eyes grew wide. "What?"

A sad smile crossed her lips. "Yes, it was a few years ago but I understand what you're going through."

Luca stared at her in disbelief. No wonder she was worried about his guards following them after the club. He bet the stalker she mentioned was her abuser. "I had no idea you've gone through something like this. I'm sorry you had to see me like that today. It probably triggered you too."

"It did a little bit, but I'm more worried about you."

A whisper of a smile tugged at his lips and a sense of relief washed over him. He shouldn't find comfort knowing that Nadia was a victim, a survivor, but it made him feel safe to open up about his torment.

He took a deep breath and looked away from her to the calming waters. "Ciara and I were put together through an arrangement that was made between our families before we were born. At first it was okay. I can't say I ever wanted to be with her, but like I told you, my grandfather's word is law and Ciara's father, Arnold, is the same way. So, we just made the best of a shitty situation," he said, relighting his blunt. "Ciara started to get violent with me when I wouldn't stop doing things I enjoyed."

"Like dancing?"

"Yeah, and hanging out with my friends." He smirked. "Cameron is the only friend she and my grandfather allow me to associate with anymore and that's because he's excellent at his job. My grandfather considers him an asset to the company and my image."

"Wow." She shook her head. "So, that's the reason you keep your distance from everyone and why you don't like to go out?"

Luca nodded. "Yes, but I wasn't always like this. I used

to be a lot like my father, carefree, happy. I used to have a very lively social life before Ciara cried to her father that I wasn't paying attention to her." He looked up at the jagged ceiling and laughed. "She was worried I'd find a way out of our arrangement and ruin her inheritance. She'd be destitute without it. Everything she has is tied to her father and I'm the only thing keeping her flush with Arnold's cash."

"That's fucked up," Nadia breathed. "So, you're both being blackmailed into this?"

"Yeah, basically."

Nadia frowned. "If you both don't want this and don't like each other, why does she treat you so horribly?"

Luca rubbed a hand over his pants. "Because Ciara likes to use me as her punching bag. She can't get angry with her father, so she takes it out on me, then she apologizes and expects everything to be okay," he said, looking away from her. "And I have to go along with it."

"Why?"

Luca looked back at her and the urge to tell her the truth about his family and the Syndicates ached to spill out of his mouth, but he couldn't do that. It could put her in danger and he was probably telling her too much, anyway.

How would he even begin to explain the Dagenham–Rodawson relationship? How his mother chose freedom over a life chained to a man who cared more about her ability to breed children with a good bloodline and strengthen his status than anything else. But she didn't find freedom at all. Against his mother's knowledge, his grandfather promised the Dagenhams one of her children to make up for her disobedience. If she didn't comply, his grandfather set out to destroy the life his parents created. Their business, his

Tutu's land. Everything.

No. He couldn't tell Nadia any of that.

"Luca?"

"Sorry." He cleared his throat. "Um, it's complicated."

"Another grandfather thing?"

"Yeah, that's why I'm stuck with Ciara, but today was the first time she ever..." he trailed off as the feel of her hand around his throat and the sound of her moans brought tears to his eyes.

Nadia slid her hand over his and the gentleness of her touch broke through the panic crawling up his spine. "It's okay. You don't have to say it. I know this is hard."

He curled his fingers around hers as if it were some sort of anchor holding him in place and blinked back his tears. "I'm weak for allowing her to do that to me," he murmured. "I should've stopped her."

"You're not weak," she said, and he looked up into her watery depths. There wasn't an ounce of pity in her eyes, only sorrow and a wealth of understanding. "She took advantage of your injury and even if you weren't hurt and fought her off, she sounds like the type of person who'd use that against you." Nadia squeezed his hand and a tear rolled down her cheek. "You shouldn't have to live like this."

"I know but, please don't cry," he said as tears pricked the corners of his eyes. Nadia had too much empathy for him. She shouldn't shed any tears for his fucked up life.

"I can't help it. This isn't right," she said, wiping her cheeks.

"It's not and I know I need to find a way out of this, but it's nice to talk to someone who gets it, at least some of it," he said, staring at her hand in his. "I don't know how good of a friend I can be, but I'd like to try if you want to."

Chapter 12

A warm smile spread across her mauve lips. "Luca, I'd love to be your friend. We still have that book club to start."

His heart swelled and nearly burst that she still wanted to be around him after everything he told her. "Are you sure?"

"Yes, I'm sure," she said, squeezing his hand. "I'm not going to let Ciara or your grandfather stop us from being friends. That's just ridiculous."

"I'm glad you feel that way and thank you for listening to me. That means a lot."

"I'll always listen. That's what friends are for," she said, slipping her hand from his to tug her phone from her pocket. She looked up at him with her green eyes sparkling with amusement. "Should we curate a reading list for our club?"

"Yeah." Luca chuckled. "I guess that's a natural progression of our conversation."

"Got you to laugh though, didn't it?" She grinned, tapping on her screen to bring up a bookshop app.

"It did." He smiled. Some of the weight on his shoulders lifted as they discussed authors they liked and novels they wanted to read. Even the nagging worry that he was disobeying his grandfather and Ciara for being with Nadia quieted for a moment. He wouldn't put her in danger because of him. He'd make sure she was protected. That was the least he could do for a friend.

***

"Thank you again for being here," Luca said as he walked Nadia down the cobbled path beside his cottage to the waiting black sedan in the driveway. "I'm sorry for taking up your day, though."

"You're welcome and don't be sorry. I'm glad I could be here for you, plus we've got a decent reading list now."

"Yeah we do," he said, tucking his hands in his pockets. "I, um, still owe you dinner."

She laughed, tilting her head to the side. "I don't think I ever answered you about that."

"Oh, well, would you want to have dinner at my place... to make up for this?"

"You don't need to make up for what happened today, but yeah, I'd love to. Then I can peep your book collection and check out the mysterious Hades' lair."

"I'm not mysterious." He chuckled softly. "But I do have an excellent collection."

"Good, I can't wait to–shit!" she said, latching onto his shirt to stop her wobbling legs from taking her to the ground.

A rumble of laughter burst from his lips as he grasped her waist and steadied her on her feet. "Are you okay?"

"I'm fine, just my design flaw getting in the way again," she grumbled.

"Aw, little Miss Clumsy was doing so well today."

"Nope, no." She laughed. "You're not giving me that nickname."

"Alright I won't. I'll just think of a better one," he said, tucking her hand in the crook of his arm to prevent her from falling again as they continued down the path to the car.

"I hope so." She scoffed. "I have far better qualities to use for a nickname than clumsy."

He looked down at her, and a blush scorched his cheeks. She did and one of those qualities was the way she eased his mind and didn't judge him for what he'd been through. "I guess I'll have to get to know you better to find out."

She looked up at him and the light in her eyes made his heart thump. "I'd like that," she said, looking away from him to Gordon standing next to the car. "I know this hasn't been a very good day for you, but I hope I helped you feel a bit better. I'm always a call or a text away if you need to talk."

"Thank you. I feel a little better and if you ever need to talk about what happened to you, I'm willing to listen."

"I don't talk about it very much, but thank you. I'll keep that in mind," she said, slipping her hand from his arm. "Well, take care of yourself and let me know when you want to have dinner."

"I will. I'll see you tomorrow," he said, looking over her head. "Gordon –"

"Before you ask Gordon to let you know that I'm home," Nadia said, cutting him off. "Wouldn't you rather that come from me?"

His cheeks flushed, and a breathless laugh escaped his lips. "Um, yes, if you don't mind?"

"I don't," she said, stepping away from him. "I'll text you when I get home as long as you respond to me this time."

"That's fair." Luca smiled. "I can do that," he said, giving her a small wave as she slipped into the car.

Gordon closed the door behind her and crossed the short distance between them to place a hand on Luca's shoulder. "She's a good one, sir. You deserve a friend like her."

"Yeah." He nodded. "Can you keep an eye on her? I don't want the Dagenhams or my grandfather to make her a target."

"Of course."

"Good and be discreet. Nadia doesn't need to know."

"Got it," Gordon said. "Your parents and Lacey are on their way out here. Jack called them a little while ago."

"I figured he'd do that." Luca sighed. "Drive safe."

"I will and don't be upset with Jack, he's just looking out

for you."

"I know and I'm not. I don't want to be alone out here tonight anyway," he said as Gordon walked back to the car and slipped inside.

Luca took a deep breath, watching the car roll down the gravel driveway. This wasn't how he thought his friendship with Nadia was going to go. After the museum, he was content with letting her go, but after today. He shook his head and walked back down the path to the cottage.

After today, he didn't think he could cut her out of his life so easily. It felt good to talk to her and it felt even better that she still wanted to be around him–not that he'd get to spend a lot of physical time with her if Ciara and his grandfather had any say in the matter, but for now he'd enjoy whatever time he could get and maybe one day she'd feel comfortable enough to tell him her story.

Chapter 13

"Where the fuck have you been?!" Minerva roared through the phone as Nadia walked into her apartment. She turned on the forest green lamp next to her yellow reading chair to brighten the dusk glow of the living room.

"I was with Luca. Something happened at the office today," she said, throwing her keys into an orange glass bowl atop her fireplace.

"That required you to go missing all day?"

"Yeah, I don't want to talk about it." She sighed, kicking off her shoes and slumping onto her couch.

"Um, you played hooky with Luca and you *don't want to talk about it?* You know I'm not going to drop this. What happened? Are you okay?"

"I'm fine, Nervy. Something happened to Luca this morning and I was the only one there, so we left and just talked and hung out," she said, biting her thumb. "I don't think I can do this."

"What do you mean?"

"I can't use Luca for information on the Syndicates."

"What? Nadia, what happened that got you thinking like this?"

"He's like me," she whispered as tears pooled in her eyes. "I think his grandfather is abusing him and his girlfriend definitely is." She shook her head and wiped the tear rolling down her cheek. "I can't use him. I don't want to."

"Are you sure? The Sholas have been the biggest lead we've had since we started investigating the Syndicates."

"Yeah, I'm sure. He needs a friend, not another person taking advantage of him."

"Okay, have you told Raquel about this?"

"No. I was supposed to drop Jonathan's note off to her –"

"What do you mean Jonathan's note?"

Nadia slid a hand over her face. "I got a card from him at the office this morning. Just one of his messages saying that he'll always find me."

There was silence on the line before Minerva heaved a sigh. "Nadia, unless you plan on quitting your job and moving again you *have* to go through with this plan. Taking down the Syndicates is the only way you're going to get him out of your life. You have to use Luca."

"No, I'm pretty sure his girlfriend is involved and I've got Raquel investigating her."

"And then what? You're already starting a friendship with him. He's your best bet at getting close to that master file we're after and you know Raquel is going to say the same thing."

"I know, but this feels so wrong. I was fine with it until I saw him today." She sniffed. "Nervy he was… raped."

"What?!" she shrieked. "How the fuck? In the office?"

she whispered. "Holy shit, that's probably why Cameron canceled our dinner plans. Is... is he okay?"

"I don't know. He seemed fine when I left, but God it brought back so many memories." Nadia scoffed. "Ciara Dagenham is basically Jonathan."

"Well, she's probably a Syndicate, so it makes sense. Luca's a pretty big guy. How the hell did she overpower him to... to do that?"

"He was already injured. He said he hurt his back lifting something, but the way he talked about his grandfather, I think he beat him. Either way, it doesn't matter. Ciara still took advantage of him and that's why I can't do this. Luca's not a Syndicate. Well, he is, but he's not like the ruthless ones I've met."

"Jesus, this is fucked up," Minerva mumbled. "And here I was planning to tell you I don't want to deceive Cameron, either. I kind of like him a lot." She chuckled softly. "We're the worst kind of spies and Raquel would be so disappointed with us."

A smile tugged at Nadia's lips as she got up and shuffled into her kitchen. "You never had to do this mission with me. I'm the one who got myself wrapped up in a man I never should've been involved with. You should see where it goes with Cameron. You might get that M.R.S. you've always wanted."

Minerva let out a bark of laughter. "Maybe, but you know I'm always going to support you, and I still think you should use this budding friendship to your advantage. Luca doesn't need to know you've got an ulterior motive. You just need something to bring down the whole organization."

"That's true, I guess. I'll talk to Raquel about it, but I know she'll just agree with you."

"Yes, she will, but I get it. I know I don't always understand what you've been through or how you cope with everything, so maybe you need someone like Luca in your life."

"Yeah, I guess you were right. It's okay to make a new friend." She chuckled, pulling out a bowl of marinated chicken from the fridge. "Anyway, I'm going to make dinner and have a big glass of wine. I think I deserve that after today."

"You do you, but don't forget to call Raquel."

"I won't. Love you, Nervy."

"Love you too," she said and hung up.

Nadia tapped the message icon on her screen and typed a message to Luca, letting him know she was home before she plucked a bottle of wine and a glass from the rack above her island.

Luca » Glad you made it home. Thanks for letting me know.«

Nadia filled her glass as she tapped her reply.

Nadia »You're welcome. Thanks for responding. How are you feeling?«

Luca » Haha. Cam and my family are here, so I'm alright.«

Nadia » That's good. I'm glad you're not alone. «

Luca » Yeah, me too. I'll see you tomorrow. Have a good night.«

Nadia » You too.«

She sat her phone down and bit her thumb as she tried to fight the smile that itched to spread across her lips. She shouldn't feel any ounce of happiness for the shit that transpired today, but as sad as it was, Luca was a kindred spirit, and it would be nice to have someone who's been through the same kind of trauma she had. It made her feel like she could tell him her story and maybe one day she would. For now, she'd just keep getting to know him.

Nadia sighed as she turned on the stove and dumped the bowl of chicken in the pan, but now she had to rethink her game plan. She swiped her phone up from the counter and called Raquel. She still worked for Shola. The master list had to be somewhere in that office.

She'd find it and get her freedom from Jonathan without extorting Luca. Maybe it would get him his freedom too.

Chapter 14

Nadia looked behind her as she slipped into the stairwell at the back of the empty marketing office. She'd gone out to lunch with Raquel to give her Jonathan's note and she'd given her the idea of going through the archived asset files to look for any contracts with Luca's grandfather. Raquel said if the master list was anywhere, it would be hidden in plain sight, because that was how presumptuous groups like the Syndicates worked.

Armed with a list of possible aliases, Nadia snuck down the three flights of stairs to the records department. She swiped her badge over the keypad and grinned when the light turned green and the lock released. She pushed the door open and peered inside the room full of old files and priceless objects stacked on rows of metal shelves. There was a lone empty desk in the corner where she assumed the archivist sat and monitored the heirlooms Shola kept as collateral for some of their investments.

If she were there for a legitimate reason, she might've done this during work hours and asked for help to locate the names on her list, but she'd just have to do this the hard way. She pulled up her notes on her phone and started with the first name on her list. *Giovanni Bianchi.*

An hour of searching went by and Nadia had nothing. None of the six names on her list had any files or heirlooms stored at Shola Enterprises. She shook her head and slid her hands to her hips as she wandered down another row of endless files and random treasured objects. This was pointless. Why would the master list be that easy to find? Gregory wouldn't be that stupid to leave valuable information like that here. Neither the Dagenhams nor Jonathan's family had anything stored away at the company, either.

She threw her head back in frustration and her eyes caught a box with G. Rodaw on a white label in thick, black lettering. Her heart thumped as she stepped closer to the shelving. No fucking way. She looked up at the J - K placard on top of the shelf and frowned. That box was out of place.

Nadia grabbed the step ladder and wheeled it against the silver shelving. Someone either misfiled those documents or it was done on purpose. She didn't know if G. Rodaw meant Gregory Rodawson. It would be awfully fucking bold of him to label his stuff so obviously, but it wouldn't hurt to look. She stepped up the short ladder and leaned up on her tiptoes to reach the box conveniently sitting on the highest shelf. Fuck. Even in her heels she was too short to reach it.

"Come on," she grumbled, holding the wobbling ladder with one hand and reaching for the box with the other.

"What are you doing down here?"

Nadia yelped, startled by the sound of Luca's deep voice. Her hand hit the top of the box below. It slid out, hitting her in the chest and knocking her off balance. She screamed in panic as she fell backwards and crashed into Luca's waiting arms.

"Are you alright?" He laughed.

"I'm fine," she breathed, clutching the box in her arms while he steadied her on her feet. "Thanks for scaring the shit out of me."

"I'm sorry," he said, sliding his hands from her waist. "I didn't expect anyone to be down here. Why are you still at work?"

"Um… I was doing some research on Johnson Corp for a new comms plan," she said, reciting her perfectly prepared response. She was an excellent spy.

Luca raised an eyebrow, checking his watch. "At six thirty at night and you needed the archive for Kirkman Industries?"

A blush burned up to her ears as she looked down at the box in her arms. "I lost track of time and I didn't mean to grab this one!"

"Right, well Johnson Corp is right here," he said, plucking a thick folder from a box on a lower shelf. "I'm not sure why you're looking into them. I'm pretty sure they plan to leave us for another asset company."

"Well, I think I should at least try to get them to stay." She held out the box to him. "I'll trade you," she said, taking the folder from his hands. "Why are you down here, anyway?"

Luca stepped on the ladder and slid the Kirkman box back on the shelf before he pulled down the box she was after. "My grandfather wanted me to go through some of his old assets."

"Oh, so how did you know?" She looked at the label. "Rodaw would be in the J-K section?"

He chuckled. "A lucky guess."

She highly doubted that. "Mm, that's pretty lucky. Well, I've got what I need now." She sighed, wishing she'd found the coveted box before him at least to have a look at what assets his grandfather was holding. "I should probably get out of here."

"Yeah," he said, hooking the box under his arm and walking down the ladder. "Actually, if you don't have any plans tonight, do you want to have that dinner I owe you?"

A smile tugged at her lips at the perfect opportunity to get a peek at those files. "Sure, why not? I just need to grab my stuff."

"Great, I'll wait for you in the garage."

***

Nadia eyed the black cardboard box sitting at their feet and she itched to comb through the many files that filled it. There must be something about the shady workings of the Syndicates in there and she felt guilty that she agreed to dinner with Luca just for the chance to look inside.

Tearing her gaze away from it, she looked over at Luca. Her heart fluttered at the way the evening sun highlighted his chiseled light brown features and set his dark hair and black suited attire in a warm glow. The bruises that stained his neck were sufficiently covered, and he looked much better than when she left him yesterday.

"So what comms plan are you working on for Johnson Corp?" Luca said, looking away from the street and turning his warm golden gaze on her. "I'm pretty impressed you're that dedicated to search the archives."

"Um." Shit. She hadn't planned to go into detail about it.

"I thought if I looked at their history with us, played on their legacy standing and reminded them of some previous successful campaigns we've done for them it might encourage them to stay."

"Mm okay, but I think you're fighting a losing battle with them." He chuckled. "They might appreciate the effort you're putting in though."

"It's worth a try," she said and a small gasp escaped her lips as the car rolled into an underground garage of a towering black high-rise and she eyed a sleek black sports car among the other prestigious cars lining the massive space. "No fucking way. Is that a McLaren 720s?"

Luca raised an eyebrow. "It is and I'm impressed you know your supercars."

"My dad is a retired engineer, so I grew up around fast cars. I've always wanted to drive one of these babies," she breathed as she got out of the car to inspect the artful vehicle sitting under the fluorescent lights.

"Well, maybe I'll take you out to the track one of these days and let you drive it."

Nadia looked up at him with a massive grin on her face. "You have a friend for life if you let me drive this beast."

He let out a bark of laughter, and she loved the rich baritone sound of it. "I'm only good enough because of my taste in cars, huh?"

She grinned. "Yep, and if your taste in books is up to par too."

He nodded toward the stainless steel elevator. "Would you like to check them out while I get dinner started? I promise not to be offended if you decide you made the wrong decision to be my friend."

Chapter 14

"Oh, don't do that to him, Miss Coleman." Jack chuckled. "This guy will be so upset," he said, holding the box of files under his arm and the rest of the five-guard entourage waited near the elevator.

Luca glared at the graying brown-haired bodyguard and she caught the twin flags of red that stained his tawny cheeks.

"I wouldn't do that." Nadia laughed. "Come on, I'd like that dinner you owe me," she said, slipping her arm through his. "I'm starving."

They followed Jack into the elevator with the rest of the black suited guards to the floors above. Nadia nearly cursed under her breath when the group of guards got off and Jack held onto the coveted box of documents.

"I'd like a report of what you find by tomorrow," Luca called after him.

"Will do, sir." Jack nodded and smiled at Nadia. "Enjoy your dinner. Mr. Shola's an excellent cook," he said, giving them a small wave.

"Thanks," she said as the doors closed and tried not to sound disappointed that her plan died before it even got off the ground. Damn it. She bit her lip and looked up at Luca, but it wasn't all bad. At least she'd get a chance to spend time with him again without it being such a traumatic event. "So, you're an excellent cook, huh? I don't like frozen or pre-packaged meals."

Luca gasped, and his eyes filled with the same playful gleam she saw at the museum. "What kind of person do you take me for? I'll have you know, miss, I only cook with the freshest ingredients."

"I'll believe it when I see it..." she trailed off as the elevator doors opened and her eyes grew wide at the spacious penthouse laid out before her. The evening sun cascaded into the open living room from the floor to ceiling windows and warmed the sleek ebon furnishings and blackwood flooring that bled into the kitchen. Gray granite countertops, black cupboards and stainless steel appliances made up the kitchen that was kitted out to professional chef standards.

Nadia stepped inside and her eyes were drawn to the built-in bookshelves that spanned the gray wall behind the long black sectional. The books were the only bits of color that gave the place any life. It was immaculate and clean, but so… empty. "Your place is amazing, but you need some plants in here, dude."

He chuckled. "Do I?" he said, shrugging off his suit jacket and hanging it on the coat rack.

"Yes. I hate to say it, but you're really living up to your King of the Underworld nickname. I'm not saying you don't have great taste, but there are more colors on the spectrum than gray and black," she said and a smile lit up her face as she looked out of the wall of windows facing the Boston harbor. "But that view is unbelievable!"

"Well, I'm glad you like one thing about my place." He grinned. "We can eat out there, if you want?"

"I'd love that," she said, slipping off her jade green heels and placing them by the door next to his. "But I want to check out that massive book collection you've got going on over there."

"Feel free. I'll start dinner. Are you allergic to raw fish?" he said, rolling up his sleeves as he padded to the refrigerator.

"Nope," she said, plopping her purse down on a stool and her heart sank at the pamphlet for coping with sexual assault lying on top of the granite island. "Luca, I'm sorry I didn't say anything, but are you doing okay?"

He looked over his shoulder as he pulled out a bowl of marinated fish. "Oh, yeah, I'm alright. I saw my therapist this morning and she left that pamphlet for me. I just didn't put it away," he said, swiping it up and shoving it into a drawer.

"You know it's okay not to be okay, but I'm glad you spoke to a professional."

"I know, that's what she said too and I promise I'm doing alright, mostly." He smiled. "You don't need to worry about me."

"Alright, and I hope you know you didn't have to make up for anything that happened. I like hanging out with you."

"That's good. I like hanging out with you too and I hope you feel the same after you check out my books."

"Of course I will." She grinned. "I still want to drive that McLaren, so you're stuck with me at least until then."

"I better not let you drive it too soon then."

A blush burned over her cheeks. "Better not," she said, crossing the room to the expansive bookcase. It had been a long time since she felt comfortable in the presence of a man like this.

Luca brought out something in her whenever she was around him. It was refreshing and she liked it. She felt like herself before her trauma and before she let Jonathan damage the lively woman she used to be.

Chapter 15

Luca stole a few glances at Nadia pour over his books while he prepared their poke bowls and set up the table on the balcony. It was nice having her there. He was glad he caught her in the archives, although he wasn't sure he bought her story about her interest in the old Johnson Corp files. She was so close to his grandfather's records, but why would she be interested in those?

"Do you need help with anything?" she asked as he walked back inside to grab a bottle of wine from the rack next to the couch.

"Nope, I'm good. Did you find anything interesting in my collection?"

"I did. Are you into secret cults and societies?" She asked, pointing to a black book with the title 'Cults: Inside and Out'.

"Um, yeah I dabble in some non-fiction. I think some of them are interesting."

"That's cool. I have this book too." She nodded. "But I wasn't aware you were into seedy fiction about BDSM?" she said, holding up a gray book with handcuffs and black lace. "You know this isn't accurate, right?"

He chuckled. "I do. That's my sister trying to ruin my impeccable collection. She thinks she's funny. She stuck some small town vampire book on there too. You'd probably like it. You have a lot in common with the main character."

"Mm, very funny." She smirked. "Is that why you keep this one?" she said, sliding the book back on the shelf. "Do you have something in common with Mr. Grey?"

"Nope. He's not a good example of the lifestyle."

Nadia laughed softly, biting her lip. "No, he's not," she murmured, looking out the open glass doors. "So, is dinner ready? I'm dying to taste your food, chef."

"It is and I hope you're hungry because I'm good at making too much," he said, glad for the change in subject. He was far from ready to think about the theme of that novel and it was too dangerous to think about Nadia in that way, but it intrigued him that she seemed knowledgeable about the subject.

"Oo, this looks amazing!" Nadia exclaimed as she sat down at the table underneath the black wood veranda. "I love poke."

"Really?" he said, sitting across from her and pouring her a glass of wine. "It's become popular recently, but I'm surprised you've had it before."

"Yeah, I've had the Japanese version tako but I'm assuming this is ahi?"

"That's right." A bright smile spread across his lips, and his heart warmed that she knew something about his culture. "My Nonna taught me how to make it and now it's comfort food for me."

"Well, thank you Nonna because this is delicious," she said, munching on a mouth full of the colorful mixture of rice, fish, and vegetables. "So, are you fluent in Hawaiian too or just in making the cuisine?"

"Yeah. My father's family is from a small village in Kaua'i called Koa Maile. They speak Hawaiian and English, but Hawaiian is actually my first language."

"That's really cool. I'm fluent in a few languages but Hawaiian is one I never thought about learning."

"I would hope you're multilingual as an international rep." He laughed, taking a sip of wine. "Hawaiian isn't exactly mainstream, but I could teach you if you really wanted to learn."

"Yeah sure. We can add language lessons to our book club," she said, taking another hefty bite from her bowl. The way her eyes glossed over in delight made his cheeks flush and his heart thump at the sight.

"I'd like that," he murmured and a part of him feared he might like her too.

***

Luca was in a fit of laughter as Nadia explained her well thought out parallel dimension theory about mythical creatures. They'd finished their meal, drank through a bottle of wine, and were still sitting on the balcony enjoying a few blunts.

"Stop laughing! It makes perfect sense! How else would people be able to describe creatures and their worlds in such detail?"

"Because people back in the day mistook things like blood disorders for supernatural ailments and then folklore was created from them. There's no parallel dimension or secret mystical world hiding in plain sight." He laughed. "You're just fucking high."

Nadia raised an eyebrow and pointed inside. "You've got a stash of high fantasy novels in there and you don't believe some of that could be real? Fuck outta here, dude."

"It's escapism, Nadia! Obviously it isn't real," he roared with laughter.

She pursed her lips. "Then how do you explain Sasquatch, Wendigos, Imps and Aliens?"

"Folklore, no one has seen Sasquatch and aliens are real."

"Ha! So you do believe!"

"In aliens because there's no way we're the only–" Luca stopped his explanation to stare at his watch blinking in quick succession on his wrist. He read the alert from his guards stationed at the entrance of the building and cursed. "I'm sorry, Nadia, but you need to leave."

"What? Is everything okay?"

"No, Ciara's here," he murmured as he read the message detailing her distressed state. "She wants to talk and I need to get you out of here."

"Oh damn. Are you okay with that?"

"Not really, but I have to be," he said, squeezing his hands together. "I don't want her to get my grandfather involved again. I don't need another–nevermind." He shook his head and took a deep breath.

"Okay, I get it," Nadia said and started picking up their wine glasses and empty bottle.

"What are you doing?"

"You said I need to leave and you don't want her to know I was here, right? Wouldn't that be bad for you?"

"Yeah but you don't have to clean up. I can do that."

"It'll be faster if I help. Grab the bowls and the other bottle of wine," she said as she got up and disappeared inside.

Luca sent a message back to his guard on the door and another to Gordon before he picked up the remnants of their dinner. Nadia had already washed and rinsed their glasses and was slipping on her shoes by the time he walked inside.

"Is there another way I can get out of here?" she said, shrugging her purse over her shoulder.

He nodded, sitting the bowls and bottle of wine on the counter. "Yeah, I'll take you to the back stairwell," he said, motioning for her to follow him. His heart was racing as he passed his bedroom to the solid black steel door at the end of the hall. He wasn't ready to face Ciara, but what fucking choice did he have? He couldn't tell her no.

Luca took a deep breath and turned to Nadia. His heart clenched at the concern in her bright eyes. "Gordon will meet you at the bottom of the stairs and take you home," he said, looking away from her as guilt washed over him. "I'm so sorry about this."

"It's okay." Nadia took his hands, squeezing them gently. "I've been in your place. You don't need to say sorry, but you need to protect yourself. Make sure one of your guards is close by."

"I will." He nodded. "Thank you for being so chill about this."

"You're welcome, but I'm pretty worried about you. Will you text me to let me know you're okay?"

"Yeah, I can do that," he said as he reluctantly let go of her hands to open the door for her. "I'll see you tomorrow."

"Okay. Don't forget to wash the bowls," she said as she walked through the door and looked over her shoulder before she started down the stairs. "Be safe, Luca."

"You too," he said, closing the door and pressing his forehead against it. Just when he was having a good time with Nadia and his mind was the furthest it'd been from the fucked up shit that happened to him, Ciara had to rear her head to bring him back to reality.

He took a deep breath and padded back to the kitchen. He watched the round light on the top of the elevator inch closer to his floor. His hands shook as he washed the bowls, threw out the empty wine bottle and shoved the other in the refrigerator.

Luca's eyes darted to the balcony, making sure there was no evidence of Nadia or their dinner before the elevator gave off a soft ding. He stiffened and held his breath as the doors opened.

"Luca, I'm so sorry," Ciara cried as she ran through the doors and crushed him with a hug. "I shouldn't have done that to you," she sobbed, looking up at him with her tearful, bloodshot eyes. Her usual kempt hair was knotted on top of her head in a disheveled bun and she was dressed as if she'd just rolled out of bed.

Ciara looked terrible, but it didn't fool him. Luca patted his hand on her back. "No, you shouldn't have done that to me."

"Please don't be mad at me." Her lip trembled. "I feel like such a horrible person."

"Ciara, I'm not ready to talk about this with you," he said, stepping out of her arms and crossing his arms over his chest.

"I know. I just wanted to say sorry. My father's been putting a lot of pressure on me lately," she said, wiping her tears. "And I took it out on you, but I went too far. Can we just start over?" she said, placing her hand on his arm. "Please?"

His skin crawled at the feel of her touch and he swallowed back the panic and bile rising in his throat. "I don't have a choice, do I?"

The sorrow in Ciara's brown eyes hardened and he saw the snarl that nearly curled over her lips. "No," she said, pulling her hand away. "But I can tell you're still mad at me." She scoffed and crossed her arms. "I'll make a deal with you."

"I'm listening."

She rolled her eyes and wiped the rest of her fake tears from her face. "Can I get a drink?"

"Fine, but what's your deal?" he said, walking around the island to stay as far away from her as possible. He plucked a glass from the cupboard, filled her cup in the sink, and sat it on the counter for her.

She raised an eyebrow. "Tap water, really?" She smirked, bringing the glass to her lips.

"What's your deal?"

"Come sit with me," she said as she went into the living room and plopped down on the couch, patting the space next to her.

Luca shook his head. "I'd rather stand."

"I'm not going to touch you like that." Ciara rolled her eyes. "At least stand a little closer."

"Fine," he said, moving to lean against the end of the island but still a good five feet away from her. "Tell me your deal."

She shifted in her seat and pushed a piece of hair out of her face. "I know I fucked up, but we have to make this work, Lu." She sighed, clenching the glass in her hand. "So, I'm willing to give you some time to cool off. Another three weeks, but you will be present at every party and every fundraiser and I promise I won't tell my father about our arrangement. However," she said, placing her glass on the coffee table and lacing her fingers together. "If I catch you with that Coleman woman, the deal is off. Do you understand?"

"I do. Does this mean no random visits like this or in the office?"

"Yes, I'll leave you alone as long as you act right at our public engagements." She hung her head. "I'm… I'm really trying to say sorry."

Luca shook his head and sighed. He guessed this was her version of an apology, but nothing would make him forget what she did. "Thank you, but it's going to take me longer than three weeks to get over this. You fucked me up."

She looked up at him, and the genuine concern in her eyes surprised him. "I know, but you have to understand where I'm coming from. You're the only thing I have control over in my life and I don't want to lose that," she said, standing up and closing the gap between them.

He flinched away from her when she pressed her hand to his cheek. "I don't want to lose you, Lu."

"You won't." He choked out a breath. "But I need time. A month at least."

She slid her hand from his face and patted it over his chest. "A month it is. We're going to be okay. You won't let me lose everything, right? You know I have nothing without you."

Luca sighed in defeat. "Of course not. I know what's at stake for you."

"Thank you," she said, leaning up to kiss him on the cheek. "You're such a good boy," she whispered.

He shuddered, gripping the edge of the island and sliding

away from her. "I think you need to leave now," he said, fighting the urge to spew his dinner over the floor.

"Alright, I'll message you calendar dates and if you want to have that talk about what happened, we can."

"Mm-hm," he mumbled, swallowing back the building saliva as sweat beaded on his forehead.

"Good night, Lu," Ciara waved as she stepped onto the elevator.

He grunted, waving back, wishing the doors would close faster. The minute the metal seams pressed together he bolted down the hall to the bathroom and vomited in the toilet. Clenching his eyes shut, he sucked in gasps of air, but the panic was closing in and he was drowning in the memory of what Ciara did to him.

"I… I am the m-master of my life," he choked out the mantra his therapist taught him in a pained whisper. "N-no one has power over me." He laid on the cool tiled floor, repeating the phrase until his racing heart and erratic breathing calmed.

Luca dragged himself from the floor to the sink, washed his mouth out and splashed water over his clammy face. He hung his head, gripping the sink and taking a few deep breaths.

That could've been so much worse with Ciara, and he was thankful she had some sense of remorse for what she'd done. At least she agreed to give him some space, but he wasn't exactly free for a month. She'd be watching him like a hawk. He couldn't be too friendly with Nadia in public, but Ciara couldn't stop him from calling or texting her.

A whisper of a smile tugged at his lips as he pulled his phone from his pocket and sent Nadia a message to let her know Ciara left and he was alright.

Nadia » Glad you're okay and she didn't stay very long. By the way, Gordon says he believes in Sasquatch. So… guess I won that.«

A rumble of laughter fell from his lips and eased the biting anxiety that clung to his nerves.

Luca » Gordon doesn't have any authority!«

Nadia »Pshh, he's ex military. He's seen some shit.«

Luca » I guess so. Anyway, I'm sorry our dinner got cut short but I had a good time with you tonight.«

Nadia » Me too. Should we start our book club tomorrow?«

Luca » Definitely. Good night, Nadia. «

Nadia » Good night!«

Luca left his phone on the sink and shrugged his clothes off before he stepped under the warm soothing water. Ciara didn't have to know he was going to keep building this friendship with Nadia. As long as he wasn't seen with her outside of work, he could keep this from Ciara's watchful eyes.

Chapter 16

Luca grinned at a message from Ciara as he leaned back in his office chair. It'd been three weeks since she promised to give him space. He was the perfect boyfriend in public and she held up her side of the deal and left him alone. Which meant he could keep his morning coffee chats and nightly book club calls with Nadia a secret.

Ciara's father had been over the moon with his behavior too and now Luca was being rewarded for his efforts. Arnold was sending Ciara away to Texas for a few weeks to lead the setup of their new hotel chain.

Luca « Good luck on your first big assignment.«

Ciara » I know you don't mean that and just because I'm gone doesn't mean I won't be watching you. One phone call to my father is all it will take, Lu. So be good. «

Luca » Safe travels.«

"You're looking mighty happy today." Cameron chuckled as he and Nadia walked into his office.

"I am. I just got some great news," he said, sliding his phone into his pocket. "And I'm hoping you two are here to give me more of that."

"Yes we are," Cameron said as they sat down in the chairs opposite his desk and he slid a black folder across to Luca. "We've been chosen to attend the Ono Medical pitching showcase in Osaka." He grinned and looked over at Nadia. "All thanks to the superb proposal by our talented International rep."

"This is amazing work," Luca said, scanning the letter detailing the week-long showcase. "Acquiring this contract would be huge for Shola."

"Yes, not only would this put us in a good position to gain more contracts like this, but the acquisition would create a surplus of funds," Nadia said as she flipped through her notes. "I spoke with Finance and they said it would give each employee a minimum bonus of five hundred dollars."

A smile tugged at the corner of his lips. "You seem like you've done some thorough research on this. I'm impressed. How likely do you think we'll be able to get the contract? It looks like we'll be going up against some big names in the industry."

"Well, we definitely have a shot. I used to intern for Mr. Ono. I know what he's looking for and how he likes to run these showcases," she said with an amused gleam in her beautiful eyes. "Mr. Ono enjoys a good competition, so we'll need a flawless presentation."

"Okay, then I want you to work on that," Luca said, chuckling at the fire that sparked behind her eyes. "Seems like you enjoy a challenge like this."

"Just a bit." She shrugged and the playful smile on her lips sent a tingle down his spine. It didn't help that he had a hard time keeping his eyes off that sultry black pussy bow top she wore.

"I hope you do," he said, dragging his eyes back to her face. "Because we need that contract."

"Then I'll do my best to help us get it," she said, crossing her red pant leg over the other. "I don't like to lose."

Luca didn't know why those words or that simple movement made his damn groin twitch, but that fire in her eyes was too damn sexy.

"Perfect," Cameron said as he clasped his hands together, interrupting the inappropriate trajectory of Luca's thoughts. "Since that's settled." He grinned. "I want to talk to you two about tonight."

Luca tore his gaze from Nadia and raised an eyebrow at Cameron. "What about tonight?"

Nadia groaned. "Is this about Minerva's thing?"

"Yeah, she told you?"

"Of course she did. I'm her best friend and I don't think it's a good idea."

Luca frowned. "What are you two talking about?"

They looked at him. Nadia shook her head while Cameron beamed. "I might have told Minerva you have the perfect theater set up and she wants to have a movie night at your place."

A smile spread across Luca's face. "That sounds like a good plan to me." He'd entertain any excuse to get Nadia in his home again. He could easily conceal her being at his place and he wanted to have her over, but he'd just been too nervous to ask her.

"Great. Is seven o'clock good for you?"

"Yeah, that's fine. Bring whatever you want to eat and I'll

provide the booze and other recreational treats."

"Wait a damn minute!" Nadia said, raising an eyebrow. "You're okay with Minerva basically inviting herself over?"

"Yeah, it's fine." Luca shrugged. "As long as you're coming too."

His heart thumped at the devilish smile that curled over her lips. "What if I'm not? Maybe I have plans tonight."

Luca leaned back in his chair. "You can bring Niklaus. That doesn't bother me," he said and bit his cheeks from laughing at the way Nadia's lips pursed together and her green eyes glared at him.

"What? Who the hell is Niklaus?" Cameron asked.

A laugh choked from Nadia's lips. "Okole puka," she muttered, shaking her head as she stood and gathered her notes. "I'm going back to my office. I have work to do."

Luca grinned at her perfect pronunciation of asshole. She was getting good at the Hawaiian he'd been teaching her. "So, I'll have Gordon pick you up then?"

"Yep, and I'll bring my *boyfriend,*" she said, crossing the room to the door.

"You do that." He chuckled as she flipped him off before she closed the door. Nadia was in love with the platinum haired God from Eyes of the Beholder. She made him read every Niklaus chapter while she sighed longingly over the green-eyed character. Her reactions to him were so adorable and Luca secretly loved reading to her and talking about whatever came to their minds.

"So, you and Nadia are getting pretty close." Cameron wriggled his eyebrows at him. "Was that a bit of flirting and who's Niklaus?"

"Niklaus is a character from a book we're reading," Luca

said as he leaned back in his chair again. "And no, that wasn't flirting, but I guess we're getting close. She's a good friend."

"Mm-hm, that seemed like flirting to me."

"Well, it wasn't, and you and Minerva need to be discreet when you come over tonight. You'll need to use the guards' entrance. Ciara's people are watching me and I don't need anything to ruin our deal," he said and a bright smile spread across his face. "Especially when I've got a few more weeks of freedom."

"What? For real? I was wondering why you were so damn chill about this movie night. What happened?"

"Arnold's sending her to Texas to open another Sapphire Hotel chain."

"Oh, that's perfect. So, that means you can go out to New York and snoop without Ciara with you."

"Yes, exactly. Raquel helped Jack decode my grandfather's files and it all points to his lake house in Watkins. This could be it."

"Mm-hm, what did I tell you about my girl? She's sharp." Cameron grinned.

"Yeah she is. My guys are good but she's got skill. No wonder she works for the Feds. She should be CIA."

"I keep telling her that." Cameron laughed. "So, do you want me to come with you on this mission?"

"Yeah, it'll make my trip look more believable. It'd be nice to have a guy's weekend out there. We haven't done that in a long time."

"We're doing a lot of things we haven't done in a while," Cameron said, pushing his papers together. "Since you and Nadia started talking I haven't seen you this happy in a long time. It's nice to see my friend again."

"Yeah," Luca said, looking down at his hands. "She just gets me, but sometimes I think I'm being selfish being her friend. I don't want her to get dragged into anything because of me."

"You're not being selfish for making a new friend." Cameron scoffed. "You've got enough guards to protect her if need be."

"Yeah, that's true. I just don't want anything to happen to her."

"Nothing will. I know the drill when you're on a break from Ciara," he said, patting his hand on the desk. "We'll have fun tonight and you're going to be fine."

Luca looked up at his best friend's warm brown eyes and smiled. "Thanks, Cam."

"Of course," he said, standing from his chair. "You just make sure you've got that good shit on offer tonight."

"I got you."

Luca smiled to himself after Cameron left. It'd been a long time since he'd had people over to his place to entertain. It'd be nice to have Nadia over again and he wondered if she'd bring him some houseplants like she said.

He wouldn't mind having something of hers in his place. A blush scorched his cheeks. He shouldn't be thinking like that. They were just friends and they both didn't want to be anything more than that, not like he could.

Unless the trip to his grandfather's lake house proved to be as fruitful as Raquel and Jack seemed to think. Then he'd have enough evidence to grant his freedom and maybe things could be different with Nadia.

***

Luca turned off the stove and poured the steaming queso dip into a black ceramic bowl. He sat it on the table in the living room before he pushed the couch further back to the bookshelf. Picking up a remote on the end table, he pointed it at the TV. It slid into the wall and a projector screen scrolled down from the ceiling in front of it. He didn't know what films they were going to watch, but he figured he'd leave that part up to Minerva.

Adding a few more pillows and blankets to the couch, Luca imagined Nadia would have something to say about the dull black and gray colors. The elevator dinged and his heart thumped as the doors opened to Gordon and Nadia, with their arms full of colorful foliage.

A smile spread across Luca's lips at the tall yuccas in Gordon's hands and the box of greenery in Nadia's arms. "You brought plants." He laughed, taking the box from her and peeking inside at the green pothos in a bright orange pot, two purple echeverias in vibrant yellow pots and three ivies snaking out of black pots with golden swirls painted over them.

"Of course, I told you I was going to bring some life into this place," Nadia said as she slipped off her black-and-white Adidas and Luca took in her curly auburn hair that was swept up in a ponytail with little ringlets escaping to frame her face. He nearly bit his lip at the tight denim jeans and fitted burgundy Boston University t-shirt she wore. God, she could wear a paper bag and her beauty would still captivate him.

Shit.

"Mr. Shola, can I speak to you in private?" Gordon asked, sitting the taller plants on the floor.

"Sure." He nodded, setting the box on the island in the

kitchen. "Excuse us Nadia, just, um, make yourself at home."

"Okay, I'll get your new babies settled in." She smiled, scooping up a few pots from the box and hugging them to her chest as she padded into the living room as if she'd already planned where they'd live. That didn't surprise him at all.

Luca tore his gaze away from her as he followed Gordon down the hall into his office. "What's going on?" he said, closing the door behind him.

Gordon heaved a deep sigh. "Well, you know I've been keeping an eye on Miss Nadia and I noticed a car parking outside her apartment every night for the past week," he said, pulling out his phone and showing him a picture of a black mustang sitting in the alley beside Nadia's brick apartment building. "I've run the plates and the car is registered to Jonathan Hatch."

Luca's face paled as he looked up from the phone. "As in, Hatch Engineering, Jonathan?" The Hatchs were known in the Syndicates for running the Juliet sex circles, as well as lending out their unethical henchmen for surveillance jobs.

"Yeah, it wasn't him in the car, but I don't know why he'd have someone watching her."

"Nadia used to work for his company, but that was years ago. This could be Ciara. The Dagenhams are good friends with them and you know they like to use the Hatch lackeys to keep themselves clean," he said, handing the phone back. "I want another guard to follow this person and make me a dossier on Jonathan Hatch."

"I will do, sir. Should we tell Miss Nadia about this?"

"No." He shook his head. "She's got a history with a stalker and I don't want to worry her. I'll talk to her once we have more information."

Gordon nodded. "Fair enough."

"Thanks for bringing this to my attention. Keep me posted with anything you find out."

"I'll talk to the team now," he said, opening the office door.

"Good. You should get some rest too. I'm not sure how late we'll be."

"I will." Gordon chuckled as they walked back down the hall. "Miss Nadia certainly looks at home here," Gordon murmured, nudging Luca's arm.

"Yeah, she does," he said with a smile tugging at his lips at the picture she made arranging the plants in his living room.

"Have a good night, Miss Nadia," Gordon waved.

"Thanks. You too." She waved.

Luca couldn't stop the wide grin that spread across his lips as he crossed the room and admired the colorful plants Nadia nestled in the stark black decor of his living room.

Nadia brought a little burst of life into his home and tonight, he was going to enjoy the company of her and their friends. He refused to let the unsettling information Gordon told him weigh on his mind. Nadia would be safe with him. "Thank you for the plants, they look nice."

"Yeah they do, right?" She smiled and her eyes danced in amusement. "I haven't even shown you the best one!" She skipped across the living room to pick up a small red potted plant sitting on the glass coffee table. "This is your baby ganja. It's tangerine kush. I've grown a few of these. It's a sativa-indica hybrid so you should like it once it buds."

"I can't believe you brought me this." He laughed. "Where should I keep it?"

Nadia squinted her eyes at him. "I thought you said you grew your own? Why don't you know where to keep it?"

"Oh, I have people grow for me. I own a distributor."

Her eyes grew wide. "You fucking cheat!" she huffed, shaking her head before she explained how to care for the plant. Luca's smile grew as he watched the excitement in her eyes and he couldn't help watching the way her lips moved and wondered what it might be like to taste her plump–*Jesus!*

What the hell was he thinking? He needed to stop having thoughts like this about her.

"Well, this is quite the setup you have here," Minerva exclaimed as she and Cameron came through the door holding a few bags of snacks and Luca was glad for the interruption to where his mind was going, but shit Nadia was so... intoxicating? Alluring? He didn't know, but whatever it was, it was distracting. In a good way.

"The greenery is new. When did you decide to change up the color scheme?" Cameron chuckled, placing the bags on the black kitchen island.

"Nadia thought I needed to add some color in here." Luca shrugged. "Welcome to my home, Minerva. Feel free to make yourself comfortable."

"I sure will!" She beamed, sitting her electric blue purse on the couch. "I'm surprised at you, Nadia. It's not like you to share your garden with anyone."

Luca raised an eyebrow at Nadia who was glaring at Minerva. "Shut up. He needed them, as you can see," she said, waving her arm over the living room. "Luca has a weird affinity for black and gray."

"Mm, you're not lying," Minerva murmured as she looked into the open black marbled kitchen and turned her excited brown eyes back on them. "So! I hear you've got an excellent selection of booze and weed for us?"

"You get right to the point don't you?" Luca laughed. "You can help yourself to the bar and I've prepared a few things for us on the balcony."

"Alright!" Minerva clapped her hands together. "This is going to be an excellent night. I hope you're into horror because I brought some good ones."

"Yeah, I love a good horror film." Luca grinned while Nadia groaned and cursed under her breath. He chuckled. "I take it you don't like scary movies?"

"It's not my favorite genre, no."

"But you don't mind watching them with me." Minerva giggled, slipping her arm through Nadia's. "Come on, let's check out this bar and get a little tipsy," she said, pulling her into the kitchen.

"She's a trip, right?" Cameron mused with a lopsided grin on his face as he tore his gaze from the light brown curly haired woman rummaging through the bar and crossed the living room.

Luca shook his head as he watched the two go through his liquor cabinet. "Minerva certainly doesn't need an invitation to make herself at home."

"No, she doesn't." Cameron chuckled. "We'll be on the balcony when you're ready."

Minerva popped her head up from the black wooden drinks cabinet and frowned. "You don't want a drink?"

"Yeah, surprise me. I trust you."

A grin lit up Minerva's warm golden brown eyes. "Alright babe, you got it."

"Babe?" Luca snickered as they stepped out to the balcony. "So are you and Minerva a couple now?"

Cameron shrugged as he sat in one of the cushioned rattan

chairs and opened the wooden box on the table. "We haven't decided to be exclusive yet, but I don't want to see anyone else."

"Wow, Minerva must be a pretty special woman to get you talking like this."

"Yeah she is," Cameron said, lighting a blunt. "But I'm surprised to see you looking so comfortable with Nadia here."

Luca blushed, plucking another blunt out of the box, and leaned back in his chair. "I don't know what you're talking about. It's only her second time being here."

"Yeah exactly, and it's like she's always been around. You look so confident with her, like you used to be."

"I don't know about all that." Luca looked away from him at the sun setting over the calm water of the harbor below. "But I like being around her."

Cameron barked out a laugh. "Okay, buddy. Whenever you're ready to admit you like her more than a friend, I'll be ready to listen."

"Fuck off. You know that's all it is. I'm just grateful Ciara hasn't caught on to it," Luca grumbled, but Cameron was right. These feelings he had for Nadia were definitely pushing over that friendship line, and he didn't mind it. He liked her. A lot. He wasn't used to feeling like this, but he'd have to tread lightly.

It was bad enough Ciara already had someone watching her apartment. If she caught on to his distracted thoughts and their frequent conversations, it would put Nadia in a lot of danger. He didn't need Ciara calling in any more Syndicate favors.

Chapter 17

While Minerva was mixing up drinks and Cameron and Luca were chatting on the balcony, Nadia slipped down the hallway to the office Gordon and Luca came out of earlier. She felt guilty for snooping around Luca's house but it was another chance for her to find some more information on the Syndicates.

Nadia »Let me know if they come back inside.«

Nervy » I got you. They're still talking. I doubt they'll suspect anything. Just hurry up.«

Nadia slipped her phone into her back pocket and sifted through the paperwork on Luca's immaculate desk. She found a few invoices for nominal amounts, but nothing suspicious or indicative of the Syndicates or his grandfather.

She tugged at the desk drawers and cursed under her breath at their locked state. Failing to find a key, she moved on to the mahogany bookshelves. Again, the ledgers were neatly categorized in date order and were full of old financial and investment deals for Shola Enterprises.

Chapter 17

Nadia sighed. There was nothing there. Luca wasn't careless at all. He didn't even have one of the telltale Syndicate Coptic crosses on the bookshelves or hanging on the walls with the abstract paintings he decorated his office with. As she was looking around another bookshelf, her heart churned at a photo of Luca and who she assumed was his Tutu. He was tall like Luca, the same golden hazel eyes and skin the same bronze shade as his father, but his hair was long and white and braided down his back. Nadia had never seen Luca look so happy standing proudly next to his Tutu on a beautiful sun kissed beach. She backed away from the bookshelf and let out a slow breath as guilt and shame wrapped its claws around her heart.

What the fuck was she doing? This felt wrong. There was nothing there that would help her. Shaking her head, she left his office and shut the door quietly behind her. Nadia slid a hand over her face as she walked down the hallway back to the kitchen.

"Did you find anything?" Minerva asked as she sat the drinks and shot glasses on a tray.

"No, just that Luca's extremely organized. I couldn't get into his desk and God, that felt so awful doing that."

Minerva placed a hand on her shoulder. "I know, but at least you looked and we've still got that information from Raquel. I'm almost glad you didn't find anything shady in his office. I like Luca, I don't want my image of him or Cam to change."

Nadia laughed softly. "Yeah, me either."

"Come on, that's enough spy action for tonight. Let's have some fun, okay?"

"Alright," Nadia said as she followed behind Minerva to

the balcony. Her heart thumped at Luca's warm golden gaze. She didn't want him to stop looking at her like that, but if he knew what she'd just done, why would he ever want to be her friend or allow her into his home again?

Nadia took a seat next to him and a smile graced her lips as he passed her a freshly rolled blunt from the wooden box on the table. "Thanks."

"You're welcome," he said, holding out his silver Zippo lighter to her.

"Alright!" Minerva clapped her hands, pulling Nadia from her sinking thoughts. "We need to toast to this night," she said as she poured four shots of tequila.

Cameron raised an eyebrow. "What are we making a toast to?"

Minerva shrugged. "I don't know, life, a good night and new friendships."

Luca smiled, taking a glass and handing one to Nadia. "That sounds about right."

They raised their glasses to each other and threw back the spicy liquor. A chorus of 'why' and 'oh dear god' filled the night air. Luca burst out laughing next to her, and she playfully shoved his shoulder.

"Shut up! Oh my God, I forgot how much tequila burns," Nadia whined as she gulped down her gin and lemonade.

To new friendships and a good night indeed. Nadia looked into Luca's humored eyes and a blush crept up her cheeks. She wanted his friendship and part of her feared she wanted more than that, too.

***

Chapter 17

Nadia thought for sure the way the night started everyone would be too distracted and forget about the dreaded horror films. But no, Minerva remembered, and she convinced Luca and Cameron to watch them. They outnumbered Nadia three to one.

One jumpy scene of a demon popping out of a floorboard had her huddled against Luca, nails digging into his arm while she watched through a tiny hole in the blanket. She buried her face against Luca's shoulder while he laughed at the horrid, nightmare inducing scenes. She clenched her eyes shut and willed the movie to end and in doing so, fell asleep amid the gunshots and chainsaws blaring on the obnoxiously large screen.

She woke a short time later to Luca gently nudging her. "Hey, the movie's over now," he whispered, pulling the blanket from her head.

She yawned. "Thank God for that."

"Mm-hm, can I have my arm back now?" his deep voice murmured in her ear and his warm breath sent a sweet chill down her spine.

Nadia bit her lip, slowly releasing her death grip on his arm and sliding her leg from around his. "Sorry," she mumbled.

"It's alright." He chuckled. "I didn't mind it."

Her heart thumped. He didn't?

"Alright you two, I think Minerva and I are going to head home," Cameron said as he and Minerva stood from the couch.

"Yeah," Minerva yawned. "Nadia, do you want us to take you home or is Gordon taking you?" she said, picking up her purse from the couch.

Dread washed over her at the thought of going home to

her empty apartment. She usually stayed with Minerva after scary movie night, but that bitch was going to Cameron's.

"Are you okay?" Luca's concerned voice pierced through her frightened thoughts.

"Yep," she chirped. Maybe… she could stay here? Shit, she couldn't ask him that. She snooped around his house and now she was going to ask him to stay? Not only would Luca think she was such a weirdo, but how much more was she going to use him? And what thirty-two year old couldn't go home by herself because she couldn't handle a movie? Fuck.

"I'll have Gordon take me home," she said with her heart pounding in panic.

"Okay cool. I'll call you tomorrow then," Minerva said, bending down to hug her before slapping a hand on Luca's shoulder. "Thank you for an awesome night. We definitely have to do this again."

He chuckled. "I look forward to it," he said, getting up to walk them to the door.

"Be good, you two," Nadia called.

"We will," Cameron said, bumping Luca's fist and waving to Nadia.

Luca pressed in a code on the elevator that she assumed was to lock the main entrance before he turned to her. "Do you want me to call Gordon for you or have you already messaged him?"

"No," she said, biting her lip. "Um, would you mind if… if I stayed here tonight?"

Luca's eyes grew wide, and a soft laugh escaped his lips. "Are you too afraid to go home?"

She cringed and nodded. "Yes, I usually stay with Minerva, but… I'm sorry. I shouldn't have asked. It's so stupid. I'll message Gordon." She laughed and wished the floor would swallow her whole.

His golden eyes softened. "It's not stupid. I don't mind if you stay."

"Thank you," she breathed as a wave of relief washed over her. She didn't want to ask him in front of Minerva. It was too embarrassing and she didn't want her blowing it up in her mind that their friendship was turning into something else. She was just scared and staying at Luca's was the best option under the circumstances.

"Yeah, I didn't know horror scared you that bad," he said, picking up glasses and empty chip bowls.

She nodded, getting up to help him. "I have a very vivid imagination. It's why I love fantasy but horror." She shuddered. "It haunts me for days."

"You're going to think I'm weird, but I envy you for that."

Nadia raised an eyebrow. "Why would you want to feel scared?"

Luca shrugged. "I don't know. I love that creepy feeling I used to get as a kid. I keep hoping to find a movie that can scare the shit out of me."

"Okay Mr. Underworld, you're fucking weird."

"Mr. Underworld." He chuckled. "I like that."

She shrugged. "Well, it suits you and your mysterious aura you've got going on."

"Fair enough. It's better than Hades," he said as he turned off the lights, setting the place in a dim amber glow from the recessed floor lights. "Let me show you to the guest room." He nodded to the hallway. "Am I really still a mystery to you?"

"Kind of," she said, plucking her gray leather tote from the black speckled countertop and followed behind him. "You just look like you have this secret battle going on sometimes."

"Well, the King of the Underworld often does," he said, opening a bedroom door.

"See, that's what I mean." She shook her head and gasped as she looked into the room at the spectacular view from the floor to ceiling windows overlooking the Boston skyline. "Holy shit. Does every room have this amazing view?"

"Um, yeah, except the bathrooms," he said, and she caught a slight blush on his cheeks. "If you want to change, some of my sister's clothes are in here, so help yourself. She won't mind."

She nodded and looked up at him. "Thank you for letting me stay."

"You're welcome," he said, pointing into the hall. "If you need anything, I'm just down there."

"I'm sure I'll be fine. Good night, Luca."

"Good night, Nadia." He smiled, closing the door behind him.

She slowly looked around the room. It was like something out of a magazine. The bed linens were surprisingly a light cream color, with hints of gold littered among the fabric. The bed's headboard was white with gold trim and the furniture was dark wood that contrasted against the sheer gold drapes hanging on either side of the enormous windows.

Luca's sister must've decorated this room. It was too warm and cozy to be his design. She padded across the plush cream carpet to the bed and plopped her purse on it. Rummaging through one of the dresser drawers, she found a t-shirt and a pair of leggings to wear. She felt a little awkward wearing his sister's clothes, but he said to help herself and she hated sleeping in jeans.

Nadia slid into the bed and moaned at the softness of it. She pulled the blankets around her and tapped the light switch next to the headboard. The room fell into darkness and her heart pounded. She pulled the blankets over her head and the minute she closed her eyes she swore she heard a small cackle and a vision of a demon's grotesque features materialized in her mind.

Her eyes popped open. She slammed her hand on the light switch and sat up.

Nope.

Leaning over the bed, she plucked a thick paperback book out of her purse. She'd just read for a while to get her mind on something else, and Niklaus could certainly do that.

Chapter 18

Luca walked down the hall with a glass of water and frowned at the light shining from beneath the guest bedroom door. He knocked lightly and when he didn't hear a response, he slowly opened the door to check on Nadia. She was sitting up in bed biting her thumb as she read the book resting on her knees.

"You're still awake?"

She looked up at him. "Yeah, I needed to get my mind on something else. I'll fall asleep, eventually."

His heart sank. He didn't believe that at all. She was really too scared to sleep. It was nearly three in the morning. She couldn't stay up all night like this. "I can't sleep either," he said, stepping inside the room. "What are you reading?"

She bit her lip and held up the book. He chuckled. "So you *did* bring your boyfriend with you?"

"Of course, I told you I would."

"Do you want me to read to you?" The words fell out of his mouth before he had a chance to analyze that damn question.

Chapter 18

She tilted her head to the side and her frizzy curls fell over her shoulder. "Sure, if you want." She scooted over and laughed. "I feel like a child."

"Nah, this is perfectly normal adult stuff." He sat his glass of water on the bedside table and slid into the bed next to her. His heart was pounding as he watched her flip through the pages of the book. His eyes drifted to the curve of her breasts in that tight pink retro Powerpuff Girls t-shirt and his groin twitched at her nipples slowly rising to attention.

"Can you read from this part?" she said, sliding the book over his lap.

He tore his eyes away from her chest as his cheeks burned in embarrassment. "Mm-hm." Fuck. He shouldn't be looking at her like that. Maybe this impulsive move wasn't a good idea. He looked at the page she wanted him to read and a laugh rumbled in his chest. "I should've known you'd want me to read this chapter again."

"What? I like it when Niklaus gets all deadly," she said as she rested her cheek against his shoulder. "You going to read it or not?"

"Alright, alright." He chuckled, looking down at her. "You comfortable?"

"Yeah, I guess." She shrugged. "Come on." She giggled. "Help me get that movie out of my head."

"Okay," he said, leaning back against the headboard and without a second thought or any hesitation, he wrapped his arm around her so she was cuddled under the crook of his arm. "Is this better?"

"Um, y-yeah this is good." She chuckled. "Now, I really feel like I'm being read a bedtime story," she said, snuggling closer to him and curling her fist under her chin. "Thank you for doing this. This is probably so weird for you."

Luca wanted to kiss the top of her head and tell her he'd do anything to make her feel safe. He cleared his throat and thought better of it. *That* would be weird. "No, it's cool. It's not like I haven't read to you before."

A smile graced Nadia's lips and her body relaxed under his arm. A warmth of pride washed over him at that simple movement. He hadn't wanted to feel the touch of a woman like this since Ciara molested him, and he didn't think he'd ever feel comfortable around someone like this again.

"You ready?"

She nodded.

"Alright," he murmured as he began reading her favorite chapter. "Miri was ripped from Niklaus' arms. Rage and fear pulsed through his veins as her deafening screams flooded his mind."

Nadia closed her eyes and sighed as he read Niklaus' battle to find the stolen queen. The more he read, the softer her breath became as she drifted off to sleep. His body relaxed against her and he rested his cheek on top of her head as he mumbled a few more passages, determined to finish his favorite part when Niklaus completed the forbidden deed of binding himself to the queen. Luca's eyes drooped closed as he whispered the last words of the chapter. The book slid from his fingers and he gave into the comforting slumber calling his name.

***

Luca scrunched up his face at the sunlight piercing his eyelids. He groaned, feeling next to him for the remote to the blackout shades. Why didn't he close them last night? A relieved sigh left his mouth when he clicked the button on the little device to block out the blinding sun. He wrapped his arm around the warm body against his side and he buried his face in Nadia's soft curls.

His eyes snapped open.

What the fuck was he doing?

Luca's heart thumped when his brain finally caught up to speed and realized where he was. Nadia's face was pressed against his chest, her arm draped around his waist and–he gulped–her thigh was resting against his fucking morning wood.

He let out a breath and eased himself out of her arms. Tucking the blanket back around her, he froze when she sighed and snuggled under the plush comforter. Convinced she was sound asleep, he tapped the light switch above the headboard and tip-toed out of the room.

Closing the door softly behind him, he leaned against it and chuckled at the tent in his pants. That hadn't happened in a while.

He shook his head as he padded down the hall to his room. He shrugged off his clothes on the way to the bathroom and stepped into the shower. The warm water ran over his head as he leaned against his forearms.

He couldn't believe he fell asleep with her. Since when did he start doing things like that? He just meant to read to her, not wake up with her tangled in his arms. Running his hands through his hair, a smile curled over his lips. He hadn't slept that well in a while, though.

"Shit," he whispered. Why did it have to feel so good lying beside her? Last night should've felt platonic. There shouldn't have been anything sexy about reading to her, but damn if it didn't turn him on.

What was wrong with him? He had excellent self-control. They both said they didn't do affairs of the heart and he couldn't feel this way. Not until he had solid evidence he could ruin his grandfather with. He didn't even know if Nadia felt the same way. She probably didn't. Why would she want someone like him? His body was full of scars and she already knew how weak he was when it came to Ciara, but he didn't feel that way around Nadia. He felt *better.*

Luca rinsed himself and turned off the shower. Wrapping a towel around his waist, he padded into his room, trying to shake his devious thoughts of her. He'd just make her breakfast, call Gordon, and send her on her way. Then he could forget this weird night ever happened.

The elevator dinged and his eyes grew wide.

Oh God, not today!

Luca fumbled to slip on a pair of jeans and a navy blue Boston Red Sox t-shirt and bolted out of his room just as his mother and father stepped into his penthouse.

"Hi honey, we were just in the city for lunch and I wanted to stop by to see how you're doing." His mother smiled and a frown knit her brow. "Did you just wake up?"

"Um, yeah I did," he said, running a hand through his damp hair. "I had some friends over last night."

Her eyes grew wide, and his father grinned. "Really? Like more than you and Cameron? You're feeling bold with Ciara out of town, huh?"

Luca laughed. "Maybe, but I have a hangover so if you don't mind –"

"Nope, we don't mind. You can tell us all about your night."

Chapter 18

His mother beamed with her golden brown eyes sparkling with excitement. She dropped her purse on the kitchen counter and twisted up her raven hair. "Let me make some coffee. This is exciting!" she said, rummaging through his cupboards for some coffee beans.

Luca groaned. "Mom, I'm coming to dinner tomorrow. Can't I just tell you then?" He didn't want them to know Nadia was still there. He didn't need them freaking out about his blatant disobedience.

She turned to him. "Yes, but I want to hear about it now. You don't look that hungover." She raised an eyebrow. "Or are you trying to get rid of me for some other reason?"

A blush scorched Luca's cheeks and he shook his head. "Nope, but it's not much of a story."

"Oh, I don't think so." His father chuckled and looked past him. "Good morning, Nadia."

Fuck.

Luca slowly turned around to find her standing at the edge of the hallway dressed in her jeans and burgundy Boston University t-shirt from last night. Her damp hair was braided back from her face and her green eyes were wide as she bit her bottom lip. "Good morning, Mr. Shola." She cleared her throat and looked at Luca. "I-I'm sorry to interrupt. I'm just going to leave now."

"Oh, don't be silly." His mother giggled. "You're not interrupting anything. You must have a hangover too. Come sit. Have a coffee with us."

Luca looked at his mother in shock that she was encouraging her to stay. Where was the worry and fear in her eyes for his seditious act?

"Um, okay," Nadia said, padding to the bar stool at the

island.

"I'm Luca's mother, Elena." She smiled, holding out her hand to Nadia as she slowly slid onto the stool. "And you must be Nadia, right?"

"I am. It's nice to meet you." She smiled, shaking her hand.

Philip chuckled, slapping a hand on Luca's shoulder. "I didn't realize you two had become so close."

Luca glared at him while Nadia choked out a laugh. "Oh, we're not. I mean we're friends, but I was just a little spooked from a movie my friend forced us to watch and Luca was nice enough to let me stay here last night."

His mother raised an eyebrow as she poured herself a cup of coffee. "That was nice of you, dear. I hope you were alright, Nadia?" she said, sitting the pot of coffee down in front of them.

She nodded. "Yeah, I'm fine now. I feel silly for needing to stay."

"It's okay. I told you it wasn't silly," Luca said, pouring her a cup of coffee.

"So." His mother grinned. "How did you two meet?"

Luca was so confused. Why was his mother entertaining this? Not that he expected her to say anything in front of Nadia, but his parents were acting as if her being here was fine, normal even.

"Oh, we work together. I'm the International Marketing and PR rep."

"And she's a damn good one, too. Nadia's the one I've been telling you about," his father said, taking a seat on the stool next to his mother.

"That's right. You're the one who's been fixing those old international investments these idiots bought."

Nadia burst out laughing. "I wouldn't say they're idiots, but yes I'm the one who's fixing their... mistakes."

A grin tugged at Luca's lips. "Feeling awfully bold with my mother here. I could have you fired, little miss."

Nadia gasped. "You would never."

"You'd better not," his father grumbled. "I'd just hire you back, anyway. I'm still the owner."

A laugh burst from Luca's lips. "Relax, dad. I was just kidding."

His mother smiled, patting a hand over his before she smiled at Nadia. "Why don't you come out to the estate for dinner tomorrow?"

"That's a great idea, Lena." Philip grinned. "It's good weather so I'm going to put Luca on the grill too."

Luca stared in utter disbelief that his parents would ask her something like that. What fucking game were they playing?

"Um..." Nadia looked over at him.

Luca tore his eyes away from his mother's encouraging wide-eyed gaze. He didn't understand what was happening, but if those two weren't concerned about this devious act, then he wouldn't either. "You might as well say yes. My mother won't take no for an answer." He sighed. "So, to make up for her demand, I'll take you out to the racetrack and you can drive the McLaren."

A dazzling smile lit up Nadia's face and he couldn't help the way his heart swelled at her excitement. "Well, in that case, I'll gladly join you for dinner."

Chapter 19

Nadia stared into her closet, a pineapple patterned bag laid open on her bed and her phone was pressed to her ear.

"What do you mean you're packing?" Minerva said. "Where the hell are you going?"

"Luca's mother asked me to dinner at their estate tomorrow."

"Wait what? You're going to have to back up. What happened after Cameron and I left last night?"

Nadia cringed and told Minerva she spent the night at Luca's because of the damn movie. She left out the bit when Luca read to her and when he wrapped his arms around her. It was only for a moment before he slid out of bed, but the irrational part of her mind missed the warmth of his body cocooning hers and the feel of his dick pressed against her thigh.

Her cheeks burned up to her ears. Nope. Minerva didn't need to know any of that. Shit, she didn't even know what to *think* about that.

"Alright, well, I can't wait to hear about this adventure. You and Luca are getting pretty close, huh?"

"Yeah, I guess so. He's a good friend." She shrugged as she pulled out a short white summer dress with little pink flowers dotted over it and placed it in her bag.

"Mm-hm, I need to get going. Cam is taking me out to dinner, but don't make that poor man shit his pants tomorrow with your crazy ass driving." Minerva smirked.

Nadia let out a bark of laughter. "I won't."

"Maybe you can do a little snooping around his parents' house."

"Maybe," Nadia said, but a twinge of guilt washed over her. She didn't want to do that. Luca's parents seemed so genuine. She didn't want to disrespect them or Luca again. "Enjoy your dinner," she said as she hung up and sat her phone on her dresser.

As she was rummaging through her closet for a pair of shoes to go with her dress, her phone buzzed behind her. She quickly picked it up and a smile stretched across her lips as she read the message.

Mr. Underworld » I'm really excited about tomorrow. You better not stall my car though, I'll be so disappointed in you.«

Nadia » Stall your car? You insult my abilities, sir. «

Mr. Underworld » I'm just basing it on your clumsy reputation. Driving a supercar isn't like a normal car you know... «

A grin spread across her lips. Minerva was right. This poor man had no idea.

Nadia » I'm well aware of that. I don't need you to mansplain it to me. «

Mr. Underworld » Haha alright. I'll see you tomorrow.«

Nadia smiled, setting her phone on her dresser again, but frowned when a series of messages lit up the screen.

Mr. Underworld » Are you going to be able to sleep tonight?

Mr. Underworld » Sorry that sounded weird. I just asked because you said you'd be scared for a few days.«

Nadia » I'll be fine tonight. I won't be too scared. I'll sleep with the lights on.«

Mr. Underworld » I don't like that. You won't sleep with the lights on. «

Nadia » Yes I will. I slept with them on last night. «

Mr. Underworld » You would've been up all night reading if I didn't come in.«

Nadia » I would've fallen asleep… eventually «

Mr. Underworld »… you're not driving my car without proper sleep.«

Damn it. She wouldn't want to risk being too tired to test that beautiful car. She'd definitely be up reading again to calm her ridiculous imagination. Fuck scary movies.

Nadia » Fine… but will you read to me again?«

Nadia stared at the screen with her thumb hovering over 'send.' She bit her lip and sent the message. She shoved her phone back on her dresser and went into her closet to find an outfit to wear tomorrow. It wasn't unreasonable for her to ask that. She bit her thumb. Then why did she feel so *embarrassed*?

They read passages to each other all the time, but the way he read to her last night didn't feel like one of their readings. His deep voice sounded so soft and sensual. It sent her right to sleep. It would be better if she were cuddled up next to him again. His body was so–Fuck! She was fucking up!

Nadia tugged a pair of pink and cork wedges from her closet and shoved them in her bag. She shouldn't be thinking about him like that, but why did he have to be so attractive? She took a deep breath to calm her nerves. Luca wouldn't think it was weird of her to ask. She just needed to squash these unsettling thoughts of wanting more than what they were.

Friendship was good. Friendship was safe.

Her therapist didn't teach her that one. She made it up to remind herself that relationships were dangerous and she didn't need to get involved with another Syndicate.

Her heart thumped at the sound of her phone buzzing behind her. She looked over her shoulder and slowly reached for it.

Mr. Underworld » Of course I'll read to you. Just call me when you're ready.«

Mr. Underworld » And it better be before 10pm. You need at least 8hrs of sleep before you get behind the wheel of my baby.«

A laugh sputtered from her lips and she forgot why she was so nervous to ask him.

Nadia » Haha yes sir. Thank you! «

Mr. Underworld » No need to thank me. I don't mind. I'll speak to you soon.«

A permanent grin planted itself on Nadia's face as she placed her phone back on her dresser. She should've known he wouldn't say no or think she was weird for asking. He probably enjoyed last night as much as she did, but she wouldn't be acting on those feelings.

A knock at her door pulled her from her thoughts, and a

frown creased her brow as she looked into the living room. She wasn't expecting anyone. It couldn't be Minerva, and Raquel never showed up unannounced.

She grabbed the baseball bat on the side of her bed and gripped it between her fingers as she went to look through the peephole in the door. She sighed in relief at her neighbor's curly haired son standing in the hallway.

"Hey Malik, does your mom need something?"

"No, I was just walking home and this guy said to give you this," he said, holding out a thin black leather collar with a silver cat face charm hanging from it. "Said ya lost it or something."

Nadia's heart sank to the pit of her stomach as she took the collar from him with shaking hands. "Thank you," she managed with a calm voice even though her heartbeat was pounding in her ears.

"You're welcome." He grinned. "Dude gave me twenty bucks to give it to ya too."

She nodded, taking a step back. "G-give the money to your mom," she mumbled, and closed the door. Nadia marched across the room, burst out the back door, and hurled the collar off the balcony. She choked out a sob as she slid her hand around her throat and stumbled into the wicker chair behind her.

Clenching her eyes shut, tears poured down her cheeks as she sucked in tiny panicked gasps. Count, Nadia. Just count.

Five. She wasn't his.

She whimpered, digging her nails into the wicker as she took a shaky breath.

Four. She was free.

She took another painful breath.

Chapter 19

Three. She had a plan.

She opened her eyes and stared at the budding flowers on her balcony.

Two. She was safe.

She sucked in a deep breath of air, expanding her lungs.

One. She was alive.

Nadia let the air out slowly and wrapped her arms around herself to stop the shiver prickling her skin.

The last time she saw a kitten collar was when she left Jonathan for good and he choked her with it. She hated wearing that thing, and he wanted to make sure she could never take it off.

"Fuck," she whispered as her lip trembled. Jonathan's mind games were getting to her. She had a small pile of notes he'd sent to her office over the last three weeks, hinting that he was watching her. It got to the point that Alex started questioning her about them. He teased her about them being love letters from a secret admirer. That thought made her gag, but someone in the office was delivering them for Jonathan and she needed to figure out who it was.

But the collar.

That was the worst of his messages and using her neighbor's son to deliver it was just another tactic to show his power.

Nadia dragged her hands over her face before she peered over the railing at the horrid piece of jewelry lying in the middle of the alley. She had to go get it. Raquel would need it for evidence.

Nadia took another deep breath, rubbed her hands over her pants, and got up. She slipped through the thick veil of ivy cascading over the entrance to her balcony and trudged down the three flights of black iron steps to the alley.

She scanned the quiet access road looking for any signs that Jonathan's henchmen were watching her, but there weren't any seedy looking loiterers hanging around, looking out any windows or sitting in the few cars parked near the dumpsters.

Nadia stared at the diamond encrusted cat-faced gem at her feet. The damn thing didn't even crack from the force of her throw. Grimacing, she swiped the soft leather choker from the ground and went back up to her apartment.

Her hands shook and tears stung at the corners of her eyes as she dug through her small desk in the corner of her room for an envelope to shove it in. "Come on, Nadia. Keep it together. He's not going to get you this time," she whispered to herself, angrily wiping her tears.

A twinkling upbeat ring sounded from her phone on the dresser. She looked over her shoulder and fear dragged down her spine at the irrational thought it was Jonathan and that he'd finally figured out her number.

She took a few hesitant steps across the room and peeked at the name scrolling across the screen. Flooded with relief, she wiped her tears, cleared her throat and answered the call.

"Hello?" she said, hating that her voice cracked in the middle of that word.

"Hi." Luca's deep voice rolled through the receiver. "Are you okay?"

"Yeah." She sniffed and cringed. "I'm fine. What's up?"

"Well, I was thinking since you're coming to my parents' with me tomorrow, do you want to spend the night here again? Instead of Gordon picking you up at the ass crack of dawn?"

Nadia's lip trembled at his offer, and she bit back the sob

that burned in her throat. Even if he called to read to her, she knew she'd be up all night clutching her baseball bat afraid to close her eyes. It didn't matter that she knew Raquel had a patrol car watching her place. Jonathan sending her that collar meant he wanted her to remember the night he broke in. He wanted her to sit in fear of what he was capable of.

At least if she stayed with Luca, she'd be able to sleep and Jonathan's bullshit wouldn't ruin her chance of driving the McLaren.

"Nadia, you still there? You don't have to stay over. I just thought it might be easier."

"No," she croaked out, wiping her tear-stained cheeks and clearing her throat again. "I'd love to stay over again."

"Alright, are you sure you're okay? You sound like you're crying."

"I'm fine," she said, taking a deep breath.

"Okay," he drawled. "You know you can talk to me about stuff if you need to, right?"

She bit her lip as a fresh wave of tears pricked the corners of her eyes at the warmth in his voice. "Yeah, I know."

"Mm, so what kind of comfort food can I make you for dinner?"

A soft laugh escaped her lips. "Mac and cheese."

"I can do that. Do you want anything else with it? Steak? Chicken? A bucket of ice cream?"

She laughed a little harder and shook her head. "Steak and a sundae might be nice."

"Steak, mac and cheese and sundaes it is, then."

"Thank you."

"You're welcome. Gordon will pick you up in an hour. Is that okay?"

"Yeah," she said, opening her drawer to pull out more clothes to add to her bag. "Are you sure this is okay? I don't want you to get in trouble with your girlfriend because you're spending too much time with me."

"Well, Ciara's not my girlfriend. Just someone I'm obligated to be with." He chuckled softly. "And she's out of town for a few weeks."

"So, that's why you were so chill about Nervy inviting herself over. You're a free man without Ciara dragging you to those fundraisers, huh?"

"I'm not completely free, but yeah, I have a little room to breathe," he said, and she could hear the wide grin on his face. "Anyway, I'm going to let you go so I can get the stuff for dinner. I'll see you soon."

Nadia hung up and clenched the phone to her chest. She wasn't ready to tell Luca what happened to her, but it was nice that he cared and understood what she needed. God, she didn't think she'd ever have feelings like this for anyone again, but Luca was truly carving out a place in her heart.

Chapter 20

Luca closed the book in his hands and looked down at Nadia sleeping peacefully against him. He brushed a curl that escaped her silk bonnet from her face and sighed. She didn't tell him why she was upset on the phone and he didn't push the matter, but the somber look in her eyes when she came over bothered him.

Her spirits seemed to lift after they ate dinner and did a few hustles in the living room because she said dance was part of her comfort process, so they did the Detroit Hustle, Cupid Shuffle, and ended with the Electric Slide. The light in her eyes returned after that and he thought for sure she was going to open up to him, but she didn't.

Luca slid out of the bed and tucked the blanket around her. "Good night, Nadia."

"Luca," she mumbled.

"Yeah?"

"Thank you," she said, snuggling under the blanket.

"You're welcome. See you in the morning," he whispered,

fighting the irrational urge to kiss her forehead. He straightened and grabbed the remote on the bedside table to close the blinds before he tapped the light switch above the bed.

Luca closed the door with a soft click and walked down the hall to his room with a smile on his face. Nadia would tell him her story when she was ready and he'd be there for her like she was for him because he cared about her.

Shit.

He cared *a lot* about her and he was really playing with fire having these feelings. He wasn't free to feel this way and he had more than enough to deal with before he could even entertain the idea of telling her how he felt.

Luca slipped into his bed and hugged a pillow under his chin as he stared out the windows at the twinkling lights of the harbor. Being friends with Nadia was dangerous enough and he owed it to her to keep her off his grandfather and the Dagenhams' hit list.

He clicked the remote to close his blinds and turned over. He also needed to tell her that he had Gordon keeping an eye on her. Heaving a sigh and closing his eyes, he'd tell her as soon as he figured out why Jonathan Hatch had his goons around her.

That was a problem for another day. Tomorrow, he'd enjoy more of Nadia's company and get a taste of her driving skills. A smile tugged at his lips as he drifted off to sleep. It was going to be a good day.

***

Luca watched Nadia ease herself into the driver's seat of the McLaren. Her auburn hair was plaited into two long braids down her back and he chuckled at her excited eyes as she clicked the seat belt over her black and orange McLaren

Engineering t-shirt. The little shit failed to tell him that her father was a retired engineer for the company and helped design a few 720s models.

On their drive to Marblehead, she told him all about her past racing go karts when she was a kid and her time living in England for a few months as a test driver for McLaren. Nadia was something else and it just made him like her even more. He shook his head as she slipped on a helmet and a pair of black driving gloves. He wasn't sure what the hell he'd gotten himself into.

"I just have two questions for you." She turned to him with her green eyes shining in amusement. "Do you trust me and did you remember to bring a blunt?"

He slid his helmet over his head. "Yes, I trust you." He felt his pockets and nodded. "And I have a blunt."

Her eyes crinkled at the corners. "Good." She looked at the open track and revved the engine a few times. "You better hang on, Mr. Underworld."

His groin twitched at the sultry tone of her voice and the use of that nickname. He laughed as she took off on the straightaway, charging at top speed toward the orange cones the crew set up for her. She weaved in and out of them like a seasoned pro and went straight onto the track. Luca slowly gripped the handlebar above him and stared incredulously at the woman next to him. He was *not* expecting her to start off this driving experience like that.

Nadia let out an excited scream as she took a corner on the track. "Okay baby show me how you move," she growled, shifting gears and speeding through the straight away.

That was when Luca realized Nadia was in a world of her own. She was so focused on the car and clipping every apex to test the car's agility. She purred her praises and grimaced at the nuisances she didn't like, muttering that her father would've made those things better.

He was so enamored by her he barely paid attention to her laps–until the car was spinning around the track. "Jesus fucking Christ woman! What are you doing?!" he roared, double gripping the handlebar above his head and preparing to skid into the median.

Nadia burst out laughing. "Calm down. I was just testing the spin," she said and righted the car as if nothing happened.

"You're insane," he breathed, sliding a hand over his hardening cock. Shit. It was turning him on too.

"Aw." She giggled. "I hope you meant that in a good way."

"Mm, I did," he mumbled, and tore his gaze away from her. His mind was going to some dark and pleasurable places, like bending her over the hood and fucking her until she screamed she was his.

He clenched his eyes shut willing that delicious thought out of his head. He hadn't wanted to enjoy someone like that in a long time and he wouldn't start now. Fuck. He needed to get out of this car.

Nadia did one more lap, weaved in and out of the cones again before she stopped in the pit lane. "So what'd you think?" she said, breathing as if she'd just run a marathon. He stared at the rise and fall of her chest, the outline of her nipples strained against her t-shirt. She looked as if she was just as turned on as he felt.

"I-I need some air," he said, ripping off his seat belt and bolting out of the car. He tore off his helmet as he walked down the sunny tree lined track and sucked in the fresh spring air. He had to calm his ass down before he could talk to her. Pulling a slim case from his pocket, he plucked out a blunt. He shook out his leg and took a few long tokes before he ambled back to the car.

The pit crew surrounded the car, putting the road tires back on while Nadia–blunt in hand–was chatting to them about the track and the car's handling of it. She looked up at him with a proud grin on her face. "You okay?"

"Yeah, I'm fine you just… surprised me." And damn near made him cum in his pants. "I needed to calm down."

"I'm sorry." She laughed. "I didn't mean to scare you. I just get in my own world out there."

"You did nothing to scare me." Nadia had no idea what she just did to him. "I'm just impressed and you looked like you enjoyed yourself."

"I did!" she exclaimed and the joy that danced in her bright eyes filled him with pride. "This baby is amazing." She sighed, running her hand over the side of the car. "Thank you for letting me test it. It's a beauty."

"You're welcome and I'm glad you like it," he said, pointing to the garage. "Do you want to see my other babies before we go?"

Her eyes grew wide. "You have more?"

"Oh, yes."

And he wanted to torture himself by watching her drive every single one of them.

Chapter 21

Nadia leaned back in the seat of Luca's pristine black Tesla and a small smile tugged at the corner of her lips. She wasn't sure what to expect going into the home of another prominent Syndicate family. She imagined it would be much like the Hatchs, flush with opulent decor and an air of elitism with the gold Syndicate Coptic cross as a staple feature in every room. If she knew what that symbol meant, she would've run then.

But Luca's family home was filled with warmth and she didn't feel one ounce of stuffy elitism. In fact, there was no sign they were members of the exclusive society at all. Their home was full of family photos and colorful island landscaped portraits on the walls and potted plants of various shapes and sizes were the staple features in his parents' home.

She felt comfortable there, and it was nice to see Luca interact with his family. She enjoyed listening to the teasing banter between him and his gorgeous little sister, Lacey, and his parents reminded her of her own with their bubbly, carefree personalities.

It made her wonder if they were genuine members of the Syndicates, because their whole vibe as a unit didn't match the high society's standards that she expected from people like them.

Nadia bit her lip and chuckled to herself, but the best part of the day was seeing that look on Luca's face when she drove his car. He went from utter shock to a dark and brooding look as if he wanted to devour her. Dear God, that was so sexy.

"What are you giggling about?" His deep voice pierced through her thoughts.

She squeezed her thighs together and choked out a laugh. "Um, nothing. I just had a really good time today. Your family is really nice."

"I actually had a good time today, too. I'm glad you came."

Her heart thumped at the warm smile on his face and the sincerity in his words. "Yeah, me too. Your family isn't what I expected."

"Oh yeah? What were you expecting?"

"Well, I've been around a few wealthy families like yours and they were so snobby like they were part of some elite society." She shrugged. "I guess I thought your family would be the same way."

"Ah, I know those types. The Dagenhams would fit that description." He nodded. "My family's never really fit in with the upper echelon of society like that." He chuckled softly. "I hope you know my mother won't leave you alone now that she knows you're into gardening."

Nadia laughed at the memory of Elena dragging her around her massive garden and sending her home with a basket of cuttings. "That's alright, I'm used to that. My mom's the same way."

So, her suspicions were right about his family. They weren't typical Syndicate members. Maybe Raquel was wrong. Luca might not lead her to any information on the Grand Duke, but he still had that box of files on him. He had to have something on the society and that elusive master list, right?

"Your mother's really into gardening and inviting random people into her home? Not that you're random to me, but my mom just met you yesterday."

"Yes." She nodded. "My mom is notorious for meeting people in a supermarket and inviting them and their family over for dinner. She's a musical theater teacher, so she naturally loves to entertain."

"Sounds like they'd make a great pair," he mumbled. "So, musical theater. Is that how you got into dancing?"

"Yep, I've been dancing since I was little. That's how I met Minerva. We've been dancing together for years. My mom used to let us help her choreograph some dances in her plays and I fell in love with choreography after that. Dance was a big part of my life besides driving fast cars."

"Ah, so that's how you sneaky little shits picked up on me and Cam's routine at the club."

A laugh sputtered from her lips. "You guys shouldn't have assumed we were novice dancers."

"I definitely didn't think you were a novice." He chuckled, and her heart thumped at the smoldering look in his eyes before he looked back at the road.

Nadia tore her gaze away from his seductive face, but not before she lingered on the curve of his firm jaw and the few buttons he left undone at the top of his salmon shirt. The thought of what lay beneath had her toes curling.

Shit.

She shouldn't think of him like that. She didn't even *want* that. All she wanted was his friendship. She didn't have room in her life for anything more than that. Not until she got Jonathan off her fucking back. She couldn't lose sight of her mission, and that was more important than figuring out how to tell Luca how she felt. God, she couldn't even bring herself to tell him about Jonathan let alone express that she liked him more than a friend.

"Nadia?"

Her eyes grew wide and a blush burned over her cheeks as she tore herself from her thoughts. "Hm?"

"You okay? You went quiet. I thought you fell asleep on me or something."

"Yeah, I'm fine," she said, but sleeping wasn't a bad idea. It would save her from stealing glances at him. She leaned back against the headrest and closed her eyes. "So how did you get into dance, anyway?"

"Dance is a way of life for my father's side of the family, but my mom was the one who put me in classes. She said I needed a well-rounded childhood and I couldn't just play soccer and football." He laughed. "And I dragged Cam with me because if I had to do that shit, so did he. We didn't take it seriously at first until we snuck into an urban dance class and then we were hooked. We used to find all the underground dance halls to work on our skills."

She laughed at that. "If I didn't see it with my own eyes, I never would've imagined you as a dancer."

"Most people don't and that was our secret weapon."

She opened her eyes and frowned at him. "What do you mean?"

"When Cam and I bust out our moves in a battle we used to fuck up the competition and when we realized the girls liked it too?" He smirked. "We were a force to be reckoned with."

Nadia burst out laughing. "Oh my God, don't tell me you two had groupies."

A dazzling smile lit up his face. "Oh, we did."

She tutted her lips and shook her head. "You two were little man whores, weren't you?"

He shrugged. "Maybe, but we were young. We liked the attention. It wasn't all about the girls, the dance battles were what we really liked."

She rolled her eyes. "Mm-hm, not the screaming groupies around the floor?"

"Nope, that was just a perk, but that reminds me, you and Minerva owe us a dance off." He glanced at her. "And since you two are so good, we're doing it freestyle. No pre-choreographed routines."

She raised her eyebrows. "Ohhh, you think we can't beat you two without practicing a routine?" She sat up in her seat. "We bested your asses just by *watching* your tired moves. I think you need a bit of practice, Mr. Underworld." He had a lot of damn nerve trying to say she and Minerva couldn't freestyle. She'd fucking dance *circles* around him and his mediocre skills.

Luca fell out in a fit of laughter. "Okay, I didn't mean to offend you." He grinned. "But damn, tell me how you really feel?"

Her cheeks burned up to her ears. "I just meant it was so

easy to follow you guys." She leaned back in her seat. "You gotta come better than that."

"Those are some fighting words, but I see you. We'll come prepared."

She smirked and closed her eyes again. "It won't matter. We'll still beat you."

"And she's so modest about it too," he mused. "So, how about a rematch in two weeks? Is that enough time for you?"

"And he's so eager to get beat." She grinned. "That's fine. You just name the time and we'll be ready."

Chapter 22

Nadia shook her head as she watched the marketing manager from Johnson Corp walk out the revolving doors. After the amazing weekend she had with Luca, her high was ruined by losing that account. They shot down every strategy she had to improve their profits, but they wouldn't budge on their decision. Johnson was taking their business elsewhere.

Damn it. She'd been on a roll fixing old investments and she really thought her presentation of Johnson's history and where Shola could take them would change their minds, but it didn't work. This was the first one she lost and she hated this feeling.

"You alright, Nadia?"

She jumped out of her thoughts and smiled at Ben, the blond-haired, blue eyed IT guy that set up her monitor a while ago.

"Oh yeah, I'm fine. Couldn't seal the deal on an old client."

"Ah, I'm sorry about that," he said, holding up a sandwich bag. "Have you eaten lunch yet? That might get your mind off things."

"No. I don't have any time for that," she said, checking her watch. "I'm late for a meeting as it is."

"Oh, if you're in a hurry, take the back elevator." He nodded to the corner of the lobby. "Everyone forgets about that one. I use it all the time when I'm on a job." He winked at her and her cheeks flushed.

"That's perfect. Thank you." Nadia smiled. "Enjoy your lunch," she said as she hurried to the elevator and pressed the button. Ben was such a nice guy. He was always saying hello to her and giving her little tidbits like this. He told her about the secret vending machine with the best snacks on the second floor too.

Nadia's smile fell and a slight chill raced down her spine when the doors opened to reveal a small white tiled and brown paneled cube. She didn't do well in small spaces like this. The main elevator was at least four of these put together, but that one took far too long to get to the tenth floor, with everyone getting on and off around lunch time.

She tugged at the hem of her shirt and gripped the folder in her hands. Fuck it. She was just overthinking again. There was nothing wrong with this elevator, and it was going to save her time. She stepped on and took a deep breath as she pressed ten. The doors were just about to close when a hand shot through and they opened again.

"Ooh, are you running late for our meeting too?" Luca chuckled as he stepped inside.

Relief washed over her to have someone else in this confined space. "Yeah, my meeting with Johnson ran over." She sighed. "I couldn't get them to stay. I'm pissed."

"I'm not surprised. Carnegie Assets has been trying to take

them from us for years. It was only a matter of time," he said, sliding a hand to her shoulder. "Don't let it upset you. The pitch you wrote got us one step closer to getting the Ono contract, and that's more important. You're doing an amazing job."

"Yeah that's true," she mumbled. "Thanks."

"Who told you about the back elevator, anyway?" He chuckled. "Only the cool people at Shola know about this."

A small smile curled at the corners of her lips. "By cool, do you mean a nerd like you?" she said and her heart clenched in panic when the lights flickered. The cube gave a dangerous shake and came to a screeching, cantankerous stop before it fell into darkness.

"Shit," Luca said, opening the service box. He mentioned something about the emergency phone, but Nadia couldn't hear him. The darkness and familiar pine scent of the wax on the floor sent her mind tumbling into the chamber where Jonathan kept her when she displeased him.

Nadia's breath came out short as she stumbled against the wall. The folder slipped from her hand as her heart pounded in her ears. She slid to the floor, clenching her eyes shut as she gripped her arms around herself and huddled against the wall. She shuddered and waited for the harsh sound of Jonathan's voice and the crack of his whip against the wall. That was the only warning he gave before the oncoming torture he'd unleash on her.

The painful memories of Jonathan's abuse swallowed Nadia's mind and the cool tiles beneath her felt like the hard wooden floors of the punishment chamber. She shook violently and sank further into the suffocating darkness of Jonathan's torment.

Chapter 22

"I think there's a power outage, but the backup generators should..."

Nadia's labored breathing muffled Luca's voice as visions of Jonathan's beatings clouded her mind and removed any rational thoughts she might've had.

"You disappoint me, kitten." Jonathan's husky voice whispered as he cracked the whip against the wall.

"No please, Master. I'm sorry," she whimpered and curled herself into a ball, waiting for the strike of the rough leather.

"Nadia, hey, it's alright," Luca whispered, kneeling beside her and slid a hand to her shoulder.

She gasped and choked out a breath as she pressed herself against the wall, wishing she'd disappear from this place. "D-don't touch me."

"Okay, okay," he cooed, pulling his hand back. "I'm just going to sit next to you, is that alright?" His voice was muffled again as she sucked in tiny breaths and sank into another memory of Jonathan's torment.

"You broke the rules again. Now Master must punish you for your disobedience," Jonathan cackled in delight as he unbuckled his belt and grabbed the back of her head. "And I'm going to fuck those screams out of your mouth."

"Nadia, you're right here with me," Luca said and his warm deep voice pierced through Jonathan's sinister tone and pulled her from the damaging visions. "You need to take a deep breath."

"I can't..."

"Yes, you can. Just try one time. I'll do it with you."

She clenched her eyes tighter and squeezed her arms around her knees. "I... can't..." she said again, struggling to speak through her panicked breaths.

"You need to breathe," he whispered.

Nadia's breath hitched. "I-I need to c-count."

"Okay, we can do that."

Nadia dug her nails into her legs as tears rolled down her cheeks. "F-five." She choked out. "I'm… I'm not his."

"Four," Luca said.

Nadia sucked in a painful breath. "I'm free."

"Three."

"I have a p-plan," she breathed.

"Two," Luca cooed.

"I'm safe," she said, taking in a deep breath, expanding her lungs.

"Yes, you are," Luca whispered. "One."

She let her breath out slowly. "I'm alive." Nadia took another deep breath. "Thank you," she muttered as her teeth chattered and a fresh wave of tears pricked the corners of her eyes. "I-I'm s-sorry."

"It's alright," he said, shrugging off his suit jacket. "You're freezing. I'm just going to put my jacket around you. Is that okay?"

"Y-yes." She nodded as he draped his warm, earthy scented jacket around her. "W-why aren't the lights coming back on?"

"I don't know. The air is still working but something isn't right." He sighed. "Don't worry, my guards will find us," he said, pulling his phone from his pocket and turning on the flashlight to create a small glow of light.

"I'm sorry you had to see me like this," she mumbled, tugging his jacket closer around her to stave off the chills of panic still rippling through her veins.

"You don't need to apologize. You've seen me at my worst

and I hardly saw you."

A soft laugh escaped her lips through her chattering teeth. "You know what I mean."

"I do, but you're still shivering," he said, sliding closer to her. "Do you mind if I put my arm around you?"

Nadia shook her head. "I don't mind," she said as he cuddled her under the crook of his arm. "I haven't had a panic attack like that in a long time," she murmured, resting her head against his side and breathing in his comforting scent. "B-but being in here… it just triggered me."

"I thought that's what happened," he said, rubbing his hand up and down her arm to keep her warm. "Are you feeling a little better?"

"Yes, thank you for talking me down. My… my ex used to l-lock me–" she said, but a violent shudder silenced her.

"It's alright, we don't have to talk about that," he whispered. "Why don't you give me your report for today? I know you have it memorized."

A whisper of a laugh escaped her lips. "I don't memorize all my reports," she mumbled.

He chuckled. "I've never seen you look at your notes in any of our meetings."

She was thankful he was trying to get her to talk about something else. It eased the anxiety nipping at her nerves and Jonathan's degrading voice floating through her mind. "True," she murmured. "I didn't think you noticed stuff like that."

"You're hard not to notice."

She smirked as tears pooled in her eyes. "Because I'm s-so clumsy, right?" she said and burst into tears.

"Hey, no that's not why," he said, holding her close. "That's not why, Nadia," he whispered. "There's far more to notice about you than that."

"I-I just w-want to get out of here," she whimpered through her sobs.

"I know. We will," he murmured, against her head. "Just close your eyes. My guards will find us soon."

"O-okay." Nadia sniffed, pressing her face into his side and clenching his shirt between her fingers. She closed her eyes, taking a few shallow breaths while Luca massaged the base of her neck.

"He nani ka pua hïnano ëhë," Luca sang in a soft whisper against her head.

She understood most of what he sang to her about a beautiful flower atop a high mountain, but his soft gentle voice quieted her sobs and caressed her in a blanket of security. Her breathing calmed and her trembling limbs settled as his deep, melodic singing lulled her into a dreamless slumber.

***

Nadia jumped awake at the sound of yelling and pounding against the elevator door as she dug her nails into Luca's shirt, cowering away from the noise.

"It's alright. I think they found us," he whispered as light pierced through the dark space.

"Mr. Shola, Miss Coleman, are you alright?" Jack exclaimed and motioned for the other guards to make a barrier around the door to block the view of onlookers.

"We're okay, but what took you so long?" Luca said, holding Nadia around her waist as he stood with her tucked under his arm.

"That's something we need to discuss after we get you out of here," Jack grumbled and his hard eyes grew soft as he looked at Nadia. "Miss Coleman, it's all right. You're safe now."

Nadia shivered against Luca and clenched the side of his shirt. "I want to go home," she mumbled as her breath hitched and she bit her lip to stop the oncoming sob.

"Okay, let's get you out of here," Luca cooed as they slowly stepped off the elevator into a circle of his black suited bodyguards. "Gordon, take Nadia home. Everyone else, Romeo, Echo, Delta, five - twenty four," he commanded.

"Yes, sir."

Luca slid his fingers to her chin, gently tilting her face to his. Her heart thumped at the warmth and concern in his eyes. "I'll check on you later, okay?"

She nodded as Gordon slowly took a step toward them. "Let's go, Miss Nadia," he said, reaching his arm around her.

"Don't touch me." She flinched away from him and buried herself against the safety of Luca's side.

"It's alright. No one is going to touch you," Luca murmured against her head as he held her around her waist. "My guards will keep a tight circle around you until you get to the car."

Gordon nodded and motioned for a quad of guards to follow. "After you, Miss Nadia."

She slowly released her nails from Luca's shirt and tugged his suit jacket closer around her. She took a deep breath and walked down the hall Gordon gestured to. The guards in her party quickly formed a circle around her, shielding her from the prying eyes of the employees peeking out from their offices.

Chapter 23

Nadia laid on her couch with a mountain of blankets around her while Minerva stroked her hair. She'd messaged her through bleary eyes on her way home. She didn't want to be alone and even though Gordon kindly offered to stay with her, she just needed to be with her best friend.

"I feel so stupid." She sniffed.

"You're not stupid," Minerva whispered.

Nadia let out a deep breath. "I have to tell Luca what happened to me."

"Whoa, are you sure? I doubt he'd expect that of you after what happened," she said softly.

Nadia sat up and brushed her frizzy hair out of her face. "But I think I need to and… and I *want* to. After today…" she trailed off. Her mind drifted back to the way Luca held her and spoke so softly to her. His voice was so soothing, like a fresh, warm blanket.

No one had ever calmed her down that quickly. It was like he reached down into her soul and kept her grounded. She'd never felt that safe with anyone before. "I… I just think he deserves to know."

Minerva raised her eyebrows. "That's a hard subject for you to talk about and I know you two are getting close, but do you think it's a good idea to tell him about Jonathan and what you're doing?"

Nadia took a deep breath. "I won't tell him about that, but Luca's become a really good friend. He's been open with me about what happened to him and I want to be open with him too."

A small smile tugged at Minerva's lips. "If you're comfortable with it, then I think that's a good step for you, but you don't have to tell him right away. You're still recovering from that panic attack. Why don't you give it a few days?"

"Yeah, maybe I should avoid that conversation for a little while." Nadia sighed, sliding her hands into her hair. "I still can't believe that happened. I haven't had an attack like that in so long and it had to happen at the office," she said, tears pooling in her eyes.

"It's alright. It wasn't your fault," Minerva said, rubbing her hand over her back. "Fuck everyone in the office. It's scary being stuck in an elevator."

Nadia wiped a tear rolling down her cheek. "God, if Luca hadn't been there, I'm pretty sure I would've been admitted to the hospital after they found me." She sniffed and shuddered. "My mind went straight back to that room Jonathan used to keep me in. I haven't thought about that in years."

"Well, with all the shit he's been sending you lately, it makes sense. Did you give the collar to Raquel?"

"No, it's still on my desk," Nadia mumbled. "I was going to bring it to her after work but this shit happened."

"Do you want me to take it to her for you?"

"You don't have to. I've already ruined your day with my bullshit."

"It's fine." Minerva shrugged. "She's on my way to Cam's place and I want to pick up that blueprint before we go to your parents' this weekend."

"Yeah, that's true." Nadia sighed, sitting back against the couch. "Thank you for being here."

Minerva hugged her tight. "Of course. I'm just glad you're feeling better."

Nadia's phone vibrated on the coffee table. She picked it up and a small smile tugged at her lips.

Mr. Underworld » How are you feeling? «

Nadia » I'm better. Minerva's been keeping me company. «

Mr. Underworld » That's good. Would you mind if I stopped by to check on you later? «

Nadia » You mean the reports from the guards you sent to patrol outside my apartment aren't enough for you? «

Mr. Underworld » Ooh she's got jokes… someone's feeling more herself. I told them to be discreet. «

Mr. Underworld » And no, that isn't enough for me.«

Nadia's smile grew even brighter. She shouldn't be feeling giddy about this; not after her dramatic episode, but she felt comforted that he cared about her safety and that he still wanted to see her.

"Mm, even I can't get you to smile like that after one of your attacks," Minerva mused. "I'm guessing that's Luca on your phone?"

A blush burned up to her ears and she slowly nodded. "He wants to come over to check on me."

A grin tugged at Minerva's lips. "That man really cares about you. Are you going to let him come over?"

"Yeah, I don't know what's wrong with me." She sighed. "But, I kind of want to see him too."

Minerva put a hand over hers and squeezed it gently. "There's nothing wrong with you. He's your friend and it's normal that you'd want to see each other after what happened today, but you still don't have to tell him anything if you don't want to."

"I know, I just want him to see that I'm alright."

Nadia wasn't sure she'd have the courage to tell him what happened to her when she saw him, but he needed to see that she wasn't the frail, broken thing he witnessed in the elevator. Her phone vibrated in her hand and she swiped her thumb across the screen to read the message.

Mr. Underworld » Don't worry if you're not feeling up for a visit. I'll be satisfied with the report from security.«

Nadia » No, it's fine. I don't mind if you stop by and your guards are being discreet. Minerva didn't notice, but you know I'm good at spotting them.«

Mr. Underworld » Convinced you were a spy in another life. I'll see you later.«

Nadia sat her phone back on the coffee table and looked at Minerva's smiling face. "What?"

Minerva shook her head. "Nothing. I'm just proud of you. You had a tough day and you're not hiding away from the world."

Nadia smirked. "I've been hiding in my apartment all day. I wouldn't call this monumental change."

Minerva laughed and wrapped her arms around her. "No, but it's progress and I'm allowed to be proud of you for it."

"Thank you."

Chapter 24

Luca tucked his phone in his pocket and crossed his arms over his chest as he watched his team of specialists dig through the computers and servers in the maintenance and IT department. He'd sent the staff home in order to allow for a thorough investigation of what happened in the elevator and why there was a network disruption.

"This wasn't the work of the Dagenhams, Mr. Shola," Jack said as he stood next to him.

"I know. I would've heard from Ciara or my grandfather by now. I haven't done anything obvious to alert them to my friendship with Nadia, but this seems like a targeted attack."

"Yeah, it does. How's Miss Coleman doing? She looked pretty shaken up."

"She said she's okay, but I'm going to check on her once we're done here."

"You can go now. This might take us a while."

"I found something, sir!" a specialist called out, raising her hand from one of the cubicles.

"I stand corrected," Jack murmured as they crowded around the young woman. "What have you got, Priscilla?"

"There's encrypted folders on this hard drive. I've decoded a few of them. One is mainly the elevator reprogramming," she said, looking up at Luca. "But this other one is disturbing, sir. This guy has been watching Miss Coleman for a while."

"What do you mean? Whose computer is this?" Luca said, looking for any sign of the cubicle's owner.

"Ben Klein, your head of IT," she said as she pulled up pictures of Nadia around the office. Some photos were of her before she worked there and a few with Minerva in what he assumed was Nadia's home. "There's videos too. The few I've decoded are from the security cameras here, but I'm going to take a guess that the others are from cameras he's placed in Miss Coleman's apartment. I can't confirm that, but judging from the timestamps, Ben has been using Shola's systems to run a surveillance operation on her for at least six months."

"What the fuck?" Luca breathed, sliding a hand over his mouth. "Jack, send a group of guards to sweep Nadia's office. Tell them to remove her computers and replace them with ones from the agency. Make sure they're discreet about it. There are enough rumors flying around about the elevator."

"I'm already on it. Her apartment needs to be swept as well, sir."

"I know, but I've got to talk to her about this before I freak her out with a bunch of agents in her place," Luca said, rubbing a hand over his face. "Why the hell would he be watching her?"

"Well, it looks like he's been sending these files to an IP address," Priscilla said as she tapped a few keys. "It's pretty heavily coded. It'll take me a while to figure out its location and who it belongs to."

"Mm, so he might be spying on her for someone," Jack murmured. "You said Miss Coleman had a stalker in the past, right? Has she told you anything more about it?"

Luca shook his head. "No, but I'll ask her. Have you started the dossier that I asked for?"

"On the Hatch boy? I have, but you don't think he's her stalker, do you?"

"I don't know. I thought Ciara hired his goons and I could be making a connection where there isn't one, but Nadia has a history at his company. It's the only thing that makes sense at this point."

"Right, you need to tell Miss Coleman what we've found today and get some answers. I'll do another background check on Ben."

"Okay, I want every server and computer replaced, but take all the hard drives. I want to make sure no one else is watching her."

"We'll get it taken care of," Jack said, placing his hand on his shoulder. "You just make sure Miss Coleman is alright. I know she means a lot to you and we'll do what we can to make sure she's safe."

"I know you will. Thank you."

Luca left the bustling room and took the elevator down to the garage. He leaned against the back of the elevator while his heart churned and stomach knotted with anxiety.

Nadia's huddled little form pressed against the wall and the sound of her panicked voice kept replaying in his mind. She was so scared, as if she were reliving whatever happened to her. And his company had been helping her stalker watch her for six fucking months. He slid a hand over his face. God, this was so fucked up.

But he could help her and at least provide her with proper protection even if she wasn't ready to give him the answers he wanted. He just wanted to do whatever he could to make her feel safe.

"Henry," Luca called to the curly black-haired guard standing by his car.

"Yes, sir?"

"Ben Klein has been suspended and I need you to make his life a living hell for a while. Subtle, but effective," he said, sliding into his car.

"Got it, Boss. How long?"

"Indefinitely," he said, closing his door. He didn't like using his guards in the same manner as his grandfather, but Ben deserved to be tortured for fucking with Nadia and if he found out that Jonathan Hatch was the one behind her torment, he'd raise hell on him too. He didn't care if he was a Syndicate–it would just make taking them down even fucking sweeter.

***

Luca parked his car between the two black sedans in the alley beside Nadia's apartment. He sighed, reading Nadia's message on the dash.

Nadia » Use the back stairwell in the alley. You won't be seen that way. I'm on the third floor and don't step on my plants, please.«

Picking up the grocery bags on the seat next to him, he stepped out of the car to speak to Gordon who was leaning against the black sedan in front of him.

"Jack told us what's going on," Gordon said, crossing his

arms over his chest. "This is fucked up."

"I know. I'm worried about her," Luca said, looking up at the brick apartment building. "She's not safe here."

"No, she's not." Gordon shook his head. "But we have the tools to make it safe and she needs a team until we figure this out."

Luca nodded. "I want you as her primary and I trust you to decide the best guards for the job."

"Yes, sir," Gordon said, pulling his phone from his pocket. "Let me know when Miss Nadia is ready for the sweep."

Luca took the back staircase to Nadia's apartment and frowned as he slowly approached her third-floor entrance that looked like a damn forest. A thick waterfall of deep green ivy leaves encased the whole side of her balcony. "What the fuck..." he whispered as he touched the green leaves and slowly stuck his hand through the dense vines to test what was on the other side before he slid through.

"Oh." His eyes grew wide at the chaotic yet ethereal garden around him. A rainbow of flowers and vines hung above him, potted plants of various shapes and sizes were bunched together in groups on the wood floor and lined against the iron railing. Two white cushioned wicker chairs and a small table sat against a brick wall in the corner, shrouded by tall leafy yuccas. The setting sun and fairy lights that weaved through the hanging vines set the balcony in a warm comforting glow.

A smile spread over Luca's lips as he tiptoed around the pots at his feet and ducked under the hanging baskets of blooming pansies. He reached up to touch a vibrant blue clematis weaving around the iron beams above his head. Nadia's place reminded him of his home and the many gardens he cultivated on his estate.

"You made it." Nadia's voice cut through his nostalgic thoughts as she stepped on to the balcony.

"I did," he said and his heart thumped at the way the sun highlighted her brown skin and auburn curls that were braided in a crown around her head. The lace cardigan over her simple yellow top and denim jeans brightened the flourishing garden around them and made her look like a modern Spring Goddess. "I have to admit, I wasn't sure about that scary ass vine you've got guarding your place, but this is really beautiful."

"Thank you." She smiled, but it didn't reach her eyes and guilt tugged at his heart at the sadness in her depths. "Did you bring me comfort food?"

"I did," he said, looking down at the bags in his hand. "I thought we could make pizza and sundaes."

Her cheeks swelled. "That sounds good," she said, holding the door open. "Well, come into my humble little abode."

Luca ducked under the flowered vines to follow her inside and took in Nadia's tiny apartment that was full of vibrant colors and a cozy warmth unlike his place that was full of clean, sleek lines and void of any clutter or color. "Your place is cute. I like it." He smiled as he sat the grocery bags on the counter.

"I'm surprised you haven't melted from all the color," she said, moving a few magazines from the island in the kitchen while he took in the plants dotted around her living room and the ivy wrapped around an overflowing bookshelf. The vibrant contemporary art pieces that hung on her exposed brick walls matched perfectly with her red couch and mustard yellow armchair, but his eyes were drawn to the framed art deco painting of Hades and Persephone on the far wall next to the Death Star hanging in the corner.

'My darkness doesn't scare you, my flower?' Hades asked.

'No,' Persephone replied. 'You've yet to see mine.'

That quote was so fitting for Nadia. The trauma of his past didn't bother her, but she had yet to tell him of hers. His heart sank, but he needed to know now. A sick invasion of her privacy tarnished the warm and welcoming home she created for herself. He'd have to ease into that heavy conversation and at least get her to agree to let him help her.

"I see you brought raw dough," Nadia said as she rummaged through the grocery bags. "I have to admit I've never tossed a pizza before."

A grin tugged at Luca's lips as he tore his eyes from the painting. "Well, little Miss, tonight I'm going to teach you."

Chapter 25

Nadia and Luca sat outside on her balcony with empty sundae bowls on the small table. The remnants of pizza and garlic bread were cleaned up and the dishes washed in the kitchen. A small smile graced her lips as she leaned back in her chair. This wasn't what she expected when Luca said he was coming over to check on her. He kept everything so lighthearted and she almost forgot what happened earlier in the day. That shouldn't surprise her anymore. She was learning that's just the way he was and it made her want to stay in his orbit.

"How long did it take you to do all of this?" he said, looking around the blooming foliage.

"Mm, about two years," she said, taking a toke of the rolled herbs in her hand. "I started gardening at my old place, but they really started going wild when I moved here. My therapist suggested I grow plants to help with anxiety and stress. So, I started with the ivy because it's hard to kill and I had no idea what I was doing back then." She laughed. "Once

I realized I could keep a plant alive, I started dabbling with other ones and I guess I just fell in love with it." She shrugged, passing him the blunt.

"Well, it's beautiful," he said, putting his feet on the wicker footstool in front of them and leaned back in his chair. "But that ivy is out of control. Shit is creepy from the other side."

She burst out laughing. "Leave my baby alone," she said, sliding her feet on the footstool next to his. "But I think it keeps my neighbors from using this stairwell."

"I wouldn't use it either," he mumbled, taking a toke from the blunt.

She raised her eyebrow. "Oh, come on, I thought you didn't scare easily."

"I don't, but I'm not going to put myself in a potential horror movie situation either." He chuckled. "Then again, I've got enough white in me to be safe, but you–" he said, pointing his finger at her. "You're the one who needs to be careful."

Nadia burst into giggles. "You're not right," she said through her laughter. "That's fucked up."

"What? You know it's true."

She grinned. "Then I guess I'll just have to use you as my shield."

He choked out a laugh and passed her the blunt. "I would gladly be your shield."

She bit her lip as her cheeks swelled from his chivalrous offer. "You're kind of a protective person, aren't you?"

He shrugged. "Only with the things I like."

That both infuriated her and made her heart melt at the sentiment. "I'm not a *thing*, Mr. Underworld."

A dazzling smile spread over his lips, and the sight of

it made her heart thump. "No, you're ka'u pua nani, my beautiful flower and flowers need protecting."

A blush burned over her cheeks. "Your beautiful flower, huh?"

"Yeah, I think it's fitting for this Spring Goddess aesthetic you've got going on," he said, waving his hand around her balcony.

"I guess so," she said and bit her lip at the adorable nickname. "But what do you think I need protecting from?"

The teasing gleam in his eyes vanished with a quickness and the worry that replaced it made her heart clench. "Nadia, I know I haven't brought up today," he said, sitting up. "But I need to apologize. That shouldn't have happened and I hope you're alright."

"I'm okay. You don't have to apologize. It wasn't your fault."

"Not directly." He sighed. "I have to be honest with you. My security agents are investigating why the elevator malfunctioned and they found some disturbing files on Ben Klein's computer," he said, clenching his hands together. "There's no easy way to say this, but –"

"He's been watching me," Nadia mumbled, sitting back against her chair and sliding a hand over her face. That son of a bitch.

"Yes, and if I knew he was your stalker, I never would have allowed him to get near you."

She shook her head. "Ben's not my stalker, but now I know he's working with him." And how those notes had been getting into her mail. Fuck.

"Working with who?"

Nadia looked away from him and bit her thumb as tears

pricked the corners of her eyes. "Jonathan Hatch. He's been stalking me for a long time. He… he's been sending me anonymous notes at the office," she said, wringing her hands in her lap. "Jonathan must've done this today to scare me. He knows I don't like being trapped in small places."

Luca cursed under his breath. "That's what I thought."

Her eyes grew wide as she slowly turned her head to him. "What do you mean?"

"Gordon ran the plates of a car that he caught watching your place and it's registered to Jonathan, but I thought Ciara hired his people to watch you."

Nadia frowned. "Gordon's been watching me too?"

Luca hung his head. "Yes. I wanted him around for your protection in case Ciara or my grandfather targeted you for our friendship."

"I-I don't know what to say to that."

"I'm sorry for not telling you. I thought it would be better if you didn't know. I didn't want to freak you out since you had a stalker, but I can see how this looks like I was doing the same thing."

"Yeah, I know you meant well, but is there anything else you're not telling me?"

"There's a lot I can't tell you for your own safety," he said, looking into her apartment. "But you're not safe here right now. Ben had photos of you and Minerva in your apartment and my agents suspect he has videos too."

Fear and panic prickled up her spine and goosebumps raced over her skin. "Wh-what?"

"I don't know how he laced your apartment, but he's been doing surveillance on you for at least six months."

"No," she whispered. If he'd been watching her for that

long, did that mean Jonathan knew what she was up to? "Oh my God," her voice cracked as she bit back the sob threatening to burst from her throat.

"Nadia, hey, it's okay," Luca cooed as he slid a hand over hers. "My guards are prepared to sweep your apartment. They can find the cameras and set up a security system for you. I'll make this right for you."

Her lip trembled as she stared into his golden depths and wrapped her fingers around his. "Can they do that right now?"

"Yes, if that's what you want."

"I do," she said, looking past him into her apartment and she felt sick. She loved her place and she made it her home, but now the thought of sleeping in there made her stomach sour. "Can I stay with… n-nevermind." She couldn't keep staying with him even if being around him made her feel safe. "I need to call Nervy." She started to get up, but stopped when Luca slid his hand to her cheek and wiped her stray tears.

"You can stay with me if that's what you were going to ask."

She wrapped her fingers around his wrist. "Are you sure that's okay?"

"Yes, I want you to feel safe until this is fixed," he said, caressing her wet cheeks with his thumb. "Call Minerva and pack whatever you need for a few days. I'll let my guards know you're ready."

Nadia wrapped her arms around his shoulders and hugged him tight. "Thank you," she whispered.

"You're welcome," Luca murmured against her head and the way he enveloped her in his arms quelled the anxiety begging to wreak havoc on her mind. She breathed in his comforting fresh soap and cedarwood scent, letting it calm her with a warmth she didn't know she needed.

***

Nadia held a mug of warm chamomile tea in her hands as she sat on the couch in Luca's living room. She felt a little better being away from her place. She spoke to Minerva who was happy that Luca was looking out for her, but she worried Jonathan might know what they were up to and they only had one chance to get the information they needed on the Syndicates.

Nadia took a sip from her mug and closed her eyes. She hoped the blueprint from Raquel led them to what she needed. She couldn't live in fear like this anymore.

"How are you feeling?" Luca said, sitting next to her with a glass of water.

"I'm alright." She sighed. "But I… I want to tell you about Jonathan."

"Only if you're comfortable with that. You know I'm willing to listen."

She sat her mug on the coffee table and folded her hands in her lap. "I think after everything that happened and what you've found out, I need to explain why I'm like this and how things got to this point with Jonathan."

He nodded, setting his glass next to hers and facing her on the couch. "Take your time, then."

Nadia took a deep breath and stared into his golden eyes. She wanted him to know, and it felt right to share this piece of herself with him. "I never should have been involved with Jonathan, but a few years ago I was out of a job for a while and my dad got me a meeting with his friend Marcus who offered me a marketing job at Hatch Engineering. Jonathan was just taking over as CEO and he was everything I thought I wanted. Smart, ambitious and extremely good looking. So when he took notice of me, I was all too happy to play his games." She shook her head. "I was so stupid."

"You weren't stupid. Naive is probably more accurate."

"Yeah." She smirked. "Minerva couldn't stand him and he didn't like her either. That should've been my first clue, but I didn't care. I was having fun. It wasn't like I was marrying him," she said, picking at a thread on her leggings. "I didn't realize what I'd gotten myself into until about six months into our relationship he took me to his 'playhouse'. That's what he called that monstrous place."

She sighed, closing her eyes. "I still remember the pine scent of the polished floors and the grand staircase lined with at least ten women dressed in black corsets standing on the steps of the staircase waiting to greet him." She took a breath and cleared her throat. "Jonathan told me they were his 'kittens' and it was time I became one too."

"And he was the Master of the playhouse, right?"

She bit her lip and nodded. "Yeah, you know about these things?"

"I do. Sex rings and Juliet circles are the vice of choice for the uber rich, but that type of power play wasn't what I was into."

Nadia hung her head. "I didn't know about that side of things until it was too late."

"Most people don't. It's not information that's usually offered when a Master is recruiting new… players."

"Yeah, but in a sick, fucked up way, I was… intrigued by it–not the circle, the idea of being a submissive. I've always been into some BDSM stuff just not on the level that Jonathan was introducing me to, but he never did anything to make me feel scared about what I was doing. I felt safe and the other women seemed alright to me." She shrugged. "So, I became a kitten."

She paused, sliding her hand over her throat. "I'm sorry, this probably isn't what you were expecting me to tell you."

Luca slid a hand over hers and squeezed it gently. "It doesn't matter what I was expecting. I'm here to listen."

She nodded, taking a deep breath. "I didn't realize how different Jonathan was as a Master until he started limiting my time with my friends, watching my every move and keeping me at the playhouse to entertain his frequent guests." She shuddered. "I didn't see how brainwashed I'd become by the lifestyle or how isolated I was until I disobeyed him," she said, threading her fingers through his and holding on to him as if he were her anchor.

"I didn't come back to the playhouse after I went out with Minerva one night, which was against the rules, but I didn't care. I needed to be with my friends." She sniffed and shook her head. "When I came back the next day he... he chained me to the floor of this tiny dark room and said it was my punishment. I don't know how long he left me there, but he would return every few hours to beat me or..." She bit her lip as if to stop herself from uttering her next words.

"You don't have to say it," Luca whispered, caressing the back of her hand.

She nodded and brushed away the tear rolling down her cheek. "After my time in the chamber I couldn't do anything right. He stopped putting me on display for his guests because I'd become his guilty pleasure and he didn't want anyone else to indulge in me after he got a taste of torturing me. The other girls were jealous that I was always by his side, but they didn't know the kind of hell I was in."

Nadia squeezed Luca's hand and sucked in a shaky breath as the memories of the catty looks from the other kittens and Jonathan's degrading voice echoed in her mind. "I had no one to talk to. I had to lie to Minerva and my family about how I was doing because he monitored my phone use. The only place I could go outside of the playhouse was the office and even there I was alone. Jonathan promoted me to a bogus executive position with an office right next to his and my only job was to service him."

"Fuck," Luca breathed, shaking his head. "How the hell did you get out of that?"

"It wasn't easy." She smirked. "I planned my escape route for weeks. I hid a bag of emergency clothes in the vents in my office and when I finally got up enough courage, I left. I stayed in a shelter for a few days, got my hands on a burner phone and called Minerva. She wanted to go to the police, especially after she saw my bruises and scars, but I didn't want to do any of that. I just wanted out. Luckily, Minerva was getting ready to take a job out here, so she offered to let me come with her and that's what I did."

Nadia pressed her tongue to her cheek and blinked back the tears pooling in her eyes. "My dad was so disappointed with me when he found out I left Hatch, but I couldn't tell him what happened. It was hard enough telling Minerva and he was such good friends with Marcus. I didn't want to ruin that for him. So, I let him believe I was just fucking up and throwing my life away."

She wiped her tears. "Everything was good for a few

months. I got a job and started putting my life back together and I thought I could put Jonathan's crazy shit behind me." She looked down at their hands. "I should've known it wouldn't be that easy to get away from him. Things started going missing in my apartment or they weren't where I left them. It was small stuff like jewelry or my lipstick. They were things I just thought I'd lost and I didn't think much of it, until I started noticing Jonathan's men hanging around my apartment building, but I shrugged that off as paranoia because there was no way Jonathan was crazy enough to follow me to Boston. He had plenty of other women around him to obsess over," she trailed off. "Sorry." She sniffed and wiped her tears. "This part is hard for me to say."

"It's alright, take your time," Luca whispered, and squeezed her hand.

Her hand shook as she took a deep breath. "I-I don't remember much from the night Jonathan broke into my apartment. I just remember waking up to him choking me with the kitten collar he forced me to wear while he yelled that everything he did was my fault before he... raped and beat me within an inch of my life."

She looked up at the ceiling as a tear rolled down her cheek. "The only reason Jonathan didn't kill me that night is because my neighbors heard my screams and called the police. I was..." Her lip trembled. "I was unconscious by the time the paramedics got there. I woke up two days later in the hospital barely able to speak or move. My body won't ever fully recover from that. I-I can't have children. My doctors said it's unlikely it'll ever happen." She sniffed. "And I wasn't always this clumsy." She laughed softly. "It's a side effect of the mild brain trauma. I almost wasn't able to dance, but

I refused to let Jonathan take that away from me too." She sighed, wiping her tears.

"Jesus, Nadia," Luca whispered. "Did you press charges?"

She nodded. "My parents were adamant that I did, but nothing really came out of that." She smirked. "The judge gave him three months' probation and they granted me a permanent restraining order against him," she said and a joyless laugh left her lips. "But that didn't help. He always finds me and he's never stopped trying to get me back. I can't tell you how many times I've moved, changed my locks, and reported him for breaching his restraining order. The last eighteen months were the longest I'd been able to live without his constant mind games, but he's just been letting me believe he's given up," she said, looking over at Luca. Her heart clenched and her lip trembled at the unshed tears in his eyes. "I'm sorry this spilled over into the office. I didn't think he'd find me there, at least not like this."

"It's not your fault. I should've been more aware of what my employees were doing." Luca shook his head. "Nadia, I… I'm so sorry that happened to you," he said, squeezing her hand. "You're so strong for going through that and still have the strength to put a smile on your face." Luca brushed away a tear rolling down his cheek. "Thank you for sharing that with me and I'm so sorry for picking on your clumsiness."

Nadia chuckled softly. "It doesn't bother me anymore. I used to get really frustrated with myself, but my family and therapy helped me find the humor in it. I learned to own it as my flaw. So, please don't stop picking on me or laughing about it. I don't want any pity."

He nodded. "Fair enough. How long has this been going on?"

"About three years and I'm tired of running. I don't want to live like this anymore," she said, her voice breaking as the weight of Jonathan's torment came crashing down on her. She bit her lip and her face crumpled as she choked out a sob.

Luca wrapped his arms around her and pulled her against his chest. "You shouldn't have to run and I'll do whatever I can to help you."

"I don't want you to get caught up in this," she cried and shook in his arms. "You're already doing too much."

He pulled away from her and wiped the tears running down her face. "As far as I'm concerned, this is my problem, too. My company enabled him to find you and I have the means to protect you. So, that's what I'm going to do."

She shook her head. "He's going to know you're involved. He's got so many connections –"

"I know the types of connections he has. I may not have had many interactions with Jonathan, but I know his social circle," he said, caressing her cheeks with his thumb and the unwavering look in his depths filled her with a wealth of security. "Trust me when I say I can protect you, Nadia."

"I… I do. I just don't want this to cause any trouble with your grandfather or Ciara."

"You let me worry about them. They don't need to know about my security agency's private contracts."

A watery smile tugged at her lips as she wrapped her arms around his waist and pressed her face against the warmth of his chest. "Thank you," she whispered.

"Anything for you," he murmured against her head and her heart swelled at that. He knew what Jonathan was and although he didn't say it, it filled her with hope that he was still willing to protect her from him. Syndicates always protect their own and Luca definitely wasn't one of them. She could've told him about her mission and her plan, but right now, the comfort and safety of his embrace was what she needed.

Chapter 26

Luca was up late reading over the plans for his weekend in Watkins Glen with Cam. Nadia's apartment was taking longer than he expected since he was adamant that Gordon installed a top of the line security suite for her after her guards discovered at least seven different cameras in her bedroom, living room and her fucking bathroom coming from the empty apartments above, below and beside hers.

Her security team spoke with the owners of the building and they were now leasing those empty apartments and would live there until further notice.

With all the work needing to be done in her place, it meant Nadia had been living with him for nearly a week. Luca didn't mind it. He enjoyed the routine they had together, having coffee in the morning, making dinner every night and staying up late reading or setting the world right over a few too many blunts.

A smile tugged at his lips as he scribbled a note over the blueprint on his lap. There was something different about the way she acted around him lately, or maybe it was the fact that it'd become natural for them to cuddle up on the couch together. Whatever it was, he was guilty of enjoying every minute he got to spend with her.

Except for her nightmares.

She didn't talk about them and he wasn't sure if she remembered having them, but he had a routine of checking on her in the middle of the night and she'd always be whimpering and tossing and turning. He'd gotten into the habit of lying with her until she calmed down, but it worried him she was in such torment every night.

Luca checked his watch and closed the leather-bound folder over his lap. He sat it on his nightstand and got up to check on Nadia. He padded to his bedroom door and his heart thumped when he opened it and Nadia was standing in front of him, hair wrapped in a scarf, dressed in leggings and an oversized stormtrooper tee with a book in her hand.

"Hey, you alright?"

"I can't sleep." She sighed. "Will you read to me?"

"Of course, do you want to go to your room or do you want to be… in here?"

"Here's fine," she mumbled, yawning as she shuffled over to his bed and climbed in as if it was a natural thing for her to do. "Why are you still up?"

"Just waiting for you, I guess," he said, slipping into the bed beside her.

"No you weren't." She chuckled softly as he took The Sound of Stars from her hand. "But I know you've been checking on me every night."

"You caught me," he said, wrapping his arm around her as she curled up against him. "You haven't been sleeping very well."

"No, I just have a lot on my mind and it manifests into nightmares about Jonathan."

He put the book down. "Do you want to talk about it?"

"There's not much to say," she said, picking at a thread on his shirt. "I'm just scared there's nothing I can do to stop him and I don't feel right relying on you for help. You have your own problems to deal with without me adding to them."

It stung that she felt that way. Yes, he had the Dagenhams, his grandfather and the Syndicates to handle, but he wanted her to feel like she could rely on him. He damn sure wouldn't leave her to fend for herself against someone like Jonathan. His lackeys were clearly a bit more tactical than he thought.

"I want to help you. I told you I have the means to do it and it won't be a problem. There's no reason for you to feel bad about this." Luca slid his fingers to her chin, tilting her face to him. "You're not a burden to me, okay?"

Her tired green eyes glossed over with tears before she blinked them back and nodded. "Okay," she said and a soft laugh escaped her lips. "You said that to me in my dream."

A smile curled over Luca's lips and a ridiculous giddiness spread over him that she found him in her dreams. "See? Your subconscious was telling the truth."

She pursed her lips. "Or you've been whispering it to me every night."

"Nope," he said, caressing her cheek with his thumb. "I sing to you."

Her cheeks swelled as she picked up the book lying next to him. "Well, tonight I want a story, Mr. Underworld," she said, sliding it over his chest.

"As you wish, ka'u pua," he said, picking up the book and

cuddling her against him. "You comfy?"

"Mm-hm, I'm always comfy with you." She sighed, closing her eyes.

A swell of pride washed over him at her sleepy admission and he pressed his lips to her forehead. "Good," he murmured before he began reading M0Rr1S and Ellie's dystopian adventure.

***

Luca woke with a smile on his face and reveled in Nadia's legs tangled up in his with her arm wrapped around his waist as she slept under the crook of his arm. He slid his hand below the hem of her cheetah print headscarf and massaged a curl that broke free. He wished their circumstances were different because every morning should feel this good. Every day should feel as good as he felt with Nadia living in his home.

"Good morning," Nadia mumbled.

"Good morning." He smiled. "How did you sleep?"

"Considering your room is like a bat cave, I slept really well." She sighed, sliding her hand over his chest. "Thank you for reading to me and letting me sleep in here."

"You're always welcome to sleep in my bed."

Nadia's eyes fluttered open and she tilted her head up to him. "Am I?"

He pressed his forehead against hers and wrapped her soft curl around his finger. "Mm-hm."

"Luca," she whispered and he ached to taste her lips.

"Yeah?"

"What are we doing?"

"What do you mean?" he murmured, sliding his hand over the curve of her waist.

Chapter 26

"This. Waking up together, you singing to me every night. Your hand on my hip," she said, her fingers finding their way to the light stubble on his chin.

"Mm, probably something we shouldn't," he said, staring into her heady green depths.

"But what if we want to?"

"Then maybe we should."

"You have a girlfriend."

"I have an obligation."

"I don't think this is a good idea," she murmured as her fingers grazed his lips.

"Do you want me to stop?" he said, kissing her fingers.

"No."

"Can I kiss you, ka'u pua nani?" he whispered.

"Yes," she breathed.

Luca closed the small gap between their lips and drowned in her sweetness. He gently coaxed her lips apart, and the moan she breathed into his mouth sent a delightful shiver down his spine. Nadia dragged her nails through his hair and kissed him back as if she were starving and his mouth was her sustenance.

And, God, he was starving for her too. He tangled his fingers in her curls beneath her scarf and gripped the swell of her ass, holding her close. He'd never felt so sated by a kiss, but in this moment she was everything he needed. Luca smiled against her lips and kissed the side of her mouth as he stared into her dazed, green eyes. "That was…"

"Real nice," she breathed.

"It was." He chuckled, kissing her softly. "I've wanted to do that for a while now."

"Me too," she whispered, sliding her hand to his cheek.

"But this is a problem."

His heart thumped as he pressed his forehead to hers. "I don't want it to be. I like waking up with you. I like being with you and I can't help the way I feel," he said, staring into her sea green depths. "You do something to me I can't really explain."

A small smile tugged at the corners of her lips. "You do the same to me, but we have no business feeling like this for each other. You're with Ciara and I've got Jonathan to deal with," she said, caressing his cheek and his heart fluttered at her comforting touch. "We can't be like this. You're not even supposed to be my friend."

"Yet, here we are. You're my best friend, ka'u pua and I never want to lose that."

"I don't either, Mr. Underworld. So, maybe we don't do this again." She sighed. "I'll stay with Minerva tonight."

"What?" His heart sank. "Are you sure?"

"Yeah, we're going away for the weekend and we're leaving after work tomorrow. Gordon said my place will be done when I come back and it's probably best if you and I aren't so close."

He slid his hand over her wrist as his heart continued to sink. "If that's what you want."

"It's not. I like being with you," she said, pushing out of his arms. "But it's how it has to be, right?"

He pulled her back to him before she moved too far away and pressed a kiss to her forehead. "You're the one I'd be with if I had a choice," he whispered.

"I don't even know how to be with anyone anymore."

"Neither do I, but we can figure it out together."

Hope and tenderness swirled in her eyes, but Luca caught

the doubt dimming the vibrancy of her sea green orbs. "I wish we could," she said, kissing him softly before she slipped out of his arms.

Hurt bit at Luca's heart as he watched her pad across the room and slip out the door without another word. What could he say or do to make how they felt for each other better? He sighed, getting out of the bed and trudging into his bathroom.

He shed his clothes and stepped under the warm running water. Crossing his arms against the damp tiled walls and pressing his head against his forearms, he heaved a deep sigh.

As much as he didn't want Nadia to leave, she was right. They couldn't be like this. How could they? Ciara would be back soon and unless his grandfather's lake house proved to be flush with shady information he could use against him and the Syndicates, a life chained to Ciara's side was all he'd have to look forward to.

But that didn't mean he couldn't keep Nadia safe. He could use his grandfather's influence to ruin the Hatch family's status within the society and terrorize the fuck out of Jonathan and his men for her.

Luca pushed away from his arms with a wicked grin on his face.

Fuck it.

He could do that shit now. He could give Jonathan the same psychological fuckery as Ben.

Luca washed and rinsed himself before he stepped out of the shower. Wrapping a towel around his waist, he padded into his bedroom and dressed in his signature three piece black suit.

The devilish grin never left his lips as he walked down the

hall to the kitchen. Not only would he fuck with Jonathan mentally, he was going to plant some incriminating evidence on him when he broke into his grandfather's house this weekend. Jonathan Hatch fucked with the wrong one, and Luca was going to enjoy watching him suffer for it.

Grabbing two black mugs from the stainless steel rack above his kitchen island, Luca poured two cups of coffee from the pot brewing on the counter and fixed Nadia's just the way she liked it. Cream, sugar and a dash of cinnamon.

A smile tugged at his lips as Nadia shuffled down the hall and he trailed over her auburn hair neatly braided into a crown around her head and the dip in her white blouse tucked into her cropped navy blue trousers that hugged her toned legs and thick thighs. She yawned and her eyes lit up when she saw the steaming cup of coffee on the island waiting for her.

"Mm, coffee." She beamed and brought the cup to her lips. The morning sun caressed her brown skin in a warm glow and heightened the contentment on her face. It filled him with a warmth that spread through him and settled in his gut.

God, he was going to miss having her here.

Luca took a sip of his coffee drinking in the warm sustenance as he drank in the sight of her too. "Would you like your team to drop your things off at Minerva's?"

"Oh, right. My team," she said, sitting her cup down. "Yeah, they can do that. Um, they don't have to come with me on my girl's trip this weekend, do they?"

"No, not if you don't want them to, but I'd prefer it if they did," he said, leaning back against the counter.

"Of course you would." She rolled her eyes and leaned

against the island across from him. "I'll be safe at my parents' house. I don't need my team."

"Alright, but you should at least tell them where you're going. Even if you don't tell me." He sat his mug on the counter and pulled his phone from his pocket. "Actually, Gordon should have your watch ready," he said, tapping a message to him.

"My watch?" She scoffed. "Is that like a tracking beacon?"

"It can track your location, but that's not its primary purpose," he said, slipping his watch off his wrist and handing it to her. "The three buttons on the outside are linked to Jack, my primary team and my secondary team. Yours will be linked the same way, so that if you're ever in a situation like the elevator, you can alert them with or without a network connection."

She nodded. "Okay, that's pretty nifty, but why can't they just fix my phone to do that?"

"Because then you wouldn't get all the other features only available on my personal network," he said, slipping his watch back on his wrist.

She raised an eyebrow. "Like?"

"A digital key to your office and my private garage, the app to my dispensary to order new seeds or bud, access to my pit crew to schedule test drives if you want –"

"Luca." She laughed. "I don't need any of that and don't you think that's a bit much?"

"No and I want you to have it."

She crossed her arms. "What would Ciara or your grandfather think of you doing all this for me?"

"They probably wouldn't approve of it, but they don't need to know," he said, sliding his fingers to her chin. "So, you don't need to worry about it. Just let me and your guards protect you."

She pursed her lips and he had half a mind to kiss that smirk off her face. Jesus, she brought out something primal in him.

"Fine, but I don't think I'll be using any of those extras," she said, brushing his hand away from her. "And stop looking at me like that."

"Like what?" he said, sliding his arm around her waist and pulling her against him.

"Like you want to devour me or something. It's distracting." She chuckled, pushing playfully against his chest.

"Maybe I do," he said, leaning down to kiss her cheek before trailing his lips to her ear. "And I think you want me to," he whispered.

"What I want," Nadia said, pressing her cheek against his and her sweet breath against his ear made his groin do a quick twitch. "Is for you to respect the boundaries of our friendship, Mr. Underworld."

His heart froze, and guilt washed over him. "I'm sorry, ka'u pua," he said, dropping his hands from her waist and taking a step back. "I won't disrespect you like that."

"Thank you," she said, moving around him, slipping her feet into her red heels sitting by the door. "We should probably get to work."

"Yeah, but we're good, right? I shouldn't have done that. I don't want you to think I'd ever force myself on you."

"I know you wouldn't do that." A smile tugged at her lips and her heels clicked on the floor as she stepped toward him and took his hand. "We're good." She bit her lip. "One day I hope you get to devour me."

Chapter 26

Luca choked out a breathless laugh as his heart slammed against his ribcage and a tingle traveled down his spine and pooled in his gut at the salacious look simmering in her green eyes. "And how I wish that day was today," he said, bringing her hand to his lips. "I'm glad we're okay."

As they dumped their coffee into the sink and took the elevator down to the garage, Luca made a promise to himself that he'd always keep Nadia safe even if he never saw the day when they could explore what they could be.

He kissed her hand as the elevator doors opened. "Let me know when you get to Minerva's tonight."

"I will." She squeezed his hand before she let go to walk across the garage to the waiting black sedan. She waved to him as she slipped inside.

Luca trudged to his car, sighing as he slid into the back seat. He always wanted to get himself and his family out of the clutches of his grandfather and the Syndicates, but he never thought he'd want it because he was falling in love. Now he understood why his mother risked her livelihood to be with his father and Nadia was the one he wanted to fight for.

Luca pulled his phone from his pocket, tapped a few numbers on the keypad and took a deep breath. If he was going to protect Nadia, he had to be smart about taking care of Jonathan while he simultaneously kept his own mission on track.

"Luca, what a surprise? You never call me and never this early," his grandfather answered with glee. "Arnold has been so happy with you lately. I planned to invite you and your parents over for dinner this evening. I think it's time we talk about you and Ciara taking the next step in your relationship."

Luca's heart churned and his stomach soured at the thought of proposing to Ciara, but he pushed back the panic. That didn't matter right now. "Sure, that sounds great."

"Wonderful. Now, what does my grandson need from me this early in the morning?"

"There was a security breach at the office and I've tracked the culprit to one of my employees who's also one of Hatch's lackeys. I'm concerned they might make moves to undermine you."

"Mm, that doesn't surprise me," his grandfather murmured. "I've told Arnold he should be wary of Marcus Hatch. His son is too ambitious for his own good. He doesn't respect the hierarchy and he thinks that sex ring he runs is enough to blackmail his way to the top." He laughed and the sharp flick of a lighter sounded through the receiver.

His grandfather was quiet for a moment as he took a long drag of his cigar and Luca could almost smell the spicy undertones of the smoke through the phone. He let out a long sigh before he finally responded. "So, what do you think I should do about this? You're going to be in my position one day. I'd like to know how you plan to keep the Syndicates in line."

Luca squeezed his hand into a fist. "I'd like to make an example of him."

"Go on."

"There's a Platinum roundtable next week. I want to invite Jonathan. He'll feel honored being called up to meet with people above his family's station. Then I'll interrogate him about his involvement in stealing information from my business and if he denies it, which he will, I'd like to take a few of his fingers to remind everyone that his kind of treachery will not be tolerated."

His grandfather let out a low whistle. "I didn't think you had it in you. You're a Rodawson after all. Would you like to do the honor of exacting that punishment or would you like me to?"

"I want to do it. I think it's time I show the Syndicates that I'm just as formidable as you, don't you think?"

"My God, what has gotten into you?" His grandfather chuckled. "I'm feeling mighty proud of you, son."

"Thank you. It's nice to hear you say that."

"Mm, you keep this up and I'll gladly hand you the reins. We can talk more about this tonight, yeah?"

"Absolutely."

"That's my boy. See you soon."

Jack chuckled softly from the driver's seat as his eyes caught Luca's in the mirror. "I've never heard you speak to your grandfather with such conviction before. The last time I heard you sound like the ali'i you are was when you led Koa Maile," he said and his brown eyes shined with pride. "He kehau ho òma èma è ke aloha, huh?"

A blush burned over Luca's cheeks as he looked away from Jack. "Yeah, it might be," he murmured, watching Nadia's car turn down the street to the alternate route to the office and the old saying warmed his heart.

Love is like a cleansing dew.

But Nadia was more than that. She was like a fountain of fresh, soothing water and he didn't think he'd ever be quenched of his thirst for the way she made him feel as if he could overcome anything in his path.

Chapter 27

Nadia smiled to herself as she stirred a bowl of potato salad in her parents' kitchen while her father was outside cooking on the grill, her mother was setting up chairs for a few of their friends she invited over and Minerva was chopping up a salad next to her.

It felt good to be home.

The calm quiet sounds of the lake gently crashing against the small shore and the fresh warm summer breeze with a soft scent of grapes was just what Nadia needed to clear her head.

She was still processing what happened with Luca and the way he kissed her as if he was starved and she was his nourishment. It was…intense but sensual and damn if she wasn't starved for him too. The only reason she didn't want to stay with him was because she was afraid of that feeling and what she wanted from him.

She looked at her shiny new rose gold watch Gordon gave her before she left on the road trip with Minerva. Her heart swelled at the message on the black background of the home screen.

Ka'u pua nani
E pakele

My beautiful flower. Be safe.

The message was so simple, but it made her feel so cherished. She wasn't used to the kind of care and respect Luca showed her. It made her feel like she could open herself to him and she wanted to. God, she wanted so much more than for him to devour her. She wanted… *love.*

Fuck.

"Someone's got it bad," Minerva giggled next to her as she tossed the salad in the bowl.

"Shut up." She laughed. "I'm just thinking about the plan for tonight."

Minerva raised her eyebrow. "Bitch, we went over it from top to bottom on the five-hour car ride and we were up until two this morning going over it again. We got it and that's not what you were thinking about." She smirked. "Someone's got that kiss on the brain."

A blush burned up to Nadia's ears. "Fuck off. I shouldn't have told you. It's stupid anyway. There's so many things wrong with the way I feel."

"Like what?"

"Seriously?"

"Yeah, what's so wrong about it?"

"Besides the fact he has a girlfriend." Nadia looked around them and leaned in closer to Minerva, keeping her voice low. "Or that we're planning to break into his grandfather's house tonight?" She shook her head, leaning away from her to grab the cling wrap on the counter. "It's no good for me to feel anything for him when I could be potentially ruining his life when I have to expose the Syndicates."

Minerva nodded. "Maybe it's time you tell him what you're up to. Luca's not stupid. I'm sure he knows more about Jonathan than he's letting on and all that security he's putting around you doesn't seem like he's that loyal to his Syndicate brethren."

"Yeah, that's what I've been thinking and I almost told him, but it still doesn't change the fact that he's with Ciara."

"But he's not with her by choice, right?"

"No, he calls her his obligation and that worries me too. He's never said what's at stake for him. So, I don't know how deeply he's tied to that obligation and what it has to do with his grandfather's leadership."

"It's probably money or some sort of bloodline bullshit. We've done enough research on cults and secret societies to know it's one of those two things or both."

"True." She scoffed. "But it still doesn't change anything and if I'm honest," she said, hanging her head. "I'm scared to feel like this. I haven't been with anyone since Jonathan and I'm not sure I can."

"I know, but that doesn't mean you should run away from him," Minerva said, sliding her hand to her hip. "If Luca wasn't tied up with Ciara and we weren't doing this thing tonight, would you be so afraid to see where it could go with him?"

"After everything that happened with Jonathan, I think I'd still be scared but." A small smile tugged at Nadia's lips. "No, I wouldn't be afraid to try with him."

"That's what I thought. He's a good man and he's worth keeping in your life even if it's just to be friends."

Chapter 27

"What man?" her father grumbled from behind them.

Nadia's eyes grew wide and she slowly turned her head to face his stern green eyes set against his stoic brown face. "Oh, it's no one. Just a friend, dad."

He raised a thick eyebrow and crossed his arms over his black 'licensed to grill' apron. "I hope he's not a friend like that other fuck, or do I need to come out there with my shotgun?"

"No." She laughed softly. "It's not like that."

"Better not be," he said and his eyes softened. "I worry about you out there. I wish you'd stay here. I can get you a job at the racetrack. They're looking for someone to do their marketing."

"You know I'm not going to do that. I've got a great job and I'm safe. You don't need to worry."

"And we're not talking about that," her mother huffed with her hands on her hips and her brown eyes glaring at her father as she walked in from the patio. "I told you not to bring that up, Charlie. My girls are home and I want to enjoy my time with them *without* talking about that asshole, okay?"

Her father hung his head. "Yes, dear. I'm sorry, but you know how I am."

"I know. That's why I came in here to remind you. Now, get those buns on the grill," she said, nudging her father out the door before she crossed the kitchen with her bright yellow dress swishing around her legs. She leaned against the counter with a grin lighting up her brown cheeks. "When your father's not around, I want to hear about this new friend," she said, patting Nadia's hand. "I think it's good you're letting someone new in your life."

"Thanks, mama."

"Mm-hm and I want to hear about that boyfriend of yours too, Minerva."

"Of course, Mama Rae," Minerva giggled as the doorbell rang through the house.

"Oh, that must be my friends from the theater." Her mother clapped her hands in excitement. "I want you to show them the routine you put together for that showcase you did last year. They'll love it!" she exclaimed as she whisked away from the counter to the door. "Put the rest of the food out. I'm so excited. It's the first big cookout of the summer!"

Minerva shook her head. "Ever the entertainer. Guess we're putting on a little show tonight."

Nadia rolled her eyes, picking up the bowl of salad and a few plates. "Does that really surprise you?"

"Nah, your mom can point out all the flaws in it like usual," she snickered. "It's good to be home, huh?"

"Yeah, it is." Nadia smiled as she sat the food on the long wooden table under the veranda of flowering vines wrapped around the black wood. She watched her father finish toasting the buns and heard her mother chattering to her guests as they walked through the house.

Her parents were like night and day nowadays. Both bubbly and humble in their own way. Her father used to be a bit more carefree, but after what happened to her, her father's concern for her well-being seemed to overpower his once free spirited attitude. But her mother, while she was a complete mess after Jonathan attacked her, she seemed to bounce back to her happy-go-lucky outlook.

Nadia needed this. She couldn't tell either of them what Jonathan had been doing to her lately or what she was planning to do. She wanted them blissfully unaware that she was going to dismantle a decades-old secret society just to get Jonathan out of her life.

And it had to work or else one day she might not have these joyous moments with her family if Jonathan had his way.

***

Nadia and Minerva slipped quietly out of her parents' home, keeping their footsteps light as they walked down the gravel path onto a woodland trail leading up a hill away from the lake.

"Alright, let's go over it one more time," Nadia said as she turned on her headlamp to illuminate the path.

"Okay. When we get to the house, you're going to jam the security system with that thing," Minerva said, pointing to the small black rectangular device on Nadia's waist. "That will unlock the house. Then we'll go in through the back door into the kitchen," she said, pulling her phone from her pocket. "I've got the blueprint on my phone and Gregory's office should be in the first hallway on our right."

"Yep. When we get into the office, I've got the USB that should extract the files from his computer. That should take no more than five minutes. Once that's done, we leave the way we came. We should be in and out in twenty minutes. Plenty of time before the jammer turns everything back on."

"Right, and what's our back-up plan?"

Nadia took a deep breath, touching the taser on her hip. "We shock the shit out of any guards in our path and get out through the garage."

"Or lock ourselves in one of the crawl spaces in the bedrooms."

Nadia grasped Minerva's hand. "Let's hope we don't have to do that."

"I know, but we've got Raquel on speed dial if we get stuck. We just have to hide and we know how to fight if we need to. I'm not afraid to use my taser."

Nadia's heart thumped as they reached the top of the hill, and Gregory Rodawson's sprawling colonial estate sat bathed in moonlight above Seneca lake. They crouched beside a thick oak tree next to a glittering pond and peeked through the brush at the manicured lawn around the house.

"You ready?" Nadia said, turning off the small flashlight strapped to her head.

"I'm ready."

"Okay, the security system should be off… now," Nadia said, sliding the switch on the device. The security lights to the house flickered for a moment, went dark, and quickly turned back on.

"That's the signal. Let's go," Minerva whispered as they ran across the lawn. Their feet crunched on the pebbled path leading to the backdoor of the house.

Nadia's hand shook as she gripped the silver door handle. She looked at Minerva, with her chest heaving. "I hope that fucking jammer worked," she said, twisting the handle. She held her breath as the door opened and she waited for alarms to go off.

"Holy shit, we're in!" Minerva whispered in excitement as they tip-toed into the kitchen.

Nadia checked the little green light on the black device on her hip and a smile spread across her face. "All that grueling practice Raquel put us through has paid off."

"Yep, and here's the map," Minerva said, thrusting her

phone out with the blueprint and their highlighted track through the fifteen bedroom house. "I still can't believe he doesn't have any guards patrolling this place on site."

"I know, right? Let's get what we came here for and get out before the jammer trips the security system," Nadia said as she followed the path on the phone into the hallway.

"Could this guy be any more full of himself? Not one family photo, just portraits of himself and that god-awful Syndicate cross." Minerva scoffed from behind her as she aimed her headlamp at an oil painting of Gregory dressed in black and gold robes, sitting against a burgundy background with his chiseled stoic face glaring into the distance.

Nadia smirked. "That doesn't surprise me. Come on, his office should be down here," she said, turning the corner and walking straight into a hard chest. She yelped, stumbling backward, dropping the phone as an arm snaked around her waist, stopping her fall. She cried out in panic and drove her fist into her captor's stomach.

"Oh, hell no!" Minerva roared, charging into them. They crashed into the wall and slid to the floor in a struggling heap. "Nadia, get his hands! Use your taser!" she grunted, wrapping her arms around the captor's neck.

"I'm trying!" Nadia snarled as she wrestled with his flailing arms.

"Hey I got the–what the fuck is going on!" a man yelled from the open office door.

"Nadia! Minerva! It's me!" The captor choked out from Minerva's crushing grip around his neck.

"Luca?" Nadia paused, pushing the brim of his black cap from his head.

"Cam?" Minerva whispered, releasing her hold around

Luca's neck. "Ohhh fuck."

"Oh fuck is right. You said you were going to New York!" Cameron huffed as he pulled Minerva up from Luca's back.

"I am in New York."

"I thought you meant the *city,*" he seethed.

"What the hell are you doing here?" Luca said, standing from the floor and scooping Nadia up with him. The annoyance and rage in his husky voice and his piercing glare in the dim light of their headlamps sent a shiver of fear down her spine.

"I-I can explain."

"You fucking better," he seethed as his watched beeped in alarm on his wrist.

"You're out of time. Take what you can. Security's been alerted. They're surrounding the house." Jack's voice sounded from Luca's watch. "We'll cover you. Get back to base."

"Shit! Let's go," Luca said, swiping Nadia's phone from the floor before he grabbed her arm and pulled her down the hall behind Cameron and Minerva, running into the office.

"Where are you going? We can get out through the garage!" Nadia yelled, tugging on Luca's arm.

"This way is safer. I know my grandfather's house," Luca hissed as he grabbed a black bag from the mahogany desk. He swung it over his shoulder before he pushed her through the open bookcase as heavy footsteps beat against the floor outside the office.

"Fuck, how did this happen?! We still had time!" Nadia whispered as Luca locked the bookshelf in place behind them as guards burst into the room.

"It doesn't matter. We just need to get out," he said, taking her hand.

"All clear!"

"We've got movement outside!" The guards' muffled voices called beyond the wall as Luca and Nadia ran through the darkened space and down a flight of steps. Nadia's heart was pounding against her ribcage as fear and regret prickled down her spine.

"What the fuck is this place?" Nadia whispered as they ran through a stone chamber that looked like something out of a medieval throne room complete with iron sconces, stone slab round table and twelve high-backed wooden chairs with a golden Coptic cross glinting in the dimly lit room. This wasn't on the blueprint. She studied it too many times to miss an underground chamber of this size.

"Somewhere you shouldn't be," Luca grumbled as they fled under a stone archway to a small cove where Minerva and Cameron were huddled and peeking outside through a small caged window in a thick wooden door.

"They're fucking everywhere," Cameron said, holding Minerva under his arm and watching the security guards patrol the back of the house.

"Give it a minute. Jack will distract them. When they do, take the path back to the house," Luca said and turned his angry eyes on Nadia. "I hope you didn't leave your car anywhere near here."

"We walked. We're not that stupid. We actually know what we're doing," she snapped back, matching the annoyance in his eyes.

"Could've fooled me." He scoffed, opening his backpack. "Take off your headlamps."

"Can we just get out of here?" Minerva hissed as they

shoved their head pieces into his backpack. "Then you two can say whatever snarky shit you want."

"Mm-hm, I got a lot of shit I want to say," Cameron mumbled as a flare lit up the night sky and gunfire rang out in the distance. The guards' footsteps crunched across the gravel as they took off yelling out commands as they ran toward the commotion.

"That's our cue! Get to the path," Luca said as Cameron pushed the door open. He ran out into the clearing, tugging Minerva behind him. Luca grasped Nadia's hand as they ran up the few steps to follow them and her foot caught on the last stair. She cried out as her knees cracked against the jagged gravel. Luca cussed under his breath as he scooped her up, throwing her over his shoulder. "The fuck would your clumsy ass do if I wasn't here?" he hissed as they disappeared into the thick cover of the woods at the edge of the graveled path.

"I wouldn't be in this situation. You ruined my mission again!"

"What do you mean *again?*"

"Over there!" A voice called from behind them.

"Shit. Hold on," Luca grunted as he ducked into the brush on the edge of the trail. "Crawl down the bank and get into the water," he said as he shrugged her off his shoulder.

"What?"

"Just do as I say!" he said, shoving his backpack into the base of a wide oak tree and nudging her forward.

Nadia slid down the muddy bank and bit back a gasp as she slipped into the cold murky pond at the bottom. Luca was quick to follow her and covered her with his body. Nadia bit her lip to stop the whimper that itched to escape her at the feel of the slick and slimy tree roots and mud touching her bare arms and smooshed against her back.

"Hold your breath. We're going under," Luca murmured against her ear. She didn't have time to think before he pushed her under the gnarly tree roots in the gently rippling water. She wrapped her arms and legs around Luca, burying her face in his chest and ignored the tickling feel of the grass swaying in the water.

She clenched her eyes shut and listened to Luca's beating heart to calm her rising anxiety. This wasn't how she'd planned this night to go. It was supposed to be a quick, in and out job. It wasn't supposed to turn into an escape from Syndicate guards. She didn't even get close to what she'd come for.

"All clear!" The muffled voice of the guard yelled above them and shook her from her thoughts. Luca peeked his head above the water before he pulled her up and Nadia sucked in a gasp of air.

"Are you okay?" he whispered, brushing her matted curls from her face.

"I-I want to g-get out of here," she stuttered as her body shivered against him and the fear of what they'd just escaped crashed down on her.

"We will, just hold on to me," he said, pushing away from the roots and sliding her to his back. Nadia molded herself to him and gripped his shirt between her fingers as he climbed back up the bank. Luca picked up his bag and ducked across the path into a sloping hill of tall grass leading toward the lake below. "They'll be headed to my house next. I've got a place we can hide."

"What about Nervy and Cameron?" she mumbled, pressing

her face against his neck.

"They'll be fine. My guards know what to do."

Tears mixed with the droplets of water beading on her face and she choked back a sob itching to burst through the panic swelling in her chest.

"We're okay, ka'u pua. We're almost there," he said as he slipped into a thick cover of trees and brush. He carried her across a small pebbled brook to the back of a small cabin a few feet above the lake. He gently sat her down and held her around her waist as he pushed open the door to the wooden cabin.

Luca turned on a small lamp next to the door and sat his bag on a dusty plaid green couch. Nadia crossed her arms over her chest and shivered as she looked around the room full of fishing lines hanging on the wall, the wide window overlooking the calm lake waters, and a small pellet stove in the corner of the room.

"There's not much here besides a bathroom. I can start a small fire to dry our clothes but we'll have to wrap up in blankets," he said, closing and locking the door. "I should patch up those cuts on your knees too."

Nadia looked down at the rips in her Lycra pants and the puddle of water around her feet. She was too shocked and cold to feel the stinging pain of the gashes across her skin. Luca touched his fingers to her chin, lifting her face to him. "And then you can tell me what the fuck you were doing breaking into my grandfather's house."

Chapter 28

Wrapped in a plaid blanket around his waist, Luca hung their dripping clothes from a small line in front of the burning pellet stove while Nadia's teeth chattered above the whirring of the fire on the couch behind him.

"Are you warm enough?" he said, looking over his shoulder at her, shivering under the thick gray wool blanket she was wrapped in.

"I will be," she said, pushing her drying frizzy curls from her face. "I didn't realize you had so many tattoos."

"I don't show them off very often, for obvious reasons," he grumbled, picking up the first aid kit on the wooden coffee table and sitting on the couch next to her.

"Because of your scars?"

"Mm-hm," he said, lifting her legs over his lap and easing the blanket to the side to assess the gashes across her knees. Anger washed over him again and he fought the urge to lose his shit at her for putting herself in danger.

"Well, I think your ink is beautiful."

"Thank you," he murmured, dabbing antiseptic over the drying blood on her knees. "I'd explain them to you, but right now I want to know what the hell you were doing tonight."

"It's a long story." She sighed. "And I didn't plan on explaining this to you half naked."

"I didn't plan on saving your ass either." He looked up from her knee and glared into her sheepish green eyes. "And we have all night."

Nadia looked away from him to his hands over her legs and took a deep breath. "I've been investigating the Syndicates for a while now. Since the court threw out my evidence that Jonathan was still stalking me two years ago. They brushed it off as me being paranoid, so I decided nothing was going to stop him unless I did. The Syndicates were the ones who made it damn near impossible for him to spend any time in jail and they enable him to treat women the way he does, so I figured I'd take down the whole society to stop it."

Luca's hands shook and his heart sank as he placed a band-aid over her knee. "So, was being my friend and getting close to me part of your plan too?"

"Not initially." Nadia slid her hand over his as tears welled in her eyes. "I didn't plan on having anything to do with you. My source told me I could get the information I needed on the Syndicates from your company, so that's why I took the job at Shola."

Luca scoffed, pulling his hand away from her. "And then you met me and thought you'd use me to get to my grandfather?"

"Yes." She nodded, clenching her fists in the blanket and his heart sank even further.

How could he be so stupid to think her feelings for him

were genuine? She was just using him and playing on his emotions like Ciara.

"I thought you were just like the rest of the sick fucks involved in that society, but when we talked after what Ciara did to you, I knew you weren't one of them." She shook her head and wiped her tears. "I could see it in your eyes that you were trapped by them just like me."

His heart stopped its heavy descent into a pool of doubt and a flicker of hope peeked through his dismay. "Why didn't you say anything?"

"I didn't know if I could trust you then but after I spent more time with you and met your family, I don't know, I felt guilty for liking you and I didn't want this to cause you any more trouble than you were putting yourself in because of me." She sighed. "I-I was going to tell you after this weekend if I found what I needed. I figured I could at least give you a warning before I ousted the Syndicates." Her lip trembled as she blinked back her tears. "I'm sorry. I know how this looks, but I didn't want to use you and I never set out to do that."

A small smile tugged at his lips as hope and relief washed over him at her confession and the truth brimming in her watery green eyes. He slid his hand to her cheek and wiped a lone tear rolling down her face.

"Why are you smiling?"

"Because I thought for a moment, I put my trust in the wrong place and you don't have to apologize for protecting yourself." He shook his head, pulling his hand away from her face. "You're brave, ka'u pua. I'm in the society and I don't have the balls to do what you and Minerva did tonight without protection." He chuckled softly. "I'm glad you were honest with me. I don't like knowing you thought about using me like that, but I can understand why you would." He sighed. "And I should be honest with you too."

"About what?"

"Why I was there tonight and why I want to take down the Syndicates too," he said, placing a band-aid over her other knee and took a deep breath before he told her the story of his mother and father's forbidden love. How his mother turned her back on the Syndicates and her duty to marry Arnold Dagenham and uphold the strength of the Rodawson bloodline.

"I never understood why my parents were so adamant about my sister and I being surrounded by bodyguards or why my mom was so upset when we first met our grandfather until we moved to Boston ten years ago. That's when I was told about the Syndicates, my duty to follow in my grandfather's footsteps and right my mother's wrongs by marrying Ciara to fix the deal my grandfather made with the Dagenhams."

"I had a feeling it was something like that," Nadia murmured. "So, what's at stake if you just walk away?"

Luca smirked. "My grandfather holds the deeds to my family's businesses, including my Tutu's land. He's also threatened on numerous occasions to auction Lacey and my mother off in the Juliet circle if I don't do what he says."

"What the fuck? He'd do that to his own flesh and blood?"

"He doesn't consider Lacey and I Rodawsons. We're others to him because of our Native Hawaiian blood and he doesn't really acknowledge my mother, either. He just deals with us because my aunt and her family passed away in a plane crash years ago. I didn't know them, but my cousin Mathieu would've been his chosen successor if he didn't die. So, everything is on my shoulders and like you, I plan to destroy my grandfather and the Syndicates to free my family from this shit."

"God, that's so fucked up."

"Yeah." He sighed. "And I'm sorry I didn't tell you the truth before, but I'm not used to talking about this with anyone besides Cam or my guards."

Nadia shook her head and slid her hand over his. "You don't have to apologize. I understand, but why haven't you told your family what you're doing?"

He squeezed her hand. "My parents would freak out, and Lacey would want to help. I just feel like the less they know, the safer they'll be."

"But what about you?"

"What do you mean?"

Nadia slid closer to him, and he tensed up when she placed her hand over his chest. "You have scars all over you from the burden you're carrying for them. Who's going to keep you safe?"

"I… I don't really think about that." Luca looked down at her small hand spread over his inked covered scars. She didn't hesitate to touch him or look at him in disgust at his marred skin. He slowly wrapped his fingers around hers. It wasn't often that he felt comfortable being bare chested like this, nor did anyone ask him about his safety.

His family cared about his well-being, but he'd always been a natural protector and the one to shield them from how he really felt. "I don't want anyone to carry this burden. My parents deserve the small happiness they have and my sister doesn't need to be wrapped up in this either."

"What about your happiness and what you deserve? You didn't create this problem for yourself."

"No, I didn't, but I'm the one in the position to get us out of it. I don't want to put them in danger because of me. It's bad enough I've told you," he said, bringing her hand to his lips. "And what about you? Does your family know you're involved in trying to take down an organization as dangerous and powerful as the Syndicates?"

Nadia shook her head. "No, but I don't have a choice. If I don't do this, I'll be running and hiding for the rest of my life. I told you I was tired of living like that and I don't expect you to take on my problems too. My fight isn't yours."

He kissed her palm. "I can respect that."

She raised an eyebrow. "I feel like there's a 'but' coming."

He laughed softly. "But, I don't want you to do this alone and you can't because I potentially have the information you need."

A smile tugged at her lips. "Is this where you blackmail me into letting you take over my mission?"

"No, I understand the importance of you having control over the demise of your abuser. What I'm proposing is that we do this together."

Her bright eyes grew wide. "Mr. Underworld, the great protector, is going to willingly allow his pua nani to join in his dangerous mission? I'm surprised at you."

"We're after the same thing and I'd rather know what you're doing than find you in a fucked up situation like tonight," he said, tangling his fingers in the hair at the base of her neck and pressing his forehead against hers. "You scared me. If I wasn't there…" He closed his eyes and shuddered at the thought of what those Syndicate guards would've done to her and Minerva.

"I know," she whispered, sliding her hands to his cheeks. "I didn't think security would've been alerted so quickly and we knew what we were doing, but I'm glad you were there. I'm not sure we would've made it out, but I'd never let them give me back to Jonathan or take Nervy into one of their sex rings. We would've fought hard."

"I know." He kissed her cheek and stared into her determined orbs. "So, can we do this together?"

"Yes, and how about no more secrets between us, either?"

"That's fair." He sighed. "Then I should tell you that soon I'm going to have to make it official with Ciara."

Her hands dropped from his face. "What do you mean? Like… marriage?"

"Yeah." He looked away from her. "Ciara will be back next week and I'm meant to propose to her at the Shola Gala after we come back from Osaka next month. I'm hoping whatever information I picked up tonight will be enough for me to stop it, but this means I won't be able to see you very much outside of the office and we'll have to be extra careful about working on our mission."

She nodded. "We can do that. We can speak in code or Hawaiian. I'm getting better at it." Nadia slid her hands to his cheeks again. "You don't want to marry Ciara and I'm not going to let Jonathan continue to dictate how I live my life. We'll find a way to be free even if we got nothing tonight."

"Ka'u pua nani…" His heart swelled at her utter determination, but if nothing came out of the books and files he swiped from his grandfather's house, then he was fucked and all the work he'd done this far would be for nothing. He and his family would be tied to the Syndicates until he found his grandfather's coveted blacklist.

"I'm serious, Mr. Underworld. You've been through enough and so have I. If nothing comes out of the information, we figure it out *together*. I'll get Raquel to do –"

His eyes grew wide. "Raquel Armentaros? Is she your source?"

"Yes… why?"

He chuckled softly. "She's one of mine too."

"Really? She's such an asshole." Nadia shook her head and laughed. "She's the one who encouraged me to get to know you. Knowing damn well we were working toward the same thing."

Luca raised an eyebrow. "You think she had an ulterior motive?"

"What? Like she knew we'd end up falling in love with each other?" Nadia scoffed and her eyes grew wide. "I-I mean… um." She cringed. "I didn't mean love."

Luca laughed softly and hope spread through his veins. "Are you falling in love with me?"

She bit her lip and shook her head. "I… I don't know. I've never been in love to know if I am."

"Me either," he said, sliding his hand to her cheek. "But I think I'm falling in love with you too."

Nadia wrapped her fingers around his wrist and her lips curled into a small smile. "I'm scared to feel like this and I hate that we're both wrapped up in something so big, but when I'm with you I'm not afraid to face it." She pressed her forehead against his. "I know I said we need to respect our boundaries, but I'm not going to let Ciara, Jonathan, or your grandfather stop us from being free. We deserve better than this. We deserve the chance to see what this is between us and I... I want to fight for that."

Her words washed over him and pierced straight into his heart. He didn't know if Raquel had some sort of hidden plan to bring them together, but God, if he wasn't thankful for this. Nadia felt the same strength from him as he did from her. They were the light to their darkness and he truly believed they could do this as long as they did it together. "I want to fight for that too." He sighed, caressing her cheek with his thumb. "I want you, Nadia," he whispered. "I want all of you, but this won't be easy," he said, pulling away from her to look into her warm sea green depths. "I might have to... do things with Ciara as much as I won't want to and I don't want to hurt you."

"I know and I won't like knowing you're with her." She sighed, looking away from him. "I knew having feelings for you would be complicated, but you're still my friend and until we get out of this, that's all we can be, anyway."

"That's true," he said, sliding his fingers to her chin and turning her face to his. "We'll always be friends and I'll always protect you. No matter what happens, I won't let Jonathan hurt you."

Nadia laughed softly. "I told you I don't want you taking on my problems."

He grinned. "Technically, I'm not. Jonathan is a Syndicate problem and it's my duty to take care of it. I'm pretty sure he just broke into my grandfather's house tonight and I doubt the Grand Duke will be too happy about that."

A laugh sputtered from her lips. "Oh, you're savage."

He slid his thumb over her bottom lip. "I can be, especially when it comes to keeping you safe."

"I like that." She smiled, leaning into him, her lips nearly grazing his. "Can I kiss you, Mr. Underworld?" she whispered.

"You never have to ask me that," he murmured, closing the gap between their lips and sliding his tongue into her mouth to drown in the sweet taste of her. Without thinking, he slid his hand up the inside of the blanket to her hip and felt three jagged scars over her otherwise smooth skin. They were like claw marks angled toward the v between her thighs.

Nadia gasped, grabbing his hand and pulling away from him as she tugged the blanket back over her thigh and the artful black and white feathers on her skin. "Sorry, I-I haven't...we should probably stop."

"You don't need to say sorry. I shouldn't have done that."

"No, it was fine. It's just I haven't really been with anyone since Jonathan attacked me and I'm..." She looked away from him. "I'm still self-conscious of my scars."

He nodded, knowing that feeling all too well. "I'm self conscious of my scars too," he said, taking her hand and placing it over his chest. "Do they bother you?"

She shook her head. "No. They have a sad beauty about them with your tattoos," she said, tracing a black pattern over his pectoral.

"And I'm sure yours have a sad beauty about them too," he said, kissing her cheek. "What I'm trying to say is, you don't have to feel weird about them with me. I'd never judge you for them and I shouldn't have touched you like that, not when we shouldn't even be this close. When we're free to explore each other the right way, we'll take this slow."

She looked up at him and the unease in her eyes melted away as she placed a kiss on his cheek. "Thank you."

"Anything for you. We should probably get some sleep," he

said, sliding her legs from his lap. "You can have the couch. I'll sleep on the floor."

"Are you sure?"

"Yeah, me and this floor are old buddies." He chuckled, getting up to turn out the light. "My dad always got the couch when we came out here to fish," he said, grabbing another blanket from the back of the couch and settling on the floor below her. "Are you comfy?"

She yawned. "Mm-hm. Good night, Luca."

"Good night." Luca closed his eyes and listened to the soft cackling of the fire. When he broke into his grandfather's house tonight, catching Nadia there and having another heart to heart was the last thing he thought was going to happen, but he was glad for it. At least they knew where they stood with each other.

"Luca?"

"Hm?"

"Will you tell me about your tattoos?" Nadia asked, and the light caress of her fingers over his shoulder left a warm tingle on his skin.

He slid his eyes open and looked up at her lying on her side, looking down at him with her tired eyes. "Like a bedtime story?"

She chuckled softly. "Yeah, something like that. They look like they have a good story behind them."

"Mm, they do, but will you tell me about yours too?"

Nadia rested her head on her arm while she traced her fingers over the tightly patterned bands of pointed spear-heads and ocean waves just below his collarbone. "I designed mine to represent my identity," she said, yawning. "Black and white feathers represent my father's Black Chitimacha heritage and they hang from a band of twisted rope like my mother's twisted gold bracelet. It's been handed down to the eldest daughter in her family since they were brought to this country and it's the only thing that ties us to our African ancestry."

"That's beautiful," he said, threading his fingers through hers. "It must be rare to have a family heirloom like that and I didn't know you were indigenous too."

"It is and now you know." A tired smile graced her lips. "So tell me the story of your tats."

"Alright," he said, sliding her hand below his pectoral to the mandala style hibiscus in the center of his abs. "This one means purity and I got it to cover scars from one of Ciara's more violent attacks," he said, moving her hand over his heart. "The patterns over my chest, shoulders and arms were done for my uhi to honor my Tutu after he passed away. I come from an old line of ali'i nui and the ocean waves and spearheads are symbols of my family's lineage. They mean courage, life and death."

"So you are a king," she murmured. "Are you the ali'i of your family?"

He chuckled softly, turning on his side still holding her hand in his. "There aren't any chiefs on Kaua'i, but I'm the one my Tutu left in charge of his lands."

"Mm, then why did your sister call you Ekeali'i? Is that your real name?" she said, closing her eyes.

"Eke is my middle name and my Nonna adds the ali'i for endearment. Lacey just likes to tease me about it."

"Is your Nonna still alive?"

"Mm-hm." He sighed, closing his eyes.

"I'd like to meet her," she mumbled before a soft snore left her lips.

Luca's eyes slid open and he looked up at Nadia. "She'd love to meet you too," he whispered, kissing her hand and closing his eyes again. She didn't know what it meant for her to say that, but he was going to have to tell her the truth about who he was.

The stories his Nonna told him about how the ali'i from the past found their wahines floated through his mind. It wasn't because their joining was predestined, but because a queen always revealed herself to a king in small subtle ways like the way Nadia made him feel like he could spill his soul to her.

A slight smile curled over his lips. One day he'd take her to meet his Nonna and maybe he'd be introducing her as the next wahine of Koa Maile.

Chapter 29

*Nadia slammed a thick manila folder of incriminating evidence on the judge's desk and glared at Jonathan's neatly coiffed blonde hair and amused brown eyes smirking at her from across the courtroom. She didn't care. Today, he'd finally get what was coming to him. "It's all there. Every dirty thing he and the Syndicates have done. They've *killed* people, Your Honor."*

"Oh we know, Nadia. Everyone knows." The gray-haired judge chuckled as he threw the folder in the burning receptacle at her feet. "We're all Syndicates and Jonathan has come to collect you."

Nadia's heart clenched and dropped to the pit of her stomach as Jonathan stood, straightening his freshly pressed stone-gray suit. Smoothing a hand over his golden locks, the smirk on his face grew wider into a deadly smile. "You'll always be mine, kitten."

Smooth, soft leather wrapped around her neck and she choked out a breath as the icy metallic touch of the kitten charm grazed her skin. The walls of the courtroom closed in as thick cuffs slithered around her ankles and wrists and the fresh pine scent of the punishment chamber poisoned her senses.

Chapter 29

A whip cracked against the walls and she clenched her eyes shut. "No," she whimpered, struggling against the chains that bound her to the smooth hardwood floor.

The whip cracked again and Jonathan's ominous footsteps stole her breath as he grasped a fistful of her hair and yanked her head back. The cruel gleam in his dark brown eyes sent fear clawing down her spine. "I've been waiting a long time for this," he said, raising his arm to crack the whip against her skin.

A scream tore from Nadia's lips as she jerked awake and was engulfed by Luca's muscular arms. She dug her nails into his chest, shuddering as she choked back a sob burning in her throat.

"You're alright, ka'u pua. You're safe," he whispered against her head.

She pressed her face against the hollow of his neck and took a few deep breaths to calm her racing heart. That was the first time Jonathan caught her in her nightmares. He always came close, but she always escaped.

"I'm sorry," she whispered. "That one was bad."

"I know," he said, kissing her head. "You've been restless for the past hour. My singing didn't work this time. What happened?"

"Jonathan caught me," she murmured. "I tried to get him and the Syndicates convicted in court, but the judge threw everything out. Then I was…" She shuddered, closing her eyes, willing herself to forget the sadistic look in Jonathan's eyes. "I was in the punishment chamber."

Luca slid his hand to her cheek, wiping the stray tear rolling down her face. "That won't happen. Not with the amount of security you have around you."

"I know." She sighed. "I think I'm still scared that whatever dirt we have won't be enough. He'll never go to prison for what he's done."

"Sure he will." Luca tilted her face to him. "We might not have enough for the whole society, but I'm sure I can conjure up something to put his ass in prison for you, if that's what you want."

"I do, but I also want him to suffer the same torment he's shown me," she said, looking away from him. "I know I shouldn't want that because no one should have to go through what I did..."

Luca caressed her cheek with his thumb. "I think it's normal for you to want Jonathan to suffer. Don't feel guilty about that. I'd say he deserves it and I'll gladly help you achieve that."

Nadia stared into his warm depths and drank in his tenacious sentiment. "Thank you." A small smile tugged at her lips as she wrapped her fingers around his wrist. "This savage side of you is disturbingly sexy."

"Is it?" He grinned. "Maybe it's because you're just as ruthless."

"No." She shook her head. "I'm pure sunshine."

"Mm, that gut punch you gave me last night would suggest otherwise."

She giggled and the last bit of anxiety tugging at her heart melted away. "Sunshine with a bite then."

"Okay." He chuckled softly, kissing her forehead. "Are you good, ka'u pua?"

"I'm good, Mr. Underworld."

Luca reached for his watch on the coffee table, squinting as he read the notifications before he clasped it around his wrist. "Cam and Minerva are on their way with Jack. Hopefully, they bring some coffee with them. We can fill them in about our joint mission, and then I'll take you back to your parents. Is that alright?"

"Yeah." She nodded and bit her lip. "Can you and Cam do Nervy and I a favor and have breakfast at my house? It'll be easier to explain our whereabouts with you two. My dad won't like it, but my mom will be too excited to entertain new guests to care."

"Of course. I'd love to meet your parents." He smiled. "I don't mind being your scapegoat, but how angry will your dad be that you were out all night with me? I need to be prepared for this."

"Um." Nadia laughed. "He might pull out his shotgun."

Luca's eyes grew wide.

"But he won't use it," she quickly added. "Just get him talking about cars and he'll settle down."

Luca raised an eyebrow. "Right, so do I tell my guards to stand down or be on alert?"

"They can stand down." She giggled. "He's a big teddy bear, really."

"Mm, okay. If you say so," he murmured. "We should probably get dressed. I'll try not to look too disheveled meeting your parents."

"It's fine," she said, sliding out of his arms to pluck her dried clothes from the line above the pellet stove. "We'll just tell them we were camping, which technically, isn't a lie."

"True," he said, getting up and a rumble of laughter left his lips as he took his clothes off the line.

"Why are you laughing?"

Luca shook his head. "It's just that this weekend has been a mess and in a weird way I'm happy about it."

Nadia smiled, leaning up on her tiptoes to kiss his cheek. "I'm happy about it too and I'm glad we talked about things again."

He wrapped his arm around her waist and kissed her forehead. "Me too."

***

After reuniting with Cameron and Minerva and talking to Jack about their new collaboration, Jack took Luca's backpack to sift through the files he stole from his grandfather in hopes it contained the Syndicates' coveted blacklist.

Nadia pushed any thoughts of Jonathan and the Syndicates' demise from her mind as she listened to Luca and her father swap stories about their love of cars.

"I don't think I've ever seen your father talk this much," her mother murmured, patting her hand before she turned her bright brown eyes on them and clapped her hands. "Alright! I want to know how all of you met."

"Nadia met Cameron and Luca at work and then we all met at a nightclub one night." Minerva shrugged.

"That's it? No, come on. Then I want to know how you and Luca met," she said with her eyes full of mischief as she looked between Nadia and Luca.

Nadia groaned, sliding a hand over her face while Luca laughed across the table. She hadn't thought about how they met since the day it happened. It pained her to relive that embarrassing moment.

"Do you want to tell this story or should I?" Luca said, leaning back in his chair with his eyes dancing in amusement.

"You can tell it," she muttered.

"Alright." He grinned, looking at her mother. "Nadia and I met on her first day of work. She was running late and I was minding my business." Luca laughed. "And she nearly tackled me when she crashed into the elevator."

Laughter sputtered from her mother's lips as she squeezed Nadia's hand. "Oh no, baby girl."

"Yep." Nadia sighed. "I was a hot mess with confetti in my hair too because *Minerva* got me drunk the night before!"

"Don't blame me for that! I didn't force you to get drunk," Minerva snickered, as she popped a strawberry in her mouth.

"Yeah, but that's not as funny as the time you missed your seat at the shareholders' meeting," Cameron said as he and Luca roared with laughter.

"Do you see what I have to work with?" Nadia huffed, waving her hand at the two giggling men across from her. "These fucking assholes!"

"When you told me about it I was picturing a room full of old men, but knowing you were in there with Cam and Luca makes it even worse," Minerva cried with laughter.

"And all of that made you want to be friends with my daughter, huh?" Her mother chuckled and shook her head.

Luca grinned at Nadia and wiped his tears. "Yeah, I just thought I really needed someone with a savvy ability to trip on air in my life and it's been going well so far."

Her father raised an eyebrow. "It better keep going well," he grumbled and patted the shotgun leaning against the chair next to him. "I like you young men, but those are my girls and I won't hesitate to use Miss Susie on you. I'm overlooking you keeping them out all night this time."

The humor on Luca's and Cameron's faces fell as they nodded to her father. "Yes, sir."

Nadia looked at her mother and Minerva before the three of them fell out in a fit of laughter.

"Hey now, I'm serious. These two need to know I'm not fucking around."

"Dad, stop. They're fine." Nadia laughed, shaking her head.

"I know." A smile cracked through his stern expression. "You two wouldn't have brought them around if they weren't."

A proud grin lit up Luca's face. "I'm glad you think so, Mr. Coleman."

"Mm-hm, but the next time you boys are in town I expect you to pick these young ladies up properly before you go out camping."

"Absolutely. We don't want to meet Miss Susie again," Cameron said as his eyes flickered to the gun. "We value our lives."

Nadia's father nodded. "As you should."

The morning bled into the afternoon, filled with their light banter and joyous laughter as Nadia's parents told Luca and Cameron embarrassing stories of her childhood with Minerva, but Nadia didn't care. She was happy to hold on to this moment and hopefully the next time she came home she could tell her parents the truth about what she'd been up to and that she was finally free.

She looked over at Luca who was helping her mother carry their empty dishes inside. And maybe when she came back, she and Luca would be exploring what they could be.

Chapter 30

Luca shuffled into his bedroom with a towel wrapped around his waist, glad to have a shower after that five-hour drive back from Watkins and the long talk he and Cam had creating a basic plan of action for the evidence he hoped they had. They just needed everything to fall into place for it to work.

Luca took a glance at his phone lying on his dresser, checking for any missed calls from Nadia. Gordon was going over her new security system and Luca offered to be with her, but she said she wanted to check everything out on her own first. He respected that. It was her home and it was good for her to get to know her team without him around.

Shrugging on a pair of black sweatpants and a white tee before flopping on his bed and closing his eyes, Luca yawned. He was exhausted. Even though the break-in didn't go exactly to plan this weekend, he was almost glad it didn't. He wouldn't have met Nadia's cheerful mother, who could've been her twin if it wasn't for Nadia's green eyes and auburn hair she inherited from her stern, but gentle giant of a father.

Luca chuckled to himself, resting his hands over his chest. He liked them a lot and he respected her father's fierce protection of her.

A series of vibrations buzzed on Luca's dresser and a tired smile spread over his lips as he got up and reached for his phone. His smile turned into a grim line as he eyed the name scrolling over the screen. He knew this was coming. Taking a deep breath, he answered the call.

"Hello?"

"You were right. The Hatch boy is making plans to undermine me." His grandfather's gruff voice seethed over the line.

"What do you mean? What happened?"

"The stupid fuck broke into my lake house Saturday night."

"Shit, how the hell did that happen? Did he take anything?"

"He jammed the network long enough to get in. I'm not sure what he took. There are a few ledgers missing from my office, and my agents are going through my hard drives to make sure none of the files were taken. He's a son of a bitch."

"Fuck," Luca whispered. "How do you know it was Jonathan?"

"He may have had the tools to break in, but he's no fucking spy. That idiot lost his hat during his escape. Fucking J. Hatch stitched right on the inside." His grandfather scoffed and a devilish grin tugged at Luca's lips that his planted evidence worked. "Not only that, my camera's caught his car driving up and down the road before and after he broke in."

Luca's heart clenched as he sat down on the edge of his bed. "What a dumb fuck," he said, rubbing a hand over his face. Jonathan or one of his fucking goons was watching Nadia that night. They must've lost her when she and Minerva went into the woods. Lucky for him, they were stupid enough to get caught on his grandfather's cameras.

"I know. I'm pissed my guys let him get away, but he had help from his fucking lackeys. They had my guards running all over my estate. I have half a mind to fire all of them for that fuck up."

"Mm, to be fair to them, I'm sure Jonathan had this all planned."

"Yeah, he just didn't think he'd get caught. I've invited Jonathan's father to the meeting this week. I think it's time we threaten the whole family for his blatant disregard for my authority."

"You sure you want to threaten them before knowing if Jonathan took anything of value?"

A rumble of laughter spread through the phone. "Even if he did, there's nothing in those ledgers, and the files on my hard drive are heavily coded and encrypted. It'll take him weeks to crack into them and by that time, I'll have his family pressed firmly under my thumb. They won't fucking dare use anything against me."

Luca raised an eyebrow. "What do you plan to do?"

"I'm going to let you question Jonathan about the Shola breach and do what you'd like with him. Then I'll strap his father up to the whipping post and beat him until Jonathan confesses. After that, I'll get one of my government buddies to freeze their assets and I'll swoop in to save them by taking their businesses as collateral so they'll have nothing left but to do as I say. That's how you make a good example, son."

And that was precisely why no one dared to mess with Gregory Rodawson.

"This will be a good bonding moment for us," his grandfather said. "I remember my first meeting like this with your great grandfather. It's how I learned what it took to be the Grand Duke."

"Yeah, but is it really necessary to torture Marcus?"

His grandfather chuckled softly. "I asked the same question of my father when I went through this, and yes. Marcus is Jonathan's emotional attachment. I'm betting he'll be ready to confess after a few whips to his father. You don't have to do that part. I'll take care of it. I just want you to watch and pay attention, okay?"

"Alright."

"I know we've had our moments in the past, but lately I'm feeling really confident about you taking over for me. I thought for sure you'd be the one to attempt to overrule me, but I'm happy to see that I was wrong. You really are loyal to your Rodawson blood."

"I'm honored to hear that. I'll try not to let you down."

"I know you won't. Your family's livelihood still depends on it, but maybe after you marry Ciara I'll remove those threats."

"I think we'd all appreciate that."

"Mm, we'll see," his grandfather murmured as if something distracted him. "I've got to go. I ordered a Juliet to calm my nerves. I'll speak to you soon."

Luca fought back the bile rising in his throat. "Yeah. Enjoy yourself."

"Oh, I will," he said and hung up.

Luca ran his hands through his hair as he fell back on the bed. "Fuck," he said, pulling at his hair as his heart pounded. He couldn't care less that his grandfather was going to destroy the Hatch family. What fucking unnerved him was Nadia being followed. That could put a wrench in things if Jonathan brought up her name and, even worse, if his men had any pictures of her near his grandfather's house.

Luca sat up with his phone in hand and speed dialed Jack. "Jonathan's men were tailing Nadia this weekend –"

"We know."

"What?"

"While we were on lookout at your grandfather's we recognized the plates on the car that kept circling the area. I had a few guys go check it out and they took care of him."

Luca hung his head. "Did he have any photos of Nadia?"

"A few around her house, but none near your grandfather's. It's fine. There's no evidence that any of you were there."

"Okay." He sighed. "Why didn't you tell me? I had to find out from my grandfather."

"I'm sorry, but it wasn't a pressing issue. We took care of it and we figured his car driving around would benefit you. I told Gordon to speak with Miss Coleman about it and the need for her to have her team around her."

"Good, and it definitely helped me. My grandfather is livid. The Hatchs are on his shit list."

"As they should be. They deserve a beating for the shit they do with those poor women in those sex circles, especially for what Jonathan did to little wahine. I-I mean, Miss Coleman."

Luca chuckled at the endearment that slipped out of Jack's mouth. "I'm sure Nadia wouldn't mind being called little queen. I'm glad you like her that much."

"I do. She's good for you."

"Yeah. Do you think the team can get everything decoded before the Gala?"

"We've got everyone working on it. They said they need

at least two weeks. Should be done when you're back from Osaka."

"Perfect. I want a meeting with you, Gordon and Raquel at the end of the week. Cam and I have a plan."

"I'll get it sorted."

"Good," Luca said as his phone beeped to indicate another call coming in. He pulled his phone away from his ear and smiled at the name illuminated on the screen. "I've got another call. I'll speak to you soon."

"Alright," Jack replied as Luca answered the call.

"Hey, ka'u pua. What's going on?"

"I'm done with my security induction."

"Yeah? How'd it go?" he asked, lying back and staring up at the sun shining its last rays of light across the ceiling.

"It went well. I like my team. It was good to hang out with them, except for the lecture I got from Gordon about the importance of having them around me. I guess one of Jonathan's guys was following me this weekend." She sighed. "I should've been more vigilant about that."

"Yeah, but my guys took care of it. You have nothing to worry about, but Gordon's right. You need to have your team around you."

"I know, and I'm glad they'll be staying here. I feel a lot safer now."

His heart swelled with pride that he could provide that for her. "That's good."

"Yeah," she murmured. "So, I guess this is the last time we can talk like this, right?"

"Not necessarily. We'll just have to come up with a code when we want to call each other."

"Okay, how about na'u nō 'oe?"

Chapter 30

"I need you, huh? I like that." Luca chuckled. "You're getting really good at Hawaiian. Are you studying on your own time now?"

"Maybe," she said, and he could hear the grin in her voice. "If I ever get to meet Nonna Shola, I want to be fluent."

"She'd love that, but she speaks English too so you don't have to be fluent."

"I know, but I want to be. You know I like languages."

"I do." He sighed, turning on his side. "So, did I make a good impression on your parents?"

"You did. My mom adores you. My dad is skeptical, but he said he likes your taste in cars."

Luca grinned. "I'll take that."

"Yeah, you're alright with them," she said and he could hear the exhaustion in her voice.

"You should get some sleep."

"Probably," she mumbled. "Would you mind reading to me?"

He chuckled softly. "I never mind that. Which story would you like tonight?"

"Mm, Bound to You."

"Oo, we're going Alpha romance, huh?" he said, sitting up to reach for the black book with a painting of a white wolf on the cover on the small shelf beneath his bedside table.

"Only because you remind me of Kayden."

Luca scrunched up his face at the thought of the white Alpha wolf whose duty was to protect his pack but feared he'd never find a mate to love and lead with. He could see the similarities Nadia saw between them, but he shook his head and scoffed. "I'd be a black wolf, thank you very much."

"Of course you would," she said, yawning. "Just read to

me."

"Alright," he said, slipping under his blankets and resting against the headboard. "You comfy?"

"Yeah, my pillows are a decent substitute for you," she murmured.

"Same," Luca said, sliding down and cuddling a pillow under his arm.

Nadia chuckled softly. "We're sad."

"A little, but it's all we've got at the moment."

"True." She sighed. "Read to me, Mr. Underworld."

"As you wish, ka'u pua nani."

Jack's nickname couldn't have been more precise for Nadia. She was a little queen in her own right, and she was definitely the queen of his heart. There was no one else he wanted to carve out a space in his life for but her.

Luca was dreading the moment he'd have to reunite with Ciara. It was easy to pretend with her when he didn't have anyone else he cared for like Nadia. He refused to hurt her, and he'd have to keep Ciara from touching him. Even if he wasn't falling in love with Nadia, he couldn't bear the thought of Ciara's hands on him ever again.

He just needed to avoid her advances for a month, at least.

Chapter 31

Ka'u Pua » Pōmaika'i i po. E pekele. «

Good luck tonight. Be safe.

Luca » Mahalo, ku'uipo.«

Thank you, sweetheart.

"Who's kay you poo-ay?" Ciara asked, leaning into his shoulder and her nauseating lavender perfume made Luca's stomach churn and sour at the scent permeating the car.

"It's kah-oo poo-ah and that was my cousin," he said, sliding his phone into his pocket. Ciara had been back for all of two days and he wasn't sure if he could last a month. His only saving grace was being able to speak to Nadia in Hawaiian and their upcoming trip to Osaka.

"Oh, you know I don't understand your Hawaiian side. Thank God your parents named you something normal," she said and slid her hand over his. "Is everything okay in… um. Where are you from, again?" Ciara asked, sliding her hand over his.

He curled his hand around hers and hated the way her long

bony fingers felt against his skin. They were always so cold. "Kaua'i and yes everything is fine."

"Good." She nodded. "I know this probably isn't the time to bring this up, but I want to talk about what happened between us. I still feel like you're hesitant around me and I don't want that."

Luca sighed. "I don't want to talk about that tonight."

"I know, but when are we going to talk about it? How many times can I say sorry to you? I've given you more time and space and you're *still* not over it," Ciara said, pulling her hand away from him.

He glared at her pouting face. "How long would it take you to get over being raped?"

She scoffed. "Don't say that word." she said, looking away from him. "It was one time and I didn't mean it. I want us to get past this." Ciara clenched her hands in her lap. "I had a lot of time to think about things in Texas and…" she trailed off, looking up at him with tenderness swirling in her brown eyes. "Luca, I'm in love with you."

Fuck.

"I don't know what to say to that."

"I hope one day you'll feel the same." She laughed softly. "My dad told me you're planning to propose, but I want you to do it because you want to. Not because you have to," she said, sliding her hand to his cheek. "I want us to try for real this time."

"The problem with that is I still don't get a choice. We'll be married whether or not we love each other." Luca wrapped his hand around her wrist and pulled her hand away from his face. "I'm doing what I need to protect my family. Maybe one day I'll be comfortable with you again, but love is something

I can't give you."

Ciara blinked back the tears pooling in her eyes and pursed her lips. "I'm not giving up that easily. You'll learn to love me and we'll be the Syndicate power couple like my father and your mother were supposed to be. You'll be the Grand Duke and I'll be your first lady." She looked away from him to the three-storey brownstone with the golden Syndicate cross carved into its bricks shining proudly on Beacon Hill. "This is the life we were born into," she said as Jack got out of the car and opened the door for them.

Ciara stepped out and her gold heels clicked on the pavement while her long black skirts and wisps of her blonde hair swayed in the warm evening breeze. She smoothed a hand over her hair and looked back at him. "Just accept it like I have."

He'd never accept this life.

Luca slid out of the car and pushed down his rising anxiety. "I'll try," he said, placing her hand in the crook of his arm.

"Thank you," she said, leaning up to kiss his cheek before they walked up the stone steps to the black suited doorman. He opened the thick ominous black door to the wide exuberant foyer of the Syndicates' meeting house.

A crystal chandelier glittered above the men and women dressed in sharp suits and elegant cocktail dresses each with their prestigious gold Coptic crosses pinned to their attire. Luca smiled and nodded hello to a few members as he scanned the room for the two honored guests.

"Oh, have the Hatchs leveled up while I was gone? Dad didn't mention they'd be inducted tonight," Ciara said, and Luca followed her gaze to two men standing at the far end of the lobby. His face went slack as he eyed Jonathan's golden tanned skin and tall stature dressed in a navy blue suit. Jonathan laughed in the small group around him and smoothed a hand over his glossy golden blonde hair before he turned his dark brown eyes to them. An arrogant smile curled over his lips as he nodded in their direction.

Luca clenched his teeth and looked away from him to Ciara who gave the sick fuck a small wave back. "I'm going to head into the chamber."

"You never do like to mingle," she said, plucking a glass of champagne from the tray of a passing server. "I'll be waiting for you after your big boys meeting." She chuckled and kissed his cheek.

Luca turned away from her and took the stairs down to the basement. He tugged out a blank black card from the inside of his suit pocket and flashed it over the scanner of a steel door. The lock released and opened to a stone hallway with iron black sconces lighting the path.

"Good evening, Mr. Shola," the guard beyond the door greeted. He stepped forward and patted Luca down as was customary to attend a meeting with the Grand Duke. Satisfied Luca wasn't armed, the guard tugged a black hooded robe hanging from the golden hooks on the wall and handed it to him. "Your grandfather is waiting for you."

"Thank you," he said, shrugging the robe over his shoulders as he continued down the hall and pushed through the doors to a room that looked as if it was erected from the medieval era, complete with iron sconces and rows of wooden benches sat in front of a long stone table. His grandfather was sitting in one of the high-backed chairs at the table scribbling some notes on a pad of paper.

He looked up at him, and a smile graced his lips. "Are you

ready for this, son?"

"More than ready," Luca said, crossing the room to take a seat in the high-back chair next to him.

"Good," he said, lying his pen over his notes. "My guards informed me that my list was taken."

Luca raised his eyebrows. "The blacklist?"

"Yes. Jonathan will never crack it, but that is the ultimate act of treason against me," he seethed.

"Then show no mercy, grandfather," Luca said as a devilish smile curled over his lips and fought the urge to laugh at his good fortune. He had the fucking list which would forever pin the mystery of its missing state on Jonathan until Luca could take the society down with it.

***

"Good evening, brethren," Luca's grandfather said, clasping his hands.

"Salutations, Grand Duke," the black robed Syndicate men replied from the wooden benches before them, raising their glasses of preferred spirits while a hazy cloud of cigar smoke hung over them and filtered into the vents above.

Luca kept his eyes trained on Jonathan sitting proudly on the front benches as if he were someone of importance. He could see why Nadia fell into Jonathan's trap. He was a handsome man who carried himself with charisma and pride, and he didn't seem to care that some Platinums looked down their noses at him. Everyone loved the Juliets he provided for them, but that shadowy profession would always be looked down upon by the society.

"Grand Duke, if I may, I'd like to ask a question." An older gentleman spoke up, raising his gold tipped cane in the air.

"You always do." His grandfather chuckled, waving his hand toward him. "I think I might know what it is, but state your question, brother Bianchi."

The elder cleared his throat and stood from his seat. "We weren't aware we'd be inducting any new Platinum members at the roundtable. Many of us would like to know why the Hatchs are here tonight?" he said, taking his seat amongst murmurs and grumbles.

"Ah yes, I'm glad you asked," Luca's grandfather grinned. "I invited them last minute because Luca and I have some matters to discuss with them that pertain to all of you," he said, turning to Luca with a devilish gleam in his dark brown eyes. "My grandson will lead this meeting tonight."

Luca smiled at the shocked expressions around the room as he stood from his chair. "Does anyone have a problem with me taking the reins for tonight?"

"No, take your place young Duke. It's about time you show us how you plan to lead," Brother Bianchi said to the murmurs of agreement around the room.

"Good, because tonight we're going to talk about loyalty," Luca said and nodded to the two guards standing at the door. "And provide you with a reminder of why you don't fuck with the Rodawsons." He glared into Jonathan's eyes as the two guards lifted him from his seat.

"Wh-what's going on?" Jonathan said as he struggled against the ironclad arms of the guards, strapping him to a lone metal chair in the center of the room.

Luca crossed the room with his hands behind his back and stood over Jonathan. The fear in his eyes filled him with delight as the guards fitted Jonathan's hand into an upright metal device designed after a cigar cutter. He was going to enjoy taking some revenge for his pua nani.

Luca smirked and turned away from Jonathan to address the gawking Syndicates. "Platinums, what is the golden rule all loyal Syndicates abide by?"

"Never attack, undermine or deceive a fellow brother," the members chanted in unison.

"Precisely," Luca said and turned back to Jonathan, shaking in his seat. "Mr. Hatch, did you or any of your lackeys hack into Shola Enterprises' mainframe?"

Jonathan shook his head. "I didn't do it for the reasons you think."

Luca raised an eyebrow. "So you admit you hacked into the network?"

"Yes," Jonathan said, and his eyes hardened. "I was tracking one of my kittens and I have a right, according to the Juliet by-laws, to monitor her whereabouts."

"That may be true, but the by-laws don't allow you to ignore our cardinal rule, does it?"

Jonathan's mouth flattened into a grim line. "No."

"I didn't think so," Luca said, taking a slow walk toward him. "Platinums, what do we do to those who break the cardinal rule?"

"Whatever the afflicted deems necessary." They responded.

"Right again, brethren," Luca grinned as he squeezed the razors against Jonathan's ring and middle fingers, drawing a trickle of blood. "Do you have anything to say for yourself?"

Jonathan didn't flinch or cry out, but kept his icy gaze focused on Luca. "Yes, why don't you tell the Grand Duke why you're really doing this? How you're trying to save your ass from being caught with my kitten."

"Why the fuck would I care about one of your women?"

A sinister smile spread across Jonathan's lips. "I don't know, but you seem to like her more than your girlfriend."

"Luca, what is he talking about?"

"I don't know," he sneered.

"Oh, he does. The young Duke has been lying to you about his dealings with *my* property and I have proof."

"He's lying," Luca said through gritted teeth.

"I'm not. Show them, dad."

Luca's heart pounded as he looked at Marcus Hatch. He was always careful about shielding Nadia from watchful eyes when she was with him, but a small twinge of doubt rose its head when Marcus stood from the bench holding up a small black USB fob.

"It's all here, Grand Duke. We've got video and audio."

"Mm, from the hacking? It better be worth it," his grandfather said as he nodded to the guards to take the USB from Marcus.

"After you see this, I'd like a formal apology and for my family to be granted Platinum status. I'd also like Luca's fingers to be on the chopping block," Jonathan said with a smug grin.

"Those are high demands for evidence we haven't seen," Luca's grandfather said, nodding to the guards. "Show it to us and restrain Luca."

"You don't need to do this," Luca said, as two guards pulled him away from Jonathan and zip tied his hands behind his back.

"Just a precaution. You know the rules. Jonathan made a fair rebuttal. Put it on the projector."

Sweat beaded on Luca's forehead as the screen made a slow

descent over the stone wall. He looked over the gathering's quizzical expressions and caught the eyes of two guards peering inside the door. One held up his fist with his pinky and thumb extended and waved it slowly.

"No, you need the blacklist to do that and I know where to find it."

Luca's eyes grew wide as he turned his head to the projector and stared at the screen in disbelief.

The Syndicates gasped.

"Treason!" a voice bellowed from the crowd.

His grandfather shook his head with his brown eyes full of malice. "I always knew it."

"This... this isn't right! None of that is true!" Jonathan roared as he struggled in his chair.

"So, that's not you and your father making plans to undermine me? The Grand fucking Duke?" Luca's grandfather roared, standing from his seat.

"Grand Duke, I assure you we would never do something like that. This... this is out of context!" Marcus said, holding up his hands.

"Disgraceful Marcus. How could you? I trusted you. I brought you into this society," Arnold said, shaking his head.

"Release my grandson and take these two imbeciles to the whipping post," his grandfather said, and his eyes softened on Luca. "I'm sorry I ever doubted you."

"It's alright," Luca said, rubbing his wrists and holding back the laugh that itched to burst from his mouth. "I suspected as much from the likes of them."

"Yes, you did, and I have more proof that what we've witnessed on this screen was just the beginning. You and your fucking lackeys stole from me, Jonathan."

"I didn't steal anything!"

"So you weren't at my lake house over the weekend?"

The color drained from Jonathan's face. "I-I wasn't there, but my men were tracking –"

"I've heard enough," Luca's grandfather seethed as he turned his eyes on the whispering Syndicates. "Let this be a lesson for all of you. I guard our secrets with the utmost respect and care. It's why you trust me and the Dagenhams to look out for all of you, but I don't take kindly to treasonous scum."

"Hear! Hear!" the brethren roared.

"All those in favor of stripping the Hatchs from their Gold member status say 'aye'."

"Aye!" Luca shouted with the rest of the gathering, and a devilish smile spread across his lips.

"You did this! You fucked with my files, Luca!" Jonathan yelled as the guards lifted him from the chair and dragged with his father to the inner chambers.

"Shut your goddamn mouth," his grandfather said and back handed Jonathan across his face before turning back to the Syndicates. "This meeting is adjourned. Enjoy the drinks and cigars upstairs, gentlemen. Luca, come with me."

"Yes, grandfather." Luca nodded and turned to the emptying room. Arnold was shaking his head in disgust as he followed behind the sympathetic brethren, giving him condolences that he couldn't have known the kind of man Marcus was. Luca looked over the group to the two guards standing just outside the doors. They gave him a small nod with knowing grins splayed across their lips.

Turning away from the gathering, Luca followed his grandfather into a smaller chamber where Jonathan and

Marcus were tied to the whipping posts in the center of the room. He couldn't hide the smug smile on his face. The guards he'd planted among his grandfather's years ago had done him proud tonight, and he couldn't wait to tell Nadia about this remarkable turn of events.

Chapter 32

Nadia bit her thumb as she paced back and forth in her living room. She checked her watch and heaved a deep sigh.

"Miss Nadia, everything is going to be fine," Gordon said as he munched on the cookies she made to keep her mind off Luca's meeting.

"What if it's not? It's almost midnight and he hasn't called or messaged me. What if something happened?"

"Those Platinum meetings can go on for hours and if something happened, we'd know about it by now. Mr. Shola's never left unprotected," he said, patting the sofa cushion next to him. "Come sit, have a cookie and then you can recite your presentation to us again."

Nadia sighed again and flopped down on the couch next to him. "I don't get how you guys can be so calm about this. Jonathan is sly and Ben probably warned him about this."

"Ben? Ha!" Henry laughed as he closed her refrigerator. "That piece of shit. It didn't take long to break him," he said, handing her a can of soda and swiping a cookie from the tray on the coffee table before he sat in her reading chair and took a bite of the sweet treat. "Damn, Miss Nadia, you make a mean chocolate chip."

"Thank you, but what do you mean Ben was easy to break?"

Henry looked at Gordon and he shrugged. "It's fine for her to know."

Nadia raised an eyebrow. "Know what?"

"Well," Henry said, running a hand over his curly black hair. "After Mr. Shola suspended Ben, he told a group of us to basically torment him for what he did to you. He usually doesn't give out orders like that, but we all knew what to do." Henry grinned, finishing the cookie in his hand. "We used our special ops skills. Hacked his shit, fucked with his finances and did a little waterboarding until Ben spilled all this shit on the Hatchs."

Nadia's eyes grew wide and a laugh sputtered from her lips as she slid a hand over her mouth. "Oh, shit."

"Mm-hm." Henry nodded, reaching for another cookie on the coffee table. "Mr. Shola's fine tonight. Don't you worry about him."

The smile fell from her lips. "Yeah, but I still wish he'd message me," she said, checking her watch again. "I know you keep telling me he's fine, but I just have a bad feeling." She'd had it all day and if she were honest with herself, the nagging worry hadn't left her since Luca told her he was going to confront Jonathan.

Gordon placed his hand over hers and she looked up at his kind blue eyes. "He's safe, Miss Nadia. He'll contact you when he can."

She took a deep breath. "Okay." She nodded and rubbed her hands over her leggings. "Are you sure you guys want to listen to the presentation again?"

"If it makes you feel better. We've got plenty of cookies," Henry said, leaning back in the chair. "Tell us again why Ono Medical should choose Shola Enterprises as its choice for international marketing and PR."

Nadia picked up her note cards from the table and stood in front of the fireplace. She took a deep breath before she recited her presentation. Even though she had every aspect of it memorized, it made her feel better to focus on work than let her mind drift to what dangers Luca might be facing.

Her guards might have gotten Ben to spill the Hatch family secrets, but Nadia knew Jonathan. He was a master at gaslighting and there was nothing he wouldn't do to keep himself free to terrorize her.

After three practice runs of her presentation, Gordon and Henry had fallen asleep during her fourth recitement. She picked up the half eaten tray of cookies and tucked them in with blankets in their respective places on the couch and chair. She loved all the members of her team, but she'd gotten really close to Gordon and Henry lately and it wasn't unusual for them to knock out in her living room. They were like two big brothers she'd never had and she was thankful for them being around her.

She turned off the light in the living room and trudged into her bedroom to flop down on her bed. She checked her watch and stared at the ticking seconds on the clock. It was two in the morning and still nothing from Luca.

Tears pricked the corners of her eyes as she reached for her phone on the bedside table and just as she was about to tap a message to him, a notification scrolled across her screen.

Mr. Underworld » Na'u nō 'oe. Are you up?«

Chapter 32

Nadia wiped the tear rolling down her cheek and smiled as she sat up and called him.

"Hey ka'u pua nani. I didn't think you'd still be awake." Luca's deep voice rolled through the receiver.

"I couldn't sleep. I was worried about you," she said, picking at a thread on her floral comforter.

"I told you there was nothing to worry about," he said, chuckling softly and the sound of it calmed her nerves.

"So, everything went okay?"

"Yes, and no. Are you comfy? Because this story is a good one."

"You're making me nervous," she said, snuggling under her blankets and hugging a pillow to her chest. "But I'm comfy now."

"Alright. So, once upon a time there was a man named Jonathan who tormented a beautiful Goddess named Nadia, but what he didn't know was a fearsome King named Luca protected that Goddess."

Nadia giggled. "Cut the bullshit, Mr. Underworld."

"What? This is an epic tale, ka'u pua."

"Tell me what happened at the meeting!"

"Okay, okay. I'll be serious," he said, clearing his throat and her eyes grew wide as he told her the events that occurred at the meeting. How Jonathan accused Luca of secretly having an affair with her and the evidence Jonathan and Marcus had that Luca was cheating on Ciara with her. "Not gonna lie, I was pretty freaked out at this point because I knew Jonathan had been watching you and I know I was careful when we were together, but there was still a chance he could've had something."

Nadia raised an eyebrow. "You seem pretty chill about this,

so I'm assuming he didn't have anything?"

"Oh no, he had something," Luca said and she could hear the grin in his voice. "I'm not sure how my guards did it, but they switched out the evidence on Jonathan's USB with every conversation he and his father had about overthrowing my grandfather as Grand Duke."

Nadia gasped, sitting up. "Shut the fuck up."

"I told you this was a good story."

"Yeah, but holy shit. I never would've thought Jonathan would try to take down the Syndicates."

"No, he was planning to become the new Grand Duke."

"Fuck. What did your grandfather do?"

"God, what didn't he do?" Luca sighed. "They were stripped of their Gold member status and got the shit beat out of them on the whipping posts. After that, my grandfather and I spent the last few hours talking about next steps to safeguard the society and tomorrow, I'll start the paperwork to take over my new engineering company."

"Oh my God." Nadia laughed. "So, you're going to own Hatch Engineering?"

"Mm-hm, it'll be Shola Engineering when I get around to making the changes. That little perk was an apology gift from my grandfather for doubting my loyalty to the society."

"Damn, that's some savage shit." Nadia grinned. "Does this mean I don't have to worry about Jonathan anymore?"

"No. The Hatchs still control the Juliet circles. For all the Syndicates' shady dealings, no one wants to tie their name to that industry and since you were one of Jonathan's kittens he still has a right to monitor your whereabouts under the Juliet by-laws."

Nadia pursed her lips and gripped the blanket between

her fists as rage rolled over her. "So even though Jonathan was caught attempting to overthrow your grandfather, he'll still be free to do whatever he wants to me because of some fucking by-law?"

Luca was silent for a moment before he heaved a sigh. "Yeah. The safety of Juliets or kittens isn't a priority for Syndicates. Jonathan will be free to do as he pleases in that realm."

"That's fucked up, Luca."

"I know."

"And now Jonathan's going to be livid for what you did to him," Nadia said, sliding a hand over her face. "This is worse," she said as tears pricked the corner of her eyes. "Confronting him made it worse."

"That was always going to be a risk and we talked about this."

Nadia bit her thumb and closed her eyes. "I know, but it still doesn't make it any easier."

"You've got plenty of protection around you and if or when Jonathan tries to come after you, you and your team will be ready, and that day may never come. Jonathan was pretty fucked up."

"Good, but we still don't know if we have the blacklist and he'll still own me because of those fucked up laws."

"He doesn't own you, Nadia," Luca said, with a deadly bite in his grizzly tone. "And we have the blacklist."

Nadia's eyes grew wide. "What?"

"My grandfather said the list was stolen. He's going to comb through Jonathan's systems looking for it, but I'm confident my specialists can decode it before he realizes Jonathan doesn't have it. We're going to take them all down.

We're going to be free."

"Yes we are," Nadia said, lying back against her pillows with a small smile on her face. "Have you figured out how you're going to break the news to Ciara?"

"I have a few ideas." He sighed. "She told me she was in love with me tonight."

"Oh." Nadia's heart clenched and a twinge of jealousy bit at her nerves. "What did you say?"

Luca chuckled softly. "That love wasn't something I could give her."

"And she was okay with that?"

"No, of course not."

"Did she… hurt you?"

"Not tonight, but I'm sure that's coming. She doesn't understand why I haven't gotten over what she did to me."

"They never do," Nadia said, yawning and hugging a pillow to her chest. "At least we'll be in Osaka next week. You'll get another break."

"Yeah, a whole week of freedom with you," he murmured. "I miss being with you."

A smile graced her lips and her heart swelled at his words. "Me too, but next week is about work and you better have your part of the presentation memorized, sir."

He laughed softly. "I do. You should get some sleep. I'm sorry I made you worry."

"It's okay. I'm glad you're safe," she said, closing her eyes.

"Nadia?"

"Hm?"

"Thank you for caring about me."

She smiled against her pillow, wishing it was him she was cuddling. "Thank you for protecting me, Mr. Underworld."

"Always, ka'u pua. Good night."

She sighed. "Night."

***

Nadia disconnected her laptop from her monitor and slipped it into her bag with the itinerary for the networking events at Ono Medical before she scanned her desk to make sure she wasn't forgetting anything she needed on the trip.

"Hey, Nadia, you got everything?" Cameron said from behind her.

She turned around to him. "Yeah, I think I do. Did you remember to print your itinerary, and do you have all your notes?"

"I've got it all right here," he said, patting his black laptop bag crossed over his shoulder. "Our plane tickets are at the airport. Luca has our hotel reservations and we just have one last meeting before we leave."

"Yes, we do. Raquel has been blowing up my phone about it all day."

Cameron let out a bark of laughter. "Yep, she's way too excited about this," he said, nodding. "Come on, let's get out of here."

"Um, Nadia?" Alex said, peeking around Cameron with his brown eyes full of concern.

"Yeah? What's going on?"

"Well, um, Miss Dagenham is here to see you."

Nadia flicked her gaze to Cameron and he rolled his eyes. "We're not available for any more meetings today."

"I told her that, but she insisted she speak to Nadia. You know how she is, Mr. Ramirez."

Nadia's phone buzzed in her pocket while Cameron and Alex were bickering over whether she needed to meet with

Ciara.

Mr. Underworld » Ciara's coming to talk to you about going to Osaka with me.«

Nadia » She's already here. Is this my jealous girlfriend talk?«

Mr. Underworld » Yeah. I'm sorry. «

Nadia » It's fine. I can handle it. I'll see you soon.«

"I'll talk to her," Nadia said over Cameron and Alex's chatter.

Cameron raised an eyebrow. "You sure?"

"Yeah, we have to keep our shareholders happy, right?" She shrugged. "I'll meet you in the garage."

"No, I'll wait for you," Cameron said, checking his watch. "She gets five minutes with you and then I'm getting you out."

"Okay, I'm sure I'll be fine," she said, grabbing her purse and swinging her laptop bag over her shoulder before following the two men out of her office.

Nadia eyed Ciara standing next to Alex's desk dressed in a short cream dress with her hair pinned up in a perfectly sculptured bun atop her head. She looked up from her manicured nails and her brown eyes filled with contempt. Nadia had been expecting some sort of threatening speech from Ciara. Luca told her she wasn't happy that he was going on this trip with her.

"Miss Dagenham, you wanted to speak with me?" Nadia asked, setting her bag behind Alex's desk.

"Yes, if you don't mind?"

"Of course not, but I don't have much time."

Ciara smiled, showing her pearly white teeth. "Oh, this won't take long."

"It better not. We've got a plane to catch, Ciara," Cameron

grumbled.

"I know that." Ciara rolled her eyes at him. "Is there somewhere we can talk in private?"

"The conference room is free," Alex said, pointing to the room across the hall with a frosted glass door.

"Thanks Alex," Nadia said, crossing the short distance and opening the door for Ciara. Nadia closed the door and sat across from her at the long black conference table. "So, what would you like to talk to me about?"

Ciara threaded her fingers together, and the slight smile on her face fell into a grim straight line. "I just want to get one thing straight with you before you spend a week with my boyfriend."

"Okay, and what might that be?"

"He's mine, and he doesn't want anyone else. So don't think for one minute you can take him from me."

"I'm not sure where this is coming from, Miss Dagenham?"

"I know you two had a *thing* a few months ago when he walked you home from a nightclub and I don't want you getting any ideas on this trip."

"Oh." Nadia laughed. "That won't happen and at the time I didn't know he was with you."

"Good," she said, leaning over her hands. "Because I know all about you, Miss Coleman."

Nadia's eyes grew wide. "What's that supposed to mean?"

Ciara smirked. "You're just one of those kitten whores and I can have you taken care of if you don't act right. Do you understand me?"

Nadia clenched her hands in her lap as her eyes grew as cold as the brown orbs glaring back at her. "I understand."

"Excellent, but just in case," Ciara said, digging into her

purse. “I thought you’d like to see this as an incentive to keep your hands to yourself.”

Ciara held her phone out to her and Nadia’s heart dropped to the pit of her stomach as she fought back the tears burning behind her eyes and the panic clawing at her spine. A naked picture of her gagged and bound in Jonathan’s punishment chamber stared back at her.

“I’ve got a nice little stash of these photos. They were a little gift from a friend and I’d hate for them to end up all over the internet,” Ciara said as she stood, sliding her purse over her shoulder. “I’m glad we talked. Good luck in Osaka. I’m sure you’ll all do great.”

The door of the conference room closed with a solitary click and Nadia wiped a lone tear rolling down her face. Jonathan was damn near incapacitated from his wounds, but he still found a way to torment her. How long had Ciara had those pictures of her?

“Nadia, you alright?” Cameron said, opening the door.

She cleared her throat and nodded. “I’m fine. Let’s go.”

Nadia was lost in her thoughts as she and Cameron traveled down to the garage. Ciara didn’t seem like she knew Luca was talking to her as much as he did or that they spent so much time together while she was away. She could be bluffing about how many photos she had, but one was enough and Nadia didn’t want to take any chances.

She bit her thumb. Those pictures getting out into the world would be devastating to her career, her family and herself. They were the one thing she couldn’t get her hands on before she ran away from Jonathan, and now they were in the hands of someone who couldn’t care less about using them against her.

Chapter 33

Luca slid his eyes open at the soft glow of light above him and his heart clenched at the worried look on Nadia's face as she sat biting her thumb while she read the notes across her knees.

"Are you okay?" he mumbled, sitting up on his elbow.

"Not really," she murmured, flipping a page in her notebook. "I can't sleep."

Luca checked the flight status on his watch. It was six hours until they landed in Osaka and Nadia hadn't slept since they got on the plane. "Are you still worried about the pictures?" he asked, sitting up in his seat. She told him what Ciara said to her and the photos she threatened her with.

"Yeah." She sighed. "I knew there was always a chance that Jonathan would do this and I should've tried harder to find them, but in the three years he stalked me, he never threw those pictures in my face or threatened to make them public and now Ciara has them."

"We don't know that for sure and our guards are on it," he

said, sliding his fingers to her chin and turning her face to him. "We won't go forward with the plan until the threat to your reputation is taken care of."

"I know, but I don't want to hold anything up, and what if they don't find all of it? I don't even know how much Jonathan has."

"They'll find it and there are other things that need to be done before we do this. You're not holding anything up. You know your safety is a top priority."

She wrapped her fingers around his wrist. "So is your family's."

"That's true, but we've been going through this for a long time. We can wait a little longer if we have to. I won't put you or anyone in harm's way for this," he said, caressing her bottom lip with his thumb. "And I don't want you worrying about it this week."

"I'll try not to," she said, but the worry never left her green depths.

"I mean it, Nadia. You worked too hard for this. Don't let Ciara get under your skin. She won't have those pictures long enough to do anything with them. You know I've got a guard on the inside at Jonathan's and my tech specialists already hacked her phone. We'll get everything."

"Okay," she said, and a small smile graced her lips. "I guess we can enjoy our free week together."

"Yes, we can." Luca grinned, sliding the notebook off her lap and sitting it on the tabletop beside her. "But you need to get some sleep," he said, wrapping his arm around her so she was cuddled under the crook of it.

"I don't sleep very well on planes."

"Mm, but you didn't have me to read to you," he said,

grabbing her favorite book from the tabletop beside him and clicking on the light above his side of their sleeper cubicle.

She turned off her light, stretching her legs along the foot rest and giggling as she snuggled against him. "You brought my boyfriend."

He pressed his lips against her head. "Of course I did," he murmured, opening Eyes of the Beholder to one of her favorite chapters. "I have all the tools to help you relax this week."

"Thank you."

"Anything for you, ka'u pua." He rested his head against hers and read softly from the pages. Luca had been looking forward to this trip since they came back from New York and he refused to let Ciara knock Nadia off her game or ruin their time together with her bullshit.

The blacklist was almost decoded. Raquel and Jack were working together on the logistics of the Gala, and Gordon was their security lead on the trip. Everything was in place so far. He just had to inform his family and make sure no one could tarnish his pua nani's reputation.

Ciara went too far with that threat. He thought about offering her compensation for the dire state she'd be in once he broke up with her, but fuck that. He didn't owe her a damn thing and he couldn't believe he was thinking of being that nice. She deserved to suffer just like the rest of them.

***

Luca enjoyed one thing about being in Osaka and that was waking up with Nadia in his arms every morning. They were exhausted every night after their packed schedules of networking engagements, tours of Ono Medical and meetings with senior management that they hardly had time to enjoy the small freedom of being together.

Luca couldn't hide the smile on his face as they presented their carefully crafted presentation to Mr. Ono and his team. Nadia was in her element in this competitive environment and it was so sexy on her. The way she delivered their strategic plans with ease, moved about the room with confidence, commanding the attention of anyone who laid eyes on her.

He was filled with pride and realized he wanted this contract for her more than the success it would bring to his company. She was amazing at this. She deserved this victory. Shit, she deserved to run her own damn marketing agency and if that was what she wanted, he'd make it happen for her.

"Thank you for that," Mr. Ono said, pulling Luca from his thoughts and gesturing for them to take a seat at the conference table amongst the management team. "I'd like to ask you one follow up question in order to evaluate your company's projection competency."

Mr. Ono waited for them to take a seat and pour themselves a glass of water before he tapped a finger over the notepad in front of him. "If I were to choose Shola Enterprises, I want you to tell me, at what date and time could I expect to see a net profit of five hundred million dollars?"

Luca tensed in his seat. Mr. Ono couldn't be serious. No company he ever dealt with asked for a projection for those kinds of figures and if they did, it was never for a specific date and *time.*

Nadia laughed softly next to him. "That's an excellent question and not something any company would be prepared to answer."

Mr. Ono nodded, but his dark brown eyes held a glimmer of amusement in them. "You're quite right, Miss Coleman, but I like to protect my companies' futures. Can you provide that kind of information?"

Luca held his breath.

"No, I couldn't provide that precise information," she said, and Luca's heart sank.

Nadia worked so hard for this and to be sidelined by a bullshit question like that pissed him off. Especially since there was nothing he could do or say to change the fact that they didn't prepare for it.

Nadia stood from her seat and picked up the projector remote.

Luca raised an eyebrow and flicked his eyes to Cameron who had the same puzzled look on his face.

Nadia clicked through a few slides on the screen, and Luca's eyes grew wide at the various graphs and charts projecting Ono Medical's profits. She walked up to the screen and studied it for a moment before pointing at a box on the graph. "February 5th, 2035 at midnight depending on your banking details."

Luca slid a hand to his chin to stop his mouth from falling open. When the hell did she do all of this?

"These numbers wouldn't be precise projections, as the economy and political climate could change. However, these would be your profits on your current plan if everything were as it is today," she said. "Would you like to know your profits on another date?"

Luca stifled a laugh and fought the urge to snatch her up in his arms and kiss the life out of her. Goddamn, she was fucking amazing.

"Thank you, Miss Coleman," Mr. Ono said and motioned for her to take a seat. "This concludes the presentation. We'll make our decision and call you with your results tomorrow." He smiled. "I'd like to thank you for coming and I hope you enjoy the rest of your time here in Osaka," Mr. Ono said as he and his team stood from their seats.

"Thank you, Mr. Ono." The trio stood and bowed to them.

Once they were out in the hall and far enough away from the conference room, Cameron looked at him and they looked at Nadia. "What was that?!"

She slowed her steps near the bubbling stone fountain in the lobby and turned around with a smug grin on her face. "What did I tell you two about Mr. Ono? He's meticulous and expects a company to know themselves inside and out."

"But when did you do those projections and why didn't you tell us about it? I almost shit my pants in there!" Cameron groaned and slid a hand over his face.

Luca nodded. "Mm-hm, I second that. Why did you keep us in the dark?"

Nadia shrugged. "Because that was my task. I'm the lead on this and it's my job to know any kind of profit projections my client asks for. No matter how crazy it is."

Cameron let out a bark of laughter. "You're unbelievable, Nadia."

"You are," Luca said with his heart bursting with utter adoration for her. "I'm so proud of you."

Her cheeks swelled as she shook her head. "Thank you, but we didn't get the contract yet."

"No, but after that I think it's fair that we officially make you Director of International Marketing and Investments, don't you think?" Cameron asked, nudging his arm.

Nadia's eyes grew wide. "What? Are you serious?"

"Yes, we are, but we can talk about that in more detail later," Luca said, sliding his hand to Nadia's waist. "I think we deserve a few drinks after that presentation and I know the perfect place for us to unwind."

Nadia smiled up at him as he guided her toward the exit to the car waiting for them. "I'd like that."

"So would I," Cameron said as he slid into the car. "I feel bad I haven't spent much time with Nervy on this trip."

"She knew what she was getting into when she agreed to come with you," Nadia said, following him into the car.

Luca grinned, ducking into the car after them. He couldn't wait to spend the evening enjoying the company of the beautiful and talented woman next to him.

Chapter 34

Nadia stood in the bathroom looking over her black jumpsuit in the mirror. The neckline dripped with a cascade of tiny diamonds that dipped low to her belly button and hinted at the salacious curve of her breasts. Chains of gold and diamonds hung from the thin straps on her shoulders and swept over her brown skin.

She smoothed the sides of her hair and patted the long braid that snaked down her bare back before slipping her feet into a pair of crimson red heels. "Where are you taking us tonight?" Nadia called to Luca as she walked out of their room to find him leaning against the bar at the small kitchenette in their suite.

Her heart thumped at the dark look in his golden eyes as he dragged his gaze over her. He pushed away from the bar and closed the gap between them. She bit her lip at his all black attire and the few buttons he left undone to show off a peek of his tattoos. Nadia ignored the fire that spread down her spine and pooled between her thighs.

"You look stunning, ka'u pua," he said, taking her hand and bringing it to his lips.

"Thank you. Your sister is an excellent designer."

"Mm, yes she is," he murmured, sliding a hand to her waist. "What did you ask me?"

She trailed her fingers over the lapel of his shirt. "Where are we going tonight, Mr. Underworld?"

He pulled her against his chest, and the earthy scent of his cologne teased her senses. "Somewhere we can dance and finally enjoy our time together."

Nadia slid her arms around his shoulders. "I'd like that and maybe later we can take a dip in that pool out there."

Luca dragged his fingers over the line of her spine, leaving a trail of fire and tingles over her skin as he pressed his lips to her ear. "I'd like that too, but first I want to beat you and Nervy in a battle."

She giggled, pulling away from him. "That's not going to happen."

Luca grinned, and she loved that playful gleam in his eyes. "We'll see."

"Yes, we will," she said, stepping away from him to grab her black clutch sitting on the counter. "You better not bust out those tired moves from Kani Kani."

Luca chuckled, sliding his hand to the small of her back and guided her to the door. "We won't, but you two better be able to freestyle."

Nadia smirked. "We're going to fuck you up tonight," she said as they walked out into the hall.

"I love this competitive side of you." Luca pulled her against his side and leaned down to her ear. "It's so damn sexy."

A devilish grin curled over her lips. "Have I been turning you on all week, Mr. Underworld?"

"Ka'u pua, you have no idea." His husky voice rolled over her skin and sent a delightful shiver down her spine.

"I think I do." She leaned back against him and thread her fingers through his. "Too bad we can't do anything about it."

He nipped her ear. "Says who?"

Her heart thumped as she looked into his heady golden eyes and a soft laugh escaped her lips. "You're being awfully bold tonight."

"Should I stop?"

Nadia bit her lip, shaking her head. "No." She was feeling bold tonight too and as fucked up as it was she'd been waiting for the moment they'd have a chance to be like this. She knew the week was going to be grueling and while she loved waking up in his arms, she couldn't help wanting to feel something more.

"Do you two need a moment before we go?" Minerva said as she and Cameron stepped out of the room across the hall from them.

Luca chuckled and kissed Nadia's forehead before he turned to Minerva. "No, we were just discussing how Cam and I are going to beat you ladies tonight."

Minerva looked at Nadia and burst into a fit of laughter. "That's cute, Luca."

"Hey now. We went easy on you at Kani Kani," Cameron said, squeezing her side. "We won't be that careless tonight."

"Okay, but you guys aren't dancing against the Furies tonight," Minerva said, smoothing a hand over her black and gold sequin dress and flashing Nadia a devilish smile. "We're the Sirens and we do shit a bit different than our crew."

Chapter 34

Luca raised an eyebrow and looked down at Nadia. "Is that so?"

"Yep, like I said, we're going to fuck you up tonight."

"Mm, these ladies are itching to get beat."

"Yes they are," Luca grinned as they made their way down the hall to the elevators and the group of guards waiting to escort them.

***

"Luca, why the hell did you suggest this club?" Minerva grumbled as they stepped out of the car in front of a long line of people eager to get into the sleek black building lit up with red lights illuminating the Makoa nightclub sign. "We're never going to get in."

"We're not waiting in that line. Luca owns this place," Cameron said, slipping his arm around Minerva's waist.

Nadia raised an eyebrow as they walked past the crowd. "You do?"

"I'm a silent owner. This is my cousin Ori's place," he said, threading his fingers through hers as they walked down a small alley beside the pulsing nightclub to a solid black door. "You need a code to get into VIP and the only way to get the code is from me or my cousin."

"Why does that not surprise me?" Nadia laughed softly. "I'm guessing Gordon has double vetted everyone in here too, huh?"

"Of course," he said, taking her hand as the door slid open and they walked up the black staircase of the mirrored corridor lit up by red recess lights lining the steps. The muffled music grew louder as they reached the crimson and gold doors at the top of the stairs.

Two burly bouncers dressed in black suits nodded to Luca

before they opened the doors and the bass filled music bled out into the corridor. A bright smile spread over Nadia's face as she scanned the bustling nightclub. Red and black lounge chairs surrounded the slick black dance floor lit up by bouncing strobe lights and iron black chandeliers hung from the ceiling lit up by faux candles.

"Eke! Cam!" a voice boomed over the swell of chatter and a tall, broad-shouldered man dressed in a black and red paisley suit moved through the crowd toward them. His long black hair was piled on top of his head and his golden brown eyes brimmed with joy as a bright smile graced his bronze cheeks. "It's been too damn long!" he exclaimed with his arms wide, pulling them both into a big hug.

Luca grinned. "It's so good to see you."

"I haven't seen you since you were that little punk in Menlo." Cameron laughed as the three men shared a few jokes between them.

"Aw, look at their little bromance," Minerva snickered. "It's so cute."

"Yeah," Nadia said and her smile grew. It was nice to see Luca like this. She loved seeing glimpses of the carefree and joyous man he said he used to be.

"And who are these gorgeous ladies you brought with you?" Ori said with his arms wrapped around Cameron and Luca's shoulders.

Cameron stepped away from him and took Minerva's hand. "This is my girlfriend, Minerva Jackson."

"It's lovely to meet you, Miss Jackson," he said, shaking her hand.

"You too, but you can just call me Minerva. You've got a nice club here."

Chapter 34

"Thank you, it wouldn't be possible without my generous cousin's support." Ori smiled at Luca before he turned his bright brown eyes on Nadia. "And you must be the infamous Nadia Coleman, right?"

"I wouldn't say I'm infamous, but yep that's me. It's nice to meet you, Ori."

"Oh, you're infamous. The whole Shola tribe knows about you."

Nadia raised an eyebrow and looked up at Luca's blushing face. "Do they?"

"They sure do, and I get to brag that I got the pleasure of meeting you first," Ori said, taking her hand. "You know this guy is a pretty big deal in our village, right? He can't just bring anyone there to meet our Nonna."

"Oh really? And why's that?"

Luca cleared his throat. "I don't think we need to get into our family history here," he said, wrapping his arm around Nadia's waist. "Why don't you show us to our table?"

"Yeah, of course. You've got the best table next to the dance floor and of course an open bar for my esteemed guests," Ori said, motioning for them to follow him through the dimly lit space, passed the bar that spanned the length of the room and overlooked the separate club below through tinted glass windows.

As they weaved through the sharply dressed crowd, Minerva gushed at the luxurious golden decor that adorned the candlelit tables, and Nadia noticed a few of the patrons bowing their heads in respect at Luca as they passed. She looked up at him and shook her head.

"Don't look at me like that, ka'u pua." Luca chuckled, squeezing her waist. "I'll tell you everything you want to know about my family, just not right now."

A smug grin curled over her lips. "As long as you know, Mr. Underworld."

"I do, but tonight I just want to dance with you."

"Me too."

Chapter 35

Luca watched Nadia and Minerva giggle to each other as they danced with a group of women. They found a crew in the short time they went to the bathroom and already found themselves lost in the bumping beat of the music. Luca didn't mind. He loved watching Nadia dance and she was a goddamn vision in that skin tight jumpsuit. The diamonds glowed on her brown skin; the fabric flaunted every bit of her beauty and he was enjoying the teasing look in her bright green eyes.

"So, you and that Dagenham chick are finally done? Or is that asshole still holding you hostage?" Ori asked as he leaned against the black leather booth and took a sip of the whiskey in his glass.

"I'm still a hostage. You know if I wasn't, I'd be home already."

"True, but something's changed," Ori said, sliding into the booth beside him. "You've never told Nonna about a girl before. That's not like you, Ekeali'i." He nudged Luca's side.

"What have you guys got planned?"

Cameron smirked. "Nothing you need to worry your young head about. You talk too much."

Luca snickered into his glass while Ori sucked his teeth. "Fuck off. I snitched *one* time and you guys won't let it go."

"Because *we* were the ones that got our asses beat over one fucking joint because your punk ass couldn't keep your mouth shut."

"I was high and we were fucking teenagers! Come on, don't be like that," Ori huffed.

"You don't need to know," Luca said, sitting his glass on the table. "And I didn't come here to talk business."

"Yeah, I know." Ori grinned. "I just hope everything works out for you. You look good with Nadia."

Luca nodded, with a blush burning over his cheeks. "Thanks."

"Mm-hm." Cameron chuckled. "And I think we're being summoned."

Luca followed his gaze to the middle of the floor and a laugh escaped his lips. Nadia and Minerva had taken over the dance floor and were doing one of his and Cameron's routines from Kani Kani - *a bit sarcastically,* he might add.

"Oh shit. They battle too?" Ori laughed as he popped up from the booth to watch them.

"Yes, they do," Luca said, holding out his fist to Cameron. "Should we mess them up?"

"Damn straight." Cameron nodded, bumping his fist as they stood from the booth and weaved through the crowd with their gazes set on the mocking duo in the middle of the dance floor.

"Excuse us, ladies," Luca said as they slid onto the floor

in front of them. He looked over his shoulder at Nadia's amused face. "You're doing it wrong." He grinned as he and Cameron matched their moves to the sound of the crowd 'ooo'-ing around them.

"Aw, we were just trying to get your attention." Nadia laughed and pushed him out of her way.

Luca caught her hand and brought it to his lips. "You always have my attention."

"Alright, stop trying to mess up her game. Get on your side, Luca," Minerva huffed and nudged him away from Nadia.

Luca chuckled, raising his hands. "Alright, alright." He laughed, backing away from them to stand next to Cameron.

"Ladies first." Cameron grinned and gestured for them to take the floor.

Nadia and Minerva looked at each other, raised their arms and snapped their fingers as they swayed their hips to the deep beat of Elderbrook's Old Friend. Crossing one foot over the other as they stepped in sync and kept their smug faces on Cameron and Luca as they popped and twirled their hips in perfect unison.

"Damn, they're *really* good," Cameron mumbled to him.

"Mm-hm, but so are we." Luca grinned. "No moves from Kani Kani tonight."

"I got you." Cameron nodded.

They crouched low and stepped out on the floor to the deep bass beat. They crept toward the dancing women and swept the floor as if to shoo them to the side. Nadia and Minerva burst out laughing as they gave them the floor.

"Okay! It's like that, huh?" Minerva hollered as the crowd cheered at their sly takeover.

Luca and Cameron popped and locked, Dougie'd and ney-

ney'd around the floor as they taunted their scheming ladies watching them. Luca kept his eyes on Nadia's devious gaze. She looked away from him to whisper in Minerva's ear, and a devilish grin curled over her lips as their eyes filled with a salacious gleam.

They slowly sauntered toward them, their hips swayed seductively as they bit their lips. Luca grinned as Nadia slid her hand up his chest. She turned around and ground her hips against him. Before he could slide his hands to her waist, she dropped low, spread his legs and slid between them. Luca choked out a laugh as the sultry pair pressed the pad of their heels into their asses and pushed them toward the sidelines.

"Those two are evil." Cameron laughed as they watched them dance and taunt them with their moves.

"Yes, they are," Luca murmured, watching Nadia's hips sway to the music. She flipped her braid over her shoulder and a grin tugged at her lips. The look in her spring green eyes sent a shiver down his spine straight to his goddamn dick. His pua nani was evil indeed.

"You watching that footwork?" Cameron said as he rubbed his hands together.

"Mm-hm, let's get 'em," Luca said with a devilish grin on his lips as he and Cameron stalked out to the floor, interrupting their routine to mimic their moves. Every single one of them, hair flips, twerks and all.

"No!" Nadia laughed, pushing Luca away from her.

He grabbed her hand, pulling her back against his chest. "I believe you just lost."

"Fuck off. You cheated." She giggled, threading her fingers through his.

Luca grinned against her head. "You shouldn't have

assumed we weren't just as good as you little Sirens."

"I'm calling that shit a tie!" Minerva exclaimed. "We didn't have a proper judge."

"Hell yeah, this isn't a regulation battle," Nadia said. "I want a rematch!"

"Whatever, but we'll still win." Luca grinned.

Nadia looked up at him and pursed her lips before she burst out laughing. "You're such an asshole."

He pressed his forehead against hers, staring into her joyful eyes. "Maybe, but I'm yours," he murmured and swayed to the gentle beat of Rihanna's Kiss It Better.

"You shouldn't say things like that, Mr. Underworld."

"It's true." He spun her around and laced his fingers through hers at the small of her back as he pressed his lips against her ear. "Aloha aku no, ka'u pua."

She pressed her cheek to his. "Me too," she whispered as they glided around the floor, lost in their own world.

Luca closed his eyes, savoring that small confession. He hoped it wasn't the booze talking for her because he meant it. His love and his heart were hers to take and while they were somewhere safe and unbothered by the dangers waiting for them at home, he wanted to drown in this moment for as long as they could.

Chapter 36

Dancing with Luca made the world melt away. Nothing mattered when she was in his arms like this. His hand splayed across the small of her bare back and her body cocooned in his solid warmth. Nadia was more intoxicated by the feel of his muscles and his decadent earthy scent than the copious amounts of alcohol and weed she'd imbibed in. She breathed him in and a burning desire to let him see her. All of her. Washed over her in a comforting wave.

There was something about being thousands of miles away from the problems that awaited them and the nagging reminder that, technically, he wasn't hers.

But none of that mattered right now. They were safe and she could let herself be the woman she wanted to be with him. The woman who wasn't scarred by her past or afraid to allow herself the pleasures she once enjoyed.

"Are you okay?" Luca murmured against her ear as they swayed to another soft ballad filtering around them.

She tilted her head back to stare into his warm, golden

eyes. "Yeah, but I think I'm ready for a swim."

"Mm, so am I," he said, pressing his lips to her palm. "Let's get out of here." He guided her through the swell of dancing bodies to their table on the edge of the dance floor to pick up their things before they made their way to the entrance.

"Have a good night," Ori said, sliding up to them before they reached the door and slapped a hand on Luca's shoulder. "Thanks for coming to see me and good luck with everything."

"Thanks. Take care of yourself," Luca said, patting his cousin's side.

Nadia smiled up at the tall man who looked nearly identical to Luca save for his long black hair, brown eyes and darker complexion. "It was nice to meet you, Ori."

His eyes sparkled and a dazzling smile spread across his lips. "You too, little wahine. I'm sure we'll meet again soon."

"Yes, you will." Luca squeezed her side and they gave Ori another wave before they descended the steps to the waiting car just outside the entrance below.

"Am I known as the little queen to all your family members, Mr. Underworld?" Nadia grinned with pride as they settled next to each other in the car.

Luca wrapped his arm around her and kissed her forehead. "Maybe."

She slid her fingers over the pattern of ink on his chest. "I want to know more about them and your life in Kaua'i."

"I know," he murmured, lifting her legs over his lap. "But not tonight," he said, sliding his hand over her thigh. "I want to get to know more of you, ka'u pua."

Her heart thumped and simmered at the desire burning behind his eyes. She slid her hand to the base of his neck and dragged her eyes down to his flush lips. "Did you mean what you said?"

"Aloha aku no?"

She nodded.

He touched his fingers to her chin and she looked into his golden depths, swirling with a soft tenderness that made her heart beat faster. "Of course I did."

She leaned in closer, her lips nearly grazing his. "I… I want you to see me," she whispered.

"I want to see you too," he murmured and caught her lips with his.

***

Nadia stood in the bathroom and tugged at the ties of the white robe she wore. Her heart pounded as Luca turned on the shower and she was regretting her impulsive request that they take a shower instead of the slightly less anxiety-inducing act of wearing a bikini in front of him.

The liquid confidence she once had was wearing thin and she was scared to let him see the scars that marred her lower half. She wanted to be open with him, but telling him what happened to her was different from showing him the lasting evidence of her trauma.

Luca closed the small gap between them, taking her hands and bringing them to his lips. "Are you sure you want to take a shower with me?"

"I'm nervous. My body is–"

"Perfect," he said, pressing her hands to his bare chest. "You never have to be ashamed of your scars, but we don't have to do this. You can take a shower on your own, ka'u pua. I never want you to do anything you're not comfortable with."

And that was the reason she wanted to bare herself to him.

Chapter 36

Luca would never pressure her into anything, yet she saw the dark desire behind his caring eyes. It didn't frighten her because she knew that covetous look. It was always prevalent in his gaze, lurking behind his golden depths whenever he looked at her and she ached for him to show her his dominance.

Sliding her hands up the rippling muscles of his chest and leaning up on her tip-toes, Nadia kissed him softly. "I want to do this," she whispered, stepping away from him to untie her robe, and the soft fabric dropped to the floor around her feet.

She fought the urge to wrap her arms around herself, but she watched his gaze instead, and the awe that filled his eyes made her nipples rise to attention. The towel wrapped around his waist joined her robe on the floor and she bit her lip as she dragged her eyes down his sinewy body to the thick, flaccid member that hung between his thighs.

Luca took a step toward her and her skin tingled as his warm hands caressed her thighs and settled over the jagged scars stretched over her hips. "You're beautiful."

"Luca," she said, wrapping her arms around his neck and pressing herself against the warmth of his hard, naked body.

"What do you want, baby?" he whispered with his golden eyes heady with need.

"I want…" Pleasure, pain and some sweet fucking release. She licked her lips and leaned up on her tiptoes. "I want you," she whispered against his mouth.

"Mm, I want you too," he murmured, kissing her softly. "But I want to take this slow," he said, lifting her up in his arms.

Wrapping her legs around his waist and sliding her fingers

into his thick locks, she gazed into his heady golden eyes. "Me too," she whispered as he carried her into the glass-enclosed shower. Her scars were miles from her mind as they kissed under the warm soothing water. The world melted away again in the safety of his arms. Nothing mattered but them and this sensuous moment.

Chapter 37

A shower had never felt so intimate and special to Luca. Holding Nadia against him while he washed her, getting to know every dip and curve of her body like she was letting him in on a secret. He wanted to know all of her deepest desires and ached to touch, kiss and cherish this side of her.

He kissed the droplets of water that rolled down her neck and smiled against her skin while she guided their hands where she wanted him to touch her. "Do you like this, ka'u pua?" he murmured when their fingers grazed her tight nipples.

"Mm-hm." She sighed, leaning back against him and rubbing her ass against his hardening cock.

Luca cupped the swell of her breasts. "What do you like?" he whispered, nipping her earlobe. "Do you like it soft?" he murmured, caressing her nipples with his thumb.

"Sometimes." She purred.

"Mm, do you like to be teased?" he said, pinching her nipples.

She gasped and bit her lip. "Yes, with someone I trust."

"Do you trust me?"

She tilted her head back and stared into his eyes. "Yes, and I know what you are. I see it in your eyes, Mr. Underworld."

He kissed her softly. "Then you understand why I'm so protective of you."

She turned around, sliding her arms around his shoulders, and his cock jerked against the softness of her stomach. "I do and I'm not afraid."

"I'll never do anything you don't want me to," he said, leaving a trail of kisses up her neck to her ear and cupping her ass cheeks. "But I want to taste you," he whispered. "Will you let me?"

Nadia slid her hands into his hair and pulled away from him just enough to look into his eyes. Worry passed through her depths. "Yes, but it's been a long time since I've done this."

Luca shook his head. "You don't have to do anything, ka'u pua." He kissed her softly and slid his hands down her sides, resting them over the rippling scars on her hips. Luca pressed his lips against her ear. "I want to hear you cum. Can I touch you like that?"

Her eyes darkened with desire as she took his hand and placed it between her thighs. "Yes, Mr. Underworld."

The husky tone in her voice and the trust that swirled in her green depths made him want nothing more than to worship the beauty in his arms. "Thank you," he said, gently pushing her down to the white-tiled seat at the base of the shower. "I'll never control you like a master," he said, kneeling in front of her. "You'll never be my slave or my kitten." He slid his hand to her cheek. "But tonight, I want you to be mine. Can you do that?"

"Yes, Mr. Underworld," she whispered.

"Good," he said, slowly sliding her legs apart and leaning into her ear. "Tell me your safe word."

"I was never allowed to have one," she whispered.

He pulled away from her and looked into her sheepish eyes. "You need one with me and you're always free to use it any time you want me to stop," he said, sliding his fingers to her chin. "So, tell me a word to keep you safe."

She nodded, biting her lip. "Petals."

"Mm, good choice." He kissed her softly. "All I want you to do," he said, sliding his hand between her thighs. "Is cum for me when I say so."

"What if I can't do that? Will you punish me?"

"No, we're taking this slow," he said, kissing the droplets of water that beaded on her throat. "No punishments, no restraints. Just me getting a taste of your limits." He stared into her eyes as he swirled his tongue over her nipple and rubbed his fingers over her clit. "Is that okay?"

Nadia's eyes darkened and a soft moan escaped her lips as she dug her fingers into his hair. "Yes, Mr. Underworld."

"What's your safe word, ka'u pua?" he asked, trailing his lips down her stomach and lifting her legs over his shoulders.

"Petals," she whispered and her breath hitched as he kissed the line of scars angled toward her center.

"Good girl. Use it whenever you need," he said as he slipped his tongue between her slick folds and moaned at the sweet taste of her honeyed nectar. His dick twitched at the beautiful gasp that left her lips and the way her nails dug into his scalp as he swirled his tongue over her clit.

Nadia gasped and shuddered when he slid his finger into

her folds. He gently thrust it in and out and added a finger every few strokes while he suckled on her clit. She rocked her hips against his face and her body tensed as a cry escaped her lips.

"Yes baby," he murmured against her as he looked up at the pure ecstasy written on her face.

"Luca." She panted. "I-I'm going to cum."

He pulled away from her and gripped her hair in his fist. He slowly fucked her pussy with his fingers as he leaned into her ear. "Not yet, ka'u pua," he whispered, licking her lips and coaxing them apart to share the taste of her on his tongue.

"Fuck," she whimpered into his mouth as her legs shook around him.

He pulled her away from him so he could watch her beautiful face contort in pleasure and agony while he brought her to the edge. She cried out and bit her lip as she fought her orgasm and his dick twitched at the sight. "That's it, baby. Don't cum yet."

God. He hadn't been this turned on by making someone cum in a long fucking time and that look on her face was going to be addicting. She was shaking and writhing in his arms as she dragged her nails over his skin. Tears rolled down her cheeks and mixed with the drool that dribbled out of her panting mouth. "Please, please…"

"Fuck, you're so beautiful." He licked her tears and smothered her mouth with his as he feverishly fucked her box. "Cum for me, ka'u pua," he whispered.

"Fucccck!" she screamed as her body tensed and her pussy sprayed her juices over his hand.

"Yes, let go for me," he groaned. The motion of her hips on his fingers made his balls tighten and he nearly spewed his seed. "Fuck," he groaned, aching to taste her again. He let go of her hair and dove between her thighs, gripping her hips as he pressed his tongue into her gushing pussy and drowned in her juices.

She panted and moaned as she tried to pull away from him, but dug her nails into his hair as if she didn't want him to move. He gripped her hips, holding her tight as he lapped up the taste of her sweet essence.

A beautiful scream ripped from her mouth as another orgasm shuddered through her body. She convulsed and cried out some incoherent blabber before her body sagged against the wall, crying and shaking as her orgasm raced over her body.

Luca wiped his mouth and gently pulled her into his arms and cuddled her against his body on the wet tiled floor. He slid his hand to her tear stained cheek and caressed her trembling lip with his thumb. "Are you okay?"

She nodded.

"I need to hear you say it, ka'u pua," he whispered and kissed her tears.

"I'm okay," she said, and a smile tugged at her lips as she touched a hand to his cheek. "I was a little scared, but you were perfect, Mr. Underworld."

Relief washed over him as he kissed her forehead and reached over her to grab a washcloth sitting on the shelf. "It's been a long time since I've done that, too. I'm glad it wasn't too much for you," he said, holding the cloth under the running water and gently washing her center, taking great care not to arouse her again.

"No, it wasn't." She sighed, tilting her head back to look at him. The faith and trust that swirled in her ardent green eyes lit a fire in his soul. He never wanted her to stop looking at him like he was the only one she'd allow to indulge in her darkest desires and he was going to keep it that way.

He pressed a soft kiss to her lips. "I should put you to bed. You look exhausted," he said, hooking his arm beneath her legs and standing from the floor.

She yawned, wrapping her arms around his neck. "Mm, I am. I just want to curl up with you now," she mumbled against his chest.

"We will," he said, pushing the glass door open. He carried her into the bedroom and sat her in the plush gray velvet chair before he grabbed a towel sitting on the bed and dried her off. He plucked a bottle of lotion from the round wooden table beside them and knelt in front of her to gently massage the lotion into her skin.

Nadia laughed softly as he lifted her foot to his mouth and kissed her toes while he spread the fragrant pomegranate cream up her leg.

He looked at her half closed eyes and chuckled. "What are you laughing about?"

"You're so attentive. I'm not really used to this."

He grinned and sat her foot down to start on the other. "You should be."

A tired smile spread over her face. "Why's that?"

He kissed her knee and put her leg down before he nestled himself between her thighs. "Because," he said, pressing a kiss to the side of her mouth. "You deserve to be cherished like this."

She wrapped her arms around his shoulders, and the light in her eyes dimmed. "Even if I don't know how far I could let you take me? I'm… I'm not as open as I used to be."

"We're still learning about each other." He kissed her softly. "And one day, we'll have all the time in the world to see how far we can take each other."

Her tired green eyes lit up as she nipped his bottom lip. "I'd like that."

"Me too," he murmured, pulling away from her to tug a robe from the hooks beside the bathroom door. "Let me take you to bed. I've kept you up long enough," he said, draping the robe around her and tugging on the other.

"Mm, I'm going to sleep so good," she mumbled as he scooped her up from the chair and carried her to the bed.

Nadia was fast asleep before her head hit the pillow. Luca chuckled, pulling the blankets around her and kissing her head before padding back into the bathroom to turn off the shower. He turned off the light and smiled as he climbed into the bed. He wrapped his arms and legs around Nadia, cocooning his body around her. Sighing into her hair, his eyes drooped and closed.

He'd do anything to make her feel safe with him because he wanted to be the one she opened up to and allowed him to take her to those dark and pleasurable places her body begged to go.

Luca's eyes slid open and watched her sleeping face and the gentle rise and fall of her chest as he traced the line of her jaw. His heart simmered and he pressed his lips to her forehead. "I love you, ka'u pua," he whispered.

To say those words out loud for the first time should've scared him, but it didn't. She held his heart and although they had problems waiting for them once they left this shelter of freedom; he was ready to let her in his life. All of it. He promised not to keep secrets from her and there was just one he had left to tell her.

Chapter 38

Nadia felt good. No, she felt amazing. A smile graced her lips as she traced a jagged line of one of Luca's scars and kissed his side. She looked up at his sleeping face, flush lips and strong jaw, and a delightful shiver ran down her spine. She hadn't cum willingly like that in a long time, nor had she felt comfortable to be vulnerable like that in a long time either, but Luca made her feel safe to allow him a piece of control of her.

She trailed her fingers over the light stubble on his jaw. He was perfect last night and he cared for her in a way she didn't know she needed. Luca satisfied her mind, body and soul and they didn't even have sex. That feeling had never happened to her before. It felt like peace and calm. Her mind was at ease and her body - oh, her body - it felt brand new.

Nadia's heart thumped and a blush burned over her cheeks when she looked up into his golden eyes that watched her through half-closed lids, and her body tingled at Luca's tender gaze. He slid his hand over hers and brought her fingers to his lips. "Good morning," he murmured, tangling his other hand in her hair.

"Good morning. I think it might be afternoon though."

"Probably." He chuckled and turned on his side toward her. "How are you feeling?"

"I feel good." She grinned. "How are you feeling?"

"I'm good." He kissed her lips and slid his hand beneath her robe to her hip. "Thank you for letting me see you like that last night," he said, caressing her skin.

She pressed her forehead against his. "Thank you for being so gentle," she said and bit her lip. "My scars didn't bother you?"

"Of course not. You're beautiful, ka'u pua. Your scars would never change that. I love everything about you."

"I do too, but I want to know about your family," she said, touching her fingers to his lips and staring into the warmth of his eyes. "You're still keeping your royal secrets from me."

"I'm not a royal." Luca chuckled. "Well, not in the European sense of the word, but why don't I make us some coffee and we can talk about this over breakfast?"

"That sounds good. I'm starving."

"Me too." He grinned. "But you were pretty tasty."

A blush burned over her cheeks and she laughed, slapping his shoulder. "Nasty man, you are."

"You liked it."

"I did. It felt good to try with you," she said, placing a soft kiss on his lips.

He slid his hand to her cheek and kissed her nose. "We need to talk about our limits, too. I never want to do anything you're not comfortable with if we're going to have this kind of relationship."

She nodded, and a wave of jealousy rolled over her. "Do you… do you have this kind of relationship with Ciara?"

Luca sighed, shaking his head. "No. I never wanted to do this with her and the subs I messed around with before her didn't make me feel like you do." He caressed her cheek with his thumb. "It's been a long time since I've wanted to do this and back when I used to, I never wanted to commit myself like this."

Nadia wrapped her fingers around his wrist. "I want to do this, but I'll never be able to wear a collar and I never want to feel like I can't do what I want."

"You have your watch. You don't need to wear a collar, if that's not something you want to do," he said, and a smile graced his lips. "A dom isn't supposed to isolate you. As a sub, you control what I do and how much power you give me. It doesn't always have to be about sex either." He kissed her cheek. "My job is to take care of you, your body and your well-being."

Nadia's heart swelled and she laughed softly. "I always thought that was how it was supposed to be, but I've never had the pleasure of having a dom like that."

"Then I'm happy to be your first."

She pressed her forehead against his, staring deep into his golden eyes and realizing she didn't want anyone else to make her feel the way he did. She pressed a kiss to his cheek. "When we're free to be like this, I want you to be my last, Mr. Underworld."

"Ka'u pua nani, I'll gladly be your last," he whispered, catching her lips with his. Tingles raced over her skin as she melted into his embrace. She was in love. She wasn't falling anymore. Luca was her one, and she wanted to share her life with him. The secrets he held about his life in Hawai'i. She wanted to be part of it.

***

Nadia snuggled into her favorite spot under the crook of Luca's arm while they spent the morning talking about their hard and soft limits while picking from the breakfast spread Luca ordered as they sat under a shaded hut on a sunbed nestled in the corner of the stone terrace. The crystal blue water bled into the horizon of Osaka's harbor below and the canopy of sheer crimson drapes billowed around the wooden posts of the hut in the soft afternoon breeze.

Nadia never had an experience like this. In her past relationships, she didn't talk openly about what she liked or wasn't comfortable with, and in Jonathan's case; he told his kittens what he wanted. It made her feel empowered that Luca wanted to know her kinks and he was open about telling her his.

"I'm glad we did that," she said, staring at his hand wrapped around hers over his chest.

"Me too," he murmured and brought her palm to his lips. "I'm sure you'd like to know about my family now, right?"

A smile tugged at her lips. "Yes, I would," she said, sitting up on her elbow. "Why did Ori say you couldn't bring anyone to meet your Nonna?"

"Because my Nonna is the matriarch of my family and the wahine chiefess who rules Koa Maile in my absence."

Nadia raised an eyebrow. "I thought you said chiefs didn't exist anymore."

"Technically, they don't, but the old Koa Maile traditions

are still very much alive. I'm the ali'i my Tutu chose to be his successor and when I'm not there, the duties fall onto the eldest in my family."

"Why not your father?"

"Because my father and his siblings were focused on building their businesses outside of Koa Maile. It's not uncommon in my village for the ali'i to skip a generation when they choose their successor and my Tutu felt I was the best one to lead my family and our people," he said, chuckling at the memory. "I was fourteen when he told me this."

"Did you want that?"

A smile spread across his lips. "More than anything. I love Koa Maile and everything I do is for them just like the chiefs before me. I was born into wealth, but my dad and my Tutu taught me we're only as wealthy as our people. So any profit I make from my businesses supports the livelihood of the village."

"Luca, I had no idea. Does your grandfather know this about you?"

He sighed. "Of course he does. He's threatened them too."

Nadia frowned. "So when you say you're protecting your family, you mean the people of Koa Maile too?"

Luca nodded. "Yes. My grandfather has some deep ties with the government. Koa Maile isn't governed by the US. We've maintained our independence for decades, but my grandfather has the power to change that. It's another reason I have to do as he asks."

Her eyes grew wide. "What? Luca! That's… you've got an entire village of people counting on you." Jesus. No wonder he always had a silent battle going on behind his eyes. She couldn't imagine what that kind of responsibility felt like.

"Yeah." He smirked, sitting up against the pillows behind them. "But they'll be safe now that we have the blacklist and I'll finally be able to go home."

Nadia's heart sank as she sat up next to him. He wanted to leave? "For good? What about Shola?"

"Not for good, but when this is over I'll spend a few months there," he said, sliding his fingers to her chin. "And I'd like to take you with me. I want you to get to know this part of my life."

Nadia's heart slowed its descent into the pool of worry as a smile tugged at her lips. "I'd love to go with you, but you still haven't explained why you can't just bring anyone to meet your Nonna."

Luca choked out a nervous laugh as he ran a hand through his hair. "It's not taken lightly when the ali'i brings someone to meet the elders in my family. To my Nonna and the Koa Maileans it would mean that I intend to spend my life with you."

Nadia's heart thumped, and her cheeks burned up to her ears. "Is that what it would mean to you?"

He took a deep breath and squeezed his hands in his lap. "We still have a lot to learn about each other, but I don't want to be with anyone else," he said, sliding his hand to her cheek. "If I met you before my grandfather trapped me in this life, there would've been nothing he could've done to take me away from you and maybe you'd already be my wahine by now."

Tears pricked the corners of her eyes and she wrapped her fingers around his wrist, staring into the love and tenderness that swirled in his eyes. "Do you mean that?"

"I do. Does that scare you?"

She nodded. "Kind of. It's a lot to process. I told you I wanted you to be my last and I meant that." She sighed, looking away from him as doubt crept up her spine. "But, I can't be your wahine. I can't have children, Luca. Wouldn't you need to carry on your name with an heir or something?"

"No, there are other ways for me to choose a successor. I have a big family and I don't need children to be happy with you, ka'u pua. You're enough for me just the way you are."

Her lip trembled as a tear rolled down her cheek. "But what will your Nonna think?"

He wiped her tears and kissed her softly. "That I've found someone who will care and love our people as she and my Tutu and the leaders before them have."

"Luca, this is crazy," she whispered. "I'm not cut out to be a... a *queen*. I'm still coming to terms with what we are and we're not even supposed to be like this yet."

"I know, but we said no secrets between us. It's only fair that you know who I really am and what it would mean to truly be with me," he said, curling his knuckles under her chin. "And you are a wahine. You command attention when you walk into a room. You're brave and so fucking smart, but what I love most about you is your kindness and the way you care about more than yourself."

Nadia's lip trembled at the truth swirling in his eyes, and she wasn't sure her heart could take much more of his confessions. This wasn't what she expected when she asked about his family. It felt like he just told her he loved her without uttering those three words. "Luca, I didn't know you saw all of that in me."

He caressed her bottom lip. "I told you, you're hard not to notice and this week with you just confirmed what I already knew."

She chuckled softly. "That I'm fiercely competitive and I have a few kinks?"

"That," he said, pressing his forehead against hers. "And I–"

A barrage of door knocks sounded from inside their suite and Luca's phone burst to life in a blaring chorus of rings on the wooden tray, shattering their sweet moment. "Great timing," Luca muttered in annoyance as he swiped his phone from the tray.

"I'll… I'll get the door," Nadia said as she slid away from him. He nodded, pressing the phone to his ear as she got up and padded around the pool with her heart pounding. Was Luca going to say that he loved her?

She dragged a hand over her face before she stood on her tiptoes to look through the peephole. Sighing as she opened the door to Cameron and Minerva's grinning faces dressed in their swimming attire, she'd never get her answer now with them hanging around.

"Good afternoon!" Minerva exclaimed. "You look well rested." She grinned with her teasing brown eyes, tugging on the tie of Nadia's robe as she and Cameron came in and plopped their towels on the back of the plush white couch in the living room. "How late did you two stay out last night?"

"I don't know," Nadia said, raising an eyebrow at Minerva. "But you two snuck out pretty quick after our battle," she said, crossing the room to the kitchenette to make a fresh pot of coffee.

Minerva laughed as she slid onto a stool and tugged her sheer cover up over her yellow and hot pink striped bikini. "We had another battle to take care of."

Chapter 38

"And I won that too." Cameron grinned, pressing a kiss to her head. "But now I'm anxious over this decision. Have you heard anything yet?" he asked, massaging his fingers in the curls at the base of Minerva's neck.

Nadia leaned against the counter and shook her head. "No, but Luca just got a call. It could be Ono," she said, nodding to the pool as Luca slipped inside.

"Yes, the rest of my team is here. I'll put you on speaker, if you don't mind," he said, crossing the room to stand beside her. "Go ahead, Mr. Ono."

"Good morning Miss Coleman and Mr. Ramirez. I was just explaining to Mr. Shola that my team and I have made our final decision and I thought it would be best to give you the news together," Mr. Ono said, sighing.

Nadia's heart dropped to her stomach. She knew that deflated sigh. She'd heard it one too many times when she lost a mock pitch war under his mentorship. Fuck.

"Let me start by saying Ono Medical reserves the right to keep your company's information on file for any potential contracts in the future," he explained.

Luca thread his fingers through hers and she looked up at his hopeful golden eyes and looked across the bar to Minerva and Cameron whose eyes were shining with the same hope.

"As you know, there was a high caliber of companies vying for this contract. Shola Enterprises is a new player in the international market and doesn't have the capacity for many big clients such as Ono Medical."

Nadia's heart was sinking to her knees as she waited for Mr. Ono to tell them what she already knew.

"My team was wary of your ability to properly handle the demands of a company of our size. The reason we asked you to this meeting was because of Luca's impeccable ability to navigate a company of its domestic size, Cameron's leading-edge domestic marketing expertise and Nadia's remarkable ability to develop and advance the businesses she works with."

Nadia's heart thumped and a glimmer of hope tingled in her gut as she squeezed Luca's hand.

"After observing your team throughout the week and watching your performance during the review, my team and I are confident in our decision to sign a marketing contract with Shola Enterprises. I look forward to working with you."

Nadia's eyes grew wide. Luca's hand shook in hers as he cleared his throat and a dazzling smile burst across his face. "We look forward to working with you too, Mr. Ono. Thank you for this opportunity."

"You're very welcome. You were the only ones who came prepared with an answer to my projection, which according to my analysts, was ninety-eight percent accurate. You've got an excellent team around you, Mr. Shola."

Nadia's heart simmered at the adoration gleaming in Luca's gaze. "I never doubted them."

"You never should. I'll be in touch to schedule an office visit. Congratulations," he said and hung up.

"We just… we just won that fucking contract! Holy shit!" Cameron burst out in a roar as he pulled Minerva's giggling form into his arms.

Luca wrapped his arms around Nadia, and she threw hers around his shoulders. "We did it!" She laughed.

He slid his hand to her cheek. "No, you did it, ka'u wahine." His golden eyes were so bright, and the joy in his eyes simmered in her soul.

Chapter 38

"Damn right she did!" Cameron clapped his hands together. "We need to break out the champagne. We need to celebrate!" he said, popping off the stool to pluck a bottle from the minibar.

"Call your guards in here, Luca. They deserve to party with us too!" Minerva said, as she rummaged through the cupboards for some glasses.

"I will." Luca chuckled and looked down at Nadia. "Should we continue our talk later?"

"I don't know. I doubt we'll be sober," she said, laughing as Cameron and Minerva pulled out bottles of liquor and shot glasses.

"True." He sighed. "I guess the moment's passed, anyway."

"Yeah. You can tell me what you were going to say some other time."

"It should be obvious by now," he said, leaning down to her ear. "You have my heart, ka'u pua," he whispered and kissed her cheek.

"We starting this party or not? Nadia, get your bathing suit on. Luca, roll up the blunts. Let's go!" Minerva clapped her hands.

"Alright, Nervy. We've got all day," Nadia huffed as she slipped out of Luca's arms to their bedroom, but she was glad for this small moment to herself to think. She sighed and sifted through her suitcase, tugging out a black and gold one piece bathing suit.

Sitting on the bed, Nadia slid her hands over her face. A tear rolled down her cheek and she quickly wiped it away. Her emotions were all over the place between the excitement of getting the contract, everything Luca told her about his life and what they did with each other. God, she felt like he reached inside of her and she let him pull her to the surface of the shell she'd been hiding in for so long.

Nadia rubbed her hands over her arms to soothe the tingles racing over her skin. She couldn't get lost in these feelings. Being here in Osaka was a pleasant reprieve from the reality of the situation waiting for them. Ciara wasn't an annoyance here and the issue of Jonathan wasn't nagging at her either.

She took a deep breath and slipped on her bathing suit and lace cover up. A smile spread over her lips. Luca didn't say he loved her, but he was right. It was obvious, and she didn't need him to say it. She loved him too, and their actions spoke louder than saying those three words to each other.

But their actions were why they had to be careful. Ciara still had her pictures and the blacklist was still being decoded. They weren't free to be like this yet.

Chapter 39

Luca wanted to tell her. He wanted that moment by the pool to tell Nadia that he loved her, but it passed too quickly and they were back on the plane to Boston without another quiet moment together. Their week of freedom dried up too fast. At least he got the chance to tell her everything, but it was torture having to pretend that they were just friends.

He took a drink from the glass in his hand, scanning the chattering crowd of shareholders on the terrace of his parents' estate. His father pulled the celebration together overnight at his grandfather's demand to celebrate the monumental contract win. Luca's eyes fell on Nadia's smiling face and trailed down her silk chartreuse dress that matched her joyous sea green depths. He dragged his eyes over her champagne heels and the peek of her leg through the delicious slit up her thigh.

"I wish things could be different for you," his mother said, slipping her arm through his. "I'm sorry you can't follow your heart like I did."

Luca looked down at his mother's raven hair swept to the side with a gold barrette. A smile was painted on her face, but sorrow filled her hazel eyes as she gazed upon the guests littering the lawn. Luca hadn't told his family about his plan and he wouldn't until he got confirmation that the blacklist was decoded, which he hoped would be soon.

"It's alright. You shouldn't have to apologize for that. At least I get to be her friend."

She squeezed his arm and shook her head. "You're more than that. I see the way you look at each other. You're very subtle, but a mother knows," she said, looking up at him. "Have you told her about us and who you are?"

"Yes."

"Then you have a plan." A warm smile graced her lips. "Your father and I suspected as much."

His eyes grew wide. "How–"

"Luca, there you are. Hiding away from everyone as usual," Ciara said, sauntering over to them in her red sheath dress swaying around her bronzed legs. He swore her fake tan grew darker every time he saw her. "Elena, it's nice to see you," she said, pressing her crimson lips against his mother's cheek.

"You as well, Ciara. You look radiant this evening," she said and Luca bit his cheeks at her sarcastic tone.

"Mm, thank you," Ciara said with a tight smile and cut her sharp brown eyes at him. "Can we talk in private?"

Luca squeezed the glass in his hand. He'd been waiting for this all night. "Sure," he said, looking down at his mother. "I'll be back soon."

"Don't be too long," she said, with worry clouding her eyes. "I think your grandfather's going to make a toast soon. He'd be upset if you missed it."

"Oh, I won't keep him from that," Ciara said, latching onto his arm. Luca glanced over his shoulder and caught Nadia's gaze through the swell of people before Ciara tugged him into the house. That small smile on her face was enough comfort for him to endure whatever bullshit Ciara had in store for him.

"What do you need to talk about?" Luca asked as they went into a small office just beyond the kitchen. Ciara closed the door and slapped him across his face. "What the fuck!" he roared, holding a hand to his cheek.

"You deserved that," she said, crossing her arms over her chest. "You've been home for two days! Why is tonight the first time I'm seeing you?" She pushed at his chest. "It's that fucking bitch, isn't it?"

"I told you I've had a lot of work to do for the new contract. Cam and I have been staying late at the office to figure out the new structure. We had a video call last night. You fucking saw me working."

"I know. I'm sorry." She shook her head, and tears pricked the corners of her eyes. "I don't like that you spent a week away from me with *her.* I don't like that you work with her either."

Luca fought the urge to roll his eyes. He hated he had to keep up this act and coddle her pouting display. "Nadia's employment status isn't going to change and as you can see tonight, she and I are just work colleagues. You don't need to be jealous."

"Well I am," Ciara said, running her fingers through her glossy locks that had a slight wave in them as if she tried to add more texture to her typically bone straight hair.

"Jonathan talked about her like she was some sort of living Goddess." She spat the word out like it soured in her mouth.

"Jonathan?" He frowned. "When did you talk to him?"

"When I asked for his help to watch her for me after your little walk home and again while you were away. He and his father have been recovering in one of our hotels," she said. "He told me a lot about her." She laughed, sliding a hand up the sleeve of his black suit. "I don't know why I'm worried. She'll be handled."

"What's there to handle? Nadia isn't a problem," Luca said, wrapping his arms around her waist and pressing his thumb over the face of his watch.

"She might not be, but I bet you didn't know she's a kitten." Ciara giggled, and the sinister sound of it made his stomach churn. "I have pictures and videos of her disgusting endeavors and I'll ruin her with them if she ever steps out of line."

No, the fuck, she won't. Ciara clearly hadn't checked on her stash since he knew for a fact his specialists had wiped everything clean from her phone and Jonathan's files.

"And Jonathan still owns her. The Grand Duke was worried there was some truth in his accusations after that mix-up during the Platinum meeting. So he gave Jonathan an order to return her to his safe keeping."

Luca's heart clenched and panic clawed at his spine as Ciara grabbed his cheek, digging her nails into his skin.

"I can't have you pulling a stunt like your mother. You know how important it is for us to be together."

"I know." Luca pushed down the fear swelling in his gut. "And I'm with you, Ciara. You didn't have to tell me any of this. Jonathan's accusations were bullshit and if Nadia's one of his kittens then he has a right to her." Luca bit back the bile and anguish for having said that, but the worry over his grandfather's order turned his stomach sour. Nadia's guards better be listening to his broadcast and making moves to heighten her security.

Ciara's stern expression lightened, and her hard gaze softened. "You really don't care about her like that, do you?" She let go of his cheek and wrapped her arms around his shoulders.

"I told you I don't. We just work together. I don't know much about her private life and I didn't want to know."

Ciara shrugged and a smile lit up her face. "Well, now you know she's just a slut and we can get back to being us." She kissed his cheek. "Have you picked out my ring yet?"

Luca stared into her joyful eyes and forced out a laugh. Ciara was fucking ridiculous. He shouldn't be surprised how quickly she moved from threatening him to asking about their impending engagement. "I wouldn't tell you if I did."

"That's fine. You know I like surprises," she said, caressing the back of his neck. "Are you ready to start over with me now?"

"I've never had a choice."

She sighed and rolled her eyes. "You'll fall in love with me one day."

Not even if hell froze over and they were the last people on earth.

Luca pressed his thumb over his watch to stop the broadcast and reached behind his head to take her hand. "We should get back to the party, unless you had something else you wanted to talk about?"

"No, that was it," she said, threading her fingers through

his. "I'm sorry I slapped you."

"I'm sorry you felt the need to," he said, opening the door for her.

"I'm trying to be better. I don't want to hurt you anymore."

"That would be nice."

Ciara squeezed his hand and looked up at him. "We can do this, Lu. We can be good together."

"It's a case of having to be, isn't it?" A small part of him felt bad for her that all she knew was what her father asked of her, but that was the extent of his pity. Her hand in life would never excuse the way she treats him or the fact that she admitted to conniving with a predator like Jonathan just to keep him by her side and put his pua nani in danger.

"I'm glad we had that little chat, Miss Coleman."

Luca's eyes grew wide at the sound of his grandfather's voice. He looked through the foyer at Nadia and his grandfather stepping out of one of the sitting rooms, and his heart clenched at the pained look on her face as they walked down the hall toward them.

"Yes, and if you'd let go of me, I'd like to go home now," she said, tugging her arm from his grasp.

"But then you'll miss my toast," he said, pulling her back to him and whispering something in her ear. Fear clouded Nadia's green eyes as she looked up at his grandfather in shock.

"Bet he wants to keep the little slut for his own needs. That's a big honor for someone like her," Ciara snickered next to him.

Luca's heart clenched in panic at the thought of him touching Nadia like that. "Grandpa, what's going on?"

His grandfather let go of Nadia and chuckled as he took a

step away from her. "I was just getting to know the star of this amazing contract win. Isn't that right, Miss Coleman?"

"Yes," she muttered, rubbing her arm where he held her. "Excuse me," she said, brushing past them into the bustling kitchen, but Luca caught the sight of tears welling in her eyes.

Fuck. What the hell did he say to her?

"She's a special one," his grandfather said with a sickening grin as he straightened his silk gold tie. "Come on, son. Let me make a toast to you and your amazing achievement."

"That sounds like a wonderful idea, Mr. Rodawson."

"Oh, it's Gregory to you, dear. You'll be family soon," his grandfather said proudly as they walked through the caterers, pouring more glasses of champagne and filling plates with h'orderves.

Luca's heart was in his stomach swimming in a pool of anxiety as he scanned the crowd for Nadia. He caught the worried eyes of his mother and followed her gaze to Nadia leaving the terrace with Gordon and Henry at her side. That was a minor relief that she knew to leave with her guards, but rage boiled through his veins and he glared at his grandfather's smug face.

"What did you say to make Miss Coleman leave?"

"Nothing someone of her type wouldn't understand," he said, pressing his hand on Luca's shoulder and keeping his voice low. "Miss Coleman is an asset to your company and she'll do well to serve us both once she's back where she belongs."

Chapter 40

Nadia held it together long enough for Henry to close the car door before she burst into tears. Gregory Rodawson was a disgusting man. Not that she thought the Grand Duke of the Syndicates would be anything different.

She pressed her face into her hands. He caught her leaving the bathroom and forced her into a private sitting room where he told her exactly what he planned to do when Jonathan brought her back into his care.

"What did he say to you, Miss Nadia?" Gordon said as he pulled away from the estate.

"How… how long until everything is decoded?"

"We should have everything soon. Why? What did he say?"

Nadia bit her thumb and stared out the car window at the tree-lined driveway. "He's ordered Jonathan to take me back and when he does, I–" She closed her eyes and shuddered. "Gregory has demanded that I be his personal Juliet."

"That sick fuck. Not on our watch," Henry huffed and shook his head.

"No, but that means Jonathan will be determined to get you back to be in the Grand Duke's good graces," Gordon said, as he turned off the main road to a dirt track and turned off the headlights as he parked the car. "You can't go home, Miss Nadia. I'm sorry."

"What do you mean? Where are we going?" she said, looking around the shrouded path as Henry handed Gordon a pair of black goggles.

"To the safe house. There are too many variables in the city. Too many places Jonathan's men can snatch you up," he said, securing the goggles over his head before he put the car in gear and continued down the brittle road.

Nadia's heart pounded. "But I have you."

"Yes, you do, but Jonathan has Mr. Rodawson now. We can outsmart his tech crew and regular goons, but if he's set on having you, he'll send his mercenaries," Gordon explained.

"Yeah, and those guys are corrupt as fuck." Henry scoffed. "They'll find and kill anyone for the right price. No questions asked."

"Won't they find me wherever we're going?"

"Yes, but out here, we have the advantage. We built this place for situations like this. After Mr. Rodawson started threatening Mrs. and Miss Shola with the Juliet circle, we needed a place to hide them."

"Oh God," Nadia whimpered, clutching a hand over her chest. "There's nothing you can do. He's going to take me," she said, gasping for air as panic clawed up her spine.

"Shit," Henry said, as he climbed over the center console to get to her. "Miss Nadia, he's not going to get you. We'd never let that happen," he said, unclipping her seat belt and grasping her shoulders. "You need to breathe."

"I… can't," she said through a strained breath as her thoughts tumbled into the depths of Jonathan's torment, which was plagued by Gregory's malicious brown eyes.

"Yes, you can. Come on, count with me."

"Once you're retrained as an obedient little kitten, I'll be your new master."

Gregory's sinister voice echoed in her mind, and the smell of a fresh cigar on his skin flooded her senses.

Tears rolled down Nadia's cheeks as she shook her head. "It won't… help." The count didn't matter when the inevitable was closing in. Why did she think she could get away from Jonathan? And now she was being targeted by the Grand Duke. How long did she have before she was chained to another Syndicate's side?

"Five!" Gordon's voice boomed through the car, shaking her from her thoughts. "What's five, Miss Nadia?"

"I… I'm not his," she whimpered, digging her nails into Henry's arms as she took a shaky breath.

"That's right," Henry cooed. "What's four?"

She stared into his concerned brown eyes and took another painful breath. "I–I'm free."

"Always, little wahine. Three."

She closed her eyes and let out another shaky breath as the panic in her chest slowly released its hold. "I have a plan."

"And it's a damn good one," Gordon said, turning the car down another brittle patch of road. "Two more, Miss Nadia. What's two?"

A shaky smile tugged at her lips. "I'm safe."

"Yes you are," Henry said. "What's the most important one?"

She sucked in a deep breath. "I'm alive."

"And we're here to keep you that way," Henry said as his usual joyful light returned to his eyes. "Did that help?"

"Yes, I-I'm sorry. I'm just scared," she said, releasing her death grip on his arms.

"We know and it's okay," he said, tugging the seatbelt back around her and pulling a handkerchief from his suit pocket. "There's nothing we won't do to protect you, Miss Nadia."

"Thank you." She sighed, taking the crisp white cloth with shaking hands and wiping her tears. The count settled her nerves for the moment and she was thankful that Henry and Gordon took to heart what she told them about her panic attacks, but fear still hung at the edge of her thoughts. "Can you tell Nervy and Raquel where I am?"

"They'll be informed. Raquel and the rest of your primary guards will be out here soon with everything you need," Gordon said, as he turned down another winding path. "We'll talk more about your security when everyone's here."

"Okay," she said, clutching Henry's handkerchief in her hands as a chill raced over her skin.

"Everything's going to be alright," Henry said, shrugging off his jacket and placing it over her lap.

Nadia tugged the jacket closer around her and stared out at the moonlit trees. She wanted to believe Henry, but everything felt like it was falling apart. Would the blacklist be enough? Or would she have to run again?

***

Nadia sat in a towel on the bed in the room she'd be living in until God knew when. She ran her hands over her face as another sob choked in her throat. A shower didn't help the incessant anxiety nagging and eating away at her.

She could run from this. She could run from everything. There was enough money in her savings to start over. Her lawyer could set her up with a new identity, in a state–maybe a new country where Jonathan and the Syndicates couldn't find her.

Nadia shook her head and slammed her fists against the bed. No. She didn't have to do that. She wasn't the one who should have to run and cower in fear. The whole reason she started this mission was because she was *tired.*

Gripping the yellow floral print bedding between her fists, Nadia stared at her tear-stained face in the oak framed mirror above the vanity. She was tired of living in fear, tired of running, and tired of being the fucking victim.

Fuck Jonathan and fuck Gregory Rodawson.

She didn't come this far to cower in fear now. Nadia got up and stalked over to the dresser in the corner of the room and tugged open a drawer.

She came this far to take them all down.

Slipping on a pair of gray sweatpants and a black t-shirt, she snarled and slammed the drawer shut.

"Glad to see that you're angry."

Nadia whipped her head to the bedroom door at the tall, curly black-haired woman standing in the doorway with her big brown eyes shining with pride and a smug grin splayed across her light brown face.

"You're fucking right I'm angry," she said, crossing the room to wrap her arms around Raquel's leather clad shoulders. "I'm so glad you're here."

Raquel hugged her tight, patting Nadia's damp hair. "We're going to get them."

"I know, we have to. I'm tired."

Chapter 40

Raquel pulled away from her. "I know you are, but we knew this was going to be hard and now we've got a badass army behind us."

Nadia laughed. "Yeah, was that your plan all along?"

Raquel tilted her head to the side. "I might've known about Luca's situation and steered you in his direction." She grinned. "But I didn't know it would get this far."

A blush burned over Nadia's cheeks as she glared into Raquel's teasing eyes. "Liar. Out here playing matchmaker."

Raquel shrugged. "Maybe a little," she said, squeezing her arms. "How are you really holding up?"

Nadia sighed. "I'm scared, but I'm not going to run. I want to see this through and now that Gregory has staked his claim on me I want to fuck the Syndicates up even more."

"Good. You're going to need to keep that energy. This shit isn't going to get any easier and we're going to have to tweak our plan now that the Grand Duke is after you."

Nadia bit her thumb and nodded. "I know."

Raquel wrapped her arm around Nadia's shoulders. "Come on, let's talk about your security setup. It might make you feel better."

"I'll feel better when we have the blacklist," she murmured as they padded down the charcoal gray carpet and crisp white hallway.

"It's eighty-five percent decoded and we can't make a move until we've at least gotten to the information on Gregory," Raquel said as they walked down the black wooden staircase to the open living room where her guards were sitting on the sleek black couches huddled over a long glass coffee table. Their laptops were open to surveillance cameras and maps in-between a spread of various snacks and drinks.

Gordon looked up at them and stood followed by the rest of her guards. "Miss Nadia, if you're ready, we've got your security detail planned."

"I don't think I have a choice, Gordon. Tell me what you've got."

Gordon, Henry, Raquel and her guards spent two hours explaining how her security would work and that she would remain living at the safe house until after the Gala. Raquel and her primary team would live with her while she worked from the safe house, and her secondary guards would keep watch at her apartment to make sure it looked like she was still living there.

"In the event the safe house is breached," Gordon said, pointing at an evacuation plan projected onto the TV above the black mantle fireplace. "You and Raquel will be taken to the vault and extracted when we have the all clear."

"What if that doesn't happen? You said these guys are ruthless."

"We also said we have the advantage here and we built the safe house for this reason," Henry said, putting down the bag of cheese curls in his hand. "You don't need to worry about anything, Miss Nadia."

Nadia took a deep breath. "That's easier said than done," she said, sliding her hands into her hair. "I… I need some air." She shot up from the couch and padded across the room to the sliding glass doors and stepped out into the cool night air.

Leaning against the black steel decking, she hung her head as tears rolled down her cheeks. She was trying to keep a brave face, but every time she thought of how much danger she was actually in, her chest tightened and threatened to cave in.

The guilt that used to plague her for getting involved with Jonathan beat at her mind again. If only she hadn't got lost in the idea of him or fell for his charismatic smile and kind brown eyes, she wouldn't be in this mess.

Nadia gripped the railing and fought back the sob itching to break free. "He's not going to get me," she whispered, taking a deep breath and said it again.

The swish of the door sliding open behind her shook her from her thoughts. "I'm fine," she said, wiping her tears.

"Don't lie, ka'u pua."

Luca's deep voice rolled over her in a comforting wave, and she turned around as he slid the door closed behind him. "Luca? What are you doing here?"

"I came to make sure you were alright," he said, closing the gap between them and gathering her in his arms. "I'm so sorry. You shouldn't have to stay here like this."

Nadia pressed her face into the warmth of his black cotton t-shirt and breathed in his soothing scent. "No, but I'm safer here," she murmured as tears spilled over her eyes.

Luca tangled his hand in her hair and kissed her head. "I promise I won't let anything happen to you."

"I know." She gripped his shirt in her fists and molded herself in the security of his arms. "Can you stay? Just until I fall asleep?"

"Of course I can."

Chapter 41

Luca hummed the melody of the lullaby his Nonna used to sing to him while he held Nadia close and rubbed her back. She'd been restless most of the night and he felt nothing but guilt for putting her through this.

"No," she whimpered.

"You're okay," he whispered against her head.

"No! NO!!" she screamed and sobbed as her fists pounded into his chest while she struggled against him. He caught her flailing arms and wrapped his leg around her kicking limbs.

"Nadia," he said, holding her tight. "You're alright. You're safe."

She shuddered and curled her head into her chest. "D-don't take me to the room, Master," she whimpered, her body shaking in his arms. "I'll be good… I'll be a good kitten."

Luca's heart broke at the fear dripping in her voice. He slowly slid his hand to her cheek, tilting her face to him. "Wake up, ka'u pua," he whispered, pressing his lips to her forehead. "You're not my kitten and I'm not your Master."

Chapter 41

Her eyes fluttered open and she let out a choked breath. "I'm s-sorry," she murmured as her face crumpled and she burst into tears.

"It's alright," he cooed, tangling his fingers into her hair and cocooning his body around hers. "I've got you." He kissed her head. "I won't let anything happen to you," he murmured against her hair. He whispered to her until her cries quieted and she fell into a quiet slumber.

Luca tightened his arms around Nadia and pressed his face into her soft curls as he listened to her soft breaths that calmed his raging heart, but a snarl curled over his lips. His grandfather went too far, and Luca was going to make sure he suffered more than the loss of his precious society for staking a claim on Nadia.

Time was running out before his grandfather realized the Hatchs didn't have the blacklist and even less before he sent his ruthless mob of soldiers after Nadia. Luca closed his eyes and let Nadia's gentle heart beat lull him to sleep for the few remaining hours of the night.

"You weren't supposed to stay," Nadia murmured against Luca's neck as his watch vibrated against his wrist, alerting him to the early morning hour.

He silenced the alarm and kissed her head. "I couldn't leave you," he said, pulling away from her to look into her sleepy green eyes. "You didn't sleep very well."

"Yeah." She cringed. "I'm sorry I freaked out."

Luca slid his hand to her cheek. "It's okay. I can imagine what my grandfather said was triggering."

She nodded, wrapping her fingers around his wrist. "It was and I thought about running, but I didn't spend the last three years planning to take down Jonathan and the Syndicates to let Gregory scare me now. I'm stronger than that and I won't let anyone own me again. I'm not going to back down," she said and her eyes filled with a determined fire that licked over his skin and simmered in his gut. "*We* aren't going to back down."

"No, we're not." Luca's heart swelled with pride at the fight in her eyes. He was prepared to fight for both of them, but it relieved him she still wanted to do this.

"I don't like that I have to stay here," she said, pressing her forehead against his. "But thank you for always having the means to protect me. I'm lucky to have you."

"You never have to thank me for this." He kissed her softly and chuckled. "I'm glad you still think being involved with me is lucky."

A small smile tugged at her lips. "I do and we have Raquel to thank for this."

He raised an eyebrow. "So she admitted to having an ulterior motive, huh?"

"She did. I don't think she planned on things getting so fucked up, though."

"Probably not." He sighed, rubbing one of her curls between his fingers. "I don't know how often I'll be able to come out here to stay with you. Ciara almost made a scene last night when I told her I was staying with my parents. I have to play my part at least until we can set our plan in motion."

"I know, but I'll be fine. I'm sure you'll be alerted if anything happens out here."

Worry trickled down his spine and soured in his gut. "That's what I'm afraid of. I don't want that call."

"I know you don't," Nadia said, sliding her hand to his

cheek. "But there's no point in making a move against your grandfather until we know for sure we have all the information we need. I don't want there to be any way for Jonathan, Ciara or your grandfather to come after us or your family ever again."

Luca gazed into the fire sparking behind her sea-green eyes. He took her hand and pressed a kiss to her palm. "I know, ka'u wahine."

"Then do what you need to do, ka'u ali'i," she said, pressing her soft sweet lips against his. He drowned in the heavenly sound of her calling him her king and it was time he truly acted like one for her and everyone's sake.

* * *

While Nadia was getting dressed, Luca took a walk around the safe house to check the security cameras, locks on the doors, and the panic room. His family spared no cost when building this place, but it gave him peace of mind to check everything himself.

Walking down the slate path in the amber lit tunnel to the panic room, he checked the recess lights dotted amongst the stone walls and any uneven flooring that could cause Nadia to trip. Luca's heart clenched at the thought of her running for her life down here, but that was the reality of the situation.

His grandfather's private security guards could find anyone, if that's what he wanted, but the panic room was made to withstand an attack from them. They'd have to get past the guards and figure out which mirror led to the steps of the tunnel.

"You checking on the panic room too, huh?" Raquel said, walking down the slate path toward him.

"Yeah, it makes me feel better to check everything myself," he said, waving his watch over one of the recess lights in the stone wall. It gave a soft click and slid to the side.

"I know what you mean." Raquel nodded as they stepped into a small one-room apartment.

Luca crossed his arms as he eyed the dark wood features of the space. Cream and wood lamps were dotted amongst the furnishings, giving the room a warm glow. Brown leather couches sat around an electric fireplace in front of an armoire full of bulletproof vests and weapons. A mahogany bar sat flush against the far end of the room with a small kitchenette tucked in the corner, masking the hatch in the ceiling to the extraction point. "She's not going to like this."

"Nope." Raquel sighed. "No books, no plants and no windows," she said, walking across the floor to the mahogany weapons cabinet. "This is pretty impressive, though. Not sure I'd trust Nadia with a rifle yet. I haven't worked on those skills with her."

"Well, you taught her how to fight pretty well. That was you, right?"

"Yes sir," she said, opening the cabinet to run her fingers down the sleek black AK-47. She chuckled, looking over her shoulder at him. "Every wahine should know how to protect herself and give her ali'i a nice gut punch."

Luca choked out a laugh. "How do you know…?"

Raquel closed the cabinet and leaned against it. "A year ago, my grandma came to visit me and told me that her sister needed my help. She wanted me to dismantle an organization called the Syndicates so her family could come home," she said, crossing her arms over her chest. "Then she told me all about our heritage in Koa Maile, how it was a great honor to assist the chiefess and my family too."

Luca's eyes grew wide and he took a step back as he processed what the hell she just said. "Raquel, you're... you're my *cousin*. Why didn't you come to me back then?"

"I know, but my grandma said it was important that I didn't get you involved. Your Nonna didn't want that shithead Duke to harm you or your family," she said, sliding her hand through her ponytail. "I guess I cheated a bit when Cam got ahold of me, but I figured it was fine since you were on the same mission."

Luca nodded. It sounded like something his Nonna would do to protect them in her own way. She must've been trying to do her own research and found a connection through her sister to help. "And what about Nadia? Didn't you realize how dangerous it was for her to get involved with me?"

"Yes, but I've watched you, researched you and learned all the things I didn't know about my culture and you as the ali'i of Koa Maile. I know what kind of man you are. I had a feeling you'd at least become friends with Nadia and be able to protect her better than I could if things got serious like this." A grin spread across Raquel's face and mischief danced in her big brown eyes. "What I didn't know was that you'd fall in love with her and not to be rude, but I'd like some sort of commemoration for finding the next wahine."

Luca laughed and a blush burned over his cheeks. "That's Nadia's decision to make, but I'm sure my Nonna would love to honor you in Koa Maile." He shook his head and slid a hand over her shoulder. "I wish you told me who you were."

She smiled, placing her hand over his. "I think part of me was scared. My mother died when I was young and my grandma never told me about any of this. I grew up thinking I was Mexican and there was a whole other side of me I didn't know. I've never even been to Koa Maile."

"When this is over, you can come home with me."

Raquel looked up at him through the tiny wisps of curls framing her face and a watery smile spread across her lips. "Thank you," she said and laughed, wiping her eyes before a tear rolled down her cheek. "I didn't plan on having a heart to heart with you. I just wanted you to know that I've got your back and Nadia's too."

"I know you do, and I'm glad you told me. Knowing who you are makes me feel better about your role in all of this."

Raquel tutted her lips. "As if you doubted me."

Luca slid his hand from her shoulder and shrugged. "I never doubted your abilities, just slightly questioned your motive to take this on as a PI."

Raquel grinned. "Well, it's good money and I like a bit of chaos. You and Nadia's fucked up lives certainly fit that bill."

Luca let out a bark of laughter. "I don't know if that's a compliment."

"It is," she said, slapping a hand on his shoulder. "We should probably get going. I think this space is sufficient, but you might want to get some books in here to help Nadia feel a bit more relaxed."

"Yeah, I'll get someone to stock it with her favorites," he said, pressing his hand against the security scanner and the stone wall slid to the side. "But I don't want her down here long enough to read any."

"Gordon and I will be the judge of that if the time comes,"

she said as they walked down the amber lit tunnel and back up the stone steps into the house.

"Yeah, and make sure she doesn't trip on those stairs. I'm regretting all the stone and slate being installed down there now."

"She'll be fine." Raquel chuckled, closing the mirrored door behind them. "There's a chance we won't have to use the panic room."

"I hope so," he murmured and a smile spread across his lips at Nadia descending the open staircase into the living room.

"Sorry it took me so long to get dressed," she said, fidgeting with the clasp of her watch. "I'm anxious all of a sudden."

"It's alright." Luca crossed the space between them. "Everything's going to be fine," he said, clasping the watch for her. "You've got a good team around you."

Nadia took a deep breath and patted the braid around her head. "I know," she said, looking around him at Raquel. "I'm sorry you're stuck staying out here with me."

"I already told you I don't mind and we're not stuck out here. Think of it as a little vacation. Nervy's going to be here for dinner tonight. I promised she could visit for a few hours a few nights a week as long as it's safe. I thought that would make you feel a little better."

A smile spread over Nadia's lips. "It does, thank you."

"Good. I mean, I plan to enjoy bossing that guy around while I'm here," Raquel said, pointing her thumb at Gordon making coffee in the kitchen.

"I'm happy I get to hang out with you too," Gordon said, chuckling as he shook his head. "But I'm in charge out here, ma'am."

"Mm, we'll see about that, sir."

"Mr. Shola, are you ready to go?" Jack said from the front door.

Luca nodded, and his heart clenched at the thought of leaving Nadia. He wasn't ready, but he knew he couldn't stay. He had to keep up appearances to keep her safe. Taking a deep breath, he looked down at Nadia, slipping his arms around her and hugging her tight. "I'll come out here as often as I can," he said, kissing her head.

"Okay, but I'll be fine if you can't. E pakele, Mr. Underworld."

He pulled away from her to stare into her bright spring green eyes and slid a hand to her cheek. "You too, ka'u pua," he said, kissing her softly before he let her go.

"We'll keep her safe," Raquel said, patting his shoulder.

"I know you will," he said, giving Nadia one more glance and a small wave before he followed Jack to the waiting black SUV on the graveled, tree-lined driveway. The sunny woodland setting of the safe house was peaceful, but Luca felt the disquiet amongst the guards like this was the calm before the storm and in a way it was.

Slipping into the car, he heaved a sigh to quell the slight anxiety of leaving Nadia. There was something comforting knowing that Raquel was family and that his Nonna entrusted her to help. It felt like she was always watching over them.

"Our guys on the inside informed me that Mr. Rodawson's techs are nearly finished with the Hatchs' files and his mercenaries were spotted scouting the block around Nadia's apartment last night," Jack said as Luca closed the car door.

"Then it's good that she's staying here," he said, pulling his phone from his pocket and tapping a message to Nadia's guards to fix the stairs leading to the tunnel, clear a space in the gym, and to bring in more plants for the panic room. He also sent a list of Nadia's favorite books and novels on their reading list.

"Yes it is. Gordon and Henry made the right decision," Jack said, as he drove down the path through the gates of the compound. "Did Miss Armentaros have a word with you?"

Luca looked up from his phone. "Yes. Did you know who she was?"

"No, she told me while you were in Japan but I should've known. Her mother and I were close. I didn't know she was pregnant before I joined the military and she left Koa Maile. She died before I saw her again. So it's been nice working with Raquel. She looks just like her mother."

"Wait Jack…is she your daughter?"

"Yeah, I think so. I've done the math and looked into her background. Her father adopted her after she was born, but I could never tell Raquel that and she doesn't need to know," Jack said, shaking his head. "I shouldn't even be telling you this. We've got bigger problems on our hands."

"Yes, but you should tell her. She deserves to know the truth about who she is. I've told her she can come home to Koa Maile with me when this is over. That would be the perfect place to do it."

"Mm, maybe you're right," he said, turning in the opposite direction of the city.

"Where are you going?"

"Back to your parents' house. They want to speak to you about what's going on and I think it's time you've filled them in. It's going to get dangerous for them too."

"Yeah, that's true," he murmured looking out the window.

It was time for everything to come to light and for them to play their part in this mission.

Chapter 42

Luca » Ha'o wau iā 'oe.«

I miss you.

Ka'u Pua » Na'u nō 'oe.«

I need you.

Luca sighed, swiping her message away and tucking his phone in his pocket before taking a slow sip of the bourbon in his glass. He needed her, too. It had been three days since he'd seen Nadia, and the charade of happiness he'd been putting on with Ciara was exhausting. The lunches, the dinners and the fucking nagging about their engagement had his stomach in constant turmoil.

Not only that, there had been two attempted break-ins at Nadia's apartment. It was only a matter of time before Jonathan and his grandfather's men figured out she wasn't living in the city.

Leaning against the lavish mahogany bar on the top floor lounge of the W Hotel far from Ciara and the gaggle of Syndicates, Luca checked the progress of the blacklist and watched the green status bar hover at ninety-eight percent. Everything was in place. His family was in on the plan now, but soon his grandfather's investigation into the Hatchs would be complete.

Luca took another sip from his glass. Nowhere would be safe for his family or Nadia when that happened. At least there was only a matter of minutes before the blacklist was decoded. He hoped.

"Do you know why I want her?"

Luca slid his eyes to his grandfather, leaning against the bar and waving away his latest Juliet on his arm. He fought the bile rising in his throat as the scantily clad brunette walked away tugging her skin tight dress down as she sat at a small table near the window. That could be Nadia forced to be his grandfather's escort. He tore his gaze away from her to his grandfather's proud face. "Want who?"

He grinned, taking a sip of the whiskey in his hand. "Nadia, your little director."

Heat flooded Luca's veins as he forced a sly grin on his face to hide his rage. "Why?"

"Mm, for one thing, she's gorgeous." He shook his head. "You know I like my Juliets as pale as they come, but I'm making an exception for Miss Coleman." He chuckled and nudged Luca's arm. "And I get to kill two birds with one stone with her."

"What's that supposed to mean?"

The smile fell from his grandfather's lips, and the humor in his eyes turned cold. "You might've fooled her," he said, nodding to Ciara sitting at a table with a few of her friends. "But it was written all over your face when you saw Nadia with me. You're in love with her and Jonathan's obsessed with her," he said, finishing the spirits in his glass. "You'll both suffer under my thumb as long as I have her."

Luca smirked. "What do you want me to say to that?"

"Nothing. I just want you to remember who has the power here. You're lucky I'm not beating you for this and that I've stepped in before you messed up my plans like your mother."

Luca curled his hand into a fist in his pocket. "Thank you for being so gracious."

"Mm, you're welcome." He waved to the bartender who sat another glass of golden whiskey on the bar. "Your marriage is important. The two founding families coming together will keep this society thriving for decades. It's my legacy. It's what I've worked for," he said, jabbing his finger into Luca's chest. "And you won't fuck this up and neither will the fucking Hatchs," he said, downing the whiskey in one quick gulp. "I'll get my list back and you'll give me a great grandchild from the *right* bloodline." He scoffed. "Not from some meaningless royal blood you've been tainted with."

Luca clenched his teeth at the insult to his people and eyed his grandfather's glossy eyes and ruddy cheeks. He'd never seen him drink like this before and he wondered if it meant he was worried or maybe he was scared.

"Are you two setting the world right over here?" Ciara grinned, sliding up to them and wrapping her arm around Luca's.

"Ah, we're just talking about how nice it'll be when you join our family. Right, Luca?"

"Of course," he said with a tight smile on his face. "I can't wait."

"I can't either." Ciara smiled and leaned up to his ear. "Why don't we get out of here?" she whispered.

His grandfather chuckled. "You lovebirds have a good night," he said, pushing away from the bar. "I've kept my date waiting long enough."

"You have a good night too, Gregory," Ciara said, threading her fingers through Luca's.

"I will, sweetheart. Be good, son."

"Mm," Luca murmured as they slipped away from the bar and said a few farewells on their walk to the elevators.

"Come home with me tonight," Ciara purred as the elevator doors closed.

"Please don't do this." He sighed, pressing the button for the ground floor. It was the same routine every night.

"I'm not doing anything. I'm just trying to be cozy with my boyfriend. Is that so wrong of me to do?" Ciara muttered. "Come on, Lu." She pouted. "You can't deny me forever," she said, sliding her hand between his legs.

"Stop." Luca gripped her wrist and tugged it away from him. "Not tonight," he said as the elevator doors opened.

"You always say that," she hissed as they walked through the lobby and out the revolving doors to the waiting car.

"I'm tired. I just want to go home," he grumbled, helping her into the open car door. Luca took a deep breath before sliding in after her.

"You always say that too." She pouted, leaning into him and wrapping her bare leg around his. "When are you going to touch me again?"

"I told you, I'm not ready for that," Luca said, pushing her leg from his lap.

Ciara tutted her lips. "It's been long enough, Luca," she said, grabbing his collar and sliding herself over his lap. "I want you," she whispered, grinding her hips against him and the stench of alcohol and her lavender perfume assaulted his senses.

Luca dug his fingers into the leather seat and fought the panic clawing down his spine. "Get o-off of me, Ciara."

"No," she said, sliding her hand to his belt buckle. "You're too weak to stop me." She giggled, piercing him with a lustful gleam in her eyes. "You're mine, Lu."

The panic ceased to seep over him, and rage replaced it instead. He wasn't hers and he didn't have to be. Luca grabbed her waist and pushed her on to the seat next to him. "I said get the fuck off me."

A snarl curled over Ciara's lips. "How fucking dare you!" She roared, raising her hand to hit him.

Luca caught her wrist and shoved her against the car door and stared into her shocked brown eyes. "You're done hitting me, Ciara."

"Oh, look who gained some balls," she said, laughing. "You can't get away from me, Lu. I fucking own you and that little bitch you like will be under your grandfather soon. I bet she'll like it too."

"You're fucking disgusting," he said, pushing away from her before he slapped the grin off her face. "Stop the fucking car." He called out to the driver.

"What? No, Lu! Don't leave. I'm sorry. I shouldn't have said that," she said, latching onto his arm.

"Fuck you," he seethed as he shrugged her arm off him.

"You can't leave me!" she screamed. "Don't you get out of this car, Luca! You know what will happen if you do!"

Luca grasped the door handle and hesitated long enough for his watch to vibrate against his wrist. He looked down at the notification and nearly laughed.

"That's right," Ciara cooed, sliding her hand over his shoulder. "Think about what you're doing. I'll lose everything. You won't do that to me," she said, tugging him back to her. "I promise I won't hurt you again. I swear."

Luca looked into her soft brown eyes and he felt nothing. The pity he once had for her dried up. She deserved everything coming to her. He grit his teeth and pulled away from her. "No, you won't hurt me again because we're done," he said as he stepped out of the car.

"Luca!" Ciara wailed as he slammed the door in her face.

Luca marched into the swell of people enjoying their night out. Tears pricked the corners of his eyes and he picked up his pace, slipping down a darkened alley as his stomach turned and rolled. He leaned against the side of the building and hurled the contents in his stomach behind a dumpster.

Fuck.

He groaned, wiping his mouth on his sleeve and held a hand over his chest to fight the anxiety biting at him.

Pressing himself against the building, Luca peered around the corner and heaved a deep breath that Ciara's car was gone. Closing his eyes, a laugh choked from his mouth.

He did it. That wasn't how he planned to break it off with her, but it was done. He looked down at the notification on his watch.

»Decoding complete «

Ciara » I'm sorry, Lu.«

Ciara » You have to come back to me!«

Ciara » Please Lu. Just answer me!«

Ciara » I love you, please don't leave me«

Ciara » I'll have the fucking bitch killed! She can't have you! You're mine! You were always MINE!«

Chapter 42

Luca dug his phone from his pocket and turned off the sync to his watch before he turned off his phone. He took a deep breath and closed his eyes. No matter what happened next, he'd never go back to Ciara.

Car lights flashed into the alleyway. Luca's eyes popped open and his heart clenched at the black sedan rolling into the alley. He eyed the license plate and let out a deep breath.

"Need a ride?" Jack grinned as he rolled down the window.

"Yes, thank you," he breathed, pushing himself from the wall and slumping into the back seat.

"You okay?"

"Yeah, I will be," Luca said, pulling a water bottle from the cup holder and taking a drink. "I just want to see Nadia."

"Fair enough. You saw the notification?"

"Yes, it was good timing too." Luca sighed. "I almost broke up with Ciara before I knew."

"I had a feeling that's why you bolted from her car. This wasn't part of the plan, Mr. Shola."

Luca rested his head against the cool glass window, staring out at the amber street lights passing by. "I know, but I couldn't do it anymore. My grandfather threatened Nadia again and Ciara tried to..." he trailed off and shook his head. "She tried to rape me and I had enough." He gripped the water bottle. "I want to finish this now."

"Well, we certainly have the tools to do it," Jack said, looking up at him in the rear-view mirror. "I'm sorry she did that, but I'm proud of you for getting out of there."

"Thank you," he said, running a hand over his face. "When Ciara tells her father what I did, everyone's going to need heightened security. My grandfather is going to be livid."

"Everyone's prepared. I'd rather you relax and spend time

with little wahine instead of worrying about what's going to happen. You both need this."

Luca leaned back in his seat and closed his eyes. "Yeah, we do."

The only thing he wanted to do was curl up in Nadia's arms, breathe her in and tell her how much he loved her.

***

Luca followed Jack up the stone steps of the safe house and his heart sank when he walked inside to find Raquel and Gordon on the couch in the living room, with Nadia nowhere in sight.

"Hey! It's finally done!" Raquel exclaimed in excitement as she popped up from the couch.

"Yeah. Where's Nadia?"

"Oh, we had a little dance party while Nervy was here and she's still in the gym," Raquel said, crossing the room to slap a hand on his shoulder. "Nadia loves it down there. You did well with it."

"That's good. Is Nervy still here?"

"No, Henry took her home a little while ago," Gordon said. "But I'm glad you're here. We can talk strategy about the next steps of the plan."

Luca nodded. "Feel free to do that without me."

"Sure. I think Nadia wants to see you too." Raquel smiled and turned her warm brown eyes on Jack. "Can I make you a cup of coffee, old man?"

Jack smiled. "Yeah, I'd like that, but I'm not an old man."

"Mm, okay. You might be in shape for your age, but you're still old enough to be my father." Raquel teased as Jack choked out a laugh.

Chapter 42

Luca chuckled softly as he walked away from them to the bathroom. He wondered if Raquel knew who Jack was to her. It wouldn't surprise him, but he hoped Jack found the courage to tell her.

Sighing as he closed the door, Luca splashed water over his cheeks and washed his mouth out a few times before he stared at his reflection. At least Ciara didn't leave any marks on him tonight. He didn't want it to upset Nadia.

A smile graced his lips, but he couldn't wait to tell her he was all hers.

Luca shrugged off his suit jacket and rolled the sleeves of his shirt over his elbows. He wouldn't mind getting lost in the music with Nadia in his arms. Dancing with her never failed to make him forget the world and all their problems.

He followed the soft music filtering into the stairwell from the gym. Luca's heart thumped as he neared the door and peered through the glass at Nadia dancing flawlessly in a black leotard and sheer purple ballet skirt flowing over her legs. He pushed open the glass door and quietly slipped inside to watch the beauty dance her tale of triumph to the moving beat and lyrics of Seinabo Sey's Breathe.

Tears welled in his eyes at her powerful twists and turns and made him feel the music in her touching routine. A tear rolled down his cheek, knowing how hard she must've worked to dance on pointe like that again.

He'd never seen her dance like this before, and he was mesmerized by the strength in the elegance of her command of the dance floor. This was her 'fuck you' to Jonathan that he didn't take this away from her.

Luca didn't think his heart had enough room to love her any more than he already did, but Nadia proved him wrong.

She was the most amazing person he knew and he only hoped he could spend his life making sure she knew it.

Chapter 43

"Don't forget to breathe," Nadia sang with her eyes closed, spinning out a final pirouette, letting the last melodic beats of the music fill her up and remind her why she had the courage to endure all she'd been through.

"That was beautiful."

Her eyes snapped open at the sound of Luca's voice. Her heart thumped at the tears in his eyes as he crossed the room to her and gathered her in his arms.

"You're here," she mumbled into his chest as she wrapped her arms around him, breathing in the comfort of his earthy scent.

"I am and you're amazing, ka'u pua," he whispered, kissing her head.

"I missed you."

Luca pulled away from her, sliding a hand to her cheek. "I missed you too."

She frowned at his watery golden eyes. "What happened?"

He shook his head, sliding his hand to her waist. "A lot of

things," he said, placing her hand on his shoulder. "But right now, I'd like to dance with you, if that's okay?"

A smile tugged at her lips. "It is. As long as you tell me what's wrong."

"Later." He kissed her softly, sliding his hand to the small of her back, pulling her close. "I just need this right now."

"Me too," she whispered as Luca twirled her around and led them in a waltz to the soft drum beat of Rufus Du Sol's Underwater.

They glided across the floor, and Luca's sensual caresses over her body as he guided her moves made her tingle and melt into the small world they always found themselves in. But this wasn't like the way they danced in Osaka. There was something deeper, more intense in the tender look in Luca's golden eyes, as if he were staring into her soul and she wanted him to have it. To have everything she could give him.

He twirled her around, catching her in his arms, and dipping her, leaving soft kisses on her neck. "Ka'u pua nani," he murmured against her ear, pulling her back up.

"Yes," she whispered, sliding her hands into his hair.

"You mean everything to me."

Her heart thumped and butterflies punched against her stomach at the affection he breathed over her. A flame simmered in the pit of her stomach and burned down to her center. And all she wanted, all she needed was him. She pressed her forehead to his. "Show me," she whispered against his lips.

He kissed her softly, picking her up in his arms, and she wrapped her legs around his waist. "I want to make love to you," he said, dragging his lips to her ear. "Will you let me?"

Chapter 43

Nadia's heart thumped as she slid her hands to his cheeks and turned his face to hers. She stared into the warmth of his golden eyes. The love and tenderness that swirled in them spread over her and sent delightful shivers down her spine. She'd never been so sure of something in her life. A smile spread across her lips. "Yes."

***

Luca laid her against the soft floral bed sheets as he kissed over her neck. Nadia sighed and trailed her fingers through Luca's hair as he took his time kissing down her stomach. He whispered sweet confessions of his affections and punctuated each one with a kiss to her skin as he slowly slid her panties down her legs.

Goosebumps prickled over her skin from the sensual way he undressed her, as if he were carefully unwrapping a precious gift. His hands were so gentle as he spread her legs, holding them over his shoulders.

He kissed the inside of her thighs and pressed his lips just above her wet mound. He looked up at her, and the tenderness that pooled in his depths sent another wave of tingles coursing through her. "You're beautiful, ka'u pua," he murmured and slid his tongue between her wet folds.

Nadia moaned as she slid her hands over her breasts, rolling her nipples between her fingers. The licks and swirls of his tongue were so tender and soft. A gasp left her lips and she shuddered as he slipped his finger into her folds.

He gently thrust it in and out, adding a finger every few strokes while he suckled on her clit. A tingle burned in her gut and slowly spread through her veins as she dug her nails into his hair and rocked her hips against his face.

Her body tensed and a cry escaped her lips as an orgasm

rippled over her. Nadia tugged on his hair and pulled his face to her. "I need you," she whispered into his mouth.

"So do I," he murmured against her lips and pulled away from her.

While her pussy fluttered in anticipation, her heart pounded when Luca crawled over her. He caressed his hands up her sides and a slight panic tugged at her heart. "Wait," she breathed, pressing her hand to his shoulder.

"What's the matter, baby?"

"I-I can't do it this way." She bit her lip and looked away from him. "With you on top. N-not initially," she mumbled. She hated she couldn't let anyone love her this way, but she felt the panic rising in her chest and even though she trusted Luca, it didn't stop her mind from seeing Jonathan looming over her.

He kissed her hand and turned her face to him. "There's nothing to be ashamed of," he whispered. He slid his arm under her waist and pulled her to him as he sat back on his knees. He straddled her legs around him and held her just above the tip of his dick. "Is this better?"

She wrapped her arms around his shoulders and a smile tugged at her lips as the rising panic subsided. "Yes," she whispered as he slowly sat her over his manhood. Her breath hitched and she moaned as his warm dick stretched her folds. He was much bigger than she was used to, but his cock felt so heavenly inside of her.

Luca groaned as she slowly rocked her hips over him. Staring into his eyes, she watched them fill with heat and desire. His fingers left a trail of fire up her back before they tangled in her hair. "You feel so good," he murmured and caught her lips with his as he guided her movements.

Chapter 43

She held him tight and whimpered into his mouth as she quickened her pace over him. He gripped her ass as he nibbled and kissed down her neck while their hips slapped together. Nadia dug her nails into his shoulders and cried out from the bliss that consumed her. "Luca…" she panted and mewled against his ear.

"Tell me what you want," he said, and his hot breath tingled over her skin and sent shivers down her spine.

"Harder," she breathed.

"Mm yes, baby," he moaned and laid her back on the bed. She tensed in his arms as panic tugged at her heart. Luca slid his hand to her cheek as he slowed his thrusts inside of her. "Look at me, Nadia."

She slid her eyes open and she stared into his warm golden depths. "I've got you." The care in his voice and his gentle, tender strokes sent a wave of pleasure rippling through her, driving away the panic in her mind.

A sizzling warmth ignited inside of her as she dragged her fingers through his hair and tugged his lips to hers. "Don't let me go."

"I never will," he murmured and slid his tongue into her mouth. She panted and moaned from his powerful thrusts and delightful cock sinking deep inside of her.

Lifting her legs over his shoulders, Luca pounded his dick into her gushing center. Nadia cried out as wave after beautiful wave of pleasure and elation rolled over her. No one had ever made sex feel this damn good and she had to fight to keep from drowning in the sea of pleasure her mind was begging to go.

"Luca!" she screamed, arching back as he gripped her hips.

"Yes, baby. Let go for me," he grunted and slammed his

cock between her thighs.

She gripped the sheets between her fists as her tits bounced up and down from the force of his thrusts. Her mouth formed an 'O' and a silent scream escaped her lips as she felt the building orgasm tingle in her gut.

"Fuck," Luca groaned, pulling her up against him. He leaned back on his knees as he continued to pound her pussy over his cock.

Nadia threw her head back and cried out in ecstasy. She panted, pressing her forehead against his. Her hips matching the plunging rhythm of his hands gripping her waist as an orgasm rose through her like a flower coming to bloom, yearning to see the sun.

She craved and feared the intensity of what he was doing to her, but it was too much and she was going to fall into pieces.

"Hold me," Nadia cried as her body shook. "Hold me!" she screamed as she wrapped her arms and legs around him. Her body tensed and shuddered violently against him as an earth shattering orgasm quaked over her. Luca cried out with her, engulfing her with his body as they fell into the bed in a tangled heap.

Tears rolled down Nadia's cheeks as she gasped for air and her body continued to spasm in his arms. She had nothing to compare this moment to. She had nothing to compare these feelings to. No one had ever made love to her and after Luca, she didn't want anyone else to.

"I've got you," he breathed. "I've always got you, ka'u pua," he murmured against her head after he caught his breath. He wiped the tears on her cheeks and his eyes filled with concern. "Are you okay?"

Nadia let out a slow breath and nodded. "I'm fine." She kissed him softly. "I…" Her lip trembled as she looked into the depths of his endearing hazel eyes. There was so much love in them she could feel it reach down to the depths of her soul and grab hold.

"What's the matter?" he murmured and caressed her bottom lip as his eyes drooped.

"Nothing." A tired smile tugged at her lips. "I love you," she whispered as a wave of exhaustion rolled over her like a soft blanket.

"I love you too," he said, kissing her softly. She closed her eyes and sighed against his lips. Her limbs relaxed and the warmth of his embrace and the calm in her heart made her feel so light that she fell into the peaceful slumber her mind yearned to go.

Chapter 44

Luca laid awake in the soft moonlit room, caressing Nadia's cheek with his thumb as she slumbered peacefully against him. He had never made love like that to anyone before. It felt like she reached into his soul and wrapped herself around him. He had never been so sure about someone in all his life. She was it for him and she said it. She loved him.

He knew she did, but it was comforting to hear the words come from her mouth and he needed to hear her say it. Luca pressed a kiss to her forehead, her eyes fluttered open, and a sleepy smile spread across her lips. "Good morning," she murmured.

"It's still the middle of the night." He chuckled softly. "How are you feeling?"

"I feel amazing." She sighed and snuggled her face against his chest. "How do you feel?"

"The same." Luca grinned against her head. "I like waking up like this," he murmured into her hair.

"Naked?" Nadia giggled.

Chapter 44

He smiled, sliding his hand to her hip. "That and with the woman I love."

She looked up at him, pressing a kiss to his chin. "I like that."

"Me too."

She slid her hand over his chest and touched her fingers to his lips. "You haven't told me what happened or why you came out here tonight."

"I wanted to see you." He kissed her fingers and tangled his hand in her hair. "And tell you I'm free to be yours for as long as you'll have me."

Her eyes grew wide. "You broke up with Ciara?"

"Yes."

"Luca." Nadia pushed away from him as panic tainted her green eyes. "But the blacklist –"

"Has been decoded." He pulled her back to him. "We have everything we need."

Her worry faded as hope bloomed in her bright green eyes and she pressed her hand to his cheek. "We're really going to be free."

He wrapped his hand around her wrist, pressing his forehead against hers. "Yes we are," he said, kissing her softly just as a loud boom erupted from outside.

Nadia and Luca's watches started blinking in warning from the bedside table as footsteps pounded down the hall and feverish knocks rattled the bedroom door.

"Miss Nadia! Mr. Shola! They're here. Get up!" Gordon roared.

"Nadia, get your shit on. Let's go!" Raquel shouted.

Fear and worry knotted in Luca's stomach as they scrambled out of the bed.

"Fuck! Oh my God," Nadia said, as she stumbled to her closet, frantically pulling out clothes.

"It's o-okay," Luca said, throwing his clothes on. "I'll get you to the panic room. You're going to be… fine," he said, watching Nadia zip up a Kevlar vest over her black shirt and cargo pants. She slid a steel blade into the pocket at her side and stuck her feet into a pair of black steel toe boots.

She looked up at him and threw another Kevlar vest at him. "You're going to need that," she said, tying her hair up into a bun.

"Um, yeah," he said, shrugging the vest over his shoulders. "I'm glad everyone prepared you for this."

Nadia looked over at him. "I'm freaking out," she said, clenching her fists. "But he won't take me that easily."

Luca crossed the room and pulled her in his arms. "He'll never take you, ka'u pua."

She gripped his waist and her hands shook as she took a deep breath. "Can you count with me?"

"Let's go! They're going to breach the door!" Gordon yelled, pounding against the door as the rapping of gunfire sounded in the distance.

Luca held Nadia tight, ignoring the impending danger. She needed this and he'd do anything to make her feel safe. "Five," he said, pressing a kiss to her head.

"I'm not his," she breathed.

"You belong to no one. Four."

"I'm free."

"Yes, you are. Three."

"I'm executing my plan."

"Damn right." He smiled. "Two."

"I'm safe."

Chapter 44

"Always. One."

"I'm alive."

"And you're going to stay that way." Luca pulled away from her, caressing her cheek. "Are you ready?"

She nodded with grit shining in her eyes. "I'm ready."

He pressed a kiss to her lips. "I love you," he said, slipping his fingers through hers. "Let's go," he said, crossing the room and opening the door to the heavy banging and popping against the doors and windows from below.

"Get down and follow us," Gordon said as he pushed them down to a crouching position while Raquel perched in front of them.

"They're going to blow the doors. We don't have much time to get to the mirror. We've got to get to the hatch in the back," she said.

"They've surrounded the compound. None of our detractors worked," Gordon said as they moved along the hallway to the back staircase at the end of the hall.

"Is… is Jonathan with them?" Nadia said as they hurried down the stairs just as a chorus of loud bangs shook the house. Windows shattered, gunfire rang out as their guards yelled and grappled with the storm of black clad military guards filtering in through the singed metal doors at the back of the house beneath them.

"Fuck," Gordon hissed. "Make a barrier," he said into his watch.

Luca grabbed Nadia's hand, pressing her between him and Gordon as a group of guards squaring off against his grandfather's mercenaries slowly backed away to shelter the staircase.

"Doesn't have to be a fight." The mercenary chuckled as

he lit a cigar. "Give us what Mr. Rodawson wants and we'll leave. Simple as that."

"Nah, we're not going to do that," Henry said, cocking his gun.

Raquel crept down the steps, waving her hand for them to follow. She quietly flipped the latch open on the floor behind the feet of the guards at the bottom of the steps.

"Thought you might say that," the mercenary said as Raquel lifted the square floorboard and a barrel of a gun pointed up at her.

"Shit."

Their guards turned around and pointed their guns at the invader as a black device shot out from the hatch.

"Get down!" Their guards yelled as the bomb exploded in a flash of blinding light. Nadia screamed as a flood of footsteps sounded around them and she was ripped from Luca's arms.

"Nadia!" he roared, trying to grab her, but the blinding light and ringing in his ears disoriented him.

"She's mine now."

A butt of a gun cracked over the back of his neck and he slumped against the side of the stairs.

Chapter 45

"No!" Nadia screamed, digging her feet into the floor as she was dragged through broken glass and shards of metal. The pungent smell of wood and metal burning assaulted her senses as she struggled against her captor.

Tears rolled down her cheeks at Luca sprawled out on the floor with a gun pressed to his head, her guards' battered faces, hands zip tied and held at gunpoint by the mercenaries blocking any path to her. Blood ran from Raquel's head as she lay limp and shielded by Gordon's bound wrists wrapped around her as he glared into the eyes of the men holding them hostage.

"Nadia!" Luca cried out, struggling against the man holding him down.

"Stay down you son of a bitch," the mercenary roared, pressing his boot into Luca's back and the rifle of a gun to his head.

"E ke koa, i ka'u wahine," Luca said with his golden eyes full of malice and his mouth in a grim line.

Be a warrior, my queen.

Nadia grit her teeth and gripped her hands against the splintered door frame. Her palms bled as she pulled away from her captor.

"Let go," Jonathan hissed. "No more games, Nadia. You belong to me."

His voice rolled over her skin in a sickening wave. She let go of the door frame and jabbed her elbow into his gut. He wheezed, releasing his grip on her just enough for her to twist out of his arms and dart around him down the steps to the stone path of the garden.

Plan B was to lock herself in the gardening shed to give her a chance to escape on one of the quad bikes and, if that failed…

"Nadia!" Jonathan roared as his feet pounded against the stone behind her.

She pushed her legs harder, running faster to the sandstone vine-covered hut shining like a beacon at the edge of the path. She cried out as her foot nicked an uneven stone. Falling forward, she skinned her knees against the rough grain.

Ignoring the pain, she scrambled to her feet to keep running, but Jonathan snatched her bun. He yanked her back, slamming her down against the ground. Nadia choked out a pained breath as her back throbbed from the impact.

Jonathan pounced on top of her, pressing his weight into her. She froze in panic at his familiar scent of pine and musk. The sinister gleam in his dark brown eyes, that seemed even darker under the amber glow of the iron lamps. The devilish smile across his golden face and flush pink lips sent her mind tumbling into the punishment chamber where he beat her for all her wrongdoings.

Chapter 45

"Good thing I fucked up your brain, huh?" he said, wrapping his hand around her neck. He leaned down to her, taking a long sniff of her hair, and pressed his lips against her ear. "I should've done this a long time ago."

She shook beneath him, sucking in tiny breaths as fear sank like daggers into her skin and whispered for her to give in. She'd never get away from Jonathan. This was always going to happen.

"But the chase was fun. Watching you look over your shoulder for me, moving from place to place because of me." He smiled, kissing the side of her mouth. "You were always thinking about me," he said, tightening his grip around her neck. "Until you met that fuck and he messed with my plans, but Gregory gave me the perfect chance at revenge." He licked her cheek. "You're mine, little kitten and you'll never get away from me again."

Fire rose through her veins at the smug finality in his words. She'd rather die than give into him and she wouldn't go out like this. She didn't have to. Nadia clenched the handle of the smooth blade in her hand and grit her teeth. "No." She choked out and stabbed the blade into his side.

Jonathan howled, releasing her neck. She took advantage of his shock, reached forward and slipped the gun from his hip holster before slamming her foot into his groin, knocking him on his back.

Nadia scrambled to her feet as he writhed in pain. He howled mercy when she stomped her foot over his chest and pointed the gun at his face. "I'm not your fucking kitten."

"Step away from him, Miss Coleman." A deep voice rang out as red lasers pointed from all directions at her chest.

She looked up at the mercenaries surrounding her as

Jonathan choked out a laugh below her. "You dumb bitch." He coughed. "You're mine. There's no one here to save you," he said, pushing against her foot.

Nadia stomped on his arm, cocking the trigger of the gun.

"Put it down," the black clad soldier said as he took a step forward.

Her heart was racing and pounding in her ears as she felt the heat of the lasers on her chest. Twelve lasers, twelve men and no one there to save her but herself.

Tears rolled down her cheeks. How long would she last with Jonathan? Locked away in the punishment chamber made to feel like she was nothing and turned into a slave to service men like Gregory Rodawson. A collar around her neck, Jonathan's men watching her every move, never able to see her friends, her family and becoming a shell of herself in front of Luca.

"No!" Nadia yelled, holding the gun beneath her chin. She'd rather die.

"Nadia! What are you doing?" Jonathan cried in panic, tugging and grasping at the leg of her pants. "Not that!"

She looked down at him, her finger shaking against the trigger. "I don't want to live in a world where you get to touch me."

"Ka'u pua! Stop!" Luca's deep voice boomed. Nadia gasped, pulling her finger from the trigger as he raced from the steps of the smoking house toward her with a swell of their guards following him.

Before the soldiers could turn their guns on him, a barrage of short staccato pings rained from the tall hedges around the garden. The twelve men thumped to the ground in quick succession as a team of combat soldiers emerged from the brush.

"Little wahine, you can put your gun down," the soldier said, holding up his hands. "It's over."

The gun shook in her hands as she looked down at Jonathan and delighted in the fear that drained the color from his face.

"Nadia…" Luca warned, stepping closer to her.

"L-listen to him, kitten," Jonathan cooed. "You won. I can't hurt you now."

Fury raged through her veins as tears blurred her vision. It wouldn't be over until he suffered for all the pain he put her through.

She had no more fucks to give. This was her moment, and no one was going to take this from her.

"I am *not* your kitten." She dug her foot into his wound, enjoying the sound of his painful cries. "I'm not going to kill you, but you're going to spend the rest of your life living in fear of me," she said, leaning down to him and pressing the gun to the center of his forehead. "So much so, you'll wish I put a bullet in your head tonight." She smacked the gun over his tear-stained face and stood from him as the combat team moved forward and dragged Jonathan from the ground.

Nadia's breath hitched as she stared into Luca's wide eyes. She trembled from the stabbing pain in her hands and knees and the lifeless bodies lying on the ground. "Luca," she breathed, her breath coming out in quick gasps. Her wobbling legs crumbled beneath her as the crushing weight of what transpired crashed down on her all at once.

"I've got you," he cooed, engulfing her in his strong arms. "You're safe," he whispered into her hair as they sank to the ground.

A sob broke from her lips. "I couldn't let him take me. I-I'm sorry I–"

"Shh, it's okay," he said, rocking her against him as he pressed his head to hers and his tears mixed with hers. "You scared the shit out of me. I'm sorry you had to resort to that."

She buried her face in his chest as another sob broke from her mouth at what she was going to do and who she was going to leave behind. "I'm sorry." She choked out through chattering teeth, shivering violently.

"We need to get you two out of here," a muffled voice said and was the last thing Nadia heard before she succumbed to the overwhelming pain and shock consuming her and fell limp in Luca's arms.

Chapter 46

Luca laid next to Nadia while she slept and refused to leave her side since they were evacuated to the lake house. Holding her hand against his chest, he rubbed his thumb over her bandaged palm. He had never been so scared in all his life.

When Jonathan ripped her from his arms and when she held the gun beneath her chin. A shudder clawed at Luca's spine as he pressed his forehead against her hand, and a tear rolled down his cheek.

Nadia never should have had to make a decision like that and it was his fault for not being better prepared to protect her. If the Koa guard had been a minute later, he would've lost her. Luca pressed a kiss to her hand. That wouldn't happen again.

He watched the rise and fall of her chest, listening to her soft breathing as tears welled in his eyes at the dark bruises discoloring her neck. He should've done better to protect her. "I'm so sorry," he whispered and kissed her forehead.

Nadia stirred, gasping as she jumped awake and her green

eyes burst to life. "Luca?"

"I'm here. You're safe," he cooed. "You're alright."

Nadia pressed her face into his neck, breathing him in. "We… we really got him, r-right?"

"Yes," he said, pulling away from her and wiping the lone tear that rolled down her cheek. "Jonathan's in a cell in my building under maximum security until you approve the plans for him."

"O-kay," she sniffed, picking her head up and looking around at the plumes of deep green foliage that caught the glimmer of afternoon sun through the sheer white drapes swaying in a soft breeze of the bedroom. "Where are we?"

"The lake house," he said, rubbing the base of her neck. "It was the safest and closest place to go at the moment."

She looked back at him and the panic in her eyes softened as she touched her fingers to his cheek. "I'm okay."

He wrapped his fingers around her wrists and his lip trembled as he pressed a kiss to the bandages over her palm. "I know. I just don't like seeing you hurt like this," he said, tears pooling in his eyes. "I don't know what I would've done if you… if you–" his voice broke as tears rolled down his face.

"I didn't," she said, pressing her forehead against his as her tears mixed with his. "I know it was a stupid move, but I thought I had no choice. I couldn't go back to that life."

"I know." Luca slid his hands to her cheeks. "I promise you'll never have to make a choice like that again and I won't fail you like that again, either."

"You didn't fail me. I'm sorry for scaring you, but I won't do that again. I have too much to live for and I love you too much to leave you," she said, pressing a kiss to his lips.

He tangled his hand in her hair and kissed her back as if he feared she'd disappear from his arms. "I love you too much to lose you like that," he murmured, kissing the tears on her cheek.

A soft knock sounded on the door before a man with thick black hair braided down his back, dressed in a black tee and cargo pants with an earpiece stuck in his ear, stepped into the room and bowed. "Excuse me for the interruption. It's good to see you're awake, Miss Coleman."

"What's going on?" Luca said, holding Nadia close.

"Miss Jackson and Mr. Ramirez have arrived and they'd like to see you. Is it alright if I send them up?"

Nadia wiped her tears and nodded. "Yes. What about Raquel and my guards? Are they okay?"

"They are. I'll let them know you're awake and ready to see them," he said, bowing again as he closed the door behind him.

"Who was that?" Nadia asked, wincing as she tried to sit up.

Luca held her around her waist and stacked a few pillows behind her. "That was Kane. He's part of the Koa guard."

"From your village?"

"Yes, they're secret specialist guards. My Nonna commissioned them to protect our village after my grandfather forced us away. I didn't know Jack called them in for support when you were taken to the safe house." He sighed, kissing her head. "They landed in Boston a few hours before we were attacked last night."

"Thank God they showed up when they did," Nadia said, looking down at her bandaged hands. "How did we get ambushed like that?"

"I don't know." Luca placed his hand over hers. "I have

a feeling my grandfather knew about the safe house. Our guards are working on that, but for now you'll have an extra team of Koa guards around you. I'm sorry. I should've been more aware of the possibility that my grandfather knew the blueprint of the safe house. It's my fault we were ambushed."

"Stop," Nadia said, sliding her hand to his cheek with her green eyes full of tenacity. "Stop blaming yourself for what happened last night. If I didn't get involved with Jonathan in the first place, your grandfather wouldn't think he had any right to own me, but now I own Jonathan and he'll never taste freedom again."

"I'll make sure he doesn't." Luca wiped the tear rolling down her cheek and a slight smile tugged at his lips. "I'm proud of you, ka'u pua." He kissed her forehead and laughed softly. "And I loved what you said to him."

A bright smile spread across her face. "It felt good too."

"Sunshine with a bite," Luca said, chuckling softly as the guilt melted from his heart. The triumph that glimmered in her eyes made him realize that while Nadia came close to ending her life, she needed that moment for herself and it filled him with strength that they were going to end this together. He slid his hands to her cheeks. "I love you."

She smiled against his lips. "I love you too."

"Nadia! Oh God!" Minerva exclaimed as she burst through the door and barreled across the room.

"I'm okay Nervy," Nadia said as her worried friend climbed onto the bed and hugged her to her chest.

"I knew something was wrong when Henry didn't come get me this morning and Cam couldn't get a hold of you Luca," she cried, looking up at him. "Are you okay?"

"Yeah." He nodded as Cam slid a hand to his shoulder.

Chapter 46

"You look like hell, but I'm glad you're alright," Cameron said, sitting on the edge of the bed. "I honestly didn't think Gregory would come after her like that."

"You should know by now how ruthless he is."

"Yeah, but shit," Cameron sighed, shaking his head as he looked over at Minerva hugging Nadia for dear life. "You think you can still pull this off?"

"I don't have a choice. What happened last night is going to set him off. Not to mention I've made it clear to Ciara that I'm done with her. I'm going to ruin his legacy."

"Damn right you are," Raquel said as she walked into the room with her forehead wrapped in a bandage with Gordon, Henry, and Jack trailing behind her. "How's my little badass doing?"

"I'm sore, but I'm okay," Nadia said, pulling away from Minerva. "You look worse than me."

"Just a little bump. I'll be fine." She smiled as Luca and Cameron moved from the bed to let her sit next to Nadia.

"You still need to take it easy," Gordon grumbled, crossing his arms over his chest.

Raquel waved him off and wrapped her arms around Nadia. "I'm glad you didn't have to go through with your plan," she whispered, kissing her head.

"Me too," she sighed, hugging her tight.

"Luca, we need to talk about what we're going to do next."

He turned away from Nadia's small reunion with her friends and stepped away from the bed with Cameron to the small huddle of guards.

"A team of Koas are with your family at their estate. Your parents confirmed our suspicions about the contractors that worked on the safe house. They were from an umbrella corporation Mr. Rodawson owned. It was a gross oversight at the time," Jack sighed, shaking his head. "The tech specialists have gone through the blacklist and it's a lot worse than we thought. You could take down the entire US government with the information we have."

"What about our guy inside? Have they finished with the Hatch files?"

"Nearly. Mr. Rodawson will know soon and after last night he's going to put the pieces together."

"We've tapped the Dagenhams devices and as far as we can tell Arnold isn't aware of the breakup, but Ciara is spiraling. She's been watching your building since last night. She's made multiple calls to Jonathan, but it's only a matter of time before she caves and tells her father."

Luca nodded. "There's a full Syndicates meeting this week. They'll try to catch me off guard with everything then, but that could help us. Ciara will want to make sure I'm forced to propose at the Gala and my grandfather will want my mother, Lacey and Nadia as collateral."

"That's true," Gordon nodded. "Mrs. and Miss Shola will be brought here to stay with Miss Nadia and the Koas until this has been handled."

"No. I'm not hiding. I'm going to work and I'm going to the meeting."

"What? Nadia no," Minerva said.

"Little wahine, that's not a good idea," Henry said, crossing his arms over his chest. "You've been through enough. We can handle the rest, right Mr. Shola?"

Luca stared at Nadia's bandaged hands, the bruises over her neck and settled on the fire behind her hardened green eyes. "We can, but it's Nadia's choice what she wants to do.

This is your fight too and if you don't want to hide, then we'll build a security plan around that."

"Luca, I can't believe you. This is crazy," Minerva huffed. "Nadia, you got Jonathan. Let those guys take care of the Syndicates. Raquel, help me out."

"She doesn't need to. I've made my decision. I deserve to see the look on Gregory's face and the rest of the Syndicates when they realize how fucked they are."

"Sorry, Nervy, but I can't argue with that. After all the work we've done, Nadia needs to be there."

"B-but what if–"

"I have faith in my guards and the Koas. After last night, I doubt any of you will let anything happen like that again."

"Never," the guards standing around Luca said, bowing their heads to her. A smile spread over his lips and a swell of pride washed over him at the fearless woman staring back at him. It would be an honor to take down the Syndicates with Nadia by his side. She deserved this moment just as much as he did.

***

"Are you sure you want to do this?" Luca asked as he sat on the bed behind Nadia gently brushing her damp hair after he helped her shower and they solidified the plans for the Syndicates meeting.

"Yes. Nervy thinks I'm on an adrenaline high, but I'm not. I know we have Jonathan, but I didn't come this far not to see the whole thing through."

"I understand that, but if you decide you don't want to be there, you can always back out," he said, spreading shea moisturizer through her thick curly locks and brushing out a few tangles.

"No, I want to do this and I want to be there for you like you were for me."

"Thank you." Luca kissed the top of her head before he took the comb lying next to him and parted her hair. "I won't lie and say I'm not a little worried about you coming with me. There's a chance everything could go wrong," he said, putting the comb down and pressing his head against hers. "Promise me you won't take your life if it does. I won't let him keep you," he whispered.

Nadia shifted and turned around, sliding her hands to his cheeks. "I promise," she said, pressing her soft lips against his. "But if it all goes wrong, Jonathan has to die. At least if we can't destroy the Syndicates, I'll know he isn't free."

Luca smiled. "I can always make the call to kill him for you. You're the one who wants him to suffer."

"It's what he deserves. Death would be too easy and too quick for him."

"Mm," he said, wrapping his fingers around her wrist and caressing the back of her bandaged hand with his thumb. "This savage side of you is disturbingly sexy right now."

"Is it?" she said, wrapping her arms around his shoulders.

He slid his arms around her waist and kissed her sweet lips. "Yes, but you need to rest. Your body has been through enough and I need to finish your hair."

"True," she said, laughing softly as he helped her turn around and settle against him. "Since when do you know how to braid hair?"

"I used to have long hair like Ori and the Koas when I was a kid," he said, braiding her hair around her head in the style she liked. "My Tutu taught me how to braid it like his and I got really good at it. I used to braid Lacey's hair all the time."

"I'd love to see you with long hair." She sighed, resting her hands over his legs. "You're full of surprises, Mr. Underworld."

"So are you, ka'u pua and I want to keep learning all about them."

A smile tugged at her lips. "Me too."

Nadia was fast asleep against him by the time he finished the intricate braids he added to her typical crown and tied a silk scarf around her head.

Luca pulled the blankets back and slipped his arm beneath her legs to lay her against the pillows. He turned off the lamp beside the bed and slipped under the blankets, cocooning his body around hers.

He closed his eyes and breathed in her floral and shea butter scent. If someone told him the woman who crashed into him months ago would be the one he'd take down the Syndicates with, he would've laughed in their face.

Luca pressed his lips against her neck, but he was glad it was her.

Chapter 47

"You're all alone, little kitten."

Nadia whimpered, struggling against the chains that bound her to the floor.

"No one's going to save you," Jonathan's voice echoed around her as his hand shot out from the darkness and gripped her neck.

A scream ripped from Nadia's mouth as she bolted upright into a cocoon of warmth and the fresh patchouli and cedarwood scent of Luca.

"Hey, I've got you," he whispered, rubbing her back. "You're safe."

Nadia fisted her bandaged hands in his shirt and breathed him in. "I'm sorry."

"It's alright," he said, kissing her head. "Did you have a nightmare about Jonathan?"

"Yeah. I was chained up again. I know it's stupid because we have him, but my mind is overreacting."

"It's not stupid," he said, pulling away from her. "Would it make you feel better if you saw where we're keeping him?"

She nodded. "Yes, I think so."

"Alright," he said, leaning away from her to grab his phone sitting on the bedside table. He sat against the wooden headboard and pulled her against him as he held up his phone. Jonathan was lying on a single cot in a plain white room that resembled a jail cell complete with a small toilet in the corner. "See? He's not getting out and he's not going anywhere."

Nadia breathed a sigh of relief. "Thank you for showing me this."

"You're welcome," he said, pressing a button on the screen that pulled up a menu function. "He'll be fitted with a tracking device like one of those probation bracelets, so you'll always know where he is and if at any point you want him terminated you can alert the guards for that. Otherwise, he's yours to do what you like to him."

"I want him trained to live in fear of me and our guards. I never want him to feel free."

"I get it. Our guards have been doing the rounds like that on Ben. Jonathan will have the same treatment."

"You have Ben in a cell too?"

"Mm-hm, I didn't ask for that, but apparently that's how my guys broke him to spill all that information about the Hatchs," he said, switching the camera to Ben, huddling in the corner of another cell.

"And no one has come looking for him?"

"Nope. It pays to have ex-military special ops for bodyguards. I don't think it'll be as easy with Jonathan, but we can keep him long enough to psychologically damage him. Marcus won't dare ask my grandfather for his whereabouts, either. They're already on his bad side. He won't risk asking a favor of the Grand Duke to find him, nor would my grandfather care."

Nadia looked away from his phone, and a wave of guilt washed over her. "Is this wrong?" she whispered. "Doesn't this make me just as awful as him?"

Luca slid his fingers to her chin, turning her face to his. "Nadia, he's held you captive for three years after he nearly ended your life. You're not a bad person for wanting to get justice for yourself. Is this unethical? Yes, but I'd say the justice system has forced your hand," he said, picking up a thick black leather bound binder from the bedside table with multicolored tabs poking out of it.

"Is this the blacklist?"

"It is. Jack delivered it to me a little while ago. I've been going through it while you were sleeping," he said, opening it to a red tabbed page. "You're not the only one who's been one of Jonathan's obsessions, but you're the only one who's survived it."

"What?" she whispered as tears pricked the corners of her eyes as she read the bookmarked page detailing Jonathan's long history of sexual assault and domestic violence against seven women who went missing and were presumed dead. Every case and every allegation was covered up by the Hatch family and expunged from the courts by various judges who were linked to or members of the Syndicates.

"Oh my God." Nadia slid a hand over her mouth at the familiar name of the judge that handled her case. "The judge knew he was going to do this to me. All those women went missing in three-year gaps."

"Yeah, that's Jonathan's M.O.. He toys with his obsessions before getting rid of them and starting it all over again. So no, I don't think what you're doing is wrong."

Chapter 47

Nadia looked up at Luca as a tear rolled down her cheek. "I want to get justice for those families too."

"We will." Luca nodded, catching her tear on his thumb. "There's a lot of good we can do with this list."

"Then I'm glad it's in our hands now," she said, pressing her forehead against his. "Thank you for showing me that. I thought I was the only one, but I was just another notch on his belt." Her lip trembled as she closed her eyes. "I would've been buried and forgotten like those other women."

"That's not true. Your friends and your family wouldn't stop looking for you as I'm sure the families of those women haven't stopped searching for them." He kissed her forehead. "But we have the answers for them and we can stop this."

"That's what I want now," she said, placing her hand over the pages of the book. "We aren't the only ones trapped by the Syndicates and we should do what we can to make some of this right."

A slow smile spread across his lips. "That's what I planned to do, but I'm glad you feel the same," he said, chuckling softly. "And you say you're not cut out to be a queen. You certainly think like one."

"I just feel responsible for this now and I know you're rich enough to help me."

Luca shook his head. "You'd do it regardless of my wealth. I know you. You'd make it your mission and drag Raquel and Nervy along with you."

Nadia laughed softly. "Probably."

"It's one of the many reasons I love you." Luca kissed the side of her mouth and smiled. "Are you good, ka'u pua?"

Nadia kissed him softly. "Yeah, I think I'm good, Mr. Underworld."

He closed the binder and placed it back on the bedside table before wrapping his arms around her again. "Do you want me to read to you?"

A smile graced her lips as they laid back against the pillows and she snuggled under the crook of his arm. "Always."

***

Nadia and Luca spent the weekend pouring through the blacklist with Raquel and their guards while they listened to the frantic messages Ciara she left on Jonathan's phone begging him to give her an update on Nadia's whereabouts. The countless messages she left on Luca's phone begging him not to leave her and finally the fatal call to her father crying that Luca left her.

"Daddy, I-I messed up. You have to help me. Luca left me."

"Again, Cici? What have you done now?" Arnold scoffed. "If you fuck this up for me–"

"You'll disown me. I know, but Luca's stuck up Nadia Coleman's ass. He doesn't care about anything but her."

Arnold laughed. "Nadia Coleman isn't the problem. Jonathan's got that handled and I'm not bothering Gregory for your fuck up. Now go fix it with Luca or should I freeze your accounts, take your house and that car you love?"

"No! Daddy, I'm serious. Something's wrong. I tried to fix it, but Luca hasn't been home and I can't get a hold of Jonathan."

There was silence on the phone before Arnold cussed. "You're right. Gregory's just called an emergency meeting."

"I told you. Luca's with her. She's ruined everything."

"Mm, don't worry. I'll fix it. Get your friends at Babble to release those photos of her. Ruin her, Cici."

Chapter 47

"I can't. They're all gone. I think Luca's assholes hacked my stuff," Ciara seethed.

"Shit. Don't say another word. They probably tapped your phone. I'll send a car for you."

Nadia shook her head as the connection was lost. She almost felt pity for Ciara at the way her father blamed her for messing up with Luca, but then she remembered how she beat and raped him. There was no excuse for that. Everyone had a chance to take responsibility for their actions.

Nadia slid her hand over Luca's. "Are you okay?"

"I'm fine. They didn't say anything I wasn't expecting," he said, bringing her hand to his lips. "But now we know a meeting is definitely happening."

"Yes, and we've got incoming. Mr. Rodawson is on his way and your family's with him," Jack said as he stood from the table, staring at his watch before he looked out the wide windows of the lake house.

Luca nodded. "I expected them to do this," he said as the Koa guards lined the front steps of the house and stood with guns raised as two black sedans crept down the cobbled path.

"Yep, they weren't going to sit this out either." Jack shook his head.

"It's fine. We've planned for this," Gordon said, tapping a finger over his watch. "Everyone is in place, and the blacklist is connected to your watches. When the moment comes, all you need to do is broadcast it."

"You're going to go willingly with Mr. Rodawson," Raquel explained, shrugging on a Kevlar vest and strapping a gun to her waist. I have a small team of FBI agents on standby if we need them, and a caravan of your guards are on their way to the Syndicate meeting house. Your men on the inside are waiting for them."

"This is it, everyone. No mistakes," Jack said, keeping his gaze on the approaching cars before he turned to Nadia and Luca. "Let's go."

"W-wait," Nadia said, grasping Luca's arm. "Shouldn't we have a vest and something to protect us?"

Luca slid his hand over hers and shook his head. "No, they'd be taken off of us anyway and my grandfather is going to separate us, but I promise everything will be fine," he said, wrapping his arm around her waist as their guards crowded around them and ushered them to the door.

Nadia's hand shook in Luca's as car doors opened and closed and the crunch of footsteps echoed in the house from the open windows. Fear and panic clawed down Nadia's spine and the courage she mustered faltered as they neared the oak door of the lake house. "Luca, I'm... I'm scared."

He turned to her, sliding his hands to her cheeks. The warmth in his eyes settled some of the panic rising in her chest, but a wave of worry flashed in his depths before he bent toward her and kissed her forehead. "No matter what happens, I won't let my grandfather take you or my family from me," he said, kissing her softly. "We're going to be free, ka'u pua."

The worry that clouded his golden eyes burned away into that of determination and the conviction in his voice filled her with the hope and courage she once had. "Yes we are, Mr. Underworld."

"I love you, Nadia."

"I love you too," she whispered, pressing her lips against his to savor the taste of him just in case–No. She wouldn't entertain that thought. This kiss wasn't just in case and it wasn't for luck. It was a promise that they would have more of this for as long as they liked because it was their choice.

"Miss Nadia, Mr. Shola, we need to go."

Luca pressed one more kiss to her lips before he took her hand. "Lanakila ke aloha, ka'u wahine."

Love wins, my queen.

She smiled up at him. "E ke koa, i ka'u ali'i."

Be a warrior, my king.

"Anything for you," he said, bringing her hand to his lips as the door opened to Gregory Rodawson standing with a smug grin on his face in the circle of a group of his guards pointing their guns at the Koas standing on the steps.

"Oh Luca, my son. You've fucked up for the last time."

Chapter 48

"Take Miss Coleman to the other car," Luca's grandfather said as one of his guards stepped forward.

"No." Nadia shook her head, pressing herself to Luca's side.

Luca grasped her shoulders, turning her to him. "Nadia, I'll be fine," he said, leaning down to her. "We talked about this," he whispered, kissing her ear.

Nadia took a deep breath, sliding her hands to his chest. "I know. I'm sorry."

"It's okay." He kissed her forehead. "I'll see you soon."

"Enough. Let's go," his grandfather grumbled as he slipped into the car.

"I love you," Nadia whispered before she let the guard escort her to the other car. Luca took a deep breath before he trudged to the open car door waiting for him.

"You just couldn't fucking listen, could you?" His grandfather glared at him as Luca slipped into the seat across from him. "Did you really think you could undermine my plans?"

Luca ignored him and stared out the car window at the

tree-lined road, praying everyone got this right today.

"Mm, not going to argue with me, huh?" His grandfather said as he smoked on a cigar, filling the car with its spicy scent. "Is that because you know you're fucked? That anything you try to do will always end up with me having the upper hand? I told your mother there was no way out of this life. I let her run away and let her keep her disgraceful excuse for a husband, but not you. You'll never get the pleasure and now your family, your woman and your people will be mine. You'll be my successor and keep my legacy alive as long as I have them."

Luca tore his gaze away from the window to glare into his grandfather's brown eyes. "And what happens when you die?"

He chuckled. "That's what Arnold is for. He's my failsafe and your marriage will keep our prominent names stronger than any other Syndicate in the society," he said, tapping his cigar on the silver ashtray next to him. "You see Luca, if my blacklist has fallen into the wrong hands it's only a problem for the others. I keep it to protect them and to keep them loyal to me and the Dagenhams, but even if the Hatchs have it, they'll never have enough power to overrule me."

"Then why are you so worried about it?"

"You may think I'm a heartless man, but I care about those that trust me with their livelihoods. I promised them I'd keep their secrets safe. We're not so different, you and I. You protect your people just as I do. It's why I know you'll make a good Grand Duke and why you'll do whatever I want to keep those you love safe. Your mother and sister will be Juliets to Syndicates I deem fit. Nadia will remain by my side, and your father will give up his business to me and return to that shitty little village. And you." He grinned. "You'll be the greatest leader of the Syndicates with a Dagenham by your side because if you fuck up again, I'll have them all killed. I'm sure I could have your village wiped off the map too and no one would give a shit that they're gone."

Luca curled his hands into a fist and fought the urge to reach across the car and shove that smoking cigar down his grandfather's throat.

"So when we get to this meeting, you're going to admit your wrongdoings and watch me beat the shit out of your father while I auction off your mother and Lacey to the highest respectable bidders. Do you understand me?"

"Yes, grandfather," Luca said through clenched teeth.

"Good."

The rest of the car ride to his grandfather's isolated estate on Nahant beach was silent while Luca grappled with everything his grandfather said. The blacklist meant nothing to him but to keep the Syndicates in line and to bolster their loyalty to him. Even if he broadcasted some of their shady dealings to the world, it wouldn't do a damn thing to hurt his grandfather, and now his family and Nadia were in tow, traveling to their demise.

Luca blinked back the tears stinging the corners of his eyes as the car rolled down a long graveled path to a gray stone house that overlooked the soft sandy beach and turbulent waves crashing against the shore. His watch vibrated against his wrist and he looked down at the message scrolling across the small screen.

Raquel » We're in position.«

Gordon » We heard everything. Don't let him rattle you. We planned for this.«

Chapter 48

"Let's go," his grandfather said as the car door opened.

Luca took a deep breath as he followed him out of the car. He looked over at his family and Nadia being ushered in behind them with their wrists zip tied behind their backs and black hoods covering their heads. "Is that necessary?"

"Yes. You're lucky I haven't restrained you, but I still want the Syndicates to see you as someone of importance when this is over," he said as they entered the lavish house full of ornate marble statues lining the dark wood hallway with pristine oriental rugs lining the hardwood floors.

Luca had never been to this Syndicate dwelling, and he assumed the place was reserved for the more sinister meetings his grandfather held. He eyed a few of the guards dressed in long black robes as they descended the steps lit up with black iron sconces on the gray stone walls resembling the chambers of the Syndicate meeting house on Beacon Hill. That was typical. His grandfather had little imagination when it came to the secret chambers he liked to do business in.

The soft rumble of chatter behind the caged wooden door of the chamber tore him from his thoughts as a guard placed a black robe over his shoulders. The brown-eyed guard patted him down and Luca felt the weight of a gun slip into the pocket of his robes. "For the right moment," he whispered, before guiding him inside the hazy room that smelled of cigar smoke and lit up by gas lamps and small candles on the round tables where black robed Syndicates from every station sat who were too eager to attend the emergency meeting of the Grand Duke.

Silence befell the room, and Luca wanted to close his eyes as his mother, Lacey, and Nadia were shackled to a stone wall. His father was forced to his knees and tied to the wooden whipping post beyond two high-back chairs facing the gathering.

Murmurs of displeasure grumbled throughout the chamber when the black hoods were removed from their heads. Luca caught the gaze of Arnold Dagenham sitting on the front table with a smug grin splayed across his face as he took a slow sip of the spirits in his glass.

"Brethren," his grandfather said, clasping his hands together as he stood in the center of the chamber. "Thank you for joining me on such short notice. I'm sure you're all wondering why I've brought my daughter, her family and my grandson's tramp in for questioning, but it seems our young Duke has some explaining to do."

Luca's grandfather turned around, his black robes sliding against the slate floor as he crossed the room to kick his father in the gut. A stifled groan left his lips, but his father refused to give his grandfather the pleasure of hearing him scream.

Smirking at the stubborn man, his grandfather continued his stroll to the three most important women in Luca's life. "The young Duke has lied to me," he said, standing in front of Luca's mother–his daughter–and smacked her across the face. "He disobeyed me."

A small yelp escaped her lips as her head rolled to the side. She clenched her fists in the metal shackles at her side, turning her head to glare heat and fire into her father's eyes. "As he should've." She spat as if her reddened cheek and bleeding lip had no effect on her.

His grandfather grabbed her chin, squeezing his fingers into her jaw. "I hope you enjoy being a worthless whore," he said, pushing her face away from him before he moved on to Lacey.

"You don't do this to your family," she said, tugging against her chains as she spat in his face.

His grandfather wiped the spit from his cheek and back-handed her. "I tolerated you," he said, turning away from her to pierce Luca with his menacing brown eyes. "I gave you a place and you brought your foreign fucking thugs to kill my men!"

He stomped away from Lacey to grab Nadia by the chin. "All for this fucking Juliet?" he said, digging into the pocket of his robes and pulling out a pair of gold plated shears. "Why don't we see what's so special about her, huh?"

"Don't touch me!" Nadia said, struggling against her shackles as tears rolled down her cheeks.

"Oh, don't do that. I don't want to cut you."

Luca's heart dropped to the pit of his stomach as the Syndicates whooped and cheered on his grandfather, slicing through the fabric of Nadia's light green top, exposing her yellow satin bra.

"Stop!" Luca roared, gripping the smooth handle of the gun in his pocket. "I… I deserve this punishment, but you said you'd allow me to admit my wrongs before you hurt them. Please, grandfather, let me explain myself."

His grandfather nodded, turning to him before he could finish cutting the rest of Nadia's shirt. "You're right, I did say that. I'm an honorable man, brethren, and we're an honorable society. It's only right to let our young Duke speak his truth," he said to the groans of the disgusting plebs around them. His grandfather slid the pointed edge of the scissors down Nadia's cheek. "You'll be a delightful treat for me later."

The foreboding man turned around, holding his hands behind his back as he strolled across the room to Luca with an amused grin on his face. "Go on, Luca. I'm sure everyone would like to know why you've put your family in this predicament."

"Yes, and then I'd like to bid on the woman who should've been my wife," Arnold said, keeping his eyes on Luca's mother.

"In due time, my friend. You'll all get to bid on these new Juliets. Go ahead, son."

Luca looked back at his family and rage burned through him at his mother's bleeding lip, Lacey's bruised cheeks, Nadia's torn shirt, and the deadly gleam in his father's eyes. "E noho ali'i, Eke," his father said, giving him a curt nod.

Be a king.

A sense of pride and purpose washed over Luca as he turned back to the waiting eyes of the Syndicates. This was his moment. His only chance to save everyone he loved and he couldn't mess this up. Too many people depended on him to get this right.

"It's no secret to most of you I didn't grow up knowing about this society. Ten years ago the Grand Duke brought me into the fold and taught me what it meant to be a Syndicate, but I didn't want this life. I didn't want to be the next leader and didn't want Ciara Dagenham to be my wife. Recently, I disobeyed my grandfather and I deceived all of you. I let you believe Jonathan Hatch was planning to undermine the Grand Duke's authority. It was a surprise to me he was, but he knew nothing of the whereabouts of the blacklist. I'm the culprit who stole it," he said to the shocked gasps from the crowd.

Chapter 48

"Luca, what the fuck are you talking about?"

He turned to his grandfather and nodded. "It was me. I broke into your house and I stole your files, but you were right. We're not so different and if I'm going to be the next Grand Duke, I have a responsibility to lead this society and do the right thing by all of you," he said, sliding his hand into the pocket of his robes. "Which is why I can't allow you to live." Luca pulled the gun from his pocket in a swift motion and shot his grandfather in the chest.

"Lu-Luca," he said, staggering back, holding his chest before he fell to the floor with a deafening thud.

"Gregory!" Arnold yelled above the shocked gasps and Syndicates rising from their seats. "What have you done?! Restrain him! He's just murdered the Duke!"

"We don't answer to anyone but our ali'i," a guard said, removing his hood to reveal his long, braided black hair.

"Or the Grand Duke," another guard said.

"Wh-what are you idiots doing? He just killed our leader!" Arnold said, waving his hand at Gregory's lifeless body.

"Yes I did, but according to our by-laws, in the event the Grand Duke is ill fitted to lead, his chosen successor becomes the Grand Duke effective immediately and that would be me," Luca said. "Take care of his body and release my family."

"Yes, sir." A few guards nodded, lifting his grandfather from the floor and tending to Nadia and his family.

"What… what are you going to do with us?" A Syndicate called out.

Luca turned to them and delighted in the fear etched on their faces. "Like I said, I'm going to do right by you. You'll go home to your families and spread the word that there's a new Grand Duke."

A swell of relief dissipated the thick tension filling the air. "Thank you for your graciousness."

"I'm not finished." Luca snapped. "When your time comes, I will bring every one of you to justice for any crimes you've committed in the blacklist."

A snarl curled over Arnold's lips. "You won't get away with this, Luca. No one in this room will stand by while you threaten us like this. We can overthrow you."

"Can you? I think you'll find that my threats are promises. I own all of you now and as your Grand Duke, I'm going to abolish this sick fucking society," he said as the twinkling sounds of notifications and phones ringing filled the room.

"Oh, fuck!"

"He ousted our government contracts and our names in the Juliet circle!"

"We need to get out of here!"

"You better run. The FBI is going to be looking for all of you," Raquel said, pushing the black hood from her head and producing her FBI badge as the Syndicates popped up from their chairs, throwing off their robes and scrambling to the doors of the chamber. "Except you, Arnold Dagenham. You're under arrest for a multitude of bullshit. Namely, the coercion of Luca, Philip, Elena and Lacey Shola, accessory to the kidnapping of Nadia Coleman, illegal trafficking and prostitution of underage minors, the murder of several women and your long-time friend, Gregory Rodawson."

Deadly brown eyes glared at Luca as Arnold struggled against his handcuffs. "This isn't over. You'll regret what you've done to me. What you've done to all of us. That bitch will never be safe," he sneered. "Dagenhams never lose."

Luca grit his teeth. "You did this time."

Chapter 48

A sick grin curled over Arnold's lips. "For now."

"That's enough out of you," Raquel seethed as she pushed him away.

Luca kept his face hardened, but fear clawed at his heart from the underlying threat in Arnold's words and the smug smile on his face as Raquel dragged him out of the chamber.

"Fuck what he said, Luca. We got them," Jack said, placing a hand on Luca's shoulder. "Everyone's safe now."

"Yeah." He nodded, looking over his shoulder at Gordon and Henry tending to Nadia and his family. "And we're going to keep it that way," he said, crossing the room toward them.

"I can't believe you went willingly with Mr. Rodawson," Gordon said, shaking his head as he placed an ice pack against his father's bruised side. "You just had to come along for the ride, huh?"

"Damn straight. This is nothing. I wouldn't leave my son to fend for himself," his father said, wincing as he pressed his hand over his side.

"Hell yeah. Eke and Nadia weren't going to do this without us," Lacey said, grinning proudly as she held an ice pack to her cheek.

Nadia chuckled softly, tying her shirt together. "You're pretty scrappy, Lacey."

"No worse than you. I heard what you did at the safe house. Should've stabbed him in the dick, though."

"Maybe next time," she said as Luca's mother wrapped her arms around Nadia's shoulders.

"I'm so sorry you got wrapped up in this," she said, looking up at Luca with joy shining in her hazel eyes. "But I'm glad you and Luca found each other."

Nadia looked up at him and the warmth in her eyes pushed

back the worry digging its claws into him. "Me too."

Luca joined them on the floor and gathered Nadia in his arms. "We're free, ka'u pua," he whispered against her head.

"Yes, we are." She smiled, pressing her face against his chest.

He looked over her head at his bruised family and took his mother's hand. "Are you okay?"

"Yeah, I'm fine," His mother said, squeezing his hand as tears pricked the corners of her eyes. "You didn't tell me you were going to shoot him. Is he… is he really dead?"

Luca shook his head. "No. It was a tranquilizer pistol. I still need him alive to get more information out of him. The blacklist isn't the end and I need to make sure whatever he's done can't harm us or our people."

"But right now," his father said, wrapping his arm around Lacey and his mother. "It's well and truly over."

For now.

Arnold's voice nagged in the back of Luca's mind. He ignored that thought and kissed Nadia's head. It was over. He had everything he needed to keep his family, Nadia, and his people safe. He was finally free.

***

Luca woke tangled in Nadia's arms with a smile plastered across his face. He trailed his fingers over her bare back and listened to her soft breathing. The morning sun filtered in through the swaying curtains in her bedroom and the scent of the blooming flowers on her balcony wafted around him in a soothing comfort.

They'd been hiding out in her apartment for the last few weeks while the media storm blew over. His family's lawyers made statements to the press and did their best to distance Shola Enterprises from the accusations made against Arnold Dagenham in the lead up to the annual Gala.

Luca kissed Nadia's head and sighed. He wanted to cancel the event, but his parents insisted it went on to show they had nothing to hide. He understood the need to host it to keep their shareholders and their clients comfortable to keep working with them, but he couldn't shake the worry that nagged at the back of his mind.

His grandfather was still under his security agency's surveillance and Arnold was behind bars in a maximum security prison while the remaining Syndicates lived in fear of when the Feds or their new Grand Duke would come for them, but Luca heard nothing from Ciara. It was a good thing. He figured she and her mother fled the state to one of their smaller holdings, but to hear nothing from her was unusual.

Luca brushed a wayward curl from Nadia's face and she stirred, opening her warm green eyes. He didn't need to worry about Ciara. She was gone and he was free to spend the rest of his days wrapped in the calming warmth of Nadia's love.

"Good morning," she mumbled, and concern furrowed her brow as she slid her hand to his cheek. "What's wrong?"

"Nothing," he whispered, kissing her forehead. "I'm just happy."

"I'm happy too." She smiled, kissing him softly. "I'm kind of nervous about the Gala tonight. Do you think it'll look weird that we're going together after being out of work all this time?"

"Maybe, but I think it's time we do something public as a

couple, don't you think?"

Nadia bit her lip. "Mr. Underworld, are you asking me to be your girlfriend?"

Luca raised an eyebrow. "You mean you weren't already?"

"Well no. Technically, I've just been the other woman."

Luca shook his head, sliding his hand to her cheek. "You were never the other woman. You've had my heart since I met you."

"Lies." She laughed. "You looked pretty annoyed with me when I crashed into you."

He chuckled softly. "Well, that's not how I expected to meet the woman I want to spend the rest of my life with."

"Me either." She grinned, kissing the side of his mouth. "But let's just start with being a couple first."

"We can do that," he said, caressing her cheek with his thumb. "So, can I be your boyfriend, ka'u pua?"

"Yes."

Luca's heart swelled as he pressed his lips against hers. He tangled his fingers in her soft curls, coaxing her lips apart and melting in her sensual embrace.

"Get the hell up, you two!" Minerva belted out as the apartment door slammed open.

"We've got hair, nails and make-up to do!" Lacey yelled as footsteps sounded from outside the bedroom door.

Luca chuckled against Nadia's lips. "I guess I'm getting kicked out now, huh?"

Nadia laughed, pulling away from him. "Yep, my girls are here," she said, sliding out of his arms and shrugging on a pair of leggings and a t-shirt. "Get up, Mr. Underworld."

"Alright." He sighed, rolling out of the bed and shrugging on his clothes. Luca smiled as he watched Nadia sweep her hair up in a ponytail. Her palms were nearly healed and the bruises that stained her neck were light patches of discoloration now. He crossed her small room and pulled her into his arms. "I love you," he said, kissing her neck.

She giggled. "I love you too. Let's go before Nervy breaks down the door."

No sooner did those words leave her lips did the door burst open to Minerva with her hands on her hips. "I don't mean to interrupt this little moment, but we're on a schedule," she huffed. "You need to get going, Luca. You've had her long enough. Cam's waiting for you downstairs," she said, motioning to the door, through the guards moving Nadia's couches and wheeling in a clothing rack and a make-up station.

Nadia gasped, pushing away from Luca. "What the hell are you doing to my living room?"

Lacey grinned. "Um, it's a salon now. I told you I was bringing supplies. Don't worry, I'll put everything back."

"There better be some damn drinks. It's too early in the morning for all this," Raquel grumbled as she barged into the apartment and slammed her leather purse on the kitchen island. "Good morning, everyone."

Luca laughed, shaking his head at the group of misfit women, and placed a kiss on Nadia's head. "I'll see you tonight. Have fun," he said, weaving his way through the guards. He looked back at Nadia, fixing drinks and making breakfast with Minerva. His sister was laughing and chatting with Raquel and a warmth spread through him. This was how life should always be.

Gordon slapped a hand on his shoulder as he stood in the doorway next to him. "It's going to be a good night, Mr.

Shola."

"Yeah, it is."

"Come on, let's leave them to it. The Koas are on duty today and I want to enjoy my day off."

Luca wrapped his arm around Gordon's shoulder. "You deserve it," he said as they walked down the hall and joined the rest of Nadia's guards exiting the building to the three black SUVs waiting for them.

There was nothing Luca had to worry about for the first time in what felt like decades and tonight, he was going to enjoy the freedom of being with Nadia to dote on her like she deserved.

Chapter 49

Nadia traced the gold embroidered flowers on the black bodice of her gown while Lacey fluffed out the small train of silk and tulle that glittered with a dusting of golden petals behind her. She turned to the side and smoothed her hands over the cascading fabric around the slit that reached up to the top of her thigh and adjusted the thin gold chains wrapped around her exposed leg.

"So, what do you think? I hooked you up, right?" Lacey grinned as she tucked a halo of diamonds and tiny golden flowers in her hair.

Nadia laughed at the crown tucked delicately between her curls pinned around her head and met in a loose bun at the base of her neck. "Yes, but don't you think the headpiece is a bit much?"

"No," Lacey said, stepping back to assess her as if Nadia was a piece of art. "It completes your look. Are you ready for your debut tonight, little wahine?"

"Debut." Nadia laughed. "You're a mess."

"What? This is a big deal. Eke's never taken a date to the Gala."

Nadia's eyes grew wide. "Wait, what? He never took…"

"Nope. The Gala is something we went to together since we were kids and we kept up the tradition until now." Lacey slipped her arm through Nadia's. "A king shouldn't be seen in public without his queen by his side," she said, opening the door.

Nadia blushed at Lacey's sentiment as they stepped out of her bedroom, and her heart thumped at Luca standing with Cameron and Minerva next to the fireplace. Her eyes trailed over his three piece black suit, the edges of his lapels were hemmed with a thin line of gold, a silk black and gold cravat was tied around his neck and tucked into his waistcoat and a golden floral pochette sat in the pocket over his chest and matched the flowers in her dress

The way his suit was tailored to his tall, broad body made him look otherworldly, and the gold in his tie made his hazel eyes glow against his warm, light brown face and midnight hair.

Luca pushed away from the fireplace, and her throat felt dry at the heady look in his golden gaze. He slowly took her hand and brought it to his lips. "You look stunning, ka'u pua."

"You do too, Mr. Underworld." She smiled and trailed her fingers over the lapel of his jacket.

"Thank you." He chuckled. "I, um, have something for you," he said, opening a slim velvet box and taking out a gold and diamond bracelet and clasping it around her wrist.

"It's beautiful," she said, touching the cluster of diamonds.

"I'm glad you like it. It's for your protection too and works like your watch. It just matches your Goddess attire tonight," he smiled.

She chuckled softly. "Of course it does," she said, leaning up to press her crimson lips against his cheek. "Thank you."

"You're welcome," he said, wrapping his arm around her waist. "Are you ready, ka'u wahine?"

She took a deep breath, nodding. "I'm ready."

It was a brief journey to the prestigious event. A caravan of black sedans full of their guards followed their limo to the Fairmont Hotel. Nadia peered out the window at the gathering of photographers and reporters behind velvet ropes lining the red carpet leading into the ballroom.

"Oh, this is serious," Raquel said as the limo rolled to a stop. "Security checks were done, right?"

"The hotel's been swept. There's nothing any of us need to worry about besides having a good time tonight," Gordon said as the limo door opened. "And I'd like to enjoy it with you, Miss Armentaros." He grinned, stepping out of the car and holding his hand out to her.

She laughed, slipping her hand in his. "Fair enough, Mr. Anderson," she said, sliding out of the car and her black sequined pants suit glittered among the flashing lights of the cameras.

"We'll see you two inside," Minerva said as she followed behind Cameron out of the car.

"Make sure Nadia's train looks good for the cameras, Eke. I put a lot of work into that dress. The fashion gurus are here and I want my work on every cover," Lacey said as she placed her hand in Henry's, who proudly agreed to step in as her date for the evening.

Nadia squeezed Luca's hand in panic. "Oh, dear God. I didn't really think about the press. I didn't prepare a statement for any of this."

"Don't worry. Just follow my lead out there. It's going to be fine." Luca kissed her head before he slipped out of the car and turned back to offer her his hand. Nadia gripped it tight as she slowly placed her gold heel on the red carpet.

The crowd of journalists and photographers took a collective breath as her glittering head and black and gold skirts emerged from the limo to stand gracefully next to him. Luca smiled, leaning down to fan out the train of her dress before tucking her hand in the crook of his arm.

"Thank you," Nadia whispered through her smile as she clenched his arm. "I'm so nervous."

"Don't be. Let's just have fun with this," he whispered back while the cameras clicked and flashed around them.

"Mr. Shola, how long did you know Arnold Dagenham was involved in a society like the Syndicates?"

Nadia's heart thumped and Luca stiffened at the reporter's bold question. "I can't comment on an open investigation, but I suspected it for a long time."

"Who's your date tonight, Mr. Shola?" Another reporter yelled out.

"The wonderful Nadia Coleman. Shola's Director of International Marketing and Investments," Luca said, as they walked through the flashing lights and posed for a few pictures.

"Miss Coleman, who are you wearing this evening?"

"I'm wearing the fabulous Lacey Shola tonight." Nadia grinned, sliding her hands to her hips, slipping her leg out of the slit up her thigh to pose for another photo.

She laughed, sliding her arm through Luca's as they continued to the entrance of the hotel. "I've always wanted to do that."

"Nadia Coleman is a Juliet!"

Nadia's eyes grew wide at the familiar voice that yelled above the camera clicks, and a roar of questions erupted from the reporters at the accusation. Luca cursed under his breath, pulling her tight to his side as he hurried them through the entrance while a group of their tuxedo clad guards filtered out into the crowd.

Nadia pressed a hand over her chest, sucking in a deep breath. "Was that Ciara?"

"I think so, but our guards will find her if it was," he said, guiding her into a small cloakroom out of sight of the guests loitering outside the ballroom. He slid his hands to her cheeks. "I'm so sorry that happened. Are you okay?"

She nodded, taking another deep breath. "Yeah. I should expect shit like that now. As long as Ciara's out there, she's going to tarnish me to get you back."

"That won't happen. Our guards will find her."

Nadia slid her fingers over his wrists. "I know and I don't want it to ruin our night."

"Of course not," he said, kissing her softly, and his golden eyes filled with amusement. "Technically, this is our first date."

She grinned against his lips. "This is pretty extra for a first date."

"Maybe." He pecked her lips. "But I'm sure I can top this one."

"We have plenty of time for you to try."

"Yes, we do," he said, sliding his hand to her waist. "Are you good, ka'u pua?"

"I'm good, Mr. Underworld," she said, threading her

fingers through his as they walked out of the cloakroom and into the ballroom to greet their excited employees and shareholders.

***

Nadia swayed her hips and tapped her golden heels against the floor while she and Minerva taunted Luca and Cameron with their moves. The evening of speeches and awards was full of laughter and far too many drinks. Her worries over Ciara melted away when she took to the dance floor with the drunken Shola employees.

"Get it Miss Coleman!" Alex cheered with the rest of the clapping crowd around them.

Nadia laughed, looking over at Minerva. "Let's fuck 'em up." She grinned, holding out her fist.

"Damn straight," she said, bumping her fist as they sashayed across the floor and circled the Dynamic Duo before they fell in sync with their moves.

"Excuse us, gentlemen," they said, looking over their shoulders. "You're doing it wrong." Nadia and Minerva spun around, their layers of jade and black skirts swirling around their legs as they pushed Luca and Cameron out of the way. They took over the floor mixing their signature twists, pops and locks with Cameron and Luca's two steps and dougies to the rapping beats of Plan B's Guess Again.

The crowd roared with whoops and cheers while Cameron and Luca burst into laughter as they raised their hands and bowed to them.

Nadia and Minerva hit their last move with a hip thrust to the side, swinging their arms in the air and punctuating the last beat with a finger snap.

"That's what we thought!" Minerva yelled as the cheering crowd filtered out to the dance floor.

"Alright baby. You won!" Cameron laughed as Syn Cole's Sway began floating through the ballroom. Nadia grinned at the soft melodic beats and she caught Luca's tender gaze amongst the joyful crowd.

Chapter 50

The familiar song brought back memories of the first time Luca and Nadia danced and he slowly crossed the floor with a smile gracing his lips at his glittering black and gold Goddess. This night couldn't have been more perfect.

That thought shattered in his mind as Luca caught sight of a black clad server barreling through the crowd toward Nadia. His heart thumped at the peek of blonde hair that glimmered beneath the brim of their black cap and the glint of a knife in their hand made the color drain from his face.

"Nadia move!" Luca shouted, but it was too late.

"You're dead, bitch!" Ciara said, shoving the knife into Nadia's stomach.

A shocked gasp left Nadia's lips as she looked down at the knife jutting from her side. Screams erupted from the crowd as Nadia fell to the floor and Ciara darted through the building crowd.

"Oh, God!" Minerva shrieked, falling to the floor next to her best friend while their guards descended onto the scene in a swift swarm aiming their guns at Ciara's fleeing form. She looked over at Luca as he ran toward Nadia. A sinister smile curled over Ciara's lips before a loud bang rang out and she fell to the ground with a thud as blood pooled from her head onto the glossy parquet floor.

"Nadia!" Luca roared as he slid to his knees beside her.

"Call an ambulance!" Cameron cried out to the panicked crowd gawking around them.

The music faded into the background as Luca held the back of Nadia's head to his chest and pressed a shaking hand to the knife jutting out of her side. "You're going to be okay," he whispered as tears rolled down his cheeks and guilt tore at his heart. "Just stay with me."

Blood spilled from Nadia's side, rolling over his fingers. Her green eyes were dazed and unfocused as she gasped for air. A tear rolled down her cheek as she gripped the sleeve of his suit. "Lu... Luca."

"I'm here, ka'u pua. I'm right here," he said, wiping her cheek. "You're going to be o-okay, I promise."

But he couldn't promise that. There was so much blood, and her skin felt cold and clammy and her breaths were shallow. Panic shot through him as his heart pounded in his ears when her eyes drooped closed. "Nadia, keep your eyes open." He pleaded, pressing his forehead against hers. "Don't leave me."

"We're not waiting for an ambulance," Gordon said, rushing to his side. His hand shook as he touched the knife. "Fuck. We need to get her to the hospital now."

"Luca, I'm not..." Nadia mumbled.

"Shh, it's okay. You're... you're going to be okay." He brushed the tears from her cheeks as their guards rushed over to them, holding a black body board. "Stay with me," he said as Gordon helped him lift her onto a black body board. Their guards rushed into the ballroom for her.

"I love…" she whispered as her eyes rolled to the back of her head, her hand slid from his arm and fell limp at her side.

The world was a blur as Luca held his hand over Nadia's side as their guards secured her in the back of an SUV.

Watching her shallow breaths, Luca begged her to open her eyes as his guards sped from the hotel to the nearest hospital. Nurses and doctors met them at the emergency bay, transferred her to a gurney, and whisked her away into the operating room.

Luca paced back and forth in the waiting room while his guards spoke in hushed, angered tones on their phones to the police and guards that remained at the hotel.

Minutes ticked into hours as guilt and worry ate away at him. How could this happen? How did Ciara get so close and why… why didn't he protect her?

He was careless. Everyone was fucking careless. What if he lost her?

Tears blurred Luca's vision as he tried to suck in deep breaths. He stared at his shaking bloody hands and bit back a sob burning in his throat. He wouldn't survive and he'd never forgive himself for this.

"Mr. Shola."

He looked up at the petite raven haired doctor.

"Y-yes?"

The somber, tired look in her big brown eyes made his heart sink to the pit of his stomach, and his blood ran dangerously cold.

"We did everything…"

Chapter 50

Ringing and pounding in Luca's ears muffled the rest of the doctor's words. He sucked in tiny gasps of air as the world toppled over, crashing down on him as a bleak black darkness clouded his vision.

"Mr. Shola!"

He failed her.

Epilogue

Six months later...

"Thank you for agreeing to speak to me about this."

"Oh, it's no problem. Renae was happy to make the trip to Hawai'i and I'm happy you asked me to be an engineering consultant on your racing team."

"Yeah," Luca said, sliding his eyes to a photo of Nadia smiling up at him in her gorgeous dress from the Gala. "I thought it was time I started getting Shola Engineering together and I think Nadia would appreciate you being involved."

Charlie sniffed, nodding. "Yeah, she would."

"Mr. Shola, I'm sorry to interrupt," Gordon said, peeking into the office, dressed in a light blue button up and tan shorts with a black earpiece stuck in his ear. "But the rest of your guests have arrived."

"Thank you," Luca said, looking away from Gordon to Nadia's father. "Are you ready for this?"

Charlie cleared his through and blinked back the tears welling in his green eyes. "Of course."

Luca stood from his chair with one last glance at Nadia's smiling face and followed Charlie into the hall of his family's home, which was decorated in Nadia's favorite flowers. Deep blue and vibrant pink clematis were weaved around the wooden beams in the airy open living room with his village's signature deep green maile vines and yellow hibiscus flowers wrapped around wooden posts between them.

They stepped out onto the vast veranda that bled into the sandy beach and kissed the clear blue waters of the ocean. The Koa Maileans were bringing trays of vegetables and fruit to the enormous firepit that would be lit later for everyone to dance around.

Luca's father was roasting meat over the grill, while his mother and Renae spoke softly at one of the many round wooden tables on the veranda that was pooling with more flowers.

"Are you alright, Eke?" Lacey said, slipping her arm through his.

"I'm okay. I'm a little nervous."

"Everything's going to be fine," she said, squeezing his arm.

Luca nodded, looking across the bustling veranda and a warmth spread through him at the joy on his people's faces. His heart swelled at his Nonna's head of white hair, and her pale pink dress brought out her glowing brown skin as she walked along the beach. "Yeah, everything's going to be fine," Luca said as a bright smile spread across his lips at Nadia's curly auburn hair billowing around her and her vibrant green eyes made his heart simmer. Her white gown dotted with blue and pink flowers flowed around her legs and bare feet as if she were truly a living Goddess walking among mortals. The beautiful sound of her laughter carried on the wind and drowned out the bubbly chatter around him.

Nadia's eyes caught his as she strolled through the soft sand toward him next to his Nonna. A smile curled over her lips as she slid a hand over her protruding belly, and that small motion never failed to bring tears to his eyes.

"What are you two giggling about?" Luca said, wrapping his arm around Nadia's waist and sliding his hand over her stomach.

"Oh, I was just telling your little wahine more stories about you when you were a child," his Nonna said, patting him on the arm. "Let's hope this little one isn't as rambunctious as you were, eh Ekeali'i?"

"I wasn't that bad." He chuckled, kissing Nadia's head. "How are you feeling?"

"I'm fine. Nonna's green juice is helping with the heartburn, but I'm good, Mr. Underworld," she said, leaning into him. "You don't need to worry."

He smiled against her head. "It's a hard habit to break, ka'u pua."

Ciara was the one who lost her life that deadly night at the Gala and thankfully, she missed any vital organs when she stabbed Nadia. It was a miracle that she survived, but even more so that she was pregnant and the tiny life they created survived, too.

When Nadia was healed enough to travel, Luca was adamant that they stayed in Koa Maile and he wasn't sure he ever wanted to go back. It would be Nadia's choice, but he already made plans to appoint Cameron as the new CEO of Shola Enterprises while he worked on expanding the company in California. Luca planned to move the International department there and offer Nadia her role as

Director of International Marketing and Investments or joint CEO.

They still had plenty of work to do righting the wrongs committed in the blacklist, too. Jonathan and his grandfather were still locked away under the surveillance of his security agency deep below the ground in the basement of his towering black building on Rose Wharf, never to be seen or heard from again if Luca had any say in the matter. Nadia still wanted to bring Jonathan to justice for the seven women he murdered, but for now, she agreed to put that on hold while they lived in Koa Maile until their child was born.

"Are you two ready to find out the gender of your little one?" A short, petite woman with graying black hair grinned, sliding up to them. Anita Vazarian, the doctor that saved Nadia's life, also agreed to take a sabbatical to monitor Nadia's pregnancy after Luca pleaded with her to take the job. He wouldn't trust anyone with the life of his child's or Nadia's but her.

"Yes! We want to know!" Renae and his mother hollered from their table.

Nadia laughed, looking up at him with joy brimming in her bright green eyes. "I'm ready if you are. Not that it matters to me. I'll be happy with a healthy baby."

"Me too, but our families want to know."

"Mm, my great grandchild is going to be a fighter just like you two," his Nonna said. "But humor us. This is such a joyous occasion."

"Wait, wait! I have a gift for my baby girl before we do this," Renae said, getting up from her seat and sliding the twisted gold bracelet from her wrist.

"Mom," Nadia said with her lip trembling as her mother

slid the gold bracelet over her wrist.

"It's yours now," Renae said, sliding her hand over Nadia's stomach. "I should've given it to you years ago, but this seems like a fitting time to do it."

"Thank you," Nadia said, wrapping her arms around her mother's shoulders. "I... I didn't think I'd have a child to pass it on to."

Renae hugged her tight, kissing her head before she looked up at Luca and tears brimmed in her brown eyes. "I had a feeling and I had hope that this would happen for you."

"I don't mean to break up your moment, Mama Rae. You know I love you, but I want to know if I'm getting a niece or a nephew!" Minerva yelled.

"I second that!" Raquel said, raising a glass of champagne as she and Minerva clinked their glasses together while the rest of their friends, guards and family seconded their request.

"Oh, alright." Renae laughed, wiping her tears. She squeezed Luca's hand and kissed Nadia's head before she took her seat next to Charlie and his parents.

Luca thread his fingers through Nadia's as they walked to the center of the veranda to a big black cardboard box tied with a blue and pink bow.

"Are you ready for this?" Nadia said as they took the ends of the ribbons.

"I'm ready." He laughed as they pulled the tie.

The village, their families and friends took a collective breath as pink balloons, confetti and glitter burst from the box.

"It's a girl!" Lacey screamed as the air filled with shouts and cheers of congratulations.

Luca smiled at Nadia's glitter covered face and tears pooled in his eyes as he slid his hands over her stomach. "We're going to have a daughter," he said, leaning down to her belly. "And I can't wait to meet you."

Nadia laughed softly, sliding her fingers through his hair. "Me too."

Luca kissed her stomach and looked up at her sea-green eyes brimming with unshed tears. He stood, sliding his hands to her cheeks, wiping away a stray tear. "I love you, ka'u pua nani."

She wrapped her fingers around his wrists. "I love you too, Mr. Underworld."

Luca caught her lips with his and drowned in her sweetness. He never thought he was worthy of the love he felt for her, but God, he would spend the rest of his days striving to be worthy of it. He still couldn't believe he was going to be a father, that they made a life together and Nadia wanted this life with him.

Luca smiled against her lips. No matter what burdens they might face in the future, he knew the strength of their love would always be enough to endure it.

-Fin-

Author's Note

Thank you so much for reading Me Too. It's been rolling around in my head since I was sixteen, so about eighteen years, and I finally decided to put Nadia and Luca's story out in the world. It started as a story to flip the damsel in distress trope on its head and put the man in the damsel character, but it developed into a story about two people overcoming trauma and finding love and strength together. I was adamant to highlight male domestic abuse because it's something that gets overlooked and isn't talked about as it should.

Domestic violence and sexual assault is a serious matter for both men and women. There are plenty of campaigns and charities across America and the UK that work toward ending this and supporting victims and survivors.

If you or anyone you know is experiencing domestic violence, sexual assault or intimate partner violence, here are a few resources for you to seek help:

ManKind - https://www.mankind.org.uk/
01823 334244

Male Victims of Domestic Abuse. Confidential helpline for male victims of domestic abuse and rape.

The Hotline - https://www.thehotline.org/resources/men-can-be-victims-of-abuse-too/

1-800-799-7233

One in 10 men has experienced rape, physical violence, and/or stalking by an intimate partner.

Women's Aid - https://www.womensaid.org.uk/

helpline@womensaid.org.uk

Women's Aid is a grassroots federation working together to provide life-saving services in England and build a future where domestic abuse is not tolerated.

Rape Crisis Network Europe - https://www.rcne.com/

RCNE is the network of European centres which support survivors of sexual violence. We aim to make sure that anyone who experiences sexual violence can get the help they need.

Domestic Violence Resources (US) - https://greatist.com/happiness/stop-domestic-violence-organizations

A list of organizations working to assist survivors, develop legal policies, and educate people about domestic violence.

As a Campaigns and Democracy coordinator and self-proclaimed activist, it would be remiss of me not to have a call to action. Please find it in your heart to donate, join a campaign or sign a petition to support the efforts to end domestic violence and sexual assault.

Stay safe and as always, thank you so, so much for reading.

Eli B

Nadia & Luca's Reading List

I know you were wondering what these two were reading!
Enjoy!

Eyes of the Beholder - Eli B

The Sound of Stars - Alechia Dow

Cobratongue University: Professors & Kings - Des M. Astor

Bound to You - S Courtney

Elemental: Shadows of Otherside - Whitney Hill

Drag Me Up - R.M. Virtues

Lord of the Fading Lands - C.L. Wilson

Dark Possession - Christine Feehan

Lore Olympus - Rachel Smythe

Me Too

Legendborn - Tracey Deonn

The Way of Kings - Brandon Sanderson

The Fifth Season - N.K. Jemisin

Children of Blood and Bone - Tomi Adeyemi

Howl's Moving Castle - Diana Wynne Jones

Luca's Lullaby

The song Luca sings to Nadia. <insert swooning noises>

Pua Hīnano by Keali'i Reichel
https://youtu.be/zUNM4T-Z1y8

He nani ka pua hïnano ëhë
I uka o 'Ähuimanu
I kumu pali wewehi
Kau ai ka maka iä 'oe
'Opu'u mai ka hïnano ëhë
A möhala i ka nahele
He lalilahi ka lihi
I ka ua Pö'aihale
Onaona nö ka hïnano ëhë
He mäpuna i ka Moa'e
Ho'olale i ka mana'o
Ia hanu i anuhea
Auhea ku'u hïnano ëhë
E lü helele'i ka 'ehu

A paoa ke kulu aumoe
Moe pono ihu käua
Haina mai ka puana ëhë
He nani ka pua hïnano
He wehi no ʻÄhuimanu
Kau kuʻu maka iä ʻoe

Translation

The hïnano is a flower of great beauty
There above ʻÄhuimanu
At the verdant base of the cliff
My eyes are drawn to you
The hïnano bud emerges
And blooms there in the forest
The sheaths are smooth and glossy
In the swirling Pöʻaihale rain
The hïnano is so very fragrant
An aroma carried on the trade wind
So stirring to the thoughts
Is that sweet scent you exude
Hear me, my dear hïnano
Let your snowy pollen scatter down
So the night shall be perfumed
You and I shall enjoy our repose
Let the story be told
The hïnano is a flower of great beauty
An adornment for ʻÄhuimanu
My eye is fixed on you

Resources

If you're reading a physical copy of Me Too and you'd like to read the resources and research that helped developed Me Too, you can find them on my website: www.elibees-blurbs.com

Koa Maile is a fictional village I made up for this story. There's no place named Koa Maile on the island of Kaua'i. So please don't go looking for it, you won't find it!

- **Hawaiian dictionary** - https://wehewehe.org/?l=en
- **Hawaiian proverbs** - https://www.tourmaui.com/hawaiian-quotes-proverbs/
- **Hawaiian heritage** - https://wanderwisdom.com/travel-destinations/Hawaii-and-Native-Hawaiians-What-You-May-Not-Know
- **Black Chitimacha heritage** - https://iamblackchitimacha.wordpress.com/our-history/
- **Senegal jewelry** (inspiration for Nadia's unknown African heritage) - https://www.npr.org/sections/goatsandsoda/2019/02/02/660636686/senegals-stunning-

gold-jewelry-and-the-controversial-women-who-wore-it

- **Detroit Hustle** - https://gluckprogram.ucr.edu/sites/g/files/rcwecm731/files/2019-08/d50_detroithustle.pdf
- **Cupid Shuffle** - https://cdn.ymaws.com/www.vahperd.org/resource/resmgr/imported/Sonna%20Longden%20Holidays%20handout.pdf
- **Electric Slide** - https://www.google.co.uk/amp/s/amp.theguardian.com/stage/2020/jun/11/how-the-electric-slide-became-the-black-lives-matter-protest-dance https://people.howstuffworks.com/stories-behind-electric-slide-moonwalk-and-other-epic-dance-moves.htm

Coming Soon

The Beast of Stornoway

When beauty meets her beast–a modern retelling of a classic story with one major twist... *this story isn't for sweet little girls.*

'Keep the Blarcum name strong.'

That is **LORD VAN BLARCUM**'s duty and his curse. All his life he's been groomed to carry on the Blarcum legacy. He lives under his mother's rule, and he does as she pleases to protect the one thing he loves most: his manor.

He doesn't care about the legacy or the empire. He prefers his isolated life on the Hebridean Isle of Lewis. His manor and his horses are all he needs.

Until she walks into his life...

AMANI BLAKE is running and searching for a new life. She's dreamed of the rolling hills of the Highlands since she was a child, but she's stuck. Trapped by a deal she made with an ex-lover to keep her family above water.

But after fleeing Detroit to live with her cousin on the west coast, she's given the opportunity to be the assistant of a Lord in Stornoway, Scotland.

Will Lord Blarcum learn to love something more than his manor? Can Amani learn to live the life she deserves?

Or will duty stand in the way of affairs of the heart?

Chapter 1

Van Blarcum poured himself a glass of whiskey and stood at his office window, staring out at the bleak gray skies and the gravel driveway. He cut his eyes to his staff standing along the steps of the manor waiting for his new assistant to arrive. "How much longer, Benny?" He grimaced. Amani Blake was ten minutes late. Van couldn't stand people that didn't respect his time. Punctuality was a must for him.

"Miss Blake should be here any minute, m'Lord. Her flight was delayed," Benny, his eldest employee and head of the manor staff, huffed. "You will be nice to her. She's the cousin of Miss Nadia Coleman and she was kind enough to help us with the dire lack of interest in this position."

"I *know*." He snapped at the old man. "You've told me a thousand times," he grumbled. No one wanted to be the assistant to someone like him and he didn't care, but he needed someone to be his eyes at the company because he sure as hell wasn't stepping anywhere near his mother or that god awful place.

Van sighed, taking another drink from his glass. There were a million things he'd rather be doing right now than waiting for his tardy assistant. He could tend to his horses. He hadn't brushed or fed any of them today, and he didn't like it when the other farmhands did it.

If Miss Blake took any longer, he'd do just that. He hated socializing. Maybe if people were more like animals, he wouldn't mind. Animals were loyal. They didn't waste anyone's time or stab people in the back, but he couldn't lose another assistant. Not when he knew his mother was making plans to take his manor *again.* That was the reason he enlisted the help of Nadia Coleman and Shola Enterprises.

Van closed his eyes. He just had to be cordial. He'd say hello, welcome Miss Blake to his home, then disappear into the stables and never speak to her again.

"Miss Blake has arrived, m'Lord," Benny called.

Van threw back the rest of his drink and followed behind him to the foyer to meet his new assistant. They were all the same. Business skirts, dress pants, hair tightly done and business written all over their faces. Only to find they couldn't handle getting their heels stuck in the mud or the dreadfully slow and quiet life of the small Hebridean island.

"Miss Blake! We're so glad you joined our staff." Benny exclaimed as he walked outside.

"Mr. Auld! It's no problem. I've always wanted to come to Scotland. Thank you for hiring me." Miss Blake's laugh and that adorable American accent nearly made Van want to laugh, too.

He stepped outside and his heart slammed against his rib cage at the woman on the steps below. A rare peek of sunlight opened up in the dreary sky and cast Miss Blake's deep brown skin and mane of long, curly brown hair in an ethereal glow. Van swallowed to wet his dry throat as he gazed upon the beauty that graced his manor.

Chapter 2

Amani squeezed her hands in her lap and looked out the car window at the rolling hills of the Highlands. Her flight was late, which meant her bags were late and now she was late meeting Lord Blarcum.

Oh God.

She hated being late. It wasn't her fault, but it made her more nervous than she already was. The only reason she got this job was because of her cousin's business ties with Lord Blarcum and because Nadia knew she needed to get the hell out of Detroit.

Amani took a deep breath and let the scenery of the beautiful countryside calm her nerves. This was going to be a new start in the country she'd been dreaming about since she was a child. She could leave all the mess of the city behind her.

"Welcome to Blarcum Manor, Miss Blake," Gerard, the sandy-haired driver with kind brown eyes and friendly smile, looked up at her through the rear-view mirror.

Amani's eyes grew wide as he turned down a graveled tree-lined driveway and an expansive stone house–*mansion,* sitting proudly at the end of the road. The driveway opened to wide open fields in a valley of the hills that surrounded it. Men and women lined the steps, some dressed in worker's overalls while others wore crisp white button-up shirts, black pants and forest green blazers.

Amani looked down at her denim jeans, Detroit Lions t-shirt and tugged her black cotton coat around her. "I'm a little underdressed for this."

Gerard chuckled as he parked the car in the gravel just before the steps. "You're alright, Miss Blake," he said as he popped out of the car and opened her door. "I'm sure m'lord will forgive your travel attire."

"I hope so," she mumbled as she stepped out of the car. Nadia already warned her about Lord Blarcum. He wasn't exactly a warm person and Amani hoped she wouldn't offend him by dressing so informally at their first meeting.

***

Everyone bowed when Lord Blarcum emerged from the house. Amani's eyes grew wide as she took in the formidable man. His rugged features were so dark, save for his bright green eyes and the flecks of blonde in his wavy brown hair that graced his broad shoulders.

His muscles strained against his dark green button-up shirt that was rolled up to his elbows, showing off his muscled forearms and beige skin. The shirt laid perfectly against his sinewy body, tucked neatly into a pair of black slacks that gently hugged his thick thighs. He was built more like a laborer than a pampered Lord.

Amani's heart slammed against her rib cage and her throat felt dry suddenly. He was handsome in the pictures she'd googled of him, but they didn't do this man *any* justice.

"Lord Blarcum, I'd like you to meet your new assistant, Miss Amani Blake," Mr. Auld introduced.

Amani was pulled out of her stupor by his introduction. She blushed, realizing she shouldn't be gawking at him. She was a staff member and should bow like the rest of them.

"Mister, um, L-Lord Blarcum, it's an honor to be here," she said, clenching her eyes shut as she bowed to him.

Damn it. She sounded like an idiot! There was no reason to get tongue tied over his impeccable looks. She needed this job and she couldn't let her emotions get the best of her like last time.

Pre-order link and cover art coming soon!
Be sure to sign up to my newsletter or follow me on my socials for updates!

About the Author

Eli B is an American immigrant who lives in Hull, UK or, as the locals say, 'Ull!

Eli has been actively writing since she was 12, but wrote her very first story when she was 10 for a 5th grade English project. Since then, Eli has let her imagination run wild, creating her own worlds and characters!

Eli writes interracial fantasy and contemporary romance. Interracial couples are very dear to her heart and she'd love to see more of these novels in mainstream lit, especially fantasy.

By day, Eli is a Campaigns & Democracy Coordinator for a

Students' Union. She trains and supports the world's next generation of rebels - *leaders* and by night she's an author who feverishly writes to her heart's content.

Eli finally shared her work publicly in 2019 when she stumbled upon Wattpad. The love and support she received from the amazing readers prompted her to continue her aspirations of becoming a published author and she has no intention of slowing down anytime soon.

You can connect with me on:

- https://www.elibeesblurbs.com
- https://twitter.com/Eliseylouwamba
- https://www.facebook.com/EliBeesBlurbs
- https://www.patreon.com/EliBeesBlurbs

Made in the USA
Columbia, SC
10 November 2021

48608320R00269